Holding Their Own XIV

Forest Mist

Joe Nobody

Copyright © 2018
Kemah Bay Marketing, LLC
All rights reserved.
Edited by: E.T. Ivester
Researched by: D.W. Hall

www.joenobodybooks.com

Other Books by Joe Nobody:

CHAPTER 1

Pete's Place was buzzing, a good number of Meraton's residents in a partying mood. A bloody civil war had been avoided for the most part, and the political situation stabilized – at least for the moment. An absolute blessing in a post-Apocalyptic world.

Given what he and his family had been through, Bishop decided to work close to home for a few weeks. Besides, the guys who normally handled the pub's security here were long overdue for a little time off. He could be close to Terri and his son while earning an honest wage.

The Texan personally knew many of the customers enjoying the evening. He'd already turned down a dozen offers for free libations. He sipped a cup of coffee instead, sitting at the bar by the entrance, keeping a watchful eye on the comings and goings of the patrons.

Like any other security assignment, Bishop's duty this night involved diligence, which translated into identifying threats. A people-watcher by nature, Bishop rather enjoyed this part of the job and was quite proficient at it.

At a nearby table, three Beltran ranch hands toasted the Alliance, threw back their brews with gusto, and arm wrestled for the top bed in the bunkhouse. To Bishop, they looked like tough, capable men, but he knew their muscles bulged more from stringing barbed wire than throwing punches. Plus, Mr. Beltran paid a full day's wages for a full day's work that started an hour before sunup. The rugged, old ramrod didn't tolerate any excuses, especially those based on excessive consumption of cold beer, or any extracurricular activities that might follow.

The two businessmen seated at the bar fell comfortably into the same benign category. Having long buried their corporate dealings in the confines of their briefcases, they loosened their ties and relaxed a bit. Business proposals off the table, they were focused more on female companionship and the bite of Pete's bathtub gin than causing a disturbance.

The far end of the bar was anchored by Meraton's very own self-appointed, political analyst – Joe Kinslow. As usual, he was spouting his party line to anyone who would listen. While the crusty, old codger's viewpoint might irritate some, his rhetoric wouldn't go over the top for at least another three beers. Harry, the bartender, knew to cut him off after two.

In fact, the crowd filling the tavern was exactly what Bishop would have anticipated, a comfortable mixture of regulars rounded out by a smattering of visitors to the fair city. Still, he maintained his diligence, scanning the room as well as all new arrivals with a wary eye, closely attending to the details of Pete's clientele.

"I'm going to get you a gift certificate for one of those fancy massages, Bishop. You're looking way, way too serious," Harry announced from behind the bar. "Then again, I don't suppose I blame you for being little uptight – given the war and all those robberies that went down."

"I'm paid to be uptight," Bishop retorted with a smirk. "Just don't drift too far away from the 12-gauge under the bar, okay?"

"You got it, Boss."

Lifting his cup for another sip of java, the sound of elevated speech piqued the Texan's attention. A suddenly sharp, male voice barked over the murmur of the crowd. A sure sign of trouble.

In a heartbeat, Bishop slid off his perch and moved toward the source. A few steps later, he found himself approaching the recipe for a brawl. The ingredients included two strapping lads, one leggy lady, and a bunch of empties crowding the tabletop.

"I don't like you looking at him like that!" one of the cowboys growled at the woman.

"She can look at anybody she wants," responded the interloper, standing abruptly and balling his fists.

In a flash, Bishop maneuvered between them. "Gentlemen! Chill! Let's talk this over."

While the Texan didn't know the two cowpokes, they knew him, at least by reputation. His presence seemed to turn down the heat to a simmer, but Bishop wanted to take the pot off the flame altogether.

"Look, fellas, everybody is in here just to have a good time... a few drinks... some good conversation," Bishop soothed, hoping a calming voice would subvert the tension. "If you two start trouble, you'll ruin what's turning out to be a nice, quiet evening... and that would most certainly piss me off."

Bishop wanted them to sit down, or leave, or at least show some sign that they were reconsidering violence. After all, this was post-apocalyptic West Texas where starvation, disease, and anarchy had long ago culled the meek from the human herd. These folks had all witnessed the practical application of Darwin's theory, and they knew that having a proper firearm decreased the likelihood of their falling prey to natural selection. These survivors stood a little taller... walked a little surer... and every one of them wore a gun.

Seconds later, the two testosterone-charged fellows casted hard glares at each other again, their bodies bowed up for a fight. Bishop had seen the signs hundreds of times before, and the prospects incensed him. Hormonal rage would lead to a shove; then somebody would throw a punch or a bottle. Within seconds, the losing man would draw a weapon. A half dozen more firearms would appear. Chaos, hot lead, and then death usually followed.

Knowing it was time to switch tactics, the forced smile melted off Bishop's face, his eyes growing cold, his voice barely a whisper. "Guys, I have to confess that I've been having anger management issues as of late. As a matter of fact, Harry, the guy holding the shotgun behind the bar, has

3

accused me of being a vampire because I always seem to have blood on my hands. So, I want to beg both of you... please... *please*... start something, right here, right now. I'm aching to tear out your throats and stomp your balls into pancakes. It's like I'm addicted to kicking ass, and I haven't had a fix all week."

The lady, as usual, was the sensible one. "I'm going home," she announced. "Alone," she added for emphasis, throwing both of her suitors a look that said, "What idiots."

As she pivoted for the door, the Romeos turned to follow, both intent on chasing the prize that was about to elude them. Bishop, however, swiftly and effortlessly intercepted them.

With a firm hand on each of their chests, the Texan halted the chase, hoping to give the woman a head start. "You guys should try humor instead of bravado when it comes to the ladies. It's always worked for me," he chuckled. "As a matter of fact, my jokes are legendary in some circles."

Bishop's attempt to take the hot air out of their balloons wasn't appreciated, and for a second, he thought they were going to test him. Now, *he* was in their sights. *He* was suddenly the root of their whiskey-induced problem.

The buff cowboy seemed to size up Bishop, his unrelenting glare boring into the Texan's eyes, his girth emphasized by shoulders thrown wide. "I am large," his posture communicated. "You should be afraid of me."

Bishop never flinched, having equated the man's stance to that of a pufferfish that swallows water to make itself look bigger and more formidable when it is threatened. The Texan's own expression hardened, and in that moment, a second, silent communiqué exchanged between them. Bishop, meeting the taller man's stare, broadcasted his own message, loud and clear.

Bishop's eyes displayed neither fear nor rage, revealing no more emotion than a mountain lion about to pounce on the hare. It was disconcerting. Primordial. Savage. Unsettling.

4

To say the least, Bishop's countenance unnerved the roughnecks.

"Let me buy you a beer, Milo," the shorter drunk interjected, a chilled wave surging up his spine, overwhelming all of his alcohol-fueled courage. "That broad wasn't worth the trouble, anyway."

There was a lengthy, uncomfortable pause, the brawny troublemaker trying to weigh his options. He had heard that Bishop was a demon in combat, an unpredictable beast without conscience or hesitation. The man standing before him was reputed to be an assassin who had put dozens of able men into the grave.

Milo had always considered such stories as gross exaggerations, the stuff of urban legends. No doubt the post-apocalyptic community was starving for the hyperbole of Hollywood's fictional superheroes, longing for a man-God to worship on their living room flat screens. People made up their own tall tales now, countering some desperate need to fill the void left after the boob tubes stopped televising 24/7... and somehow Bishop fit the bill. *I don't see what the big deal is about this guy. I could take him in my sleep,* Milo mused. Nobody was as good as the rumors about Bishop suggested. He wasn't especially tall, didn't seem physically intimidating, and surely didn't possess any mystical, superhuman powers. He was just an average man who had probably gotten lucky more than his fair share of the time. The rest was all bullshit, embellished by those who didn't have the balls to put their fingers on a trigger. It occurred to his foggy mind that no man's good fortune lasted forever.

Yet, a warning sounded inside of Milo's head, ringing as clear as a church bell on Sunday morning. "Here is a predator," some deep instinct cautioned. "The reaper is standing right in front of you. Walk away. Survive. See tomorrow's sunrise."

"To hell with this... to hell with all of you," Milo finally growled from his throat. He then broke eye contact with Bishop and stormed toward the street.

Just like that, the background din of a pub on Saturday night returned, and that was just fine with the West Texan. "Don't fall off your horse on the way home," he chuckled, watching as the antagonist staggered out the door.

Exchanging looks with Harry behind the bar, Bishop nodded to his coworker, and the scattergun was returned to its roost.

"I need some fresh air," Bishop announced to the barkeep, heading toward the entrance. "Be back in a minute."

He needed to make sure Milo didn't reconsider his course of action. More than once, the Texan had vanquished a drunk, only to have the man reappear a few minutes later, his loud mouth demanding retribution for being exiled. Several times, the returning customer supplemented his newfound bravery with a firearm and lead.

For the late hour, Main Street was busy. These days, more cars lined the streets, evidence that the government's effort to refine oil was paying dividends. Gas was still expensive however and was beyond the financial reach of many citizens. The carriages of Detroit and Japan had to share the road with far more horse-drawn wagons and solo riders than before the collapse. The tie-up rail in front of Pete's was still packed with horseflesh.

Milo was nowhere to be found, prompting Bishop to finally release his grip on the .45 pistol in his belt.

"Hey, Bishop!" someone shouted from the sidewalk. The Texan peered up to see two of Sheriff Watts' lawmen hustling his direction.

"Evening, Deputy. Are you guys here to police up the horseshit from the street?" Bishop grinned, nodding toward tie-up rail. "Harry would be happy to loan you his shovel."

Ignoring the insult, the older one spouted, "We just ran into a woman who claimed there was trouble down here at Pete's Place."

"All over now. Everything's under control," Bishop replied.

"Let me guess," the older deputy began. "You busted somebody's head? Again."

At first, Bishop thought the officer was joking. "No, I didn't get to do anything *that* fun tonight. As a matter of fact, this job's getting downright boring," he stated rather matter-of-factly, "I asked a couple of good, old boys to move along, and they did. End of story."

The cop stepped close, his nose stopping less than an inch from Bishop's. "You should have called us, tough guy. People are getting sick and tired of thugs like you taking the law into their own hands. They want order and due process, not some bouncer being judge, jury, and executioner."

"Now you're going to tell me how to do my job, Deputy? I broke up a fight, probably saved that gal from getting a black eye... or worse.... And nobody got hurt."

"This time," the cop spat. "From what I hear, that's not always the case with you and your kind. Sheriff Watts warned us about men like you... ruffians who think that it's still every man for himself and have no respect for law and order. I got news for you, Bishop, the public is fed up with cowboys, violence, and vigilantes. You don't work for the government anymore. The shit I took this morning has more authority than you."

"If I've broken any laws why hasn't Watts arrested me?" Bishop replied, his anger barely in check. "Better yet, why don't you boys try and take me in?"

Instead of answering, the deputy pointed at Bishop's pickup. "Is that your truck? Parked illegally?"

Bishop didn't take the bait, his eyes never leaving the officer. These lawdogs were new and obviously full of

7

themselves. "It's not parked illegally, and yes, that's my pickup."

A huge grin spread across the lawman's face. "Well, look at this. It's outside the marked parking spaces. That is a violation," he chided, reaching for the citation book in his pocket.

"There isn't a painted parking line in the entire town," Bishop protested, his wide arms indicating all of Meraton.

"Exactly," the cop replied, turning to his partner. "In fact, every one of Pete's customers is parked illegally. I wonder how long this bar would stay open if we decided to strictly enforce the local ordinances? We could even have all of these cars and trucks towed." The second officer crossed his arms in defiance and sneered at Bishop, amused by the clever abuse of power employed by his partner.

For a second, Bishop considered knocking the cocky deputy on his ass, and if his partner interfered, he would take him on, too. It would be easy. There were only two of them, and he doubted they were all that skilled. If they pulled their weapons... well... so be it.

On the other hand, he was well aware that it would be stupid to get Pete's business on the wrong side of the law. The men now writing him a senseless ticket were just like the two cowboys in the bar, the only difference being that they were drunk on authority rather than cold brew. They were trying to escalate, to goad him into a fight. He wouldn't give them the pleasure. Instead, Bishop decided he would have a quiet conversation with the sheriff... later.

Shaking his head in disgust, Bishop accepted the citation without another word. Now wasn't the time to confront the two cops leering at him. He would take it up with Watts later, try to straighten things out through proper channels.

While he fully understood the need for keeping the peace, the Alliance's recovery was going too far, too fast. Electricity was great, as was the reduction in crime resulting from the reformation of various law enforcement agencies and a judicial system. With those advances also came the negatives of society, like stupid regulations and ordinances, along with chickenshit parking tickets and other minor violations.

The subject was an ongoing dispute between him and Terri. "Civilization isn't all roses and chocolates," he complained just yesterday. "I saw a notice today that we're going to be billed for property taxes starting in January. In the blink of a post-apocalyptic eye, the government is getting too big again."

"People want services from the government. They want a fire department, better schools, police protection, and healthcare. Those things cost money, and it doesn't grow on trees," Terri had responded.

He felt out of sync with the transformation of his native West Texas and didn't make any secret about it. He and Terri could teach Hunter what he needed to know to survive and thrive. That education included both book learning and the skills a man needed in the field. "Next thing you know, they'll be telling my son what to say and how to think," Bishop grumbled. "And I have had enough of that over the top, 'politically correct' bullshit to last a lifetime."

Even his recent change of careers had been due to the recovery and how it was being managed. The SAINT teams were blunt instruments, equally capable of delicate negotiations and extreme violence. Now, with the expansion of government, the politicians in Alpha had decided they were no longer necessary. Bishop disagreed.

The deputies continued walking down the street, the tavern's customers evidently benefiting from their benevolence.

Stepping around the corner to find solitude, Bishop was in no mood for socializing. He decided to check the back of the bar, an excuse really, a chance to reset his attitude. He was just admiring the West Texas starfield when the crunch of gravel under a boot caused him to pivot with a start.

A shape appeared in the shadows. Bishop's hand flashed like a striking cobra, finding the grip of the 1911 pistol on his belt.

"You son of a bitch," hissed a voice from the darkness. "You think you're God."

Bishop was already moving, knowing instantly that Milo had indeed returned. Two steps into his egress, the first shot ripped through the quiet air.

The expanding ball of red flame erupting from the muzzle, combined with its thunderous roar, told him Milo was firing a 12-gauge. Bishop automatically tensed, expecting the stinging bite of buckshot tearing into his flesh. It never came.

Diving headlong behind a nearby car, he couldn't believe he hadn't been hit. Was the shooter that drunk? How did anybody miss at that range?

A human form staggered from the alley, nearly falling before entering the light. Milo looked like an unmade bed, his clothing dirty and disheveled. A sizeable section of filth stained his shirt, and the stench permeating from it told Bishop that his antagonist had fallen into a pile of horse dung.

Again, the drunken man raised the shotgun to his shoulder, slurring, "Where in the hell are you? Come out and fight like a man, Mr. Hero. I'm going to cut you in half."

Bishop noted he was facing an old-fashioned, double barrel, break-action shotgun. That meant Milo only had one shot left. The Texan also realized he had taken cover behind a police car.

Rising to show himself, Bishop yelled, "I'm over here, Milo!"

As expected, the belligerent man pivoted toward the sound of Bishop's voice and fired. The pattern hit the windshield, a spiderweb of glass appearing just above the steering wheel. "Sorry, Deputies, the cruiser was the closest cover," the Texan grinned.

"That wasn't even close," Bishop muttered, reaching the rear bumper. "Maybe he hit his head when he fell?"

Chancing a glance, the Texan spied Milo standing with the shotgun's action broken open, fumbling in his pocket for a reload. Bishop charged.

Covering the gap in five steps, Bishop's shoulder slammed into the larger man's midsection with enough force to send both of them sprawling. Somehow, Milo maintained his grip on the scattergun, which caused the Texan no small amount of vexation.

Am I getting that old? Bishop thought. *Am I that slow and out of shape?*

Bishop quickly rose to his feet, sobriety assuring him an edge against his attacker.

The cowboy had managed one knee when Bishop was on him, grabbing the shotgun with one hand while throwing three, rapid, sharp jabs with the other. The Texan wanted that weapon out of the fight.

All three strikes landed squarely, Milo's head snapping back with each blow. Due to either alcohol, adrenaline, or just plain meanness, the ranch hand somehow maintained his grasp on the 12-gauge.

What the hell is wrong with you? Bishop cursed himself. *You should have put him down by now.*

Bishop's tactics changed when it became clear he wasn't going to disarm the larger foe. Doubt entered his mind again when he realized that his surprisingly-strong adversary was about to regain his feet. *You're going to get your ass kicked by a drunken fool,* he thought. *You need to get off that damned barstool a little more often.*

With a growl of massive effort, Milo was up, both men clutching the shotgun with every ounce of strength they could muster. Bishop swiftly focused on a new, critical priority – keeping the business end of the cowboy's street-sweeper pointed away from his body.

Lashing out with a kick, the Texan tried to take out Milo's leg and missed, adding to his embarrassment.

Milo, on the other hand, realized that he was stronger than Bishop and concentrated all his significant girth on wrestling away his weapon. Around and around they went, both refusing to loosen their grips, the shotgun acting as the axis of their two-man merry-go-round.

As he was pulled around in a circle, Bishop wondered if his opponent had managed to replenish the weapon at the center of their dispute. Struggling to keep his own footing, he tried to replay the last few moments before they had gone down. *If that blaster is loaded, I'm going to have to kill him*, Bishop thought, his confidence only somewhat bolstered by the weight of the .45 still tucked in his belt.

The problem was, Bishop couldn't be sure if Milo had inserted two new rounds or not. Even in West Texas, shooting an unarmed man would raise more than a few eyebrows. Killing a defenseless, drunken cowboy was worse. Yet, he was defending himself against and attacker and couldn't take the chance.

With his grasp weakening, Bishop was about to let go and draw when a new voice screamed, "Freeze! Police!"

Releasing his hold, Bishop lost his footing and nearly fell. As he struggled to regain his balance, he spotted the two deputies rounding the corner, each with his weapon high and ready.

Milo, suddenly finding himself in command of the shotgun, started to bring the barrel up just as Bishop shouted, "It's not loaded!"

The cops either didn't hear, or didn't care, and opened fire.

Diving for the gravel as the first two rounds whizzed over his head, Bishop's brain screamed, "What in the hell are you shooting at me for?" As he skidded across the rocks, the unmistakable roar of the 12-gauge answered. "Oooops."

One of the deputies went down, the other centering his front post on Milo's chest. Two slugs slammed into the brawny cowboy, his body jerking in a spasm as he collapsed in a heap.

Bishop started to rise but then thought better of it. A moment later, the remaining deputy stood over the Texan, shouting commands at the top of his lungs. "Put your arms out! Put your arms out! Like a fucking airplane! Get them out!"

Doing as he was told, Bishop made wings. The cop then holstered his weapon and put a knee into the Texan's back. Less than 15 seconds later, the handcuffs were on.

Harry then appeared out the back door of Pete's. Somebody went for the doctor. Sirens sounded in the distance. A crowd gathered on the fringe of the back lot. All the while, Bishop lay on the sharp gravel, staring at Milo's empty eyes just a few feet away. At some point in time, he heard an angry voice announce that the wounded deputy had died.

"This is all so stupid," he mumbled under his breath. "So unnecessary. So avoidable."

Terri had just gotten into bed when she heard Bishop's truck pulling into the driveway. He was late. She sensed trouble. Throwing back the sheets, she grumbled, "So much for having a *regular* job."

She padded to the front door, glancing through a slit in the curtains. It was Bishop all right, her husband's clothing ripped and dirty. "Oh, my heavens! I should have bought hydrogen peroxide by the gallon," she breathed, reaching to undo the deadbolt.

While doing security work for Pete was far less stressful than commanding a SAINT team, Terri fully understood her husband's work was dangerous. She still worried about him every time he walked out the door.

"You okay?" she whispered, checking the lacerations on his arm.

"Yeah. I'm fine. Just a rough day at the office. I need a shower."

Terri knew instantly that her husband was anxious, and by the expression on his face, there was a lot more than a bar fight on his mind. He would tell her about it when he was ready. "I'll get you some clean clothes. Coffee? Something to eat?"

"No," he grumbled. "Thanks, but I'm not hungry."

He headed toward Hunter's bedroom, quietly peeking in at the sleeping boy. After an admiring pause, he made for the bathroom. Terri heard running water a minute later.

She laid out a fresh pair of pants and a shirt on the vanity and then took a seat on the commode. "How bad was it?" she eventually asked.

"Two men died outside of Pete's tonight," Bishop replied, his soapy face appearing around the shower curtain. "One of them was a deputy. It was all so... so unnecessary. I'm having trouble deciding who to be mad at."

"Sounds like you're directing most of your anger at yourself," she ventured, peering deep into his eyes. "What happened?"

While he washed and scrubbed, Bishop told her exactly what had occurred. Twice she stopped him to ask a question or clarify a point.

"You didn't do anything wrong, Bishop," she eventually proclaimed. "There's no need for you to be mad at anybody."

"Watts doesn't think so," he replied, rubbing a towel across his chest. "He gave me a pretty rough time about all this. Some shit about how death seems to follow me around. I don't think we'll be on his Christmas card list this year."

Grunting, Terri nodded. "I think the good sheriff is just getting tired of burying his deputies. Who can blame him? It was just a bad set of circumstances that swirled out of control. No one is at fault as far as I can see."

Bishop was silent while he buttoned his shirt. He wanted to tell her that he had been too slow, that he had lost a step, that he felt old, worthless, and weak. A year ago, he would have stopped the incident long before things got ugly. Two men would have still been alive. But the words just wouldn't come.

Finally glancing up, he said, "Enough about my shenanigans. How was your day?"

"I met with the contractor today," she gushed with newfound energy. "He's completed the drawings for our new home out at the ranch. He's come up with a great design, including thick, bulletproof stone walls just like you wanted."

Bishop wanted to see the drawings. Terri was happy to provide a distraction.

"Wow," he said after studying the blueprints. "Those walls should hold back anything short of a tank round."

"There's plenty of rock lying around to skirt the bottom of this fortress. The problem is the logs used for the upper half of the proposal. According to the builder, the only place you can get wood like that is in East Texas."

Rubbing his chin, Bishop asked, "Can he take care of it? Does he have a source for the material?"

Shaking her head, Terri replied, "He's going to check, but he didn't leave me feeling warm and fuzzy. In fact, he tried for half an hour to talk me out of using any wood on the exterior."

"And?"

Terri stood just a little too quickly, her frustration obvious. "I don't want to live in a citadel, an underground bunker, or a fortress, Bishop. I don't want the Great Wall, guard towers and a moat incorporated into my landscaping... or belt-fed weapons in my living room. I want a warm, loving, comfortable home to raise our children and grow old

15

together. I've gone along with your security requirements and have tried hard to integrate everything on your list."

"And you've done a great job," he responded, tenderly brushing a lock of her hair back into place.

She smiled up at him, his gesture prompting her to relax. "I want a log cabin, my love. I've dreamed about living in a log cabin since I was a little girl. This might be the only chance we have to build a home, and I want it to be perfect for both of us."

"Then let's go find some logs," he shrugged.

"What?"

"Pete's Place isn't going to reopen for a while with the parking lot being a crime scene. Besides, I could use a little change of venue. Let's take a road trip and ensure my queen is happy with her castle."

Terri wasn't convinced, "I don't know if that is a good idea. We've not had the greatest luck with vacations, Bishop. Remember that trip when we got involved in the Salt War? Or the time I was bitten by that snake? Besides, Hunter is older and more mobile now, and he won't just happily cruise along in his car seat for hours at a time."

The idea of a holiday break seemed to be growing on Bishop, "We'll be in Alliance Territory the whole trip. Hasn't everyone been shouting to the heavens that things have settled down? That civilization has returned to Texas? That it's time to store my weapons in my gun cabinet?"

"Well... yes... sort of," she began, hating it when he reversed her logic.

Bishop interrupted, wagging his finger, "We don't need SAINT teams anymore, Bishop. You can't carry your rifle into government buildings anymore, Bishop. You need a license to drive, Bishop. We have to pay taxes, so we can have government services, Bishop."

She sensed his argument was based on more than just the need for a change of scenery, but she kept her observation to herself. "Okay, okay, you've made your point. How long would be we gone?"

"Four days," he shrugged. "Six at the most."

Terri began to pace the room, her mind working on everything from what they would need to pack, to how they could keep Hunter entertained. Her contemplative expression made Bishop think he was about to lose his Great Piney Woods vacation before it even started.

The Texan suddenly brightened and then played the winning card. "Besides, isn't our anniversary next week? We could make this a romantic getaway."

She stopped, mid-step, her head snapping up to stare in amazement at her husband. "You remembered!"

"Of course, I remembered. Don't I always?"

"I don't know. The last two years, you were away on some secret mission or out in the mountains training. How would I know if you remembered or not?"

He pulled her close, gazing deep into her eyes, "Please. Let's do this. We'll have a great time."

She brushed a tender hand on his cheek, caressing and thinking at the same time. "I suppose I could ask Mrs. Ramirez to watch Hunter for a few days. I know she's short on money this month. I could offer her extra pay, and we could leave our son here where it's safe."

"Would that allow you to relax and have a better time?" he asked.

"You're not the only one who gets a little tired of the daily grind. Yes, I would feel better if we left Hunter here with people we trust. Besides, I think he's been flirting with Mrs. Ramirez's granddaughter. She's as cute as a bug's ear."

Bishop pretended to be concerned, puffing out his chest and a smirk crossing his lips. "Is this young lady good enough for our son?" he teased.

Terri laughed at his reaction, then added, "I hope we never have a daughter. I can't imagine what you're going to

17

put those poor teenage boys through when they come calling."

Wringing his hands like a mad scientist hatching a plot, Bishop responded in an almost evil tone, "I can."

CHAPTER 2

The pickup was loaded for a road trip, Bishop stuffing everything he thought they might possibly need into the bed. "Good thing I put that camper shell on," he mumbled, having to push hard on the last box to close the tailgate.

"All ready?" Terri called from the porch, lugging one last suitcase behind her.

Shaking his head while pointing at the bag, Bishop replied, "Well, I was."

Terri grinned, her expression betraying her complete lack of remorse for contributing another piece of luggage to the bed. "Sorry, I thought of a couple of last minute items. Is there room?"

"We're only leaving for a few days, darling," he grumbled.

"Don't give me any crap, Bishop," she answered, her small fists now perched on her hips. "Half of that stuff in the truck is your 'just in case,' items, like extra ammo, all of your fighting gear, and two spare rifles."

"You never know," he countered. "As you pointed out, our road trips sometimes don't go according to plan."

"You promised me this time we would be safe," she sighed.

As he hefted her case into the back seat, Bishop nodded, "Should be. Like I said, we're not leaving civilization or anything. We're in Alliance territory the entire way. Given the law and order speech Watts gave me the other night, you'd think all of Texas is as tame as a toothless, old hound." He grunted to exaggerate the work involved in accommodating the new bag before continuing, "Besides, you *do* have a history with slithering serpents, my love. Best to carry some spare ammo."

"Good thing we're not taking Hunter," she challenged after scanning the stuffed bed. "You would've never made it all fit."

The mention of his son caused Bishop a twinge of guilt. Or was it worry? Despite having only dropped the boy off an hour ago, he already was missing his child. "Oh, rest assured that I could manage a spot for our little guy. Maybe we should take him?"

"I know what you're feeling," Terri replied. "But I'm sure he'll be fine. Still...."

"Let's get going before we change our minds," Bishop suggested. "Always go with your gut, not your heart."

Ten minutes later, they backed out of the driveway, both of them working through a mental checklist, worried they were leaving something behind.

It occurred to Bishop that even with the recovery, traveling wasn't as simple as it used to be. A hefty percentage of the pickup's bed was consumed by gas cans, the availability of precious fuel spotty at best, especially for strangers journeying through unknown territories. There weren't any brightly lit neon signs along the interstate advertising food or billboards indicating the price per gallon of diesel.

Meals were another unknown. Unlike before the collapse, truck stops, fast food joints, and roadside cafes no longer bustled with an influx of travelers. No, most of those areas looked like ghost towns now. Here at least, Bishop's employment helped a little. Pete's series of restaurants and food trucks were a known commodity. Regardless, Terri had insisted on packing enough grub for the entire trip.

Shelter was their largest single concern. Well-run hotels, like Meraton's Manor, were rare, and advertisements for such establishments were not reliable. Most roadside billboards had not been updated, so travelers might follow them to a luxurious inn that had been burned out years ago. Local knowledge of resources was critical to find clean and safe sleeping quarters. Therefore, another section of the bed's real estate was dedicated to their tent and camping equipment.

Currency was another issue. While the Alliance's new printed money was widely accepted in the major population centers, Bishop had heard stories of some businesses refusing to accept the notes. Coinage was still issued by the United States. Gold was universal, as were medicines and ammunition. The West Texan had plenty of the latter on hand – just in case.

Still, with all the potential roadblocks to a proper holiday, they needed timber for their home and a break from the everyday grind. Despite all their concerns, Bishop looked forward to spending some quality time with his bride, as well as adding a little spice to his routine. Terri felt the same way.

With the stereo's volume cranked, West Texas passed by the pickup's windows quickly, Terri having stashed a few of their favorite music CDs in the console. The miles rolled by with both passengers singing, playing air guitar, and pretending to bicker over which melody was the best.

At one point, they stopped at a former border patrol checkpoint and enjoyed a quick brunch of cheese and homemade bread. They picnicked in the shade of the abandoned building's metal canopy, enjoying their entire meal without another vehicle approaching. "Well, I gotta admit," Bishop commented once they had resumed their journey, "there's nothing quite like Armageddon to solve lunchtime gridlock. We've got the whole road to ourselves today."

"Now, Bishop," Terri chided, "I hope you don't mean to suggest that the collapse of society solved your road rage issues." She chuckled before continuing, "you know, though... I gotta admit that the West Texas landscape is even more stunning without the constant distraction of passing ragtops, SUVs, muscle cars, hatchbacks and clunkers.

Four hours into the journey, Bishop veered off the state highway onto a smaller paved road. Hoping to infuse a little romance into their little excursion, he had planned a special meal at Pete's newest eatery. Located in Round Rock, Bishop was sure the employees there would be able to provide information on available fuel and shelter.

By mid-afternoon, they pulled into Pete's new digs, the travelers impressed by the facility's ease of access. "Pete's got the Midas touch, for sure," Terri observed. After her mate stowed the pickup on the grass just beyond the parking lot, Terri hopped out and stretched her road-weary, cramped muscles.

Bishop sprang out the driver's door, responding, "Well, I am glad he does since the old boy's success is what pays my salary. Although, if it stays this busy, I am going to have to speak to him about adding a little more asphalt out here," he light-heartedly teased.

The distinct aroma of sizzling food accompanied by a country music ballad floated across the parking lot and beckoned the couple inside. Bishop, on his best behavior, bounded to the pickup's passenger side to escort his date properly. He smiled at her, brushing the hair from her cheek to admire the natural beauty that was his bride. "This way, little lady," he flirted, wrapping his hand over hers, the lovebirds now meandering toward the restaurant's entrance.

After a round of introductions, Terri was shown to their table. She perused the menu while Bishop took a perfunctory tour of the place, happy to play his role as VP of Security. Everything seemed in order, the newly hired staff anxious to impress.

The house specialties were fried chicken, chicken fried steak, deep-fried catfish, and when available, fried shrimp. Terri was concerned for the local population's cardiovascular system, "I sure hope there's a qualified heart surgeon in the area."

"As a matter of fact, he's seated by the drink station," Bishop countered, turning to point out a table near the window. He leaned in close and continued in a voice barely louder than a whisper, "Rumor is that Pete's got him on retainer." Terri giggled at her mate's quick wit, all the while making a mental note that her husband seemed more relaxed than he had in months.

The coleslaw was excellent, as were the baked beans, their waitress boasting about how all the veggies were locally grown. Today, however, Bishop couldn't get enough of the buttery, soft rolls. Round Rock had become a production center for yeast during the recovery, making beer, wine and bread so much tastier these days.

Bishop received directions to a local gas station that wasn't price gouging, as well as a campground that was considered safe and offered running water for showers. "I have been assured that this place is clean, so it looks like we're pitching a tent tonight, my love," Bishop advised his wife.

"Wow, Bishop, sounds like a regular 5-Star resort," Terri responded, "running water can be such a luxury item these days."

"Wonder if the showers are co-ed," Bishop mused, an unmistakably suggestive and slightly mischievous expression on his face.

After a round of "See you soon," and "Have a good trip," the couple was off, Bishop relieved to fill up his tank at the local station. "Now, with the cans I have in the back, we have enough fuel to make it home. Cross one worry off the list."

They drove another 20 minutes through the Hill Country, each fascinated by the changing topography and landscape. Colorful rock formations poked out here and there, offering evidence of ancient volcanic eruptions that had formed a long-forgotten mountain range, leaving rolling hills and a sandy plateau dotted with limestone and granite. The sun hung late in the afternoon sky when Terri noticed a brood of wild turkeys strutting across a grassland, nibbling on native wildflowers and weeds. Bishop slowed the truck for a better view.

Once the feral birds became aware of the human spectators, they became skittish and headed for cover. Built for speed, their lean and agile bodies sprinted across the savannah. Like planes accelerating on a runway, they took to the sky, eventually settling in the trees that framed the prairie. Yes, the Hill Country was spectacular.

Eventually, the carbohydrate-laden meal combined with the warmth of the day caught up with Terri, and her lashes became heavy. She was just nodding off when Bishop noticed a metal sign that stretched over an intersecting lane. "Next stop... Shady Acres Campground," he announced in his best tour guide voice as he signaled to exit.

A series of rustic, hand-painted directionals marked the way to check-in. "Travelers welcome," Bishop read aloud as Terri shook herself to full consciousness. "No Smokers, Vagabonds or Tramps."

"Smokers?" Terri questioned, her mind now absorbing the mixed bag of messages. "Good thing I left my cigars at home."

"I don't think that's what they meant," Bishop grinned. "But we'll see. Frankly, I'm a little more concerned about the ban on tramps," he continued, his eyebrows arched in a suggestive manner, his mouth curled in a smile.

Terri playfully jabbed him in the arm to let him know he was straying into no man's land before she artfully steered the conversation. "There probably is a dress code that goes along with that restriction, Bishop. Sort of a modesty requirement. I bet you have to leave your speedo thong in the suitcase," she teased.

With that, Bishop launched a retaliatory tickle fight, his left hand on the steering wheel while his right arm stretched to the far side of the truck. Terri was prepared for the attempt to one up her and skillfully maneuvered out of his reach.

A short distance later, Terri read another notice, "Maximum Stay – 3 Nights. Alliance issued identification is required. We are not a waystation for Smokers!"

"Looks like management has had some issues," Bishop nodded. "And would you believe it? I think I left my passport and my birth certificate in my other pants."

"No worries," she responded, waving her arm as if to dismiss his concerns. "Pay in advance, and you can probably get by with leaving a hair sample for DNA typing. You know... just in case," she laughed.

The pickup rounded a bend through a stand of scrub oaks and pecans, entering the parking area for the campground. A pre-manufactured home in a previous life, the repurposed building clearly housed the facility's office. Terri offered her assessment quickly, "Look at the way the pecan tree canopy grows over the driveway. The whole place looks welcoming, neat and clean... well maintained and charming."

They dismounted from the truck, both stretching before securing accommodations. Bishop spied a middle-aged lady discreetly studying them from behind a curtain.

The entrance was locked, a small note mounted above the doorbell. "Press for service," it read. Bishop did just that.

A mechanism on the door buzzed, allowing them entry. Bishop immediately noticed a shotgun leaning against the wall behind the counter. "Can I help you?" the proprietor asked, standing beside the conspicuously displayed weapon.

"Hi," Terri began, "we're traveling to East Texas on business and need someplace to camp tonight. Do you have any sites available?"

The woman relaxed after Terri's greeting, but only a little. "How did you hear about us?"

"I'm in charge of security for Pete's restaurants throughout the Alliance," Bishop explained. "I was just visiting our new facility in Round Rock, and they recommended your campground."

The lady's eyes darted toward the pickup, obviously searching for any clues that might help her judge the veracity of Bishop's story. "Do you have Alliance identification?" she asked.

"Yes, ma'am, we do," Terri responded, reaching for her purse and providing the newly minted driver's license. Bishop did the same.

The owner carefully examined their credentials, before warily looking over the couple one more time. Maintaining eye contact with Bishop, she moved closer to the counter, leaned toward her prospective customers, and gave Bishop a big sniff. Taken aback by the tactic, Bishop tilted backward, away from her. "Ma'am?" he questioned, throwing Terri a 'what the hell?' glance.

"Checking to see if you're a Smoker," she bluntly replied.

"I don't smoke," Bishop stated. "Maybe a cigar once a year, but other than that, I'm tobacco free."

"No, no, no," the lady fussed. "That's not what I mean. I'm checking for campfire smoke. The vagabonds and drifters always smell like burning wood because they live out in the open. We call them Smokers."

Finally satisfied, the woman smiled, the stress exiting her shoulders. "I'm sorry to appear unfriendly," she replied. "You don't know how much trouble we've had with bums and gypsies."

"Really? Is it a big issue?" Terri inquired.

The innocent question seemed to fuel the proprietor's anger. "Yes, it is, and it seems to be getting worse every single day. Most of the troublemakers come from the east, places like Louisiana and Mississippi. It seems like every mother's son has heard that Texas is now the land of opportunity, so they head west. Most of them don't have a pot to piss in, let alone the basics to survive. They get here and expect to be taken care of... by ME... and that's just not

26

going to happen. Don't get me wrong; I am a kind and compassionate person, but I am not the Alliance Welcome Center, or a soup kitchen, or a homeless shelter, or a refugee camp."

"I had no idea this was a problem," Terri replied. "We're from West Texas... around Alpha and Meraton, and I have not heard of any issues there. In fact, our leaders are concerned about a potential labor shortage if the recovery continues at its current pace."

"I've got no quarrel with people looking for legitimate work," the lady replied. "It's those that are seeking a handout or something to steal that cause us headaches. Just two days ago, somebody tried to make off with my well's pump handle and broke it in the process. Last week, some yahoos dug up an entire row of my radishes and green beans after they pulled my corn and helped themselves to the tomatoes. These pilferers will rob you blind if you turn your back. Damn lazy, shiftless drifters. I've got no use for them."

"We're won't cause you any problems, ma'am. In fact, if you have a campsite for us, we'd like to invite you to share a meal with us this evening. We've got fresh sausage and greens. Terri is a great cook, either on a stove or over a fire," Bishop offered.

While their host declined the offer, the couple from the west could tell it served the intended purpose of allowing her to relax. "Thank you, but no. These days my stomach is especially sensitive. I'll sign you up for our best site. It sits off a small lake, has good shade, and offers a smooth spot of ground to pitch your tent. You're welcome to gather any firewood lying around. Just please don't cut on my trees."

"That sounds just perfect," Terri chirped.

"We'll take it," Bishop declared, adding, "Do you accept Alliance currency?"

"Yes, or US greenbacks. The price is $10 per night Alliance, $15 US."

After receiving cash from Bishop's pocket, the proprietor produced a hand-drawn map with directions to site number 14. "We have two RVs and a motorhome over on the other side of our property," she noted. "You two are the only tent campers here right now, so you shouldn't be disturbed. Checkout time is 10 a.m."

They drove over a narrow lane, through a pasture, and into a lightly wooded area. As the trees grew thicker, so did the outcropping of rocks, Terri noting the unusual white hue of the limestone that was so much different than West Texas. A few hundred yards later, they arrived at number 14.

Bishop was pleased with the layout, a thick hardwood tree dominating the area, providing shelter and shade under its massive trunk. "We don't see trees like this around Meraton," he whistled, admiring the ancient oak.

The site was bordered on two sides by a 15-foot high wall of stone, Bishop's truck and the oak providing the remaining two walls of what was essentially a makeshift fortress. He decided not to mention the tactical advantage to his wife. They were here to enjoy some time together, and he didn't want to come across as paranoid or of having been spooked by the stories of the grouchy, facility owner.

They both wanted to move around a bit and stretch their muscles before unloading the truck, so Bishop tucked a pistol inside his belt, and they headed off to explore the area. He locked the pickup, just in case.

A few steps later, Terri stepped in close, wrapping an arm around his waist, "This is like an oasis... so green and alive," she cooed as they walked. "Not at all like the desert. It reminds me of Houston, only not as humid and with better trees."

Bishop agreed, "You got that right."

They found the lake, a half-acre body of water just over a slight rise. Bishop wondered if it were stocked with fish, Terri secretly wishing she had packed a bathing suit. She didn't say anything, though, knowing her suggestion would send her mate's mind down a mental path that led to skinny dipping.

Navigating the bank, the Texan spotted two flat stones and decided to impress his bride with his rock skipping skills. He managed three jumps on his best throw.

"I got this," Terri replied, searching the ground for the perfect projectile.

With a sideways whip of her arm, she watched with glee as her toss bounced and skimmed across the surface, "One! Two! Three! Four... five... six! I got six, Bishop!"

"Nice," he replied, his male ego only slightly dinged.

After a 20-minute long, meandering stroll, they returned to the pickup and began setting up camp. "Do you want the tent or a hammock?" Bishop asked.

"Just a second while I get the weather report," she replied, licking her index finger and holding it up to check the wind while she scanned the sky.

"Funny," he laughed. "You know damn good and well that there are no more weather reports."

"Oh, I know, that's one of the things I miss the most." Terri continued in her best announcer's persona, "Expect it to be hot in Houston today folks... with a 92% chance of heat and humidity till the end of time."

Bishop chuckled. "Well, I don't know about that, but I didn't wash the truck before we left home, so I have no reason to expect rain," he reasoned. "So, which will it be, my love? Want to sleep under the stars... or take advantage of the privacy of our portable boudoir?"

"Both," she announced, crossing her arms in anticipation of his protest. "I want both. That way, I can sleep in the comfort of the hammock, but if it starts raining, I can hightail it into the tent."

"How about I set up the hammocks and if it starts to pour, we can catch some Z's inside the truck?"

Terri wrinkled her brow in disdain, her eyes narrowed to slits. In her opinion, Bishop's Plan B clearly came up short.

"Uhmmmm, I am not engineered to sleep in the pickup," she retorted.

"The seats recline...."

"Bishop, I am not a pretzel."

Holding up his hands in surrender, he capitulated, "Okay, okay, I'll set up both. Can you gather the firewood?"

"Sure thing," she nodded, feeling only slightly guilty.

"Now... watch out for rattlesnakes," he teased before she'd managed two steps.

"There are poisonous snakes here?" she squeaked, stopping mid-stride.

"Yes, but they're rare. Just be careful when you reach to pick up the wood."

He had to chuckle when she returned to the truck and retrieved her pistol, her eyes now scanning each footfall. "Beware, you venomous vipers. I am prepared to use you for target practice," she cautioned. "I am *not* going to get bitten again," he heard her mumble.

Keeping an eye on his wife, Bishop began setting up their sleeping accommodations. After unloading a cooler full of food and the tent, he set about securing one end of his survival net to the tailgate, the other to the oak's trunk.

Normally, in the field, Bishop would have used rope or double-stranded paracord to tie each end of the net. Now, he was eager to try a new trick a friend had passed along in Pete's. A moment later, a soft clicking sounded from the campsite.

"What's that noise?" Terri called.

"I'm using ratcheting cargo straps to secure the hammocks," Bishop replied as he worked the small handle. "It's always tough to get rope or cord tight enough, but not with these babies. Why didn't I think of this before?"

He'd packed another net in his wife's pack, and soon, both suspended bunks where swinging freely in the breeze. Terri returned just then, dumping an armload of branches next to the stone-lined firepit.

She wasted no time in testing the lodgings, plopping onto one of the nets and then rolling her up her feet to get horizontal. "Nice," she said, gently swaying. "Where's my pillow and mint?"

"It's not bedtime just yet," Bishop protested, bending to separate the kindling. "I have to finish setting up camp, and you've got to make supper. It's been at least a half an hour since I had a snack," he teased.

Grinning from her perch, Terri's voice dropped low and sexy. "Will these fancy straps of yours hold two people?" she asked, running the fingers of one hand from her chin to her throat, traveling down as far as the top button of her blouse.

Bishop's head tilted back in laughter, "If I didn't know better, I would think you were trying to distract me from my chores, Terri. Be careful, because you know I have a weakness for those beautiful legs of yours."

"I don't know what you mean," she replied, batting her eyelashes while she feigned innocence. "You're just trying to get in my pants, Mister. I can see right through those sugary words. They're a dastardly attempt to circumvent my virtue."

"Why, Madam, how did you know?" he grinned, standing and then bowing deeply. "I salute your perception... and that sexy smile of yours."

Pretending to refocus on the fire, Bishop half-turned, and then moved like a striking cobra. In a flash, he grabbed the side of Terri's net and dumped her into his arms, cradling her like a newborn.

Yelping in protest, she had no choice but to throw both arms around his neck to keep from being upended. For a precious moment, they stared, and then kissed passionately.

"Later," she whispered, "I'll alter your perceptions of the universe. But for now, if you'll put me down, I'll make you a culinary masterpiece."

Hesitating, Bishop finally nodded, gently lowering her to stand. "The way to a man's heart," he teased, returning to the fire.

"Well, that too, I suppose," she winked. "But really I was just thinking that I needed for you to keep your strength up."

A short time later, the crackle of burning wood accompanied the odor of a campfire as Terri worked a knife and pan. Bishop kept himself occupied unfolding their blankets and double-checking the straps holding his wife's net.

He had just finished erecting the tent when she announced their meal was ready. Rubbing his stomach, Bishop took his plate and hopped up to sit on the tailgate. Terri joined him.

They feasted in silence, watching the sun as it dropped behind the trees to the west. High, red streaks accented the Columbia blue sky, providing the perfect dinner show. After devouring the fresh sausage and garden-picked green beans, Bishop pulled her close under his arm. "This is perfect," she whispered. "I'm glad you talked me into this."

After throwing another log on the fire, Bishop eyed the spool of fishing line lying beside his pack. After a quick mental debate, he decided against putting out trip wires and noisemakers.

"Just a year ago, I wouldn't have considered going to sleep in a strange area without some sort of early warning device," he informed Terri. "Am I getting slack? Lazy? Overconfident?"

"No," she smiled. "You're coming to grips with the recovery. There's no one around and no reason for anybody to bother us. Besides, we need to get going early in the morning, and it always takes you forever to roll up all that fishing line. We'll be fine."

Shrugging, he replied, "I suppose you're right."

After a second, longing glance at the line, he returned his gaze to the fire. It was quiet here. They hadn't even seen or heard the people on the other side of the campgrounds. He just needed to relax and chill a bit. Hell, he might even pull off his boots before going to sleep. "We're all nice and civilized now," he whispered to the night.

He remained fireside, contemplating everything from tomorrow's drive to his job working for Pete. Hunter filled his mind, as well as the intimacy he had just enjoyed with his wife. "You're a lucky man," he decided. "A great wife and son. A generous employer. Good friends and hope for the future. Maybe society's collapse isn't all that bad."

A yawn signaled it was time to turn in. After tossing one more log onto the campfire, Bishop made sure the truck was locked and Terri was asleep.

Hefting his carbine, the Texan then unlaced his boots and gently rolled into his net, pulling in the cold metal and sharp edges of his rifle. "I know, I know," he mumbled quietly, glancing over at the oblivious Terri. "I'm being paranoid. Maybe next year I'll be able to sleep with only a pistol."

Bishop had no idea how long he'd been asleep when something made his eyes pop open. Had he dreamed the noise? Was it his imagination? The fire?

Without breathing or moving his head, he scanned the campsite, noting the reduced level of flame rising from the embers. He'd been out... maybe two hours, perhaps even three.

Again, the crack of a snapping branch sounded from the far side of the pickup, the Texan's mind racing to calculate the distance. Whatever, or whoever, it was, the trespasser was close. His grasp tightened on the M4.

Coiled for violence, Bishop's mind raced with his priorities. The highest was obviously protecting his wife, Terri sleeping soundly in her nearby nest. If some intruder came in from the front of the truck, he would roll left; from the back, he would have to go right.

He focused on remaining motionless, even pacing his breathing. He strained his ears, hoping for a break in the still

33

night, when the crackle of a boot crunching leaves alerted him, this time from the far side of the campsite. The realization shook him to his core. *There is more than one. They are approaching from two different vectors.*

Before Bishop could recalculate his first move, a human shape appeared in the shadows. Standing just beyond the dying fire's sphere of illumination, it seemed to be studying the campsite's layout.

"Cover the tent," hissed a low, barely audible voice from behind the pickup. "I'll get the cooler and search the truck."

Bishop knew he and Terri were in trouble. The angles were all wrong, the raiders sporting superior numbers as well as being on their feet and able to maneuver. It would take him at least a second to roll out of the hammock and bring his weapon into the fight. That was an eternity in combat.

What if there are more than two? he pondered. *I should have set up the trip wires. Damn it! First, you're too slow and weak behind Pete's, and now you're caught here with your pants down. Idiot!*

The shape from beyond the fire turned into a person, then morphed into a woman. She was holding a Louisville Slugger wooden bat.

Bishop assessed her quickly, noting her rail-thin arms, dirty, torn dress, and wild, ratty hair. She was unsteady, scared to death, and filthy. She didn't even have shoes on her feet.

What the hell, Bishop thought, his mind revisiting the campground owner's bitch session. *Who brings a club to a gunfight?*

Another form appeared just then, slinking quietly from the pickup's back bumper. This intruder was male, his clothing tattered, an unkempt beard and long, dirty hair trying to escape the baseball hat on his head. He carried a long gun.

Bishop waited several heartbeats, wanting to make sure more raiders didn't appear from the murky darkness. He wasn't worried about the woman with the bat. It was the firearm that held his attention, and its owner was obviously more focused on the cooler than anything else.

I'll wait until he lifts the food and kill him, Bishop plotted.

Step by cautious step, the gunman crossed the campsite, his eyes never leaving the ice chest. *He's like a thirsty man in the desert, mesmerized by an oasis*, Bishop thought, his thumb now on his carbine's safety.

"Gordon," whispered the woman. "This isn't right. Let's leave... now."

"But we need the food," Gordon protested, his voice a little louder than it should have been.

"Not this way," she replied. "I'd rather starve. Let's go, before we wake these people up."

The female burglar didn't wait for Gordon to respond, pivoting quickly to walk away. Her partner in crime, however, didn't want to leave without food, rocking back and forth as he tried to reach a decision.

"Are you that hungry, Gordon?" Terri asked.

He pivoted to turn, startled by Terri's words. The bolt-action in his hands made it only a few inches higher before she stuck the barrel of her pistol against the back of the wannabe thief's head. "Don't," she warned. "You won't make it."

Bishop, stunned by his wife's unexpected appearance, took longer than he should have to roll out of the net. *Where in the hell did she come from? Had she been using the restroom? Did she hear them long before I did?*

Once clear of the hammock, his weapon was up, his voice snapping, "Drop the rifle! Drop the rifle now!"

Bending slightly at the knees, keenly aware of the gun pressed against his skull, Gordon slowly lowered his weapon toward the ground. The woman reappeared at the edge of the fire, "Please... please don't kill him," she begged. "There aren't even any bullets in his gun."

35

Not about to sucker for that old line, Bishop dashed across the campsite and bent to snatch Gordon's firearm from the dirt. The woman, believing the Texan was attacking, rushed to defend her man.

Her intent was unclear to Bishop, his carbine moving to cover her advance. Gordon, thinking his partner was about to be shot, leapt to grab the Texan's weapon.

Bishop's foot shot out, catching Gordon's leg just above the ankle. In a howl, the scarecrow fell, clutching at his limb.

Stunned by how easily his foe had been felled, Bishop took the bolt-action and stepped back. Dropping to her knees, the woman tried to comfort her fellow burglar. "Are you okay?" she cried, her throat already choked with emotion.

Checking the weapon, Bishop was surprised to find it was indeed void of ammunition. "Who in the hell tried to raid a camp with an empty gun?" he mumbled to Terri.

"I traded my last two rounds for a cup of rice," Gordon explained from the ground. "Our kids wouldn't stop crying. We had to eat."

"Stand up," Terri commanded. "Lift up your coat... I want to see your waistline. Any weapons?"

"No," Gordon replied. "I sold my knife last week. I got four ounces of beef jerky. I'm unarmed."

The robber did as Terri instructed, Bishop stunned by how his attacker's hip bones jutted from his torso. "You said you have kids? Where are they now?" the Texan barked, scanning the darkness beyond the edge of the fire's light.

The woman turned, facing the direction she had come. "Matt, Daisy, come on in here. It's okay. Come on in."

Two soiled ragamuffins shuffled into the light, neither of them having seen their 10th birthdays. Both children looked like hell, their eyes glued to the ground while their thin bodies shivered with fear. Even Bishop's heart was touched.

"Okay, what's your story, Gordon? Start talking," Terri demanded.

"We're from Baton Rouge. Before the collapse, I worked in a chicken processing plant, and Stacey taught second grade in the local elementary school. Since the government fell, things were bad there... really bad. There was never enough to eat. Our suburb was controlled by some crazy warlord dude who siphoned off every food shipment and demanded protection payments. There were no police, no courts, no services whatsoever. We finally got desperate five weeks ago and headed for Texas. Our car was stolen just before we crossed the border, along with most of our supplies. It's been pure hell ever since."

"And you can't find work?" Bishop asked.

"No. I've stopped at every town and village since we crossed. I don't have any tools, nor do I have any experience with the building trades. I worked two days for a farmer just west of Beaumont, but he accused me of stealing and threw us off his land at gunpoint without paying me a cent."

Stacy jumped in, "I lost my eyeglasses when our car was stolen. I can't see well enough to read without them. Everything we've heard about Texas was a lie or exaggeration. The people here have been cruel, rude, and downright violent. There's no work anywhere, nor will anyone help a stranger. We were better off starving back in Louisiana."

Bishop and Terri exchanged troubled looks, the couple wondering how much of their captives' story was true. While there had been a few rumors and accounts about sections of the Lone Star Nation where the recovery lagged, it was difficult for the couple to believe things were that bad.

"First, I'll take that baseball bat. Then, open the ice chest," Terri ordered. "Feed yourselves and your children. We can talk after you've eaten."

The couple from Texas moved out of earshot yet remained close enough to keep watch as their famished guests descended like a pack of ravenous wolves on the cooler.

"What are we going to do?" Terri whispered to her husband.

"Not much we can do," Bishop answered. "We can give them some food, maybe even a little money. If they can make it to West Texas, then I'm sure they could find work. Problem is, that's several hundred miles. They look to be in bad shape."

"You got that right," Terri nodded, watching as the youngest child alternated between chest-deep coughing and trying to swallow a mouthful of food. "No way they'll make it without help."

A period of silence followed, both Texans trying to think of some solution to help the pitiful immigrants. There just weren't any good options.

After nearly an hour, the travelers stopped eating, almost embarrassed at how much they had consumed. Bishop approached cautiously, reaching for his wallet. "Here's $50," he began. "If you can make it to West Texas, a lot of the towns there have church groups that will help newcomers find work and shelter. Go to Meraton, Fort Davidson, or even Alpha. There are bulletin boards in those towns where jobs are advertised. Along the way, look for churches as well. Take another loaf of bread and a pound of jerky. I even have a spare map. Other than that, there's not much we can do to help you."

Gordon and his wife were amazed, gushing with thanks. The children smiled for the first time.

By the time the two families separated, the sun was rising. "Might as well start breaking camp," Bishop announced. "No way we're getting any sleep now."

The campground's showers were excellent, the sun-steamed water still bearable due to the warmth of yesterday's rays. Bishop had just finished pulling on a new shirt when he spotted Shady Acre's mistress approaching with her shotgun.

"Did they give you any trouble?" she barked, clearly upset.

"Ma'am?" Bishop responded, quickly growing tired of everybody they encountered having a damned 12-gauge pointed in his general direction.

"Those drifters," the woman answered, "did they take anything?"

Shaking his head, Bishop grinned, "No. They tried, but my wife had gotten up to powder her nose. She got the drop on them, and everything turned out okay. We gave them some food and money, and they went on their way."

"You did what?" the old grouch snapped. "Lord in Heaven, Mister, I wish you hadn't done that. Now they'll tell all their gypsy friends and every other hobo they bump into. I'll be inundated with bums!"

"They're headed for West Texas," Bishop countered, quickly growing tired of the woman's negative bias. "They had starving children, and we're not the sort of people to turn our backs on those in need."

Waving him off with a dismissive hand, she spat, "Easy for you to say, young man. Your business isn't going to be full of prowling tramps. You're not welcome here anymore. Kindly pack up and leave and do not come back."

With that, she spun angrily and stomped off, cursing and mumbling with every step.

Terri appeared from the women's shower just then. "Who was that?"

"That lovely, generous woman from the front desk," he answered, quickly repeating the conversation.

"No good deed goes unpunished," Terri replied, shaking her head. "Let's hit the road."

CHAPTER 3

Bishop navigated using state highways, passing between Houston and Dallas as they headed to the far, northeast corner of the Lone Star Nation.

Their destination was a town called Forest Mist, a small berg residing where the Texas, Louisiana, and Arkansas borders met. According to their contractor, a sawmill operating outside of the town was the best source of hardwood logs in all the Alliance.

Located at the northern end of the great Piney Woods, Forest Mist had been a lumber town since the 1850s.

And what a forest it was.

Mile after mile, the couple passed through nothing but trees and met no other vehicles on the road but trucks transporting logs. No farms, businesses, or even homes came into view. Just lots of pine, oak, birch and other patterns of bark they couldn't identify.

At over 12,000,000 acres, "The Thicket" as the massive woodland was nicknamed by the locals, had been a source of timber for the United States during the expansion years, as well as both world wars. Hardwoods dominated the northern reaches while the south was thick with pines. Many of the post-WWII homes constructed for returning veterans had been framed and roofed with East Texas lumber.

Even today, in post-collapse Texas, the region was the primary source for critical resources, especially housing and commercial building.

Nearly 50% of the Alliance's population hadn't survived the apocalypse, which should have translated into half of the available housing being unoccupied. There should have been plenty of roofs for every citizen, even given the increased immigration to Texas. That supposition, however, was completely wrong.

To begin with, high-rise housing was practically unusable without consistent and reliable electricity for elevators and city water with enough pressure to reach higher floors. The units in these multi-story monstrosities were among the first abandoned homes when society collapsed and remained so to this day. Each of the now-empty buildings had once sheltered hundreds of residents.

Like most of the United States, the citizens of Texas had been heavily concentrated in the larger cities. While Houston, Dallas, Austin, and the other major metropolitan areas still offered plenty of available single-family living, their homes were sited on postage stamps, incapable of supporting sustainable living. After the downfall, people migrated en masse out of the urban areas to the countryside where there was enough open land to grow food, dig wells, and survive. Despite the Alliance's efforts to restore utilities in the population-dense metropolitan areas, people were still leery of residing there. Folks wanted land, gardens, cows, pigs, chickens, and a safe distance between themselves and neighbors who might turn violent.

Who could blame them?

Bishop remembered living in Houston after things had gone to hell. The raiders, gunfights, and entrenched fear that spread through his neighborhood were still fresh in his mind. He and Terri had gotten out. Procuring enough food, water, and security to survive in a compactly inhabited area was nearly impossible.

The Texan had heard the stories told by those who had experienced far worse. During the lowest periods of the collapse, mankind's worst tendencies had reared their ugly heads. It was no wonder that the metropolises were struggling to recover their citizenry while quaint, rural areas were beginning to realize housing shortages and population booms. People had been the problem and would be again if the apocalypse ever returned for round two.

Bishop had travelled to East Texas twice since the collapse, both visits due to a mission assigned to his SAINT team. The area was very different from his native desert in the west, almost as drastic a change as visiting a foreign country. The Piney Woods had its own unique vegetation, terrain, and culture.

"I'm going to look up the local marshal when we get to town," Bishop announced.

"Oh? Is something wrong?" Terri frowned.

"No. It's always a good idea to let the authorities know when you're around," Bishop replied. "Besides, when I told him we were leaving town for a few days, Sheriff Watts gave me a package to deliver... probably secret law enforcement papers and official documents. He said this guy was a friend of his, and he suggested I stop in and introduce myself."

"Okay," she shrugged. "Seems a little weird, but given how trouble always follows you around, I suppose it's not a bad idea."

Pretending to be hurt, Bishop retorted, "Trouble follows *me*? Now isn't that the pot calling the kettle black?"

"I only get in hot water because I'm bailing you out of one mess or the other. I'm a nice girl... innocent and chaste. I can't help it that you're a magnet for dark clouds," she teased.

"*Innocent and chaste?* Why you little shit," he grinned. "You and Diana are the ones always conjuring up these hairbrained schemes, sending us men into Indian territory... or some hotbed of nefarious activity south of the border. Hunter and I just want to live the quiet life, do a little hunting and fishing, chill in a mellow, stress-free state of bliss."

The image of Bishop holding a fishing pole, complete with bare feet, bib overalls, and straw hat made her laugh. "Sure... you bet."

Terri tried to envision Bishop relaxing in a sparsely populated forest like the one surrounding her. "This scenery reminds me of that old television show with the town called Mayberry. For the life of me, I can't quite place the sheriff's name," she mused, drumming her fingers on the console as if doing so would encourage her neurons to fire a little faster and come up with an answer. Finally, after searching the recesses of her childhood memories, Terri remembered. "Please tell me that sheriff's name in Forest Mist isn't Taylor?" she questioned.

"No, I don't believe so," the driver grinned, pointing to the surrounding ocean of foliage. "I think his name is Woods."

"Bishop."

"Or was it Timberlake?" he continued, barely choking back a chuckle.

"Bishop...."

"I've heard he's thinking of *branching* out and getting away from law enforcement and into the private sector," the Texan deadpanned. "A lot of people think his *bark* is worse than his bite, but I don't believe that's the *root* of his problems. I've heard he's nothing more than a *sap*."

"Bishop! Stop! Please!"

"Sheriff Watts knew his father, said the man was a *chip* off the old block," he added.

"Do you ever want to have sex with me again?" she demanded, staring at him with a puzzled expression, her arms crossed on her chest, wanting to laugh, but knowing that if she did, he would never stop.

"Okay, okay. I am going to go out *on a limb* and guess that you're getting *board* with this."

She couldn't help it any longer, a deep, belly laugh finally busting loose. "Such sophisticated humor. Next thing you know, you'll be asking me to pull your finger," she managed between guffaws.

"Speaking of fingers," he said with a straight face and holding out a digit, "Could you check this for me? I think I picked up a *splinter*."

44

That did it, Terri's eyes watering as she hooted out of control. "Please! Stop! I have to pee!"

They arrived in Forest Mist a few hours before sunset, driving slowly through the main drag, gawking at every storefront and sign. It wasn't a big place, the business district less than 10 blocks long. Like most Texas towns, the center of the village was dominated by a courthouse and its surrounding square.

The couple noted two cafes, a gas station, a local coffee shop and a second-hand clothing store. A smattering of boutique businesses dotted the downtown landscape. Bud's Small Engine Repair was the only service industry represented on the square, and according to his rudimentary window advertisement, he specialized in chainsaw repair.

"Bud's is a cut above the rest," Bishop mumbled as they drove by, his comment eliciting a playful punch on the arm from his wife.

The town's shopping traffic was modest, but busy. People hustled along the sidewalks, many carrying purchases from one shop or the other. They all wore clean clothing and looked like they bathed and shaved on a regular basis. A gaggle of small children kicked a ball around an empty lot, their energy a sign of good nutrition, their unsupervised activity a sign of security.

Bishop and Terri passed a grocery store, the front of the building boasting several stacks of small, wire cages. Terri noted both chickens and rabbits were for sale. A hand-painted sign on the window advertised, "Fresh Milk."

Bishop had learned a lot of lessons during his time with the teams. While Terri focused on the goods and services available, his eyes were scanning for other indicators. There were a lot of firearms on display, but they were carried casually, a few rifles slung over shoulders, most pistols concealed under jackets. Weapons, in Forest Mist, were accessories, not primary tools, and that was a positive. *The recovery is in full swing here*, Bishop noted.

His light surveillance detected no indication of tyranny either. Another, even bigger plus.

In many of the communities his SAINT team had visited, some strongman or bully had taken it upon himself to fill the void of leadership after the local government had collapsed. Sometimes it was a businessman; other oppressors had been the local deputies or previously elected officials. Many had begun with their hearts in the right places and had ultimately been corrupted by power. It was an age-old tale that repeated itself time and again.

Not here, however. A bulletin board full of notices advertised community meetings and gatherings. Bishop noticed a single sheet newspaper on sale for five cents per copy. That same rag was being read by two men on the next corner. The white clapboard church's sign not only listed 10 a.m. services on Sunday, but a Bible study class on Tuesday night. The elementary school was having a PTO gathering on Wednesday, as well as a bake sale for the band on Saturday.

Dictators and warlords couldn't tolerate public gatherings. Towns that were under the heel of a tyrant weren't allowed to hold such events. Unrest might follow if people met in large groups and talked. Questions could be asked, and the answers might not promote the oppressor's agenda. Conspiracy might find welcoming ears. The foundation for an uprising could be established.

The clearest example of freedom and democracy, however, was a series of faded, yet still-readable posters hanging from the utility poles. "Vote," they advised. "Election on November 6th. Exercise your most important right at the Oak Street Fire Station."

At the next stop sign, Bishop turned, following a small green sign with an arrow. It read, "Courthouse."

A moment later, they pulled into an empty parking spot adjacent to a police car.

"I hesitate to ask," Terri ventured, "but what is the marshal's real name?"

"Plummer," Bishop responded without any hint of deceit in his voice. "Dallas Plummer. According to Watts, he's been a lawman around these parts for four decades."

The couple entered the time-worn courthouse, Bishop following the signs indicating that the city jail was located in the basement. The building smelled of old-fashioned floor wax, ammonia-based window cleaner, and musty cigars.

Strolling inside the marshal's office, they found themselves facing a chest-high counter. Behind the thick wooden barrier was a twenty-ish female deputy perched on a tall stool. Her nametag read, "Plummer."

"May I help you?" she inquired politely, her eyes giving the two visitors a serious once-over.

"My name is Bishop. This is my wife Terri. We just arrived in Forest Mist from Alpha, and my friend, Sheriff Watts, asked that I stop in and say hello to Marshal Plummer."

"Who's out there, Allison?" a gravelly male voice boomed from some unseen office.

"You have visitors, Dad. Say they're from Alpha," the deputy answered.

An older man appeared around the corner, Bishop judging the officer to be in his mid-50s. He had a slight paunch and wore civilian blue jeans and a flannel shirt. A .45 automatic, complete with pearl grips and a hand-tooled holster, hung from the gent's belt, keeping a shiny, silver badge company. "I'm Dallas Plummer. To what do I owe the pleasure?"

Extending his hand, Bishop repeated his introduction.

Nodding and accepting the handshake, Plummer said, "That old law-dog Watts sent a message that you were coming our way. How's that worthless piece of worn-out cowhide doing these days?"

"The sheriff is well," Bishop responded, handing over the small box he was assigned to deliver. "I think he's like everyone else, stressed over trying to make things like they were before, but other than that, he's doing just fine."

"His shortwave message said you were both heroes of the Alliance, that the two of you played important roles in reestablishing the rule of law. Heck, even out here in the backwoods, we've heard of Miss Terri. So, allow me to welcome you folks to Forest Mist. I appreciate your delivering this package and stopping in. If there's anything we can do for you while you are here, just let me know."

The couple from West Texas watched as Plummer produced a pocket knife and quickly opened his bundle. A moment later, he pulled out a hunk of cheese, wrapped in plastic. Bishop was puzzled.

Noting his visitor's perplexed expression, the local lawman explained, "Watts lost a bet to me last year. I staked a quart of our best local honey, and he wagered a pound of goat cheese. I won."

"What was the bet about?" Terri inquired.

"Who would retire first," Plummer announced with a huge grin. "Last month, I announced I'm not interested in reelection. I hope my daughter decides to run for my job," he continued, nodding toward the attractive deputy. "She's a better cop than I'll ever be."

The polite conversation continued for several more minutes, small talk about Forest Mist, the marshal's pending retirement, and of course, the recovery. Allison, it turned out, had earned a master's degree in criminal justice, graduating at the top of her class, and she was without a doubt her father's pride and joy.

"Before the downfall, I had planned to turn in my badge for a rod and reel," Plummer explained. "When things got really bad, I couldn't just sail off into the sunset. Now, with the Alliance and all the progress we're making, it's time to hang up my gun belt and do some fishing. Hopefully, the worst is behind us."

The conversation easily turned to how the apocalypse had changed the world. Though they had only met, the four of them shared a defining, common experience... one that would no doubt frame their lives for as long as they drew breath. They had all lived through an Armageddon, and they all lost friends and family in the process. They each shared a survival story or two as they reminisced about the poignant experience of survival. Eventually, Terri changed the subject, asking the lawman, "Can you recommend a hotel or a safe place to hang our hammocks?"

"There's a bed and breakfast operating over off Walnut, about three miles outside of town. If they're not full, you should be able to get a room. You'll see the sign."

"Thank you for your hospitality, Marshal," Terri replied.

"And don't wait too long to begin that extended vacation," Bishop interjected as they headed out the door. "You know, even a *bad* day of fishing is better than a *good* day at the office."

Following Dallas' directions, the couple soon approached the lodge. A white sign edged with lattice welcomed them, advertising Angel's Porch – Bed, Breakfast, & A Friendly Smile.

Before them stood an impressive 'Painted Lady,' a turn of the century Victorian home bejeweled with detail and colorful paint. The wide, front steps beckoned them to the veranda that spanned the front and two sides of the home. Terri felt that she had just stepped back in time to an era where the occupants took time to relax, unwind and socialize. She envisioned herself sitting in one of the old rockers, reading a book while she sipped a cool drink. Bishop noticed the hanging swing, the yard shaded by majestic elm and oak trees, and the sidewalk that bubbled up where the roots had displaced it. The place looked warm and inviting.

Terri observed that there was only one other vehicle in the driveway, a good sign that there was room at the inn. As they trekked over the uneven sidewalk, Bishop spotted a series of hand-painted signs mounted in a vertical row on an antique, cast iron, Victorian era lamp post. The first read, "No Soliciting." Below that, another message, "No Handouts." The final warning, "Beggars & Trespassers will be Prosecuted."

Again, next to the front door, another sign: "No free lodging. This is not a shelter. Paying customers only."

Exchanging looks with her husband, Terri commented, "Just like the campground. This must really be an issue around here."

Bishop knocked, then stepped back from the door so as not to appear threatening. A dog began barking immediately. A minute later, a female voice answered from behind the still-closed door.

"May I help you?"

"Marshal Plummer suggested we stop by and see if you have an opening. My name is Terri; this is my husband Bishop. We're in town from West Texas and need someplace to stay for a night or two."

"Do you have cash?"

"Yes, ma'am, we do," Bishop replied, patting his backside to indicate his wallet.

The door inched open, but only just enough for the round face of a young woman and the sneering teeth of a German Shepherd to peer through. "Please accept my apology. I don't mean to be impolite, but we've had quite a few problems with Smokers and people on the dodge," she explained. Her canine companion merely growled another greeting.

Since the collapse, dogs had been nearly as popular as chickens, cows, and other farm livestock. People still felt insecure, many families having lost loved ones to violence, malnutrition, or disease. Bishop understood that some folks still considered their pooches as the first line of defense, so he kept his eyes glued to the bristling canine. Seeing Bishop's continued interest, the proprietor warned, "This is Thor, and he doesn't like strangers trying to pet him."

Believe me, lady, I have no intention of moving anywhere near those lethal tusks, Bishop thought. Producing his billfold, Bishop opened it far enough to display a significant amount of green currency. "You must be Angel. Let me assure you that we are only hoping to be your paying guests. Do you take Alliance or US?" His question seemed to reassure Thor, the canine relaxing his attack posture somewhat. Bishop still wasn't convinced that the big, snarling fangs were not a threat toward him or Terri. *That beast is still a long way from winning Mr. Congeniality in the Forest Mist Dog Show,* Bishop thought.

The innkeeper blushed momentarily, almost as if embarrassed. "Angel was my mother. My name is Carlie. After mom passed away, I kept the business name. Besides, having a new sign painted is expensive. A room, with breakfast, is $25 per night Alliance. We could also work out a deal for gold or silver. Still interested?"

Bishop thought the price was high and was about to ask if a filet mignon was included with the breakfast buffet, when Terri jumped in, responding, "That's fine. Do you need payment in advance?"

"How many nights?" Carlie asked, opening the door and waving them inside.

"Probably one, maybe two," Terri answered, crossing the threshold and scanning the interior.

"If you can pay me for one night, then we can settle on any extra before you leave," the innkeeper replied. "I serve coffee, fresh eggs, and homemade bread for breakfast."

"Where did you get coffee?" Bishop inquired, wondering if Carlie's source might be the same as Pete's top-secret vendor.

"There is a man from South America who owns his own ship, a small freighter I'm told. Twice a year, he brings a load of coffee beans into the port at Beaumont. People come from all over and sometimes camp out for days to buy his product. He only sells it in 40-kilo burlap bags of beans, but it is excellent, and the only game in town."

Smiling broadly, Bishop asked, "Have you ever seen a shorter, thick, balding man in his late 50s buying up large quantities of the beans?"

Shaking her head, Carlie said, "I've never personally been down to the harbor to buy. About six months after the collapse, Marshal Plummer organized a few men to head down there with a wagon and team. How he knew about the shipments, I have no idea."

Rubbing his chin, Bishop decided he would have to stop in and ask Plummer some questions. This definitely warranted further investigation. Despite a fair amount of badgering, Pete had never revealed his source for coffee. When no one else in the entire Alliance had java, the tiny bar in Meraton brewed a fresh pot every day. There had to be a connection.

Terri, however, wasn't as nosy. "May we see the room?"

Carlie put the dog away and then showed them into the parlor. The B&B was clean, adorned with simple, antique decorations that generally accessorized a rural residence, and was well-appointed with old, solid, plain furniture.

"The room is this way," Carlie offered, leading the way to the sleeping quarters. The couple from West Texas was escorted up a narrow, creaky wooden staircase. At the top, Carlie opened a heavy, pine door and motioned them inside. "If you decide to stay, breakfast is in the main dining room at 8 a.m. Your bathroom would be through that door. We even have hot water," she turned to identify the facilities before continuing, "but please don't steal the toilet paper. I'm down to my last case and have no idea where I'll get more."

Terri thought the room was tastefully decorated and charming. Bishop still had questions. "How many other guests do you have for this evening?"

"You folks and a cattle salesman from Port Arthur," Carlie answered. Then, to cover the uncomfortable pause where her potential customers debated whether they would be her guests, she rattled on. "You see, the two big lumber mills in town have taken to buying beef on the hoof to feed their crews. We have electricity most days, but every now and then the power is out for two or three days in a row. It's hard to keep food from spoiling when that happens."

"We'll take it," Bishop announced after exchanging nods with his bride. "I like the noisy stairs and the fact that I can see the truck from this window."

"Speaking of lumber mills, we're here to see a man named Whipsaw Jones. Have you heard of him?" Terri inquired.

"Oh, yes, everybody knows Whip. He owns one of the two mills I was speaking of."

"We are here to purchase logs for a home we're building out in West Texas," Terri went on to explain. "Our contractor told us about Mr. Jones. He said your friend had the best lumber in all of the Alliance."

A fleeting flash of some unknown emotion crossed Carlie's eyes, just a shadow of reaction that Bishop couldn't quite read. "He is Forest Mist's largest employer. I'm sure he'll be able to help you."

The Texan wanted to ask more questions, still confused by her unintentional response. Terri, however, had other ideas. "Bishop, you should probably get the truck unloaded. It's getting dark outside."

Assuming his wife wanted to quiz their host girl-to-girl, Bishop nodded and replied, "Sounds like a good idea."

Breakfast was as advertised, the bread excellent, as was the coffee. It helped that the visiting couple got to sleep in a real bed and that no one tried to sneak off with their truck or its contents.

Carlie gave Bishop directions to Whipsaw's place of business while Terri finished her shower. It was 9:30 a.m. on a pristine, cloudless morning when they backed out of the driveway at Angel's Porch.

In reality, Bishop could have probably found Whipsaw's mill without directions. The perpetual parade of empty log trucks led right to the right to the establishment's front gate.

He steered the pickup into what appeared to be a substantial operation, including an expansive, gravel parking lot, several metal structures the size of three city blocks, and the unmistakable rumble and clatter of Herculean machinery at work.

Terri pointed out a sign indicating visitor parking, the vacant spots relatively near the front of a single-story building sporting blue paint and a towering sign that announced, "Jones Lumber, Inc."

"Looks like they've got plenty of wood," Bishop noted, gazing at a massive pile of logs that must have been 60 or 70 feet long and taller than his head.

"Big place," Terri nodded. "Let's go see how much this is going to cost us."

Terri stepped onto the pickup's side rail before springing to the crushed rock below. A wide smile spread across her face as she grabbed a folder from the truck. Almost giddy as she reviewed the information inside, she turned to Bishop and gushed, "Now... I have all the specs for the wood in here." Flipping the pages, she murmured, "I wonder if they have a price list."

Bishop smiled as he walked toward her, pleased to see her enthusiasm for their building project. Terri had worked hard to make the modest camper, as well as a series of rentals, a home. Clearly, she missed having a space she could personalize for their family – a place to really make their own. Now, for the first time since they bugged out of

Houston, she would have a spot to put down some deep roots. Bishop rested his palm on the small of her back, gently guiding her through the parking area, her focus immersed in the papers in front of her. Satisfied that indeed she had what she needed, Terri stopped short and turned to Bishop, fairly beaming, "You know, most people don't know this, but seven US presidents lived or were born in log cabins.... And besides that, log cabins are energy efficient, so the house will stay cooler in summer and warmer in winter.... Plus, the wood breathes, so we will have better air quality, too."

"And this whole time, I thought you got this idea from Hunter's Lincoln log set," Bishop teased. He grinned at her obvious exuberance, grabbed her hand, and took a moment to search her eyes. "Seriously though," he began, his tone becoming soft, "our lives changed when society collapsed... in ways that we never saw coming. This is a dream of ours that has been on hold for a long time, and I can't think of anyone I'd rather share this with than you." He leaned over, brushed back her hair and kissed her on the cheek, and then closed his own eyes for just a moment as if trying to preserve the memory in his mind forever.

"Oh, Bishop, I haven't been so excited about anything in a long time," she responded. Then taking a deep breath, her entire demeanor changed, "But now... I have to put on my poker face. Time to negotiate." Her expression quite stoic, she became all business on the outside. "Let's do this."

Now almost across the lot, the couple was just a few feet from the sidewalk leading to the mill's main office when Bishop paused, pointing out a notice that said, "Not hiring. Not accepting applications."

Terri shrugged, dismissing the message. "Clearly sales must be down," she speculated. And then with a twinkle in her eye, she continued, "I believe we can fix that."

"I hope we aren't going to singlehandedly jumpstart the local economy," Bishop fired back, grinning at his beaming bride. The couple mounted the steps to the extensive front porch, noting yet another sign, this one created by hand, scrawled in thick magic marker, and stapled by the front door. "No Trespassing. Gypsies and Smokers Not Welcome." But it was the last message that really caught the couple's attention. A wood placard trimmed along the outer edge with crude drawings of pistols, long guns and semi-automatic weapons, conveyed its message with absolute clarity. It simply read, "We DON'T Dial 9-1-1."

Opening the door for his wife, Bishop waited until Terri had stepped inside before crossing the threshold. Before his back foot had even planted, a large fellow wearing work clothes and a hardhat shoved Terri back out the way she'd come. Had it not been for Bishop's chest acting as a backstop, she would have surely fallen.

"Can't you fucking people read!" Bellowed the oversized fellow, moving toward the visitors with clenched fists.

Surprised, shocked, and not completely understanding what was happening, Bishop took longer than he should have to respond. He managed, "Hey, asshole, we're looking for Whipsaw Jo...," just as the behemoth took a swing.

Ducking under the haymaker, Bishop shoved Terri out of the way with his left hand as his right delivered a punishing jab dead center in the buffoon's crotch. Three quick rabbit punches followed, the Texan pissed to high heaven that someone would dare lay a hand on a lady, let alone his wife.

As the attacker staggered backward and howled in pain, Bishop charged after him, another blow snapping the hefty man's head back with a sickening thud a nanosecond before a brutal kick deflated his chest.

Just like in the Bible, Goliath fell to David's assault, jarring the floor as he landed in a heap. Bishop, not feeling like the ass jackal had paid with enough pain, stepped in to deliver more punishment. He was also determined to make sure his much-larger opponent didn't regain his feet.

"Freeze!" a new voice shouted, Bishop detecting the outline of another hardhat rushing in. The new arrival was pointing a pistol at the Texan's chest.

In a flash, Terri's 9 mm was up and ready, counter-covering the gunman as she screamed, "Drop it!"

For several seconds, a standoff was in play, everyone's eyes darting among the weapons and fighters, all of them afraid to move. "Why did you attack us?" Terri hissed. "We're here to buy logs, not start World War III!"

"Bullshit!" the injured guy barked from the floor, blood running from his nose. "You're another pair of those worthless bums, in here wasting my time, looking for something to steal!"

Bishop drew back his leg to deliver another motivational kick to the loudmouth at his feet, but was interrupted by yet another new, booming voice that rolled through the room. "Everybody stand down! Right this fucking minute. Everybody put those damn guns away. This is a business, not a Wild West saloon. What is going on here?"

Another larger than life shape appeared from the hall, Bishop positive Whipsaw Jones had just joined the fray. "Is everybody deaf?" he bellowed a second later. "Lower your weapons! What in the hell is going on here?"

"I caught these two sneaking into the office!" declared the bleeding gent at Bishop's feet. "I tried to move them back outside, and this guy sucker-punched me!"

"You ever put a fucking hand on my wife again, limp-dick, and I'll do more than put you on your ass!" Bishop responded, his weight shifting forward to the balls of his feet.

"We're here to buy lumber," Terri interjected, her voice steady and her pistol never wavering. "We simply walked in the door, and that man shoved me... hard. Do you always greet customers this way, Mr. Jones?"

"That's bullshit, Boss. I had to use the john, and they snuck in," Mr. Bleeding Badly claimed.

At nearly 6'6" inches and well over 300 pounds, Whipsaw Jones was built like a proverbial oak himself. At least 60 years of age, time had rounded out his mid-section, and there was a stiffness in his back and legs that came to men who had performed heavy labor for decades. Still, Bishop sensed tremendous power in the giant's arms and shoulders. His eyes were clear. He was unphased by the weapons and blood. He was in charge, and he had been for a long, long time.

As Bishop concluded his evaluation, so did Mr. Jones. The logger's eyes were quick, noting the strangers' clothing, body language, and weapon. Finally, he stepped to the window to assess the pickup truck parked outside.

His attention then returned to the workman still bleeding on the floor. "Use the john, my ass," Whipsaw spat. "You left your post and were back in the office flirting with Alice, you lazy piece of shit. Worse than that, you let this little guy put you down? I ought to fire you and hire him to keep an eye on things. Now get up, before I let him finish you off."

Before the weighty guy could rise, Whipsaw reached out and lowered the employee's pistol. "I said put that down," he ordered.

Terri mimicked the other weapon, lowering her own blaster as things began to settle.

"Who are you?" Whipsaw asked, "and what do you really want?"

"We're from West Texas," the female gun holder answered in a strong, but polite tone. "My name is Terri, and this is my husband, Bishop. We're building a new house, and our contractor advised us that you could provide the logs we need for the construction. We drove here from Alpha, hoping to find the materials we need."

"Terri, you say? Are you the same Terri that helped form the Alliance?" Whipsaw asked.

"Yes, I used to work closely with Diana Brown, but I am retired from public service now."

The battered guard, with the help of his pistol-wielding co-worker, finally managed to stand upright. Bishop never flinched, his ire barely under control after seeing his wife blindsided. Deep inside, he prayed the guy would make another move.

"Get out of here. Go fix your nose," Whipsaw ordered his injured employee. "Come see me after I'm finished here. We're going to have a very serious chat."

After his two workers had left, Mr. Jones stepped forward and offered his hand to Bishop. "I'm sorry," he began. "It's very, very rare for customers to walk through that door. Normally, we only get Smokers begging for work or trying to steal food or tools. I can't tell you how much fuel and equipment we've had pilfered this last year. Two weeks ago, one of them actually strolled right in here and took two computers, a fire extinguisher, and all the groceries in the breakroom."

Bishop, in no mood to apologize, merely nodded his acceptance of the other man's words. "I'm sorry to hear that. We'll be on our way, Mr. Jones."

Motioning for Terri to go first, Bishop opened the office door to leave.

"After all that trouble, you're just going to walk away?" Whipsaw asked, seemingly annoyed.

"I don't think we want to do business here," Terri responded over her shoulder.

"Fine by me. We don't need your type around here anyway."

Making their way cautiously back to their truck, Bishop had to smile when he noticed Terri had never put away her blaster. The couple didn't exhale until they were a few miles down the road.

"You okay?" Bishop asked.

"Yeah. Fine. You?"

"I'm good. I guess our options for shopping have been narrowed by 50%, though. What's up with these people around here? I've never seen such paranoia."

"I can't answer that," Terri frowned. "Seems like a complete overreaction on the surface, but then again, we've not walked a mile in their shoes. Maybe there is a real problem here?"

"Or maybe there was," Bishop countered. "I lost count of how many times we saw towns making a mountain out of a molehill when I worked with the teams. Either that, or someone is utilizing the old method of creating a fictitious enemy out of thin air... to attract attention to a common lightning rod for hate."

"I don't follow?"

Bishop explained, "Like Hitler did with the Jews, or the communists did with capitalists, or our government did with the Commies – you make some group or segment of people the dreaded, to-be-feared enemy so that folks rally around your way of thinking. It's a tried and true method of directing hate and instilling terror so that the average Joe Nobody forgets about his own problems."

"Do you really think that's what is happening in Forest Mist?"

"I don't know, and to be blunt, I don't care. We're here to buy materials for our new house and to have a little fun in the process. I'm just not in the mood to become embroiled in local problems. The Alliance honchos determined that the SAINT teams are now obsolete, so I am definitely off duty."

Reaching across the console to gently touch his arm, she shared her observation with her mate. "You sound bitter," she whispered. "I thought you were past that. Besides, the opportunity Pete has offered you in the private sector is quite lucrative, my love."

Bishop nodded and said, "I still think it was the wrong decision. My sour grapes aren't because I lost my job, but from my concern about the future of Texas. Hell, Terri, you and I made huge sacrifices and even risked our very lives to establish a stable society. What we built can easily be destroyed if this fledgling civilization is not nurtured and protected... and neither you nor I is in a position to protect it. It isn't as though the issues the SAINT teams addressed just disappeared overnight. They didn't vanish in the blink of an eye. The need to guard... encourage... develop what you and I worked so hard to create is still as strong as ever."

She didn't respond for almost a mile, and Bishop appreciated the silence. When she finally spoke, she abruptly changed the subject suggesting, "Let's get something to eat and find out about that other lumberyard. Perhaps Mr. Jones' competitor is a more reasonable supplier."

Having consumed a rather lackluster lunch, the couple returned to the pickup, this time heading to the south side of Forest Mist. Their destination was a lumber operation called Highland Hardwoods, recommended by the waitress at the cafe. The proprietor was another long-time resident named Leonard Yarborough.

Just over eight miles outside of town, Bishop steered the pickup down a badly paved, county road, entering a constant stream of log trucks. The asphalt was barely wide enough to allow two of the commercial vehicles to pass each other, had not maintained for several years, and was well beyond needing a few potholes filled.

After cresting a gradual rise, Bishop had to hit the brakes again. "A traffic jam? Out here in the middle of nowhere?"

Glancing up from the case of music CDs in her lap, Terri spotted several cars and trucks ahead, then quickly realized they were parked along the shoulder. "Must be a church picnic or something. Either that, or one hell of a garage sale."

Now barely creeping along, the couple soon got a good look at the first vehicle.

It was a late 1980s pickup, its bed and hood rusted, the tires' tread smooth and threatening to expose the wire in the steel belt radials. A man stood behind the truck, a woman and three children resting in the bed. "Carpenter will work for food," the large sheet of plywood advised. "I have my own tools. Quality work. Reasonable."

Indeed, spread over the ground at the man's feet, laid several saws, hammers, toolboxes, and a variety of other implements. He waved as Bishop passed, his eyes following the Texan's truck, hopeful it would pull over and hire him out.

Less than 20 yards further sat another pickup, this vehicle announcing it was the property of a drywall expert. Again, the claim, "Have Tools," was highlighted on his mini-billboard.

They passed at least two dozen examples of what Terri quickly termed a "Post-apocalyptic job fair."

One man advertised "Management experience," while another quipped, "Certified Mason. Brick, stone, or tile. 20 Years' Experience." An assortment of tradesmen including handymen, plumbers, and roofers rounded out the career expo.

Further off the road, Terri spied children playing in the weeds. Beyond them, someone had started a fire, the smell of sizzling meat permeating the area. Several people had pitched tents, others apparently living in makeshift structures constructed of cardboard, scrap lumber, and anything else available.

"A shanty town of day laborers," Terri proclaimed. "There must be 100 people living here, hiring themselves out for contract work."

Some of the trades were not construction related. "Housecleaning," announced one sign, two Hispanic women with aprons offering to tidy residences or office space. An older woman offered to do laundry, "50 cents per pound, you provide the soap."

"Look at the license plates," Bishop nodded, "they're all from other states. These people must be... what do the locals keep calling them? Smokers?"

While no one looked affluent by any measure, Terri didn't see any signs of malnutrition. These people were thin, but not starving. Their clothes were old and worn, but not filthy.

One of the last job seekers that drew Bishop's attention was a single, mid-20s fellows standing next to a newer model Ford pickup. "West Texas or bust!" the hand-painted, cardboard banner declared. "Skilled carpenter. Will work for food, money, or gasoline."

Tempted to stop and discover the young man's story, Bishop decided to keep on going. They couldn't leave Hunter with the sitter forever, and so far, they weren't having much luck finding Terri's building materials. *Water, water everywhere, and not a drop to drink,* he thought, scanning the sea of trees that dominated the area.

The entrance to Highland Hardwoods was only a short distance after the last of the shanty town's residents. The Texan pulled in slowly, taking his time to look for any notices, warnings, or armed security guards. He saw nothing but a lumber mill, less than half the size of Whipsaw Jones' operation.

The main office was a repurposed house trailer, supported by concrete blocks at the edge of a gravel parking lot that was in bad need of a few truckloads of rock. Still, men in hardhats hustled about, the sound of a distant saw competing with several working, diesel engines in the background.

"I'll go first this time," Bishop told his wife. "You cover my back. These people are jumpy and weird."

"Gotcha," she smiled, patting the pistol under her shirt.

Bishop knocked on the office door, waiting several seconds before checking the knob. "Hello," he ventured after opening the door about an inch.

"Hello?" a male responded. "How can I help you?"

The couple entered a modest reception area, occupied by a man in a hardhat who was working at a cluttered desk.

"We're looking to buy some logs and other lumber. You were recommended to us in town," Terri responded.

"Well, you've come to the right place," the greeter answered with a smile. "I'm Len Yarborough," he added, standing and offering a hand. "I'm the head cheese around here."

After a round of introductions, Terri explained their log cabin project while producing a shopping list of required materials.

Len seemed relieved, "When I first saw you pull in, I thought you were more of the townsfolk from Forest Mist, coming back to complain about the camp."

"Camp?" Bishop asked.

"You didn't see all those poor people alongside the road on the way in?"

"Oh, *that* camp. Yes, we did pass a lot of people looking for work," Bishop replied.

"I let them set up there, allowed those poor souls to use my property, and some of the long-term residents around here don't like it," Mr. Yarborough sighed. The lumberman then produced a pair of glasses from his shirt pocket and began reading Terri's wish list.

Whistling, he smiled and said, "You must be building quite a place out there. I can provide most of these items right now, but some of the larger pieces we'll have to cut."

"Can you ship them to West Texas?" Bishop asked.

"Yes, but it won't be cheap. Of course, you knew that before you drove all the way over here, right?"

"We had a pretty good idea," Bishop nodded. "I can guarantee diesel fuel in Alpha, as well as a crew to unload the lumber and logs."

"That helps," Len smiled. "Fuel is always an issue, and a truck large enough to haul this order is a thirsty machine. Would you like to go see my operation?"

Nodding, Bishop and Terri motioned, "After you."

It took nearly an hour to tour Highland Hardwoods, Mr. Yarborough's business encompassing several large buildings, storage facilities, and nearly a dozen saw houses. An assortment of forklifts, pickers, bulldozers, and trucks littered the grounds. The couple was also shown equipment specific to the logging industry, odd machines with names like tracked feller bunchers, grapple skidders, and knuckleboom loaders.

"Most of our product is going to north Texas right now," Len advised. "There is a lot of agriculture in that part of the Alliance and a strong demand for new housing. But I can assure you that we can supply you out in West Texas as well. Now, I have everything on your list but the exterior logs."

Pausing, Len then added, "Speaking of logs, you're the second person this week that's mentioned a log cabin. We had a traveler stop by a few days ago, a young man from up north who claimed to have experience building log homes. If I remember right, he was even from West Texas."

"Really?" Terri said. "Does he live around here now?"

"You probably passed him on the way here," Len responded. "He said he had family back in... in... Meraton, I believe. Was trying to get back to that part of the country."

Bishop remembered the young man with the sign. "Yes, I think we saw him."

"Seemed like a nice fella. He sure knew his lumber, that much I can say. I even offered him a job, but he said he wanted to go west. Was worried about his kinfolk."

After returning to the office, Yarborough began working on their order. "I'll need a 50% down payment, the rest on delivery," he stated, passing Terri a handwritten bill of goods.

Scanning the items listed, she frowned. "This is really going to stretch our budget," and then turning to Bishop, she showed her husband the estimated cost.

Again, a long whistle filled the room, Bishop's eyes stretching wide after reading the dollar figure at the bottom of the document. "Holy cow," he mumbled.

"A lot of that is transportation costs," Yarborough explained. "I will have to hire out a trucker to deliver your goods, and those guys don't work cheap these days."

Terri began doing some quick calculations in her head, finally nodding her agreement. "Pay the man," she said to Bishop. "We don't have much choice."

Standing, the Texan unbuckled his money belt and then worked an internal zipper. A moment later, he began removing several $100 bills from the hidden compartment, Sam Houston's image at the center of the Alliance's new currency.

As he counted the money, Terri had another thought. "My contractor was very adamant that the logs for the exterior of the home have no more than five-degrees of warp in any direction. Are you sure you can provide that quality of material?"

Rubbing his chin, the mill's owner responded, "That's a new one on me. But, as I said, we don't normally provide timber for log homes. I'm not even sure of how to measure for something like that. It will be about 10 days before we cut the exterior pieces. Maybe you can have your man come and inspect the product before we load it on the truck?"

Exchanging a questioning glance, Terri wasn't sure. "I suppose that would be the smart thing to do. Probably cost us less than a second shipment or sending the materials back. I'll have to see how much he'll charge us to do that."

After Bishop finished counting out the deposit, Len took the bills and locked them away in his drawer. "You'll see our truck by the middle of the month. Thank you so much for this order."

Feeling good about their purchase, Bishop and Terri stood and shook Len's hand before exiting. "I like him," both said at the same time.

On the way out, Bishop again slowed to pass the shanty town. "I've got an idea," the driver announced, quickly cutting off the pavement to park next to the man holding the "West Texas or Bust," sign.

"Hello," the fellow greeted, his smile genuine and wide. "My name is Nathan Hill. Are you looking for a carpenter or handyman?"

"Do you know anything about log cabins?" Bishop asked, accepting Nathan's offered hand.

"Yes, sir, I sure do. I worked for a development company in Tennessee for four years while I was in college. Their specialty was log homes. I learned a lot."

"What were you going to college for?" Terri inquired, instantly liking Nathan.

"Construction engineering at the University of Tennessee," Hill replied. "But everything went to hell my senior year, so I never got my sheepskin."

"So, you've built log homes?" Bishop asked again.

"Yes, sir. Sure have. Where is your home, and what's the problem?"

"We're building a new home," the Texan answered. "Between Meraton and Alpha."

The young man's eyes lit up like the Fourth of July. "Meraton? Oh, my goodness. I'm desperately trying to get back to Meraton. My uncle lives there, and he's the only family that I've got left."

Neither Bishop or Terri knew the uncle, but that didn't mean much since they had only arrived in the village after the collapse. Both secretly hoped Nathan's relative had survived.

"Let's go get something to eat," Bishop suggested. "Maybe we can do business and help you get home at the same time."

Nathan, rubbing his stomach, eagerly agreed. "I haven't found much work out here, and I hate to say this, but I don't have any money, sir. But if you're buying...."

"Don't worry about it," Terri grinned. "We'll take care of it. Why don't you ride with us, and we'll bring you back here after our meeting is finished?"

"I don't have a choice," Hill said, nodding toward his truck. "I'm almost out of gas."

On the ride into town, Nathan shared his story. Everybody had a story.

It was like so many Bishop and Terri had heard. Confusion when the terrorists had attacked. Trying to hunker down and wait for the government to get the grid back up and establish order. Eventually figuring out that things were never going to get back to normal.

"Us college kids really had no clue," he shared. "We had always had our parents, family, professors, and teachers guiding us through life. It never dawned on us that we were consuming everything from beer to toilet paper, and none of it was being replaced. Eventually, things ran out. Hunger matured some of us, heightened some deep-rooted need to survive. I was one of the lucky ones. I was already working a job to pay tuition, so I had a better understanding of how life really worked outside the academic bubble. That pickup I'm driving was actually a company truck. I looted enough diesel fuel to get home after it was clear our business was never going to reopen."

"Where's home?" Terri inquired.

"Gulfport, Mississippi," Nathan replied, his tone dripping with sadness. "My parents were divorced years ago. Mom and her sister, my aunt, lived along the Gulf of Mexico. They didn't make it. I found what was left of their bodies in the house, probably killed by looters... or worse."

"So why come to Texas?" Bishop asked, thinking he already knew the answer.

"I tried to make it along the coast. I fished for a while, scavenged whatever I could, always hoping and waiting for the government to come back to life. Gangs eventually took over, extorting protection money to even walk along the beach or travel through town. If I did manage to catch a few fish, I had to give them half. Everyone was shooting, pillaging, killing. I lasted over two years, hungry, scared, and lonely the entire time. Finally, I just had enough. I kept hearing rumors about the Alliance and how good things were in Texas. While I hadn't seen my uncle in years, I figured it was worth a shot. To be honest, I looted some diesel fuel and left in the middle of the night, packing my tools and whatever else I could gather."

"And?" Terri prompted.

"And life here is better, but not as good as what I had hoped. I guess I should've expected the resentment and distrust, but I didn't actually realize that I would be an outsider. I mean, I still think of us all as Americans, and I never considered that I would be entering a foreign country, you know? And, well, immigrants have always had a tough road to travel. While I didn't anticipate open arms and brass bands, the hostility toward anyone not 'from here,' has been a bit discouraging."

"I think you'll find things are a bit more welcoming in West Texas," Terri offered. "While there are probably a thousand reasons why the people here are responding like this, Bishop and I have been surprised by the overall attitude."

"That's good to hear," the passenger smiled from the back seat. "Not everybody has been an ass. In fact, Mr. Yarborough has been more than generous."

They arrived in Forest Mist, Bishop choosing to sample the other local café this time.

Marshal Plummer and one of his deputies nodded politely from their booth, and the couple entered and took the first open table.

A waitress appeared a few moments later, handing out three single-paged, handwritten menus. "The special today is pork tenderloins and mashed potatoes. We also received a few quarts of strawberries, but they're going quick."

The smiling server had no sooner left with their order than Bishop sensed a presence over his shoulder. Half-turning, he spotted Plummer standing nearby, the deputy a few feet away.

"Heard you had a run-in out at Whipsaw's place," the elder lawmen stated. "Heard things got a little tense."

Terri addressed the question, even though both officer's eyes were locked on her husband. "You might say that," she replied with her warmest smile. "You see, I don't like being assaulted, and neither does my husband. Mr. Jones and his goons are lucky they're still drawing air."

"According to what I heard, it was both of you that were the aggressors," the deputy said.

"You heard wrong," Bishop replied. "We went there to buy lumber and were greeted with violence. We only defended ourselves, and that's the truth."

"Neither of you have a mark on ya," the deputy continued, his words dripping with skepticism. "Yet, the man I saw out at the mill had clearly been pummeled. Kind of makes me question who was doing the assaulting."

Bishop turned in his seat, the Texan's eyes boring into the questioning lawman. "He struck first and missed. I defended myself and didn't miss. Do we have a problem here, Deputy? Marshal?"

Plummer seemed to be marinating Bishop's side of the story, the marshal finally taking a deep breath and saying, "Watts said you were good people. He also said you weren't afraid to mix it up, and that dead bodies seemed to sprout like weeds along your trail."

"Did you find any dead bodies out at Mr. Jones' mill?" Terri snapped, her temper beginning to surface.

"Not this time," Plummer nodded.

"Look, Marshal, we just purchased a truckload of lumber from Highland Hardwoods and will be leaving town tomorrow. We'll be out of your hair and heading west,"

Bishop stated, his opinion of the local lawman declining with each passing moment.

"All right then," Plummer said, evidently deciding that diplomacy was his best out. "I hope you enjoy the hospitality of Forest Mist for the remainder of your stay."

With that, the two lawmen headed for the front door, the encounter apparently forgotten as they exchanged greetings and friendly hellos with the other patrons.

"That was weird," Terri mumbled to her husband after the marshal had vacated the establishment.

"Naw," Bishop shrugged. "He's just doing his job. Remember, we're strangers here."

"Sounds like you all had a similar, less-than-hospitable 'welcome' at Jones Lumber as I did a few days ago," Nathan offered. "Only I thought they were going to shoot me."

"It wasn't the finest example of customer service I've ever seen," Bishop grinned. Then, rubbing his sore knuckles, he added, "but I filed a complaint that I'm positive got management's attention."

Wanting to change the subject, Terri produced Len Yarborough's invoice. "This is a list of the materials we purchased. Our contractor was adamant that the exterior logs had no more than five degrees of bend or warp. Do you know how to measure that?"

"Sure," Nathan smiled, happy to be back on familiar ground. "You only need a carpenter's square, a chalk line, and measuring tape. Easy."

Before Bishop could comment, Nathan continued scanning Len's invoice, "He's charging you a ton of money for delivery. One of the men back at the camp has a trailer big enough to hold most of this order, and my truck could pull it. Since I'm going to be driving to West Texas anyway, I could save you a lot of money by hauling your lumber on my own."

Terri liked the sound of that. "Really? Do you think it would hold the entire load?"

Hill studied the items again, finally shaking his head. "No, it would take two trips. Still, even with the cost of fuel, we could cut that delivery charge in half. I could follow you home with the first load, and then come back when Mr. Yarborough finished cutting the rest."

Glancing at her husband, Terri responded, "That would also save us some time. Our contractor could get started with the initial load and not be sitting on his hands for 10 days."

By the time they had finished their meal, an agreement was reached. Nathan was hired.

Outside, the Texan handed the younger man two $100 bills while Terri was distracted by a window display of the neighboring shop. "Rent the trailer. Buy a tank of diesel for your truck and some food for the trip. In the morning, go to Mr. Yarborough's mill and load up the initial materials. We'll meet you at that empty lot across the street tomorrow at 4 p.m. From there, we'll head for West Texas."

"Sounds good," Nathan nodded, reaching to accept the money. "Where will you be in case I run into any problems?"

Putting his arm around the younger man's shoulders, Bishop pulled his new friend further away from Terri and whispered, "I'm taking my wife for a little side trip. It's our anniversary and a surprise."

"What are you two plotting?" Terri grinned, trying to sneak up and eavesdrop. "I smell a rat."

"Oh, nothing dear," Bishop answered, his face a picture of feigned innocence. "Just some boring details. Ready?"

CHAPTER 4

Bishop and Terri pulled into Forest Mist, laughing and joking, giddy from their perfect day. "That was an excellent anniversary you pulled off, my love. One for the history books," Terri cooed.

It had been Carlie's idea, their host at the bed and breakfast telling Bishop that the most wonderful place in the world was less than 30 minutes away.

"Where might that be?"

"Rocky Falls State Park," the hostess had bragged. "You folks couldn't ask for more – a crystal-clear stream for swimming and a shady forest for a picnic. The waterfall is unspoiled, flanked by smooth, granite stones and centuries-old woodlands of sycamore, oak, spruce, and cypress supported by a leafy green understory and banks of fragrant, climbing honeysuckle. During the week, nobody is there, so you could have the place to yourself."

Not only had Carlie recommended the pristine location, but she'd also packed a gourmet basket for lunch, complete with a tasty bottle of wine for their peaceful hiatus.

It had been a special, relaxing day. Just what the couple from West Texas needed.

Driving to the intersection where they'd agreed to meet Nathan and his trailer of their lumber, Bishop was only mildly concerned to find no sign of their new friend. "It's probably taking Mr. Yarborough longer to load our stuff than anticipated."

Thirty minutes later, Bishop was starting to get concerned. After an hour, he put the truck in gear.

"Where are you going?" Terri asked.

"I'm driving to Highland Hardwoods. Either Nathan has had engine trouble, or he's taken our money and headed for parts unknown."

He was just pulling away when the waitress from the café darted across the street, waving her arms as if something was wrong.

Exiting the truck, Bishop and Terri met her on the sidewalk. "Sir! Sir! I'm glad I saw you. I think there's trouble with that young man you were dining with yesterday."

"What kind of trouble?" Terri asked the exasperated woman.

"He pulled up with a load of lumber about three hours ago, came in the café and ordered food. He even tipped me on a to-go order. When I glanced up a few minutes later, I saw Mr. Jones and three of his men surrounding his truck. They had their rifles out, pointing them at your friend. They took him away at gunpoint while one of them drove off with his truck and trailer."

"Did anybody tell the marshal?" Terri asked, her panicked expression betraying her worry.

"I told the cook to go to the courthouse, but the marshal wasn't there," the frightened server reported. "I just have the worst feeling about this."

"Please, try and find the marshal. Tell him we're on our way to Whipsaw's mill," Bishop snapped.

Without waiting for the waitress's response, Bishop rushed toward his truck. Opening the tailgate, he pulled out his carbine, armor, and load vest. "Get my rifle while you're at it," Terri instructed.

It took Bishop just a few minutes to throw on his gear, Terri slamming home a full mag into her own blaster. "This is bullshit," she growled. "They had no business with that kid or our lumber. If they have hurt him..." she began, silently finishing the thought.

The miles to Jones' sawmill passed in silence, Bishop's brain in high gear, recalling the layout, surrounding terrain, and any other detail he could remember from their first visit.

Half a mile before the turn to Whipsaw's operation, Bishop exited off the highway and onto an old logging road.

"They might be expecting us," he informed his puzzled wife. "Let's come in the back way."

He guided the pickup far enough where it wasn't visible from the main thoroughfare and then stopped. "We'll cut right through these woods. It's not far."

It was easy to navigate, the sound of Whipsaw's machinery their guide. Less than 10 minutes later, they had a good vantage of the main office. Nathan's truck was parked outside, a full trailer of lumber still attached to the hitch.

"Let's go get him," Terri announced, rising from behind a tree.

"Hold on a second," Bishop barked, motioning her back to cover.

A moment later, Terri spotted what had given her husband pause.

Across the parking lot strutted Whipsaw, his over-sized figure being followed by a gaggle of his men. Three of them toted rifles, the rest armed with nothing more than sweaty shirts and hardhats. "That should give those thieving curs something to think about," the boss proclaimed in a loud voice. "We'll cut down his body tomorrow before it starts stinking up the place."

"He didn't even die well," Jones continued after a few more steps, "begging and crying like a little girl. I'm telling you boys, these vagrants are scum... pure, worthless scum!"

Throwing his wife a look that was a combination of sadness and pure rage, Bishop motioned her back deeper into the forest. "I think we're too late," he whispered. "I have a feeling we'll find Nathan at the entrance."

Staying at the edge of the thickest growth, the couple quickly made their way to location where the mill's driveway met the county road. Sure enough, hanging by the neck from a large tree was Nathan's lifeless body. Next to his swaying corpse was a hand-painted sign, "This is what happens to thieves in Forest Mist."

"Those rotten, murdering bastards," Bishop hissed. "I'm going to bleed them all. Every, last one of them is getting a ballistic message."

Terri had seen her husband in similar states, unspeakable violence and carnage sure to follow. She had no words to stop him, a seething sense of injustice building in her own core. She was incensed as well, a boiling fury that encompassed her normally compassionate soul with an undeniable need for revenge.

"Go back through the woods, stay at the edge, but out of sight. You're going to be my sniper. If I get in trouble, keep them off my back," he instructed, his words icy with contempt for the men's heartless actions.

Nodding her understanding, Terri hustled away, remembering a tree stump that would make the perfect rest for her weapon.

Giving his wife a minute's head start, he double-checked his weapon while taking a knee. He had 28 rounds in the rifle's magazine, another three full boxes of pain pills on his vest. Terri could add half that amount of lead to the fight.

Bishop wanted to kill Whipsaw Jones as badly as he had ever craved to take another human life. The man was a murderer, vigilante, thief, and a danger to countless innocent people. Someone had to stop him cold.

Standing, the Texan moved with purpose toward the mill's office, marching boldly up the driveway in plain sight.

He didn't notice the sound of gravel crunching under his boots, nor did Bishop pay any attention to the background hum of machinery. As he approached what was sure to be a deadly encounter, he suddenly realized that killing Jones was too good for the man. Wouldn't it be better to see him stripped of his business, assets, and freedom? Surely that would inflict more pain than 62-grain lead missiles piercing his body. He should suffer a death similar to the judgment he imposed on bright, young Nathan. Being hung in public as a criminal was the proper ending to such a man.

A quick death was too good for men like Jones. The pain was but momentary, the agony far too fleeting. Besides, Bishop was tired of being chastised for the number of men he'd put down. About how *he* was a killer. He was sick of being looked at like he was carrying the Grim Reaper's scythe. Even the Alliance council had decided that men like him were too blunt an instrument for civilized society. Mankind had advanced beyond the need for his methods and tactics, had no place for those who made a living with a battle rifle.

No, Bishop decided as he approached the mill's office, *I'm going to haul this asswart into the marshal. Sheriff Watts says Plummer is a good man. He'll put this animal behind bars. Terri and I will come back for the trial and probably hang around for this bastard's execution.*

Surprisingly, he made it to within 50 meters of the main door without being challenged. Nathan's truck was there, as was the trailer full of lumber. "Whipsaw Jones! Whipsaw Jones, you cowardly fuck! Come out with your hands up!"

Someone peered out a window, then the door opened. Two men with long guns stepped out on the porch first, followed by the oversized lumberman. "What can I do for you?" Whipsaw bellowed. "You still mad about yesterday? Coming back here with a rifle seems like a bit over the top."

Ignoring the killer's words, Bishop got directly to the point. "You're going to tell your boys to drop their weapons, and then you're going to come with me. I'm taking you to the marshal, and you'll be charged with murder."

Whipsaw seemed genuinely surprised. "Murder? Who in the hell do you claim I murdered, Mister?"

"Nathan Hill," Bishop responded. "The young man you and your crew of jackals just lynched at the entrance to this mill."

Jones' face burned crimson red, his nostrils flaring in anger. "That wasn't murder, you pompous piece of shit. That was justice. We caught that lowlife bum red-handed, a trailer full of *our* lumber behind his pickup. He was heading out of town with his ill-gotten gains."

"That is my lumber," Bishop corrected. "I purchased it yesterday from Highland Hardwoods. I've got a bill of sale. I hired Nathan to haul it to West Texas for me. You've murdered an innocent man, and I'm going to see you pay dearly for that."

For the first time since the confrontation had begun, a shadow of worry passed across Whipsaw's eyes. Still, he was far from conceding. "Innocent man, my ass. He was living in that camp, alongside the rest of those guttersnipes and vagrants. Maybe he didn't steal *this* wood, but I'm sure he's guilty of a dozen other crimes. You can have your lumber back if you produce a bill of sale. Otherwise, get the hell off my land."

"I'm not leaving without you. Now you can be either dead or under citizen's arrest," Bishop warned. "We can do this the hard way... or the easy way. That's up to you."

"You're talking an awful strong game for a single man facing a lot of guns," Whipsaw spouted. "Why don't you get off my property before I tell my boys to ventilate your carcass and hang you up next to your friend?"

"You want more blood on your hands, Jones?" Bishop countered. "How many of these men do you want to see die today? Your specialty is trees, my vocation is death, and I'm a leading exporter. Man-up and own your actions. Face a jury of your peers. Accept justice before you get a lot of people killed."

Movement distracted Bishop. At the edge of his peripheral vision, he noticed human shapes rushing across the mill's lot. Evidently, Terri spied them as well.

Just as Bishop was moving his head and sights to identify the threat, Terri's rifle unleashed six shots in rapid succession, the impact of her rounds throwing geysers of gravel and dirt directly in front of three men trying to flank her husband's position.

The trio nearly fell backward, trying desperately to halt what had been a full-out dash for a tactical advantage. With clumsy movements that reminded Bishop of the Keystone Cops, they retreated, hightailing it back the way they'd come and out of sight.

Terri's escalation served to uncork a series of simultaneous events.

Seeing their cohort's efforts spoiled, two of Whipsaw's henchmen raised their weapons. Bishop dove for the cover of Nathan's nearby trailer and its load of bullet-stopping lumber. Men scurried both away and toward the main office. Terri moved as well, remembering her husband's lessons involving "shoot and scoot."

Whipsaw remained standing on the porch, screaming, "Cease fire! Cease fire!"

Bishop, now behind the trailer, centered the big boss' center-mass in his optic, ready, willing, and able to put an end to all this with one squeeze of the trigger. A single realization prevented the annihilation of the lumberman. "They haven't shot at you, yet," he whispered, hesitating for a moment. "If you shoot him now, you will be a cold-blooded killer as well... and just as guilty as the vile man cowering before you. You can't kill him."

Yet, it would be so easy. Whipsaw was a sizeable target, less than 50 meters away. The Texan could have almost thrown his knife and saved ammunition. Bishop was convinced the man was behind Nathan's murder, had just heard the man confess. Justice could be served with a single bullet.

Sirens and flashing lights then filled the lumberyard, three police cars racing into the parking lot at breakneck speed. Before Bishop could reconcile using his trigger finger, Marshal Plummer and his deputies screeched to a halt and poured out of their vehicles.

"Drop your weapons! Drop your weapons!" the lawmen shouted, mostly at the lumberjacks gathered around Whipsaw at the front of the building.

Moving slowly, Bishop did as instructed, raising one hand into the 'don't shoot' position while slowly pulling his carbine's sling over his head.

With his weapon on the ground, Bishop stood with both hands in the air. "Am I glad to see you," he said as Plummer walked his way.

"What in the hell is going on here?" the marshal barked, clearly upset at having an armed standoff disturb his afternoon.

"Whipsaw murdered my employee," Bishop replied, nodding toward the lumberman who was now surrounded by deputies.

"Why?" the marshal demanded. "I saw the corpse hanging at the entrance. What did the deceased do?"

"Does it matter?" Bishop responded as Plummer pulled the Texan's pistol from the holster at this belt. "He killed an innocent man."

The marshal, now convinced that Bishop was unarmed, seemed confused. "I've known Whip Jones since we played high school football together. He's an overbearing asshole and a bit of a bully, but he's not a murderer."

"He is now," Bishop answered, suddenly wondering if surrendering his weapons had been the smart move. Was Plummer in cahoots with Jones? Was the local lawman corrupt?

"Come with me," Plummer ordered, pivoting instantly. "I'm going to get to the bottom of this."

Bishop followed the marshal's brisk pace, his mind wondering if Terri still had a good angle. Again, he was proud of her for not showing herself when law enforcement arrived.

"Whip, what in the hell is going on here? Why is there a body hanging from your driveway? What's all the shooting about?" Plummer snapped.

"We caught a drifter with a trailer full of our wood," Jones replied, pointing toward Nathan's rig. "While this crazy son of a bitch claims it's his lumber, I still have my doubts. We confronted the pilfering bastard, and he did exactly what you'd expect, denied everything. I sent one of my boys to get you, but you weren't in the office, and the door was locked. The thief tried to get away as we tried to apprehend him... to hold him until you got back. In the scuffle, the bum was killed."

As the deputies collected a small mountain of firearms, more and more of Whipsaw's employees began to gather. Bishop could feel the loathing directed his way, could see the hatred in the local men's eyes.

"I heard you confess, claiming the victim cried and begged like a little girl," Bishop spat. I also talked to witnesses in town who saw you take Nathan away at gunpoint," Bishop interjected. "He was alive when you left Forest Mist. That's why I rushed out here, to try and straighten all this out. I was too late."

If nothing else, Jones was quick on his feet. "Yes, that's true, he was still alive. On the way back here, he tried to escape. He wouldn't stop fighting, made a grab for a gun. One of my boys put him in a chokehold, but he wouldn't stop resisting. Since he was dead anyway, I decided to use his body as a message to all the rest of that thieving hoard."

The lawman seemed to be buying Whipsaw's story – hook, line, and sinker. Turning to Bishop, he said, "See there, your man's death was an unfortunate accident. There was no murder here."

"I know a doctor in Alpha who can tell in a heartbeat if those rope burns on Nathan's neck came before, or after he died," Bishop bluffed. "Arrest him, Marshal, and let's get an expert in here to prove or disprove the charge of murder."

Everyone started to talk at once, Whipsaw's men all voicing their support with voices that were growing angry.

Plummer was obviously on the fence, the marshal's expression indicating he wished he had retired years ago.

Turning to one of his men, he ordered, "Go cut that body down and put it in my SUV. One way or the other, we have an unlawful disposal of remains."

"You can't be serious," Whipsaw protested. "When everything went to hell around here, we were burning bodies every other night. Hell, I buried my own sister in nothing more than a bedsheet out behind the church. Unlawful disposal? That's a joke!"

"Besides," jumped in one of Jones' assistants, "The guy we strung up wasn't a citizen of the Alliance, he was a drifter. Look at his license plates, they're from Tennessee, for God's sake. You can't arrest Whip for nothing, Marshal. The dead man had no protection under Alliance law!"

Several of the surrounding crowd voiced their support, a chorus of "Damned right," and "Hell, yeah," swirling over the lot.

"Quiet!" Plummer shouted, "Or I'll haul all of your asses in for obstruction!"

"He was a human being, not some wild, dangerous animal," Bishop said once things had settled down. "He was a man, a freeborn American, just like the rest of us."

"I bet you were one of those liberal snowflakes who didn't want any borders before the collapse," Jones laughed, pointing at Bishop. "You're an outsider here, Mister. You don't know the trouble we've had with those worthless drifters and bums! We don't want them here. We want them to leave us alone and stop stealing everything that isn't nailed down. Hell, you probably think Texas should be a sanctuary country!"

Another outburst of laughter and support arose from the gathered mob. Bishop ignored them and stepped toward Plummer while saying, "So now we can kill at a whim over economic status? No longer is race the excuse. We're enlightened, so religion isn't a problem. Nor is a man's creed important, ladies and gentlemen. Now, we kill based on how poor a person is. We hate, shun, discriminate, and murder because this man didn't get back on his feet as fast as everyone else? I believe in borders, and I know that there are no statutes against a man crossing into Texas from Louisiana. I also believe in the law. Do you, Marshal?"

Again, the Texan was stunned by the marshal's next statement, "Well, Bishop, Whip might have a point about protecting a non-citizen of the Alliance. Things have changed so much during the recovery, that I'm not even sure what the law is nowadays," Plummer stammered, clearly caught between the devil and the deep blue sea.

"Bullshit!" Bishop hissed, his eyes narrowing to slits. "Did none of you ever step foot in a church? 'Thou shall not kill?' There's not a society on earth that accepts murder. It is morally wrong, and if Jones gets away with it this time, what is to stop him from visiting any of your homes in the middle of the night the next time you have a disagreement? Arrest him, Marshal Plummer. If you don't, I can guarantee you'll have an avalanche of heartache fall on your head from the Alliance. You'll be up on charges, sir, and probably won't be spending your retirement with a fishing pole."

"And you'll testify?" Plummer demanded, repeating the obvious while buying time and hoping for a way out.

"Damn right!" Bishop hissed, his temper near the boiling point.

"And you have other witnesses in town who will back up your side of this story?"

"Yes, sir, I do," the Texan responded, quickly growing impatient with the marshal.

"Who are these supposed witnesses?" Whipsaw snarled from the porch.

"I'll be glad to bring them to the prosecutor when the time is right," Bishop grinned. "Until then, I'm going to keep their names under wraps. I wouldn't want them to be victims of an untimely accident or perhaps a similar 'misunderstanding.'"

Nodding, the local lawman had little choice but to concede. Bishop had him pinned. No escape. "We do have legitimate charges here. Whip, you've got to come with me, and if any of you men cause an ounce of trouble, you're going get a free tour of my jail. Understood?"

Again, Bishop was surprised. Most crowds would have mumbled; some might have even shouted their support for the man being arrested. Not here.

Several of the bolder men actually began chastising the deputies as they moved to put cuffs on Jones' oversized wrists. "This is wrong!" somebody shouted. "We'll get you out of this, Whip," another angry voice added. "There's not a jury in this county who'll convict you for this!"

For his part, Bishop wanted his rifle back.

Walking with purpose toward the stack of firearms resting by the front door, Bishop reached in and scooped up his carbine before anybody noticed.

"Hey! What's he doing?" someone shouted.

Ignoring the eruption of protests behind him, the Texan walked briskly toward the forest and what was sure to be an anxious wife.

More and harsher comments followed Bishop, a few threats even reaching his ears. "You'll get yours, asshole," and, "We're going to fuck you up for this, Mister," two of the more G-rated examples.

"I see you're doing a great job of winning friends and influencing people," Terri greeted, stepping around a tree trunk where she'd been watching.

"Yeah, up to my old tricks," Bishop grumbled. "Let's get back to the truck before serious trouble comes our way. We want to be clear of Forest Mist once word gets out. In a way, I feel sorry for Plummer."

"He's a wimp if you ask me," Terri stated.

"He's just a man who has to live around here. You know what these small towns can be like. Everybody knows everyone else and has since they've been kids. The marshal has to wake up every day and look at the same faces around him. Now, that's not going to be so easy."

"If Jones goes to trial," she replied. "And I have my doubts about that."

"Yes, you're right there. A whole lot of things can go wrong before that happens."

"So, are we going back to West Texas? Without our lumber?"

"No. Let's go find someplace to camp for tonight. We'll go into town early and talk to Plummer, tell him we want our wood returned, and arrange for Len to haul it back to Alpha according to the original agreement."

They reached the pickup without incident, Bishop scanning the surrounding woods like he expected an army of Jones' supporters to descend on them at any second. "You drive," he said to Terri. "At least for a few miles, I'm going to ride shotgun. Remember our escape from Houston?"

She actually smiled at the recollection, "We made it. Together. That seems like a lifetime ago."

"I thought we were past all that, but I guess luck isn't on my side this time. Remind me of all this next time I suggest a road trip."

Five miles later, without any sign of pursuit, they traded places. "We'll go settle up our bill with Carlie and let her know what happened. Somehow, I got the impression she wasn't a big fan of Whipsaw Jones. Maybe she can recommend another place for us to stay until this all blows over."

Thinking word of the incident wouldn't have spread across town just yet, Bishop drove right through Forest Mist. They found Carlie working in the kitchen, their hostess baking something that smelled wonderful. "Decide to stay another night?" she asked in a cheery voice.

It took almost 20 minutes for Bishop and Terri to explain that afternoon's events, Carlie's expression shifting from concerned, to sad, to angry. "That man Jones is a bully. Always has been, always will be," she spat. "And it's gotten worse since the collapse. I can't even count the number of timber leases that he's taken over. Before everything went to hell, there were five sawmills in this area. Now, it's down to two. He parades around like he owns this town, and quite frankly, he just about does."

"Where can we stay until this all settles?" Terri asked.

"Why here," Carlie replied without hesitation. "I'm no fan of Whipsaw Jones, and I'm definitely not intimidated by him or his crew of thugs."

"That's not a good idea, Carlie," Bishop said, shaking his head. "There's a good chance that Jones' boys will come looking for anyone supporting us, or the case against their boss. We wouldn't want to put you in harm's way."

Waving a dismissive hand through the air, the B&B's owner didn't seem concerned. "I know the majority of that lot, and they are mostly bluster and pomp. The only one of them worth worrying about is Whip's son, Ketchum. He was in the Army but got kicked out years ago. Heard he was doing serious time over in Georgia someplace. They call him Blackjack. He's a mean one, but nobody has seen him around here in years."

"I appreciate the offer, Carlie, but we can't put you or Angel's Porch at risk," Terri responded gently. "Unfortunately, Bishop and I have some experience dealing with this sort of people, and I think it best for everybody if we find someplace to stay out of sight – at least during the night."

Lost in thought, Carlie seemed to be considering all the options, thinking hard about a safe place for her guests to stay. Finally brightening, she responded, "How about a compromise? There is a small, unused apartment above the barn. You can hide your truck in there at night, and no one will know you're here. It was finished just before the collapse. Mom and I were hoping to rent it out for extra money. You could even use my car... if you can put some gas in it."

Bishop had to admit that camping, for what could be several nights, didn't seem nearly as attractive as having modern amenities like a bed, roof, and toilet. Nor would it be as secure, their experience on their journey into Forest Mist still a fresh reminder. "Let's have a look," he conceded.

CHAPTER 5

It took a while for the marshal to clean things up at the mill. Cutting down Nathan Hill's body was the easiest part.

After nearly an hour of statements, searching Nathan's truck, inventorying the lumber on the trailer, and snapping at least 100 photographs, a deputy was finally ready to book Whipsaw Jones.

Seeing things were about to wrap up, one of the lumber tycoon's most trusted foremen approached. "What can I do to help, Boss?"

Whip didn't respond at first, holding his tongue until the deputy was out of earshot. Finally, assured of a little privacy, he answered, "In my top desk drawer you will find an address book. On the back page is an address where you can find my son, Ketchum, down in New Orleans. Get to him. Tell him what has happened. Tell him I said now was the time to come home."

The foreman didn't like the assignment. "In New Orleans?" he mumbled, fear in his throat. "You want me to find Blackjack?"

"Yes," Whip responded, frustration at the man's hesitation evident in his tone. "You'll be okay. Ketchum runs the entire north side of the Big Easy. Take one of my business cards. It will act as a pass to get you through. Tell my son I said to hurry. I am not going to enjoy sitting in a cell. Besides, it's not like there is a big backlog of cases at the courthouse. This trial might start any day."

Nodding, the employee responded, "I'll get it done, Boss. You can count on me."

"Hurry. Take a company truck and anything else you need."

Marshal Plummer appeared just then, taking Whip by the arm and guiding him toward the closest police cruiser. "Come on; it's time to go."

As the short convoy of law enforcement vehicles exited the mill, Plummer spoke to the prisoner in the backseat. "Do you want me to find you a good lawyer, Whip?"

"I don't need a lawyer, Dallas. I plan to represent myself. Plus, you don't need to worry about me. After all, you're going to have enough on your mind in the next few days."

Frowning, the marshal retorted, "Are you threatening me, Whip?"

"Why no, Marshal. I would never do such a thing," the prisoner sarcastically replied. "Besides, I'm in handcuffs, locked in the back of a police car. How could I possibly threaten you?"

"You know damn well what I mean, Whip," Plummer responded.

Shaking his head, the arrested man's tone became optimistic. "Seriously, Dallas, I'm not all that concerned. I don't think the prosecutor can seat a jury that will convict me. I don't think you'll get any witnesses to testify."

"I wouldn't count on that, Whip," Plummer warned. "This guy Bishop has a reputation and so does his wife. They aren't the type to let water like this flow under the bridge. From what I hear, he's one hardheaded SOB and knows a lot of important people back in Alpha. You might want to rethink that part about hiring an attorney."

"I'm not going to jail, Dallas... at least not long term. In honor of our *former* friendship, I'm *letting* you take me in. That way, you can still pretend that you're doing your job. But... after this... we're done. You're now officially on the wrong side of my ledger. Now please, just shut up and drive. I'm tired of hearing your traitorous voice."

They stepped out the back door, strolling across the sizeable yard toward what had been a corral or livestock pen. On one side of the faded, white barn was a pasture, Bishop estimating it offered at least 200 meters of open space that would be a challenge to cross without being seen... and shot. On the other stood a patch of oak trees, another unused field, and then a dark, thick forest of pine.

"Wait till you see the best part," their tour guide hinted as they continued their jaunt toward one edge of the property. Then, pointing to a barely visible path of slightly shorter weeds leading into the distance, she continued, "You see that lane over there? That's actually a gravel trail my dad used to access the back of our property. It heads into that far woods and comes out on a county road. You could come and go using it, and no one would ever know."

"It's a promising piece of property," Bishop nodded in approval. "Let's see the barn."

The interior still smelled of hay, several bales lining one wall, no doubt acquired to feed Carlie's modest herd of milk cows. Crossing the hardpacked dirt floor, Bishop noted a rusty shovel and rake hanging from another wall, a workbench on the far side that was cluttered with worn tools and an assortment of jars brimming with screws and nails. The center of the building was practically empty, plenty of room to hide the truck, the double-wide doors opening toward the back of the property providing private and easy access.

"This barn used to be always full of hay," Carlie reflected. "So many of our cattle died during the darkest hours. At one point, we had over a hundred head. Our pastures just weren't big enough to support them without extra feed, and we didn't have any money to buy food for ourselves, let along the cattle. I suppose I'm lucky to have any of our herd left."

Leading them to a broad, wooden staircase, Carlie motioned for them to climb. "It's probably a little dusty up here... maybe a few cobwebs. The well is close by, and the toilet works just fine. There's no heat or electricity, but it's dry, and the window opens for fresh air."

They entered what would be called an efficiency apartment in most real estate markets. Broad, planked beams made up the floor, the walls constructed of painted plywood. A set of lower kitchen cabinets topped by open shelving defined the kitchen, the space completed with a modest gas stove, a sink, and a lot of dust.

Bishop stepped to the apartment's sole window. Like the big doors below, it too faced away from the road. Unless someone were watching from a distance, he and Terri could have light at night with careful management of the curtains. *We can defend this*, he thought. *It's not Fort Knox, but we can make it extremely difficult for anyone to get inside.*

The bed and two chairs were covered in drop cloths, a closet-sized bathroom rounding out the space. "This is perfect," Terri acknowledged, seeing her husband's approving nod. "If you're sure you don't mind, we'll take it."

"I can give you a break on the price," Carlie began.

"No, we'll pay the same as long as breakfast is still included," Bishop interrupted. Terri's puzzled look prompted a shrug from her mate before he continued, "A man's got to eat."

The three co-conspirators huddled quickly, deciding that Bishop and Terri should make a show of moving out. After loading their bags into the truck, the couple from West Texas paraded through town slowly to make sure they were seen heading back west. "At least we'll get one night's sleep before I'm seen at the jail, and people realize we really didn't leave," Bishop predicted.

After driving for ten minutes, Bishop turned around and used the back way into Carlie's property. Twice, the pickup's engine whined as it struggled to manage the weeds in the old, overgrown lane. With dusk approaching, shadows grew long, and the fading light further complicated their little mission. By the time the sun had disappeared below the horizon, they were pulling the truck into the barn.

Carlie appeared at the stairs, a broom, mop, and bundle of dust rags in her hand. "I got the first layer of dirt off," she announced, wiping back a strand of hair from her damp forehead.

"Thank you so much," Terri said, hurrying to help the innkeeper bring the cleaning supplies down the stairs. "You should let us fix supper for you. We've got some great sausage in the cooler."

As Carlie went to freshen up, Terri lit a candle and fired up the gas stove while Bishop unloaded their gear. "You should leave tomorrow," he began. "Go home, get Hunter from the sitter, and let Nick know what's going on here."

"Our son will be fine," she replied, her voice making it clear that she didn't want to leave. "You need me right now more than Hunter does. Send Nick a message via shortwave if you really think there's anything he can do."

Clearly worried about his family, Bishop wasn't going to back down. "Look, this should all blow over in a few days. Plummer and the other town leaders will come to their senses, put Jones on trial, and that will be the end of it. There is a chance, however, that it won't go that smoothly. My gut says that if things do go wrong, this could get ugly."

"Then let's both head back. We'll brief Diana and Nick and let the Alliance government handle it. It's not our responsibility. You're not on a SAINT team anymore, remember?"

"I have to stay to testify," Bishop countered. "You don't. Besides, if I'm still hanging around, it will keep the pressure on the locals to do the right thing. If they believe you've gone back to Alpha to report in, it will add even more incentive to act like they're part of the Alliance."

Turning from the sizzling pan of meat, Terri firmly propped her hands on her hips. "I'm not leaving, no matter how much you fuss. If things do get messy, you're going to need me. Just like our bugout from Houston, and a dozen other situations since, we survived because we were together. Now isn't the time to break up the team."

Bishop knew from his wife's expression that she wasn't going to change her mind. Truth be told, he was secretly glad she was going to be at his side. Of all the military contractors, special forces operatives, and highly trained experts he'd worked with over the years, Terri was the best teammate he'd ever had. He trusted her judgment, intellect, and bravery more than anyone else on the planet.

Sure, she wasn't the fastest or the most physically impressive. She couldn't outshoot even the least-skilled member of the teams, nor could she run as fast, carry as much gear, or rule in unarmed combat.

What she did bring to the table was unequaled intelligence, a cool head under fire, a relentless drive to dominate, and the willingness to put others before herself. She had an uncanny ability to perceive what the enemy was thinking and enough experience to predict how they would react. He'd seen it over and again, having lost count of how many times she'd pulled his ass from the fire. In summary, she was a winner, and in an all-out fight to the death, that was the type of person Bishop wanted at his side.

He took a moment to reflect on his feelings toward his wife, realizing that without the apocalypse, he would have probably never really appreciated how strong a woman she was.

Sure, trusting his spouse with the checkbook was one thing. Working together to overcome life's typical challenges created a unique bond, adding a deeper level of confidence and faith in each other. Admiring how his mate parented offspring was another common milestone of conviction and commitment.

None of those "normal" events could compare to combat, however. Compared to the ultimate contest of life and death, overcoming the loss of a job or the stress of buying a home was no big deal. There was a brotherhood known by battlefield survivors, a feeling every veteran experienced and understood. Bishop shared it with many men, and because of a world gone insane, his spouse was a member of that elite club as well.

It was a potent glue, an unbreakable weld that would always keep them together. It didn't replace love, trust, and commitment, but amplified those elements and emotions. The little bumps in life were put into perspective, the true, live-or-die issues shared and solved together. For a moment, he considered how many other couples might have enjoyed the same bond. Two cops on a dangerous beat? Male and female soldiers fighting in the same war? Bonnie and Clyde? Bishop doubted there were many others who had experienced the relationship depth and solidarity that he and Terri had.

And she looks damn good in a pair of tight jeans, Bishop thought, chuckling at the silliness of the male mind. *What more could any man ask for?*

"Okay. I guess you're staying," he whispered. "And I'm glad."

Setting the spatula down on the counter, she wrapped her arms around his neck, drawing her face close to his. "I guess it was the jeans that got ya, huh?" she teased.

"How did you know?"

"Because you've been gawking at my butt since I put them on this morning, you perv."

"Sorry," he replied, lowering his gaze.

"Don't be," she smiled. "It makes me feel good to still be able to draw your eye."

"As long as it's only *my* eye that matters," he grinned, pulling her tight.

As expected, Forest Mist's courthouse was the benefactor of additional security, especially the area where the jail was located.

There were at least four armed men patrolling the exterior, AR15 rifles in full display. Two more uniformed officers were stationed just inside the courthouse's entrance.

Bishop was required to check his weapons at the door, his M4 drawing special attention from the two deputies posted there. Fortunately, both of them recognized the Texan. "The marshal is in his office," the female officer announced after patting him down.

To say Dallas Plummer was surprised to see Bishop walk into his department would have been an understatement.

"You're still in town?" the lawman greeted, eyebrows arching high.

"Why wouldn't I be?" Bishop responded with an innocent expression.

"I... well... someone told me that they had seen you leave town yesterday," the marshal stammered.

"We just relocated to a spot nearby," Bishop replied. "I'm not going anywhere."

With a grimace on his face, Plummer motioned Bishop into his private office and offered the Texan a chair before closing the door behind him. "This is a hell of a mess," the marshal began.

"Sir?"

"The county prosecutor recused himself from the case this morning. So has the county judge," Plummer announced.

Shrugging, Bishop responded, "So? They probably know Whipsaw just like everyone else around here. I'm actually reassured they took that step."

The marshal clearly didn't share Bishop's enthusiasm. "That means that it will be at least three or four days before

96

an Alliance prosecutor or judge can be assigned to the case. In the meantime, I'm holding an increasingly hostile prisoner in my jail and exceeding my overtime payroll budget like money is growing on trees. Whip is demanding his right to bail, a hearing, and a speedy trial."

Waving a dismissive hand through the air, Bishop replied, "So? He can demand any damn thing he wants. Doesn't matter. He's a killer... a murderer. You believe that don't you, Marshal?"

Shaking his head, Plummer replied, "I don't know what to believe, Bishop. Ever since the collapse, I've struggled to divide right from wrong. Forget about legal and illegal; all that went out the window a long time ago. I've kept the peace in this town by using a moral compass, and now its dial is spinning out of control."

Bishop didn't understand the lawman's dilemma and said so. "He killed an innocent man, Dallas. It doesn't take the wisdom of Solomon to grasp that assassinating an innocent man is wrong. Like I said yesterday, if Jones gets away with it this time, what's to stop him next week or next month? Before long, you'll have an entire town full of folks who commit homicide on a whim."

The marshal sighed deeply, "Do you know where I was yesterday when Whip sent his man to report what they'd found?"

"No."

"We were called out to the Larry Amherst's place, about 10 miles from here. I've known Larry and Ima since I was in elementary school. Somebody had killed both of them, probably for the meat that was in his smokehouse. They had been brutally stabbed and hacked to pieces; God rest their souls. One of the neighbors spotted a bunch of men hurrying back toward the border. The witness said two of the gang were carrying machetes. Claimed they were all hauling bundles of what looked like meat."

"I'm sorry, Marshal. Truly I am. But that doesn't make it okay for other people to commit crimes in my book. That doesn't justify Whipsaw Jones' actions."

"You're right," Plummer nodded. "Absolutely correct. And yet, you weren't here when Whip and his men passed out food to our starving community or helped to fight off marauders who tried to slaughter us during the night. A lot of his people died in the process. You don't know how many lives he saved here in Forest Mist, or what sacrifices he made to keep our citizens safe. From what I heard from Sheriff Watts, you of all people would understand what we went through. How can you ask a man to fight for his life on Monday, and then on Tuesday tell him he must turn off the switch and play nice? Before the Alliance came into existence, shanty towns like the one outside of Len's mill would have never been tolerated. Those folks would have been run off or shot if they didn't heed the first warning. When society collapsed, we did what we had to survive. We had no choice."

Shaking his head, Bishop disagreed with the marshal's analysis. "I'll use that same logic, Marshal. During those bad times, everybody begged for the rule of law. We all wanted things back the way they were, hoping, praying that the government would somehow regain control and keep the peace. You can't have it both ways. Preventative killing isn't justified in an orderly society. If we don't maintain the cornerstone of innocent until proven guilty, we might as well declare Diana Brown dictator and dissolve the council."

Again, Plummer nodded his head in agreement. "Those are strong words, Bishop, and I'm going to do my absolute best to hold up my end."

"That's all anybody can do, sir," Bishop replied. "If you want me to get in touch with Alpha and request they send you some additional manpower, I'll be happy to."

"No," the marshal answered. "There's enough resentment about the Alliance leadership around here all ready. That last election divided a lot of our citizens, and some of the new rules and regulations coming from the capital are rubbing folks the wrong way. If I need additional manpower, I can always call on a few of the neighboring lawmen for help. Lord knows I've sent them men when necessary."

"Up to you, sir," Bishop agreed. "Just let me know."

After extending his hand to the troubled official, Bishop turned to leave but was stopped by Plummer. "One more thing," the marshal began, his tone filled with hesitation.

"Yes, sir?"

"Whip has a son... a bad apple from the get-go. His name is Ketchum. Years ago, when the kid was only 17, I brokered a deal between father, son, our judge at the time, and the US Army. It was one of those 'enlist or do serious time' arrangements. Ketchum, at the urging of Whip, enlisted in the Army rather than become a resident at our state prison."

"And?" Bishop replied, having already been warned by Carlie.

"Well, Ketchum did well for the first few years. Heard he made Ranger and was trying for Special Forces. Then his true colors surfaced again when he tried to relieve his commanding officer of his duties with a bullet. He went to Leavenworth but was released about a year before the collapse. Time served. I've heard rumors Blackjack Jones was in Louisiana, but I can't swear by it. If he is, and he decides to come back home, there's going to be serious trouble. He's a bad hombre and won't hesitate to kill."

"You think he'll come back to break his father out of jail?"

"I don't know. For years, after his kid had gotten into trouble, Whip acted like my intervention was exactly the right thing to do. Thanked me over and over again for keeping his son out of prison. Still, you just never know about domestic relationships. Nothing surprises me anymore after 38 years on this job."

"What did Ketchum do to get into trouble?" Bishop asked.

"Tried to kill his mother," Plummer grunted. "Beat the shit out of the woman in an argument."

"Wow," Bishop replied, "and the Army took him?"

The marshal's eyes glazed over slightly as his mind returned to another time, his voice dropping low and quiet with reflection. "Oh, you know how these things go. After a few days, both parents were downplaying the entire incident. Mrs. Jones didn't want to press charges. Their son needed some counseling, not jail. Their boy had simply lost his temper, and one wrongdoing shouldn't ruin his entire life. I didn't buy it for one second at the time, but Whip was an outstanding member of the community and promised he'd get the boy help if we could keep him out of the hoosegow."

"Let me guess. The boy had always been trouble?"

"I heard his name mentioned a lot, that's for sure," Plummer grinned. "Again, just like a lot of law enforcement situations, nothing was ever black and white. Sure, Ketchum was a bully, but he was also the star of the local football team. Plus, he seemed to have a sense of civic responsibility. When a tornado wiped out 20 homes years before the collapse, nobody worked any harder than Whip and his son to clean things up and help out those who were impacted by the storm. I heard stories of a few incidents at the school, but in those days, I let the principal handle all but the worst transgressions."

"I see," Bishop said. "What does Blackjack Jones look like? How will I know the man if he comes walking up to me on the street?"

"Oh, you'll know him. He has a jack of spades tattooed on each arm. He's the spitting image of his father, only with crazy eyes. Big son of a bitch, that's for sure."

"Roger that, Marshal," Bishop replied, clearly not impressed.

"You watch out for that one," Plummer added. "He's mean, ruthless, and clever. If that wasn't bad enough, he carries around an ass full of military training. He's not your normal thug or felon."

"Will do. Let me know if I can do anything to help, okay?"

"Stay out of sight and trouble is all I ask. You'll know when the Alliance prosecutor gets to town, and they will no doubt want to talk to you and any other witnesses. Until then, please lay low and keep out of my hair."

"Yes, sir."

Exiting the courthouse, the Texan drove to Highland Hardwoods and explained to Mr. Yarborough exactly what had happened. "The marshal will have our wood in the town's impound lot by this afternoon," he said. "We need to go ahead with the original plan and have it delivered to West Texas."

"I'll take care of it," Len promised. "And you be careful, young man. Whipsaw Jones is one mean son of a bitch, and half of those men working at his mill are seedy characters at best. Watch your back."

Next, Bishop decided to stop by the café and place a take-out order. Terri was stressed enough over Hunter and the situation in Forest Mist. Not having to make lunch would help a little.

The waitress who'd sent them to Jones' mill was working, giving Bishop a sly nod as the Texan entered the front door. "I'd like to place an order to go," he requested with an innocent smile.

Five minutes later, Bishop was handed a brown paper bag with two cheeseburgers, a large order of coleslaw, and a bill for $9.35 Alliance.

As Bishop fished for his wallet, he whispered, "Stay low. Keep quiet. No one knows you're going to be our star witness, and we want to keep it that way. Understand?"

"Okay," she mumbled, fear now filling her eyes.

"You'll be fine as long as nobody finds out. If you need help or are threatened, go and tell Carlie out at Angel's Porch... the B&B."

"I know where it's at," she replied, counting out his change.

"You're a brave girl," Bishop nodded, stuffing the coins into his pocket. "You're doing the right thing."

CHAPTER 6

Whipsaw's foreman expected the worst from his journey to locate the boss' son.

He remembered Ketchum well, having been a year behind the school's most notorious bully and football team captain. Fear and loathing were the two words that came to mind when recalling the oversized brute.

Anticipating some run-down biker headquarters or worse, the lumber man was pleasantly surprised when he was escorted to what had been a 5-star hotel before the collapse. Ketchum was obviously moving up in the world.

Sure enough, lounging by the pool between two curvy, blonde women, sat Whip's only son. The years showed on Ketchum's face, but not his body. Shirtless and displaying a multitude of dark ink patterns across his shoulders and chest, Blackjack looked to be in peak physical condition. A long, dark ponytail of hair rounded out the gangster's façade.

Several heavy, gold chains adorned Ketchum's neck, both of his wrists wrapped in precious metals as well. Enormous rings sparkled with jewels on both hands. The girls accompanying him sported flat tummies, large breasts, clean hair, and painted toenails. A large-bore pistol rested on the lounge side table.

A nearby cooler was the obvious source of the beer supply, rings of humidity staining the concrete deck next to the chaise lounges. Nearby, the messenger noted a table covered with food, the likes of which he hadn't seen in years. An impressive assortment of crawfish, corn on the cob, potatoes galore and several other dishes comprised the culinary display.

"Gus?" the large man inquired, pulling up his sunglasses and standing to tower over his guest. "From Forest Mist? Oh, my gawd, man, how many years has it been?" the former bad boy gushed, his friendly greeting absolutely unexpected. "You got here just in time. We were just getting ready to have a bite."

"He claims to have a message from your father," announced one of the burly biker-types who had escorted Gus to see their leader. "Says it's important."

"I'll get right to the point, Ketchum. Your father has been arrested for murder. He wants you to come back and help him straighten things out," the foreman explained.

Blackjack's face grew grey, his expression grim, as he recalled the fear he had experienced while in the man's presence long ago. "Murder? Dad? What has that old coot gotten himself into now?"

Gus explained a summary of recent events as quickly as possible, desperately wanting to return to his doublewide, wife, and kids. He prayed Ketchum wouldn't shoot the messenger.

"And who is this Bishop guy?" Blackjack asked after digesting the news from home.

"Don't know much about him," the foreman replied. "Some say he was one of the founders of the Alliance, and that his wife was a heavyweight on the council. One of Plummer's deputies told me that he was one badass dude and had killed over 50 men."

"Plummer? That old blowhard is still carrying a badge?" Ketchum laughed. "Hell, it would be worth a trip back there just to stomp that old fucker's bones into dust."

"Your dad is locked up in Plummer's jail. They're waiting on an Alliance prosecutor to show up from Port Arthur," the messenger continued.

"Okay, Gus," Blackjack nodded. "Thanks for delivering the news. Do you need a room for tonight? Someplace to rest? Can you stay and have some dinner before you go?"

"No, thanks, but I've got to get back. With your dad behind bars, I'm running the show at the mill, and I want everything to be ship-shape when he gets out."

Blackjack extended his hand and then addressed his henchmen. "Make sure this man gets out of our territory safely."

As Gus turned to leave, Ketchum added, "I'll see you tomorrow. Don't tell anybody I'm on my way. I want my arrival to be a surprise."

The six-hour drive from New Orleans passed quickly, Blackjack's convoy drawing curious glances as they rolled through a handful of small towns.

Ketchum's large, German sedan led the caravan, its front license plate boasting an image of the jack of spades.

Next followed a raised 4x4 pickup with large tires, lots of chrome, and a bed brimming with supplies. The extended cab was crammed with human resources as well.

A parade of Harley Davidson motorcycles shadowed the truck. Riding in pairs, they stretched the length of a football field, their powerful motors creating a low rumble as they passed. Some of the bikes were occupied by solo riders, others having their "bitch seats" filled with female companions. Leather, club colors, patches, and beards were in abundance.

Behind the bikes rolled three motorhomes and another pickup, all transporting additional manpower and supplies. Except for the Harleys, all the vehicles had been what Blackjack termed spoils of war. The big man had been busy since the collapse, building an empire, collecting loyal employees, and partying like a rock star.

Louisiana politics had always been a bit edgy. From the days of the French freebooters settling along the Gulf Coast, to the criminal reign of Governor Huey Long, corruption had always seemed to have a foothold in Cajun Country. Even after the horrific events surrounding Hurricane Katrina, a time when the public needed their leaders the most, countless elected officials were convicted of crimes where they preyed on their own constituents and thwarted the recovery. Several studies had labeled the state as the most corrupt in the union.

Nothing had changed all that much since the downfall. Louisiana offered little in the way of critical assets that the struggling federal government in Washington needed to kickstart the recovery, and thus was low on everyone's priority list.

New Orleans, with its multitude of low-income households and her dwindling population, had practically been ignored since the collapse. The brief civil war with the Independents had severely depleted local military assets, those that remained being charged with securing the port, the Mississippi River, and the state's two nuclear power plants. Effectively, everybody else was on their own.

Ketchum Jones had always loved the Big Easy. As a teenager growing up in the region with Bourbon Street, all-night festivities, readily available prostitutes, and look-the-other-way drug enforcement had been a magnet for a young man seeking to indulge some of his most primal instincts. The city's charms had endeared themselves to young Blackjack, and after his release from military prison, there was no other destination as attractive to a man who needed to blow off a little steam.

Despite his public state of embarrassment over his son, Whipsaw had continued to support his offspring with money. "One of these days he's going to grow up," the father had confided in a friend. "I pray every night that he'll be a good enough man to take over the lumber mill when I get too old to run the show."

Like father, like son, Blackjack did indeed develop an entrepreneurial spirit. After drinking, whoring, and buzzing his way from one end of the French Quarter to the other, Ketchum woke up one morning experiencing a rare moment of introspection. What was he doing with his life? Where was all this heading? His father's benevolence wouldn't last forever. Besides, he wanted desperately to be his own man, and running some backwater sawmill didn't fit the bill.

Given his size, military-honed skills, and willingness to become violent at the drop of a hat, a career in collections was the logical fit. Through a hooker friend, he contacted one of the local drug pushers and offered his services as an enforcer. Within a year, he was managing an eight-square block territory of the Fourth Ward.

By the time civilization tumbled over the cliff, Blackjack was a celebrity in the New Orleans underworld. Expanding into illegal gambling, various recreational pharmaceuticals, protection rackets, and high-end prostitution, his name became known more for his intelligence than his muscle.

Ketchum was smart and ruthless... and desperately wanted to avoid jail at all costs. Unlike most of the other criminals operating along the Gulf Coast, he kept a low profile, settled disputes as peacefully as possible, and used significant portions of his profits to bribe the authorities. He was maturing, just like his father had predicted.

New Orleans, like most major American cities, took the brunt of the apocalypse. Food shortages, disease, violence, and a lack of leadership resulted in complete anarchy. With a loyal, well-armed organization already in place, the entire west side of the city soon fell into Ketchum's lap. He had the manpower, weapons, and management hierarchy to fill the void left after the government disappeared.

For months after the downfall, if you wanted to eat, drink, sleep or work in New Orleans, you went to Ketchum.

The strongman quickly took control of the large staging areas surrounding the port, killed or recruited any competition, and deployed his forces in a fashion that would have made his old commanders back at Fort Benning proud.

Liquor stores weren't looted in Blackjack's territory; they were secured. Instead of sending his men to the corner gas stations with five-gallon cans, Ketchum sent a platoon of shooters to secure the fuel distribution companies and took control of their enormous tanks full of precious gas and diesel. He didn't bother with the local grocery stores – he commandeered the warehouses that supplied them.

Fireteams of his men stormed up gangplanks at the port, taking over every freighter and cargo vessel tied to a pier. At one point, someone bragged that Blackjack should be renamed Black Beard. Another smartass boasted that Ketchum now controlled the third largest navy in the world.

By the time the first hint of a recovery appeared in the region, Ketchum had consolidated his power, his organization deeply engrained in practically every aspect of life.

Now, driving toward his hometown, Blackjack felt a deep sense of gratification. His father's support had never faltered. The old man hadn't lost faith, nor forsaken his troubled son. Ketchum hated the concept of unpaid debt. He wanted to owe no one and looked forward to paying off the only man who had believed in him throughout the worst of times.

There was also a materialistic side to this endeavor. Ketchum was smart enough to realize that eventually, authority and government control would erode his hold on the Big Easy. It was time to branch out, and his father's lumber operation was a profitable, legitimate enterprise. It would give him a solid foothold in Alliance territory, and with that, the possibilities were endless.

Stopping at an abandoned furniture factory just on the Louisiana side of the border, Blackjack gathered his men around. "We will operate from here for the time being. If there's work to be done in Forest Mist, we will do the job and then dash back across the border. This will hamstring any nosey Alliance cops and keep them off balance. Now get your lazy asses busy making this place defensible. I want those restrooms over there clean and functional by nightfall. Somebody get busy fixing those showers as well. You people already smell bad enough as it is!"

A round of laughter arose from the colorful mob as they dispersed to perform their assigned tasks. Within an hour, BBQ was cooking on three grills while others pitched cots, swept floors, and configured the location's security.

The Crescent Furniture Company had been a household name in the region during Ketchum's childhood years. Originally constructed to take advantage of the industry's primary raw material, wood, the enterprise had grown and prospered in the years following WWII.

Blackjack had made deliveries here, riding with his father in the cab, fascinated by the largest building he'd ever seen.

The place was enormous, the main structure covering nearly six acres under one roof. Several smaller constructions had been added as the company had expanded, including the newer office facility that had been built in the late 1970s.

Giant, brick smokestacks rose from the what Blackjack knew were massive kilns used to dry the raw lumber before it was lathed and molded into dressers, beds, tables, and desks. There was the pad, a poured concrete apron where logs were stacked, inventoried, and sorted. Ketchum had once heard a worker claim that 17 football fields would fit inside the fenced area.

Crescent was a monument to the golden years of American manufacturing, but like so many industries across the country, it had eventually fallen to cheaper foreign labor, a lack of economical, raw materials, and the burden of environmental regulation. The company had declared bankruptcy a few years before Ketchum was shipped off to the Uncle Sam's Army.

As he scanned his new home, Ketchum's attention moved to the rail yard. There were five sorting tracks there, now overgrown with weeds and brush. He knew this area was connected by a branch line to the main freight terminal in Shreveport.

On the other side of the facility stretched a large lake. Ketchum couldn't remember the body's name, but that didn't matter. Just like the manufacturing processes of old, his small army would need a lot of water.

His primary concern, however, was defense. Smiling at his choice for a base camp, he continued to take in the surrounding area and was pleased with his selection. The walls were thick like a fortress, and between the lake, railroad tracks, pad, and employee parking lot, a mouse couldn't get close to the place without being seen. "Fort Apache," he whispered, "we could hold off the 4th Infantry Division from here. Perfect."

The smokestacks loomed at one end, a water tower at the other – both excellent locations to post marksmen and spotters. The buildings had been sited for the efficient movement of the plant's product, which also happened to make then easily defendable. He noted enough old logs remained on the pad to supply their cooking fires for a month.

There was plenty of room to hide their vehicles inside the abandoned operation's primary structure, an option that might prove important if things got really out of hand. The saws, lathes, and other heavy equipment that once filled the interior had been sold by the auctioneer's gavel decades ago.

Several of the larger walls had become bulletin boards for the local youth, spray painted graffiti advertising various adolescent artworks, including tags that covered everything from "Led Zeppelin," to the "Class of '82." Ketchum himself had taken advantage of the abandoned, remote facility as a youth, bringing his prom date there for a heated make-out session.

Satisfied with the group's efforts, Ketchum turned to his lieutenant and ordered, "Keep an eye on things here. I'm heading into Forest Mist. I'm going to pay a visit to an old friend."

It was late-afternoon when Bishop began preparing his kit. Terri had seen her husband perform the same task dozens of times, and it was never a good sign. "Going to war?" she asked sheepishly.

"I hope not," he replied with a quiet voice. "Still, it never hurts to be prepared. Remember the Boy Scouts' motto?"

Grunting, she played with his hair, "You, my love, were *never* a Boy Scout."

"True," he nodded, pulling a rifle from its case, then changing the subject. "I want to take another pass through Forest Mist... take a serious look at the town from a tactical perspective," he stated.

"I thought that's how you always looked at everything?" she teased.

Giving her body a quick up and down assessment punctuated with waggling eyebrows, he quipped, "Not everything."

He continued, checking magazines, squirting beads of oil into critical places, and switching his optics on and off. "You really are expecting trouble," Terri noted.

"Why not be prepared?" he responded, pulling items from his pack. "It won't hurt anything. If things remain calm, then all I have done is check my weapons and gear, something I should do on a regular basis anyway. Now, if it does get nasty around here, then I'm ready."

"Well, if you can't beat 'em, join 'em," she whispered, taking a seat on the floor beside him. "Where's my rifle?"

He pointed to a separate duffle, saying, "All of your stuff is in there. I'll make sure it's okay, if you want."

"No, I'll do it myself," she grinned. "Besides, it's been so long since I used some of this stuff, I've forgotten exactly what's in here."

"Remember, we're not expecting a fight this afternoon. All I want to do is scout the town, draw a few diagrams, and then come back here to regroup. Later, tonight, I plan on going back and making sure things remain peaceful."

"Okay," she replied. "I'll ride along with you. My artistic skills are better than yours anyway, and it will be good to get out of the house... err barn."

Shaking his head, Bishop responded, "I don't think that's a good idea. I don't want people knowing we're both still in town. Besides, I plan to wear a disguise."

"Huh?"

"I'll show you in a little bit," he promised.

For another 20 minutes, Bishop continued his preparation routine, considering his options while things were still calm. Angel's Porch was close enough to easily hike into Forest Mist, but the offer of Carlie's vehicle seemed like the more logical approach. She evidently didn't drive it often, so there was a good chance the vehicle wouldn't be noticed.

Donning a baseball cap he'd found in the closet and adding dark sunglasses, he turned to his wife and announced, "My disguise."

"That's not going to fool anybody," she laughed. "I'd know you a mile away."

"Yeah, but you know and love me. Unfortunately, most of the townsfolk don't."

"So why can't I put on a disguise and go with you?" she inquired.

"Because every guy in town was checking you out. This has always been a problem, my love; the price I pay for marrying such a beautiful woman. Unless we have a world-class makeup artist, every stud in town is going to take one look and know who you are by your silhouette."

She swatted him on the chest, "You're as full of shit as a Christmas goose."

"Seriously, I want you to hang out here. It wouldn't surprise me if some of Whipsaw's boys dropped in on Carlie to see if she knows where we're hiding out. You and your rifle might be required."

"Okay, but if I catch word of you flirting up that pretty waitress at the café, my rifle and I will have other work tonight," she teased.

Emptying a five-gallon can of gas into Carlie's Volkswagen, Bishop then tried the ignition. After three weak cranks, the engine finally turned over. A blue cloud of exhaust signaled the motor's protest at being disturbed after such a long slumber.

It was a cute, little sedan, just the perfect car for a single gal to tool around the countryside. Compared to his pickup, Bishop felt like he was commandeering a skateboard.

Just in case, he loaded his pack into the back seat, the carbine placed on the passenger side and covered with a small blanket. You just never knew.

With a pad of paper and a semi-dull pencil, Bishop headed for Forest Mist. It would be dark soon, and he wanted to get a good look at the lay of the land.

As he drove, Bishop began the mental part of his exercise. If he were one of Whipsaw's men, how would he go about breaking his boss out of jail?

"I'd put a gun up against Plummer's head and force him to hand over the keys," he declared, knowing that the methods employed in the Old West wouldn't work against a modern police force. "Pulling out the window-bars with a rope tied to my saddle probably would fail as well," he chuckled.

No, it would take an assault of some sort, and that wouldn't be easy given the stout walls and narrow entrances to the courthouse.

Plummer had been wise enough to post men outside. Bishop was sure the marshal had increased the internal security as well. So, how could he break Whipsaw Jones out of his cell?

"I'd wait until they relocated him," Bishop whispered, approaching the edge of town. "The jail is too tough a nut to crack without a platoon of infantry."

Problem was, there was no reason to ever remove Whipsaw from the facility. The courtrooms were in the same building. Meals would be delivered, as would any medical care required by the prisoner.

"Fire?" Bishop suggested to the empty car. "If there were a raging inferno, wouldn't they have to evacuate the accused?"

His first pass alongside the old building extinguished that idea.

The exterior was constructed of solid stone, thick and sturdy. "They probably designed it to withstand a tornado," Bishop decided. "No way a Molotov cocktail is going to do much damage. You would have to get inside to start a threatening blaze, and Plummer's deputies aren't going to let anyone just carry in a can of gasoline."

Bishop then recalled the tunnels he'd encountered at another small-town courthouse while on a SAINT mission. He made a mental note to ask the marshal if there were a similar feature here in Forest Mist.

He continued driving around the square, the late hour allowing the Texan to gawk at will. Not many folks were out and about. "Do they sense trouble is brewing?" he wondered out loud. "Do they see the storm clouds gathering on the horizon?"

After two orbits of the jail, he determined that Plummer's men held the upper hand. "If I had to bet on either the jailbreakers or the marshal, I'd put my money on Whipsaw remaining behind bars."

His next goal was to determine how he might be able to help the marshal's forces keep the murderer in his cell. Patrolling the grounds with a rifle would be redundant and stupid. A stakeout probably wouldn't work either. He couldn't just sit in Carlie's car for hours and wait for the black hats to make a move. He would be spotted, probably by both the marshal's men and Whipsaw's rescuers.

"The most effective tactic would be an overwatch," he decided, his attention darting to the small berg's skyline. "Where could a man with a long-range blaster set up and perhaps foil an escape attempt?"

Wishing Kevin was at his side, Bishop began scanning the horizon as he drove around. The tallest building in the area was the courthouse itself. The square was lined with two-story structures... massive, mature trees blocking all but the narrowest fields of fire. Only one church steeple was visible in the distance, and after a quick drive-by, Bishop determined that the narrow tower was barely wide enough to house the bell, let alone a sniper. "There's no room at the Marksman's Inn."

"How would you do it?" he kept repeating as he maneuvered through the quiet streets. "Where would you strike?"

Then a realization dawned on him. *A distraction. I would draw off Plummer and his deputies, pull them away from their patrols on the courthouse lawn and surrounding area. But how to best get their attention? Rob the bank? Start a fire? Attack the school?*

It then occurred to Bishop that he was at an extreme disadvantage compared to the locals. They would know where the soft spots were located. They would understand what was important to the people of Forest Mist. He was an outsider. He could only guess where the community's Achilles' heel was.

The sun was almost down, the last vestiges of day casting stretched shadows across the pavement. Still not willing to admit failure, Bishop wanted to make one last pass of the courthouse. Perhaps there was a way he could climb up the exterior and hide out on the roof? Maybe there was a rooftop on one of the nearby buildings that offered a wider view?

Turning onto the square for the third time, Bishop knew instantly that something was wrong. One of the patrolling deputies was in a hurry, moving toward the side entrance closest to the jail.

As Carlie's commuter moved closer, the Texan spied a rather brawny man with his hands in the air, three deputies covering him with weapons high and ready. In an instant, Bishop knew Ketchum Jones had returned to Forest Mist. "That certainly didn't take long."

Pulling into a parking spot with a view, Bishop watched as Whip's son was patted down not once, but twice. During the process, a lone figure appeared at the top of the courthouse steps.

Marshal Plummer didn't look happy.

"Hello Ketchum," Plummer greeted. "What brings you back to town?"

"You know damn well why I'm back, Dallas. I want to visit with my father," the prodigal son hissed.

"Visiting hours are over, Ketchum," the marshal replied, his hand never drifting far from the pistol on his belt.

"Don't be a drama queen, Dallas," the big man snarled, nodding toward the lawman's sidearm. "You've got three, maybe four men with rifles pointed at my back. I'm not here to cause trouble. I just want to check on my dad."

Hesitating, Plummer rubbed his chin. He knew it was a bad idea but couldn't come up with a good reason to deny his ex-friend a few minutes with the lad. The delay in scheduling a bail hearing was already ginning support for the accused, plus, the case had not yet been reviewed by a prosecutor. No one on the jury would like the way Whipsaw was being treated, and the marshal didn't want to add to what was already a negative perspective. "Okay, Ketchum. Come on in."

For a third time, Blackjack was patted down, this time by the marshal himself. No weapons were found. "You have 10 minutes, Ketchum. I would make them count."

Ketchum was shown to his father's cell, the marshal informing the visitor, "You can talk through the bars. I'll be right outside, watching through the window. No physical contact. No hugs, handshakes, or passing contraband. Understood?"

"Yes," Blackjack nodded.

Whipsaw, hearing the activity outside of the holding area, was rising from his bunk when he spotted his son. "Ketchum! You came! My God! Son, it's good to see you."

"Hello, Dad," Blackjack greeted. "I wish our reunion was under better circumstances."

"They tell me I'm in a lot of trouble, but I'll be damned if I understand why. I guess having trouble with the law is in our DNA," the senior Jones began.

"Don't worry about it, Pop. I wanted to stop in and let you know I was back in town and ready to help," Ketchum replied with a wink. "I also have a suggestion regarding your case. Something I need you to seriously consider."

"Oh? What's that?" Whipsaw asked.

"You need to request a change of venue," Ketchum stated. "There's no way you can get a fair trial here in Forest Mist."

"What? What in the hell are you talking about?" Whip began to protest. "If anybody can understand what happened, it's the people here in...."

Blackjack interrupted his father, "Because they would have to *move* you to the new venue... to a *different* town and jail."

Puzzlement clouded Whip's eyes for several seconds. "Yes," he mumbled, going along with his son's stated concern, "yes, I suppose it would be difficult to seat a fair jury of my peers here in Forest Mist. Still...."

Seeing his father didn't grasp his veiled message, Blackjack continued, "There are too *many obstacles* to your freedom here in Forest Mist. Support for Plummer is too *strong* here. If you want justice, you're going to have to get it someplace else."

Whipsaw finally realized the unspoken communication, now understanding what his boy was trying to convey. The jail was too well protected, Dallas having scheduled too many deputies to ensure their inmate stayed right where he belonged. A breakout was impossible unless he were transferred to a new location.

"No," Whip spat. "That's not how this is going to go down, at least not initially. I want my name cleared, and I want it done in front of my friends and neighbors. I want that courtroom full of people from Forest Mist, and I want them to hear every word of my trial. We're going to stand and fight."

"That's a bad idea, Dad," Ketchum hissed, shaking his head at the old man's stubbornness. "I've been asking around, and with an Alliance judge on his way to town, you're risking a death sentence. Do you really want to chance dangling at the end of a rope?"

Whip moved away from the bars, pacing the small area afforded by his cell. Finally, he concluded, "We'll do it my way at first. If things go badly... if it looks like I'm going to lose, then we'll give your idea a shot. Agreed?"

"I have resources, Dad. I can have you down in New Orleans and out of the Alliance's reach in six hours. Within a week, I can have you on a boat to the Caribbean. I know some people down there."

"And sacrifice everything I've worked so hard to build here? Throw it all away? I control 80% of the timber leases in this county. The mill is my legacy... my life's work. I'm not going to just walk away and leave that, Son. Think about it. One of these days, I hoped you would take over and expand what I've built, make it even stronger. I can't just turn tail and run... hide for the rest of my days. That would surely kill me the same as a rope."

119

Grunting, Blackjack retorted, "You're the same hardheaded, old mule I remember. It's your life, I guess, but I'm telling you that you're taking a huge risk... the ultimate risk."

Again, Whip paced, his mind working through his son's words. Finally, moving closer to the bars and dropping his voice to a whisper, he suggested, "Let's play it both ways. There's no case against me without the witnesses. If they don't show up, the charges will have to be dismissed. Understood?"

Smiling for the first time since he entered the jail, Blackjack brightened. "Why you crafty, old fox. You do still have a few working brain cells after all. Let me get to work on that."

"Do so discreetly, Son. But do so."

CHAPTER 7

"Well, well, well," Bishop mused, "this certainly changes things." Seeing Whip's son enter the jail was a brilliant stroke of luck and set his mind in motion. Finally, something had gone right. "I can follow him," the Texan determined. "It might come in handy to know where he's holed up."

Witnessing the lost lamb's return to the fold also eliminated any element of surprise should things get ugly in the coming days. "I know you're here, Mr. Blackjack. I can keep an eye on you."

Watching as the muscular man exited the lockup, Bishop started the car and prepared to back out of the parking space. He had to be careful not to get too close, and yet he couldn't risk losing sight of the target. Dusk was fading into night, a situation which was going to make following Whip's son even more difficult.

Marching briskly across the courthouse lawn, Ketchum crossed the street and then proceeded along the sidewalk. At the next intersection, he turned right and continued to stroll past the storefronts like he didn't have a care in the world. Bishop would have sworn the guy was whistling.

Backing away from the curb, Bishop was so intent on watching Blackjack that he almost bumped into a vehicle that suddenly appeared behind him. Pressing the brake hard, he motioned, "Sorry," to the other driver with a lighthearted wave. After glancing in the rearview for a better look, he realized it was a police car.

Finally having a clear road, Bishop proceeded slowly toward the spot where Ketchum had passed out of his view. As he made the next turn, a posh Mercedes sedan slinked out of an empty lot, its license plates indicating the car hailed from Louisiana. "That must be him," whispered the Texan.

There weren't many vehicles on the town's streets, a fact that gave Bishop pause. Besides Blackjack's car and his own wheels, there was only one other set of headlights visible in any direction.

"Stay back," Bishop cautioned himself. "Don't make him think he's being followed."

Three blocks later, the German performance vehicle turned, heading east down a two-lane highway. "He's heading back to the Pelican State?" Bishop guessed.

The Texan couldn't follow, his headlights appearing in Ketchum's mirror a sure giveaway. Instead, Bishop continued north, planning to eventually flip around and race to catch up with his quarry. He could only hope Blackjack wasn't paying close attention to his mirrors and wasn't a lead-footed driver. His plan was thwarted when Bishop noticed that the third set of headlights plying the streets of Forest Mist were now behind him. "We're having a three-car parade."

Bishop turned on the next street, and the headlights followed him.

"What goes around comes around," the Texan mumbled, now wondering if Blackjack Jones hadn't ventured into town alone. "It would make sense for him to travel with personal security or a backup. Let's test that theory."

Two blocks later, with his tail keeping a reasonable distance, Bishop suddenly cut hard left and hit the accelerator, racing down a gravel alley. Before he'd managed the next block, there were headlights behind him. "Shit," he mumbled, unsure of what to do.

He turned onto the next paved street, now travelling through a residential neighborhood of craftsman homes, desperately trying to formulate a plan. Should he confront the henchman on his tail? Maybe try to lose the follower? What message did he want Blackjack to receive from his backup?

It was after the next turn that Bishop caught a glimpse of the tenacious car behind him. It was a police cruiser, probably the one he'd almost backed into at the courthouse. A second later, the Texan had a sinister thought. "What if that's Blackjack's game to free his father?" he grunted. "What if he has someone on the inside? A corrupt deputy?"

A hundred scenarios flooded Bishop's thoughts as he drove. *Could Ketchum be blackmailing one of Plummer's men? Had someone accepted a bribe?* Hell, for all he knew, Whip's son could have kidnapped somebody's child and be forcing them to help free the accused.

Another turn revealed the First Baptist Church, a property Bishop had scouted just an hour before. He remembered the narrow driveway that encircled the buildings and the mature trees that garnished the grounds. An idea popped into his head.

Accelerating hard, Bishop turned into the church's lot and fast-tracked past the sanctuary toward the wing that probably housed Sunday School rooms and a fellowship hall at the rear of the facility. Just as the headlights followed, the Texan turned hard left, cutting behind the structure and out of sight. He slammed on the brakes, skidding to a stop in the crushed stone.

The police car gave chase, probably thinking Bishop was trying to elude. When the Texan observed the front of the cruiser appear around the corner, he threw the transmission into reverse and hit the gas.

Surprised by the sudden appearance of the Volkswagen's bright reverse lights, the cop slammed on the brakes and swerved, coming to a rocking stop with its grill less than two feet from a massive oak.

Bishop hit the brake as well, skidding to a halt with his rear bumper positioned inches from the squad car driver's door. The M4 was in the Texan's hand as he jumped out. He snapped the blaster to his shoulder as he charged at the stunned, trapped deputy. "Let me see your hands! Let me see your hands!"

The officer couldn't get out, the door pinned by the Volkswagen's bumper. The cruiser couldn't move forward because of the tree, backing out impossible due to the angle of Carlie's car.

Bishop spotted the uniformed body inside try for the passenger seat, but the cop was too slow. "Let me see your hands!" he commanded again, now positioned immediately outside the deputy's window, the barrel of the M4 less than an inch from the glass.

The window rolled down, Bishop finding himself staring at Plummer's daughter. "Allison?" he questioned.

"What in hell are you doing?" she blustered. "Assaulting a peace officer! Eluding the police! Get that damn gun out of my face, right now!"

Lowering his weapon, Bishop smiled, "And I was about to ask you the same thing – what in the hell are you doing?"

"I saw you spying on the courthouse and was trying to figure out what you're up to... and how you got Carlie's car."

"Hold on a second," Bishop responded, stepping back toward the Volkswagen. "Let me move so you can get out."

A minute later, Allison flew out of her cruiser with the speed and fury of a woman with a bee in her bonnet. Bishop was pretty sure it was faked rage, embarrassment probably the more accurate description. Nothing would piss off a cop more than being pinned in their own car.

"I'm of a good mind to arrest you," she barked. "I should haul you down to the jail and let you share a bunk with Whipsaw. He'd probably enjoy that."

Not being able to help himself, Bishop laughed and then held up his hands to calm the irate deputy. "Hold on now. Before you slap the bracelets on me, please, let me explain."

"You've got 20 seconds," she hissed, resting a hand on the pistol dangling from her belt.

"I spotted Ketchum when he left the jail and realized it was a prime opportunity to determine the location of his hideout. I was following him and then noticed I had picked up a tail. When I realized my stalker was driving a police car, I was worried Blackjack might have bribed or blackmailed one of your coworkers."

"Haven't you already caused enough problems? Do you ever get enough? The whole town is up in arms over this stunt, and now that Blackjack is back, I'm positive there's going to be bloodshed. My dad doesn't deserve this... the people of Forest Mist don't deserve this."

It was the Texan's turn to be surprised. One statement from the marshal's daughter had changed him from the good Samaritan to one of Satan's minions. He didn't like it.

"Now just a damn minute, Allison. Are you saying Whipsaw should get away with murder just because the town has had a rough go of it? Really? Think about your words, Deputy. Think about rule of law."

His push-back seemed to have the desired effect, her eyes suddenly finding the gravel beneath her boots interesting. "I know. I know. You're morally right, legally correct, standing on the high ground from every angle but one."

With his eyebrows darting skyward, Bishop replied, "But one? And what angle would that be, Deputy?"

"This is uproar going to tear Forest Mist apart. Even if not a single shot is fired, even if Jones is found innocent, this community is never going to be the same. Our department has already been called to break up two fist fights over this mess. We've got people who are now scared to defend themselves over the fear of being arrested, other families wondering if there will be jobs at Whip's mill if he is hanged. He is the largest employer in town, you know. The mill offered the only work around here during the bottom of the collapse and still supports the largest segment of the population. All this pandemonium because of two stupid, pigheaded men."

"What two men? Whipsaw and me?" Bishop asked, his own temper starting to rise.

"Yes. Both of you. If you hadn't stuck your nose in, my father would have arrested Jones, scared the crap out of him on some lesser charge, and then let the whole thing blow over. He would have probably talked the judge into fining Whip a ton of money and used the funds to help all those homeless vagabonds move on. Now, you've made a federal case out of it, threatening to bring in your Alliance bigshots... even intimating our department with your promise of calling in the authorities from Alpha. Thanks. Thanks a lot for nothing," she barked.

"So, the people of Forest Mist place that low of a value on human life?" Bishop countered. "Murder is justified because some guy is down on his luck, or because other people in a similar situation as Nathan Hill have committed crimes? Struggling people are the new justification for hatred and bigotry? Think about it, Allison. Think real hard. I don't believe for one second that deep down inside, you roll down that lane. Now, if you're not going to arrest me on some trumped-up charge, I'm going to head back to my wife."

"Don't cause us any more trouble, Bishop," she warned as the Texan moved toward his car. "The citizens of Forest Mist don't want or need your kind of help."

As he bent to climb behind the wheel, Bishop paused and responded, "The citizens of Forest Mist don't deserve my help if they think like you, Allison."

Bishop complied with the deputy's suggestion, laying low, enjoying some quality time with Terri, and working on a few projects to help out around Carlie's B&B. He fixed a door, reattached some guttering, and removed a dead limb from one of the pecan trees.

For two days, he didn't venture far from Angel's Porch, playing the role of handyman while keeping an eye on things. He hoped it wasn't the calm before the storm.

Only once did he and Terri chance leaving, the Texan wanting to drive to Louisiana using the same route he'd seen Ketchum Jones take out of Forest Mist. "There's a slim chance we might spot that big Mercedes," Bishop told his wife. "Even if we don't, it's a beautiful day for a drive. Let's go scope out some countryside."

Beginning to suffer the effects of cabin fever herself, Terri wholeheartedly agreed.

"He's more comfortable outside of the Alliance," Bishop noted as they tried to figure out where Jones' son might be staying.

"Why do you say that?"

"Whipsaw has a nice home, the lumber mill, and probably a lot of friends around here. Why drive all the way to a neighboring state? Why not stay close to town, your father, and the legal proceedings about to take place?"

"Maybe he doesn't like it here?" she shrugged. "Perhaps he's so unpopular in this area that he feels like he can't stay in Forest Mist? I know Carlie wouldn't let him near her place."

"While I don't know why he prefers the inconvenience of Louisiana, the fact that he is out of state presents some serious challenges for any scheme he might try to implement. It seems to me that he would have a better chance of success if he were staying local. I guess it just depends on what he has planned."

After driving around for a few hours on both sides of the border, the couple decided it was a hopeless exercise. "He could have set up a satellite operation anywhere," Bishop announced, turning the Volkswagen around.

The fourth morning's dawn kissed the earth with color and light so splendid that Bishop and Terri lingered over their morning coffee in silence, mesmerized by its ever-changing palette.

The couple sat in wonder, their attention divided between the light show offered in the eastern sky and the pearl-like visions created by morning dew hanging on broomsedge and Bermuda grasses alike. The whispered rustle of a soft breeze stirred the trees near the barn, bringing the couple back to the real world.

Bishop announced, "The Alliance prosecutor and judge are supposed to arrive today. I don't know where Marshal Plummer will have them stay, but there aren't exactly a ton of 4-star hotels in the vicinity to choose from. He might resolve that Angel's Porch is the best option, in which case, we have to find other digs."

"Maybe they'll decide to change the venue?" she replied, making it clear that her husband wasn't the only one worried about the situation. "Maybe you can make a sworn deposition, and then we can go home."

"That would be nice," Bishop shrugged, "but I doubt that is going to happen. I think they like to have a witness they can cross-examine on a felony charge like murder."

Before she could respond, the rumble of several motorcycle engines assaulted the morning's respite, Bishop immediately reaching for his rifle. "Honey, we have guests."

"You don't know that it's trouble, my love. Remember that," she warned as he bounded down the steps.

Bishop had just exited the barn when four motorcycles pulled into the driveway. Keeping out of sight, he waited until the riders had dismounted and then began working his way toward the B&B.

They were a motley-looking crew, an assortment of leather and patches only partially obscuring their abundance of body ink. Three of the riders sported ratty, long hair and beards, the leader of the pack offering an entirely different fashion statement, his shaved head shining like a newly minted penny. Their exposed muscles indicated these were men who got plenty of exercise, the kind of body-building that guys didn't get from the local gym or yard work.

"Only four?" Bishop whispered. "Maybe Blackjack Jones isn't such a monstrous threat."

Mr. No-hair sprang for the porch as Bishop carefully worked his way to the far side of the house. He wanted a flanking angle and the property's thick tree line provided excellent cover. As he passed the main structure, the distinct sound of growling and snarling swelled like a developing thunderstorm. *Thor is on the job,* Bishop thought, remembering his own close up look at the beast's healthy chompers.

The lead biker beat on the front door just as Bishop reached his desired spot at the corner. From there, he could listen, as well as engage the visitors if necessary.

He heard Carlie's voice, muffled through the heavy wood of the door. "Can I help you?"

"I just want to talk," the biker replied. "Just looking for some information, lady."

"Go ahead... talk," Carlie answered without opening the door. "I can hear you just fine."

"Seriously, ma'am, we're just trying to find two old friends of ours. We heard they were staying here with you and wondered if you can point us in the right direction."

"There's no one staying here right now," Carlie responded.

The determined biker continued his saga, "Our friends are from Alpha. Their names are Bishop and Terri. I know they were renting from you, and I heard in town that they were seen driving your car. Please, lady, I have some important information for them."

"Why you clever, bastard," Bishop whispered, wondering if Carlie was going to fall for the scam.

"Yes, there was a couple staying here, and yes, I loaned them my car, but that's all I know."

It was the biker's turn to become agitated, "Ma'am, can you please tell me where they are staying?"

"They checked out of the inn several days ago, and I don't know where they are anymore," Carlie replied, holding her ground.

Realizing his charade wasn't working, Mr. Chrome-dome switched to Plan B. "Look, lady, you've got a very pretty house here, and I'd hate to see anything happen to it. Fires are a big problem these days, and an old, wooden place like this could be a burning match in seconds. Now please, before my buddies get restless and mean... can you tell me where to find Bishop and Terri?"

"Those are some very shiny motorcycles in my driveway. I'd hate to see what two barrels of buckshot would do to them, and accidental discharges are a big problem these days, too. Now get the hell off my property!" the voice inside angrily retorted. Thor chimed in with a low growl, just to remind the man on the porch that he wasn't intimidated either.

The rider turned to his comrades and shook his head. The other three bikers then began to spread out, all of them reaching for their belts and producing pistols. Bishop flicked off his rifle's safety.

"I did hear them talking about Rocky Falls State Park," Carlie's voice continued. "They did mention having camping equipment with them. Maybe they are staying there."

"Excellent play, Carlie," Bishop whispered. "Making them think the guns scared you into talking. A frightened woman is believable. Nice."

Mr. Egg-head held up his hand to stop his comrades, Bishop noting that they all halted immediately. It was a telling sign of discipline that he wouldn't have expected. The leader stood quietly for several seconds, contemplating what Carlie had just shared.

"If you're lying to me, we'll be back," the biker finally warned. "It will be in the middle of the night, and we won't knock," he added, storming off the veranda in a flurry. A minute later, all four motorcycles roared down the road, heading back toward Forest Mist.

Waiting until the echo of their motors had faded, Bishop stepped up onto the porch and announced, "Carlie, it's okay. They're gone."

She opened the door, pale with fear, a sheen of perspiration on her face. She was still shaking as she clutched the double-barreled shotgun. "You okay?" Bishop asked, noting Thor had remained at her side and didn't appear to be going anywhere.

"Yes, I'm fine," she blushed. "In fact, that was sort of fun."

Knowing the woman was covering, Bishop tried to be supportive, "You did a great job. That was pretty quick thinking... the part about Rocky Falls."

Terri then stepped out on the porch, a rifle cradled in her arms. "I'm sorry this has happened," she apologized, reaching to gently reassure their host.

"They'll be back," Carlie mumbled, her eyes never leaving the road, almost as if she expected them to reappear at any moment. "When they don't find you at the park, they'll come back here. I don't think it will a social call the next time."

"Yes, they will return," Bishop agreed, his gaze following Carlie's. "And now we know what Blackjack's strategy is. He's smart... very smart and has better people than I anticipated. Those guys may have looked like a bunch of ruffians, but they were disciplined. That ploy about us being their old friends was inspired."

"What is Ketchum's play?" Carlie asked. "I don't get it?"

"He wants to eliminate any witnesses," Terri answered for her husband. "That's why they're looking for us. At least we know where they are, for a few hours anyway."

Turning to his wife, Bishop acknowledged, "Yes we do, and maybe I can use that information to our advantage.

Carlie, is there anywhere you can go for a few days? Any friends you can stay with until this all blows over?"

"I'm not leaving," she sternly replied. "This farm is all I have left. I don't have the money to go anywhere, and I wouldn't leave even if I could."

Terri tried her turn at convincing the innkeeper, "You just saw what happened, sweetie. You said yourself that they would be back. Bishop and I can't be here all of the time. Even with Thor by your side, they could hurt you badly. And I don't mean just your property, Carlie."

The proprietor wasn't having any of it. "This is my home. If I pack up and leave town, I'd be the same as those poor drifters. I know what people think of them, and I'll die here before I run."

In a way, Bishop couldn't blame her. How many times had he decided his ranch was the Alamo? The fortress where he would make his last stand no matter what? How would he feel if placed in a similar position?

"Okay," the Texan nodded. "I understand. In my experience, the best defense is a strong offense. I'm going to Rocky Falls and wait for the arrival of our new biker friends. After they come up empty at the park, I'm going to follow them to see where Blackjack and his buddies are hanging out. Maybe we can take this fight to them."

Terri didn't like it but understood her husband's logic. "You're not going to try and take them on while you are there, are you?"

"No," Bishop stated. "But like any enemy, if you know where their headquarters is located, you can inflict a lot of damage if necessary. I promise I'll keep out of sight. This is a reconnaissance mission, not an attack."

"You better take the truck," she said. "The secret's out about Carlie's car, and being seen in the pickup will lend credence to her ruse."

"I should have been more secretive about driving the car. Being seen in it was a mistake," Bishop grimaced, now regretting his weak attempt at stealth. "I don't know what it is with me lately – I seem to be off my game."

It was the third time Terri had heard her mate lament his actions, and it worried her. "It was a good idea, Bishop. Hindsight is always 20-20."

"We brought them right here," he moaned, his voice full of disappointment. "I might as well have left a trail of breadcrumbs. No matter. What's done is done. We need to get out in front of this, and figuring out where Blackjack is hanging his hat is step one."

Ten minutes later, Bishop pulled the pickup out of the barn. The heavier, more robust vehicle was reassuring in a way. "I'm going to stop in town and see if the prosecutor and judge have arrived and try to get an idea of the schedule going forward."

"Okay. Be careful," Terri replied, raising up on her tiptoes and kissing his cheek.

Figuring the bikers would have to report in, travel to Rocky Falls, perform a search of the park, and then return to their leader, Bishop calculated he had at least an hour to be in position. That was plenty of time.

He left via the back lane, worried that Mr. Skinhead would have left one of his gang to keep an eye on Angel's Porch. He then took a few extra turns that allowed him to enter Forest Mist from a completely unique direction.

Hard stares and unfriendly glowers met the West Texan as he rolled into town. Bishop tried to brush off the dark reception, "Wow, you are becoming paranoid, my friend. Might be time to book an appointment with the local shrink."

For a moment, he was tempted to stop by the café and check in on the other star witness. Given the number of cars and trucks parked outside for breakfast, he decided against the idea.

Turning onto the square, he found the courthouse was still an armed camp. Two deputies with long guns patrolled the perimeter, Allison running the checkpoint at the door.

"Have the Alliance officials arrived?" Bishop asked as he stepped forward to be searched.

"Yes," she responded, clearly unhappy to see the man from West Texas. "As a matter of fact, my father was just asking if I'd seen you skulking around town. I think our visitors would like to speak with you."

"That's why I'm here," he grinned as another officer patted him down.

Bishop found Marshal Plummer's office guarded by yet another pair of lawmen, both wearing badges, but dressed in plainclothes. These fellows were clearly not locals. After introducing himself, he discovered that the two new faces worked directly for Nick's department and were assigned as protection for the judge and prosecutor. One of the men knew the West Texan, his previous job being a member of SAINT Team Four.

After taking a few minutes to warn the new security men about what they might be facing, Bishop was shown into the marshal's office by one of the bodyguards.

There, seated behind Plummer's messy desk, was a gray-haired gent wearing a white button-down shirt accented by a red tie, projecting a rather distinguished air. He was introduced as Judge Crawford.

Seated across from His Honor was a lady. As she turned to greet Bishop, he had his second surprise of the morning.

"DA Gibson?" the Alpha resident stammered. "Pat? Why, ma'am, I'm surprised to see you here in East Texas. Last I heard, you were in Austin, trying to organize a department of justice for the Alliance."

She smiled and then reached to hug Bishop. "Diana asked me to make a special trip out here to handle this issue personally. How's Terri doing?"

"She's holding up pretty well, considering. I'm sure she will want to get together as soon as possible and catch up," Bishop responded.

As everyone settled back into the chairs, Bishop recalled the first time he'd met the former district attorney. Long before the Alliance had been formed, when the people of Alpha and Meraton were working to establish rule of law and a regional government, word had come that the nearby town of Fort Stockdale was under the control of a ruthless tyrant who had enslaved the local population.

Nick, Bishop, and a group of men had formed a team and traveled to the small town, loaded and ready to put down a tin pan dictator. After overthrowing the local warlords, they were going to ask the citizens if they wanted to join their growing movement.

Despite dozens of downtrodden souls wandering into Alpha and claiming brutal treatment by the leaders of Fort Stockdale, Nick and Bishop had eventually discovered that the opposite was true. District Attorney Gibson had actually saved the town, and while the lack of resources required she rule with an iron fist, her leadership had kept hundreds of people alive.

Later, the first Alliance council had invited Patricia Gibson to be one of the founding members. She had a reputation as a forward-thinking legal mind and was also one of Terri's favorite people.

"I didn't know Diana was aware of the situation here," Bishop responded sheepishly. "I know she has a lot on her plate, and I didn't want to bother her with this."

"Marshal Plummer actually apprised Sheriff Watts of recent events," Judge Crawford announced. "In turn, the sheriff informed Miss Brown."

"Oh, I see," Bishop nodded. "Well, regardless, I'm very concerned about how this is all going to play out. My gut senses trouble on the horizon, and in fact, it's already started as of this morning."

Explaining what had occurred at Angel's Porch just 30 minutes ago didn't take long, both prosecutor and judge listening intently. "Who is the other witness, Bishop?" Gibson finally asked.

"The waitress at the café. Her name is Margaret. She's scared to death," Bishop replied.

"We'll take her into protective custody," Patricia stated. "Nick assigned Judge Crawford and me a security detail. It sounds like we're going to need a few more men. I assume you and Terri can take care of yourselves?" she added with a wink.

"Yeah, we'll be okay, but I'm worried about Carlie. Speaking of bikers, I've got to get going. I want to see if I can figure out where Whipsaw's son is holed up."

"Be here tomorrow at 9 a.m. sharp, young man," Crawford announced. "We're going to have a preliminary hearing for the accused. You may be called."

"Yes, Your Honor. I'll be here with bells on."

Retrieving his firearm before hustling back to the truck, Bishop scanned the surrounding streets, his eye tuned for anything that appeared out of place. He spotted no Mercedes sedans or motorcycles.

A minute later, he rolled out of Forest Mist, heading north toward Rocky Falls.

The drive passed quickly, Bishop formulating his plan as he raced for the unoccupied nature preserve. The Alliance hadn't recovered far enough to worry about parks and recreation areas, and Rocky Falls was no exception.

The green information sign announcing the entrance to the park was the first indication that the facility had been forsaken. Vines entangled the posts and were beginning to obscure the white letters. He and Terri had almost missed the turn on their trip here a few days ago.

Someone had crashed through the chain-link fence years ago, probably in search of food or someplace to pitch a tent... or just out of pure meanness. The windows at the small entrance building, normally where visitors would pay a fee to enter the park, were all smashed. The door had been kicked in, hanging at an awkward angle from one hinge.

Despite the lack of lawnmowers and maintenance, the park had been constructed at this location for a good reason. Bishop didn't know the name of the small stream that ran through the grounds, but it did feed one heck of a pretty waterfall and rock formation. The pool at the bottom of the cascade was large enough to welcome dozens of swimmers and sunbathers. No doubt, in better times, it had been a popular destination on those sultry weekends in the Lone Star State.

Other than that main attraction, the West Texan remembered a picnic area, campground, park office building and gift shop, and two smaller structures that were the facility's restrooms. The parking lot was large, weeds sprouting up between the cracks in the blacktop. Someone had hauled in large, bathtub-sized boulders to create a border around the paved area.

Steering the truck toward the administration office, Bishop pulled behind the structure and onto the grass. Carefully, he maneuvered behind a thick stand of briars, dead brush, and waist-high weeds. After satisfying himself that he was well hidden, he switched off the pickup's motor and pulled his carbine from the passenger side.

Exiting the truck, he hiked to the corner of the building and took a knee. "Now it's a waiting game," he sighed, wondering how Terri and Carlie were making out.

He anticipated the sound of motorcycle engines, sure the bikers who had accosted Angel's Porch would come here to the park in search of the prosecutor's star witness. He was here, but not where they expected to find him. With any luck, they would check out the campgrounds, perhaps other areas of the facility, and then leave empty-handed. He would follow them back to their lair, and that intel would no doubt prove useful.

For 20 minutes, Bishop just sat and waited. Passing the time by chewing on jerky, listening to the birds, and watching a colony of fire ants working on their kingdom, he found it difficult to remain focused. Twice he stifled a yawn, wondering if the day would present the opportunity for a nap. "Are you getting that old?" he questioned, shaking his head and standing.

The first man-made sound he heard wasn't a motorcycle, but a 4-wheeled vehicle. "Showtime," he whispered, disappearing back around the corner and setting up to spy on the facility's main road.

In fact, it was two SUVs that roared past the entrance shack.

In a flash, Bishop's weapon was up, the former contractor studying the new arrivals through the magnification of his optic. The first thing he noted was the Louisiana license plates. The second was the fact that each of the units appeared to be full of men.

As expected, they zoomed past the headquarters building without even a glance, turning down the narrow lane, following a sign that pointed toward the park's campgrounds. So far, so good.

After waiting 10 minutes, Bishop was mildly annoyed at how long it was taking the ne'er-do-wells to search what was a tiny campground. He and Terri had driven through the small roundabout on their anniversary day jaunt. It shouldn't take them all afternoon to determine no one had pitched a tent.

At 15 minutes, he was getting worried. Maybe the bikers had decided to take a dip at the falls? Perhaps the ignoramuses had gotten lost?

It was 21 minutes after their arrival when Bishop's heart rate shot sky high. In the distance, less than 100 meters away, he spotted a man stalking across the grounds, a long gun in his hands. "Shit! They've dismounted and are

139

searching the park on foot? Who would have thought?" the Texan hissed.

Now on the lookout for foot patrols, Bishop quickly spied a second and then a third rifleman. They were slowly moving a dragnet toward his position. If they continued on the same trajectory, they would surely spot him or at least his truck.

Surviving the next 30 minutes quickly replaced Bishop's grandiose plan of playing super-sleuth. He was outnumbered at least 10 to 1. He had to find someplace defendable to hide – and quick. If they stumbled onto his truck, a gunfight was inevitable.

His first instinct was the park building's roof, but that idea was quickly dismissed. That plan was like climbing up a tree and hiding among the branches. If the trackers found him, he would be a trapped raccoon, and Blackjack's boys would be the hungry hounds snapping at their meal.

His second thought was to run for the truck and make a mad dash for the open road. A quick estimate of the distances and times involved quickly quelled that idea. They would be on him before he could back his ride out of the brush, making swiss cheese out of the pickup, and everything inside, including Terri's husband.

As he watched the approaching crew, Bishop had to acknowledge that he'd underestimated Ketchum's gang. Four of the henchmen were now visible, perfectly spaced, taking their time, and working with military-like discipline. No one man got too far ahead or behind. There were no gaps in their line. They always maintained visibility with at least one of their teammates. "Plummer said Blackjack had been a Ranger in the Army. I should've expected as much from his crew," the Texan admitted. "He's probably recruited other skilled criminals from Leavenworth, or from the streets of New Orleans. Birds of a feather."

Bishop's only hope was that the men surrounding him didn't venture too far into the surrounding overgrowth. Going prone, he began belly crawling toward a dense patch of vegetation, less than 20 meters from the office building. He considered going deep into the surrounding forest but dismissed that concept. He didn't want to lose the pickup, and it was possible that he might be able to spring an ambush.

If he could disable a few of the searchers, it might create enough confusion for him to escape. If such an opening appeared, he could make a run for it as they regrouped.

It was with no small amount of relief when Bishop made it to the thicket undetected. Ignoring the thorns and tangling vines, he wiggled his way in like a rabbit and said a quick prayer that it would be enough to keep him hidden. He was less than 50 meters away from the truck and had a clear line of fire to three sides of his ride.

Onward the line advanced, making their way past the picnic tables, faded blue trash cans, and shady patches of elm and oak. Bishop, watching from the briar patch, estimated his odds at avoiding discovery less than 50-50.

It was several minutes before Ketchum's men descended on the office building. Mr. Shaved Head, from Carlie's front porch, was clearly the leader.

Motioning his team to hang back, he approached the building with his weapon high and looking for work. Slowly he pied each corner while his men looked on, eager to join in if a fight broke out.

Once he'd cleared the perimeter, the boss waved his team forward. The crew quickly huddled while hushed, grunted instructions were relayed, and then the men rushed inside.

It took less than three minutes for the disappointed hunters to emerge from the abandoned building, Mr. No-hair clearly not pleased at coming up empty-handed. "Let's head back. Blackjack is going to be pissed," one of the men complained, just loud enough for Bishop to hear.

As they began walking back toward the campground and their vehicles, the leader paused less than 20 meters from Bishop's truck. Acting like he'd heard something; the hairless gunman stood completely still and scanned the underbrush with a careful eye. "Oh, shit," Bishop whispered. "He's seen the truck."

It seemed like an eternity before the man moved, and when he did, Bishop's blood ran cold. Turning only his head, the gang's leader looked right at Bishop, his eyes boring into the brush pile as if he knew exactly where the West Texan was hiding.

Flipping the safety off his carbine, Bishop centered his optic on Cue Ball's chest. He'd cut the hairless head off the snake and deal with the subordinates next.

"What's up, VooDoo?" one of the other searchers asked. "You see something?"

"No," the leader replied. "Thought for a second... but no. Let's head back."

Exhaling in relief, Bishop waited several minutes before exiting his hide. He wanted to be next to his truck when the bad guys left the park. He wanted to follow them if possible.

Again, he scanned the area with his optic. These guys were far more skilled than he'd anticipated, and he wouldn't have put it past their leader to leave someone behind – just in case. He was up against professionals.

When the sound of two starting engines drifted across the park, Bishop hustled for the office building and prepared to make a dash for his truck.

CHAPTER 8

The SUV's motors were racing, the whine of their exhaust striking Bishop as odd. As he darted for his truck, he noticed something that made him pause mid-step. Tire tracks. His pickup had pushed down the weeds, the trail clearly visible from where he was standing. Mr. Baldy had seen it. That's why he had paused in this exact spot.

Looking up, Bishop spied the two SUVs now, barreling across the park grounds, on a direct course for the office. They knew he was here.

He turned, watching a rooster tail of dust approach from the camping area. Egress via the pickup was now out of the question. He would have to stand and fight it out here, and in a way, he was ready to get it over with.

He quickly scanned for cover, wanting someplace that would allow him to move... to avoid being pinned down. The wall of small boulders surrounding the parking lot was his only option.

Not wanting to be trapped inside the office, Bishop scrambled for the rocks. Going prone behind the nearest stone, he brought the carbine up just as the first SUV careened into his sights.

The rear window rolled open, a rifle barrel poking through. Two bright flashes sparked, Bishop hearing the rounds whiz over his head. Any thoughts of talking his way out of the engagement evaporated.

A man with less experience might have aimed for the windshield or the tires. Bishop knew both targets would be ineffective. Instead, he aligned the red dot of his holographic optic six inches below the hood ornament and began slamming home a steady stream of lead.

It was a natural reaction for the men inside the first vehicle to duck low, desperately trying to get under the vulnerable windshield glass as Bishop's rounds began to thunk and whack into their ride.

Some of his bullets were stopped by the radiator, others deflected by the air intake and mechanical apparatus attached to the big SUV's firewall. Some, but not all.

The first lead to avoid those obstacles streamed right through the glovebox and slammed into the passenger's chest while still traveling at over 2,000 feet per second. It shattered two ribs, clipped an artery, and then tumbled and tore through the hapless man's right lung.

The second lucky shot punched a perfect .223-inch hole in the speedometer, glancing off the steering wheel before it plowed into the driver's chin. The bullet fragmented, shredding the driver's tongue, pallet, and sinus cavity before the largest fragments came to rest in the already-deceased man's brain. His body, spasming from the violent penetration, forced his leg muscles to tighten and lock down on the accelerator.

For a horrifying second, Bishop thought he was shooting at some sort of up-armored SUV like he'd seen used by the president. The lead vehicles kept coming, pointed at his rock like a missile. His bolt picked that moment to lock open. Empty.

Reaching for a new mag, Bishop realized there wasn't time. With his vision filled by the charging SUV's tires, he buried his head in the dirt just as the front wheel slammed into the boulder. The West Texan felt the rock move and prepared himself to be crushed.

The racing behemoth's front tire shot skyward, propelled into the air by the physics of its mass, velocity, and angle of impact. The body of the SUV had no choice but to follow, the entire left side launching into the air as it roared over Bishop's head.

With its center-mass no longer low and spread evenly across four tires, the airborne vehicle fell victim to gravity and began to tumble as it raced back to earth. Its landing, at over 40 miles per hour, was on the passenger door.

Momentum took over, the vehicle bouncing a full two feet into the air as it continued to flip. Finally opening his eyes, Bishop spotted his target slam roof-down into the parking lot as it continued to roll toward the office building.

It managed two spectacular flips... mirrors, trim, and a blizzard of glass flung in all directions before the still tumbling wreck crashed into the park's headquarters with devastating force.

The concrete block wall crumpled like a sheet of tin foil, the SUV continuing into the structure and punching through the opposite wall before coming to rest with its rear half protruding through a cloud of dust, drywall, and crushed blocks.

It took Bishop a full second to blink away the fantastic violence of the crash, the sound of the second attacking vehicle's motor helping him to regroup. Punching in a fresh box of pain pills, his M4 was up and ready to fight.

The second driver, no doubt swayed by what had just happened to the point man, slammed on his brakes and yanked the wheel hard left.

The cutting tires threw up a wall of pale dust and burning rubber as the SUV swerved off the pavement and into a patch of brush and undergrowth. Bishop snapped a shot just as all four doors flew open, shooters with long guns piling out before the wheels had stopped rolling.

Despite the cover of the foliage and fog of thick dust, Bishop continued to squeeze the trigger, sending the assaulters to ground just a few feet from their ride. Half expecting them to panic and expose themselves, he continued to lay down a steady stream of suppressing fire while his eyes darted right and left looking for a real target.

After several shots, no human shapes appeared. Bishop took his finger off the trigger, his eyes desperately scanning for the attackers. The weeds and grass were too thick for him to see the earth, the West Texan sure the men out there were on the move. Hell, he would be.

Rage surged inside Bishop, the adrenaline dump commanding his body, pure fury hijacking his emotions, his mind replaying the attempt to crush him like a bug and the absolute viciousness of the act. Glancing over his shoulder at the crashed Suburban, his anger boiled over.

Raising his rifle, Bishop squeezed the trigger hard. He raked the undercarriage with a series of shots, relentlessly concentrating his fire on the passenger compartment, desperately seeking to kill any survivors. "You sons of whores," he growled, sending round after round tearing through the interior.

His wrath somewhat satiated, Bishop returned his attention back to the second Chevy. "They'll split up," he whispered. "They'll hit me from two sides, and this rock isn't big enough to protect me. I need to get out of here."

Yet, there was no place to run. He could retreat to what remained of the office, but that would only buy him a few seconds at most, and then he would be hemmed in. Bishop knew he was outnumbered, and in that situation, maneuver provided the best chance of survival. "I can't see them. They can see me. I need to fix that."

Vowing to even the odds, he darted toward the brush, hissing, "Good for the goose, good for the gander."

Four steps from the edge, a shot rang out, the bullet kicking up a small spout of soil at his feet. The spent round gave Bishop an excellent tactical image of where at least one of his foes was hiding. He dove for a sizeable clump of grass and weeds, hitting the ground with a teeth-jarring thud and rolling hard to his left. Just to keep everybody honest, he fired three rounds in the general direction of the shooter.

Bishop knew the secret to his longevity was to keep moving. Yet every time he fired, he flashed a big, bright neon arrow that pointed at his position. Given the headcount on each side of the fight, it was key that he didn't allow them to engage force-on-force.

Crawling on all fours, he scrambled for a downed thatch of short oak. The attackers could be anywhere, which meant he had to remain diligent at each and every one of those 360 degrees. His only chance at survival would be exhausting and risky... and oh my God was it going to suck.

Catching his breath, Bishop decided that the hunters probably hadn't managed to flank him. If he continued to move to the south, there was a good chance he could stay in front of them.

He figured there were at least four of them out there, maybe five. He didn't think anyone had survived from the crashed SUV, but had they left a man or two at the campgrounds? Were they sneaking up on him at that very second? He prayed there weren't more of the bastards.

During the next few minutes, Bishop played the scoot and hide game, always trying to keep himself within a reasonable distance from his truck. If they decided to leave or try and capture his wheels, he wanted to be close enough to ruin their day.

The rustle of a bush made Bishop's head snap to the south. Before he could send a shot that direction, a branch cracked to the west. "Shit. They're trying to envelop me," he hissed. "Standard small unit tactics."

Bent at the waist, he ran hard for the trunk of a felled pine lying less than 20 yards away. Before he'd made three strides, a string of bullets ripped through the air, the zipping lead chasing every footfall. Bishop was forced to zig and zag, ricochets singing off the ground.

He dove for the downed tree, landing badly as he skidded across the ground on the far side. Just as suddenly as the barrage had started, the shooters held their fire.

Whoever they were, Bishop had to admit they were skilled. They communicated silently, moved well in the field, and had excellent fire discipline. Special Forces? Rogue law enforcement from some godforsaken part of Louisiana?

His last, desperate move for cover had resulted in a ripped shirt and missing skin. Massaging his throbbing shoulder, Bishop pulled back a hand covered in blood. It was nothing in the grand scheme of things, a hell of a lot better than wearing a marble hat. He'd gotten lucky. They had advanced a lot closer than he had realized.

Scanning the thick vegetation, the witness on the run knew he was in trouble. The forest was thinning out, giving way to a grassy pasture beyond, the men behind him pushing him further and further away from the office and his only method of escape. Pretty soon they'd herd him out into the open, and that would be the end. The men trying to slaughter him were pressing, trying to wrap up Whipsaw's trial before it ever got started.

Bishop moved again, crawling through the dirt to a patch of briars and wiggling his way into the undergrowth. The thin branches wouldn't stop a bullet, but at least his ass wasn't fully exposed. A quick scan brought home the realization that there were only a couple more places left to hide. After that, it was open, bare pasture.

Fueled by desperation, an idea surged into Bishop's brain. It was a long shot, but he had to try.

His rifle sling was wrapped with a length of paracord, a super-strong string that had hundreds of uses. It was just one of a dozen insignificant things a man collected for those "just in case," moments. Bishop's wrist became a blur of small circles, unwinding the cord in a rush.

He tied one end to a high branch above his head and then began playing it out as he crawled to the next clump of brown vegetation. The hunters were closing in, no doubt believing they had him cornered. If he read them right, they would be eager and aggressive, furious over the loss of their comrades, convinced they had him surrounded, and willing to take risks.

Bishop waited for nearly a minute, scanning the forest for any sign of movement as he quietly stacked a few rocks and branches in front of his head. It wasn't much, but even the thinnest cover might make the difference.

Finally ready, he took a deep breath and tugged on the cord, the tension making the distant bush rattle and sway.

Trying to sell the feint, he stopped for several seconds, then gave the limb another tug.

Less than 20 meters away, a square of red cloth appeared behind a thicket of scrub. Slowly, Bishop moved his rifle barrel to point in that direction.

A light twitch of the paracord followed, the lassoed bush barely moving at all. Next, he heard the rustle of a footfall to the right. The plan was working. They were moving to hit him from two sides. He let go of the paracord, the killers needing no more convincing.

He spotted just a sliver of a cap, the blue cloth visible for only a second. Bishop knew where to look now, making it harder for the man to conceal himself.

Three more times there was a glimpse or noise. Bishop was confident he now understood their plan, but he didn't dare spring his trap just yet. He wouldn't get a second chance.

In they rushed, guns high, totally focused on the place where they thought their quarry was hiding. Two of them wielded sub-machine guns, the other two armed only with pistols. They hadn't been expecting an extended fight. He would take out the two more powerful weapons first.

They opened up on the brush pile, no shouted warning, no mercy. The West Texan was fine with the rules of this engagement, images of the SUV's bumper inches from his skull serving to melt away any sense of clemency.

The M4 gently pushed against his shoulder, two 5.56 mm rounds exploding the first target's head. The assailants probably wore body armor, and he didn't have the time to take any chances. Before the empty brass had landed on the desert floor, his optic was centered on the other automatic weapon. He squeezed again, and again.

Blackjack's boys were quick, reflexes honed from training and combat. Bishop didn't have time to move his aim before the remaining two shooters were into the fight.

A pistol round found Bishop's back, his body armor protecting his vitals but still transferring enough kinetic energy to hurt like hell. He ignored the pain, forcing his ribs to expand and draw air. He fired again at a shadow, rolled hard right, and loosed three more rounds where his instincts told him a man had gone to ground.

A shape appeared out of the brush, the shooter moving like a big cat. He scooped up one of the MP5 machine guns and dove for cover before Bishop could center his optic.

Still outnumbered, Bishop sensed it was time to move. He had them back on their heels, but there was still plenty of opportunity for the tide to turn. Just as he rose to run, the MP5 sang its deadly song.

Hot lead buzzed past Bishop's head as he scrambled back toward the park's office, the swarming bullets so close he thought he could feel the heat of their passing. Again, he launched into the air, landing on his bad shoulder with a grimace and moan.

Pushing the agony aside, he flipped over and fired three rounds back the way he'd come, shooting from his back, between his legs, and barely missing his own boots.

With a grunt of determination, he was up and running again, swerving and dodging to keep as many patches of vegetation between him and the pursuers as possible.

After scrambling 50 meters, Bishop realized two things. The first was his exhaustion and pain. The second was the fact that he was no longer being shot at. The men behind were smart, saving their ammo for when they had a proper target.

Bishop dropped to a knee, his eyes seeking any sign of his nemesis. None appeared.

Drawing deep breaths while he rested, he slapped home a fresh magazine. He had evened the odds somewhat but was still on the short end of the equation. Outnumbered two to one, and given the quality of men he was facing, he couldn't get sloppy.

He rose and scurried for the rocks beside the parking lot, cutting hard between the last two bordering trees, trying to be as difficult a target as possible.

Reaching a spot between the office and his truck, Bishop went prone to scout the yard. He hadn't seen any sign of the pursuers now for several minutes. Had they decided to call it quits? Were they circling back? Trying to reach the surviving Suburban? Come back later with reinforcements? They were very skilled men; anything was a possibility.

Bishop's trained eyes noted no movement in the brush beyond the ruined park building. Neither was there any sign of life around the crumpled SUV still resting on its side under the collapsing roof of the office. As he started to rise for the final sprint to his truck, Bishop caught a glimpse of color through the undergrowth. He dropped down again, waiting for a maelstrom of bullets to rip into his flesh. None came.

He saw them clearly then, rushing through the woods, all discipline lost. They were on a direct course for the unharmed SUV. Bishop's angle was bad, the corner of the damaged structure blocking his line of fire. He raised his rifle, on the fence as to whether to engage or let them go and make his own escape. "They'll be back," he whispered. "Here, in Forest Mist, or at Carlie's... they'll be back. Finish it now."

The smell of gasoline reached him, Bishop's vision taking in the wounded SUV. Their course would take them right past it, and they would probably check to see if any of their friends had survived. The West Texan could discern something glistening in the sunlight, the underside covered in a shiny liquid. He waited, trying to estimate when the two attackers would be close enough to make his last stand.

As anticipated, a man rushed from the woods, bent at the waist and running hard. He made a beeline for the leaking vehicle.

Bishop aimed at the axle, hoping to generate a spark. He fired once, then again, then began emptying his magazine into the exposed steel.

For a few seconds, Bishop thought his plan was flawed. Then there was a flash of white, followed by a sizzling red mist of flame. The vapor cloud of petrol detonated with an enormous clap of thunder.

A yellow and red fireball expanded instantly, blowing pieces of the doomed Suburban in every direction. That shrapnel was immediately followed by chunks of the park building's walls and roof, a dark column of swirling smoke rising into the Texas sky.

Bishop felt the blast's heatwave skim across his face as he rose to charge. It took only a second for the explosion to consume its fuel, leaving several small, sprouting fires in its destructive wake.

As he rounded the corner of the damaged office, he spied a man on the ground, his leg posed at an unnatural angle, his life blood leaking on the dirt. He was clearly out of the fight, so Bishop kept on moving. Circling the hot area with the carbine at his shoulder, he found the remaining hired gun, Mr. Cue Ball, racing through the underbrush, running as if the devil himself was on his tail.

For a heartbeat, Bishop considered letting him go. The brush near his truck was now burning, the fire spreading in all directions. He decided not to press his luck. A column of smoke that large would be seen for miles. He had no idea who might see it and come to investigate or help Blackjack's remaining thug.

Turning to run for his own truck, Bishop heard the surviving SUV's engine turn over. "Shit!" he hissed, "I forgot about that!"

He spied VooDoo backing out of the undergrowth, the reverse lights making an excellent target. Bishop began squeezing the trigger, his carbine gently nudging into his shoulder.

One taillight blew out as the big Chevy jerked right, then swerved hard as the driver fought to straighten the wheel.

Bishop felt his bolt lock back, his rifle empty. Cursing his lack of weapon management, the West Texan ejected the spent magazine and yanked a fresh box of lead missiles from his vest. By the time he slammed them into the well and slapped the release, the Chevy was racing down the park lane, out of reach.

"Damn it!" he cursed, reaching for the empty magazine and throwing it into the dump pouch on his belt. "You had better get your shit in one, neat bag soon, Bishop, or these guys are going to kill you *and* your wife."

Stomping back to his pickup, Bishop's anger at his own stupidity continued to boil. "You had all the time the world to switch mags. You stood there, watching the pretty fire like a mesmerized schoolboy. What was that all about anyway? Were you opining for hot dogs and mustard? You better start thinking, old man, and un-fuck that brain. These guys aren't common bullies or bumbling amateurs. You can't give them a second chance and expect to walk away the next time."

During the entire drive back to Forest Mist, Bishop continued his negative introspective. For some reason, he kept making mistakes, was plagued with bad judgment, and knew his luck wouldn't hold out forever.

By the time he reached the village's outskirts, his ferocity was fading, gradually being replaced with cold, logical assessment. Despite his missteps, he *had* managed to deprive Blackjack of seven henchmen, one vehicle, several weapons, and several dozen rounds of ammunition. He *had* sent a message.

"They won't be so bold the next time," he reasoned, turning to take the back road to Carlie's. "I shoved a load of hurt right up Ketchum's ass. I wonder how much more he can take before he decides his father isn't worth it?"

Ketchum knew instantly that something had gone badly wrong. Only one of the Suburbans pulled into the camp, and only one occupant sat inside.

Ignoring the circle of concerned onlookers that surrounded the SUV, VooDoo exited the driver's door and made a beeline for his boss. "All of the others are dead," he reported.

"What? What in the hell did you run into?" Ketchum replied, motioning for his second in command to move away from a dozen pairs of ears.

"I'm sure it was this Bishop character we keep hearing about," VooDoo stated. "It was one guy. He moved like nothing I've ever seen before. Excellent fire control, aggressive as hell, and damned lucky."

"Was he waiting for you? I can't believe you stumbled into an ambush, Sergeant."

Shaking his head, Ketchum's subordinate grunted, "No, actually he was hiding. I saw a sign of his truck hidden in the brush and tried to surprise him."

VooDoo continued, recounted the events to his superior in a concise, accurate, military report. As he listened, Ketchum not only absorbed the facts, but also considered the man relaying them.

He'd met the sergeant at Leavenworth, the two prisoners sharing a cellblock. The fact that both men had been convicted of similar charges was a natural attraction, and a friendship soon developed.

Attempted murder of a superior officer, known as "fragging," hadn't been all that common since the final years of the Vietnam war. Given that both Jones and VooDoo had attempted to permanently relieve their commanding officers of duty was yet another link in the bond between them.

In fact, VooDoo claimed his innocence, swearing that he hadn't tried to execute his lieutenant. A witness had spied the sergeant carrying a Claymore Antipersonnel Device toward the officer's latrine and had warned his commander. Later, at the trial, the accused had testified that he was setting up the deadly mine to protect that section of their perimeter. The tribunal didn't buy the story.

"I should have bled him," the sergeant had told Blackjack later. "He was an incompetent fuck and bound to get us all killed."

Ketchum, on the other hand, blamed whiskey for his incarceration. "My LT was a dumb shit as well," he confessed to his new friend. "We lost two good men on patrol that day because he was a coward. I got stone-faced drunk and rolled a grenade in his general direction. I only wanted to scare him, but some of the shrapnel hit that West Point puke in the leg, and I was brought up on charges."

As they served their sentences, their bond grew. When Ketchum was finally released, he told VooDoo, "Come to New Orleans. I'll set you up. We can do great things together."

Less than two years later, VooDoo had served his time and remembered his friend's words. With no place else to go, he had headed to the Big Easy. By that time, Ketchum had become widely known as a ruthless, skilled operator in Gulf City's underworld. The addition of a trusted, disciplined, equally violent second in command had served to accelerate Blackjack's rise to power.

The two men had been inseparable ever since.

"So, Bishop and his wife are staying at Carlie's Bed and Breakfast. Just like we were told," Ketchum announced after digesting his man's report.

"What makes you say that?" VooDoo asked, his brow knotting in confusion. "I can't connect those dots."

"You said Carlie lead you to believe that they were staying at Rocky Falls. When you got there, Bishop was waiting for you, hiding in the bush. You said the tire tracks were fresh, so he must have arrived just before you got there. That can't be a coincidence. He knew you were coming, probably was on a scouting expedition, curious about what he was up against."

"And?"

"How much time passed between when you were at the B&B and when you arrived at the park?" Blackjack inquired.

"About 90 minutes, give or take," VooDoo shrugged. "I came straight back here, briefed you, and then rounded up a team. We drove directly to the park."

"Bishop was either at Carlie's place or very close by. She got word to him. That's the only way he could've have gotten there before you," Ketchum proclaimed.

The sergeant had to admit that Ketchum's reasoning made sense. "Thinking back now, she was awful brave when we confronted her on the porch. Hell, he might have been in the house, waiting to engage if we tried to enter. She must have known he was there."

Ketchum began pacing, his mind working through all the variables. Bishop was the star witness against his father. Without the stranger's testimony, there wasn't much of a case.

"Our friend from West Texas is skilled and extremely potent," Blackjack offered. "Since arriving here, I've been gathering what information I can. Everyone's been telling me that this Bishop is a capable man, a dangerous individual who understands the rhythm of combat and has the will, training, and experience to execute at a high level. I think he's proven that beyond any doubt today."

"I agree one hundred percent," VooDoo replied, watching as his boss continued walking the tiny race track, rubbing his chin.

The sergeant remained confident, Ketchum having demonstrated his brilliant strategic skill hundreds of times since the disgraced NCO had arrived in New Orleans. His skills as a tactician were beyond question. The man had an abundance of both balls and brains.

Most leaders would have been furious at the loss of seven men, but not Ketchum. Every officer VooDoo had ever served under would have been irate, challenged his leadership and decisions in the field, and invoked some sort of disciplinary action. Not Blackjack Jones.

Secretly, deep inside, Ketchum was worried. While he still considered New Orleans his kingdom, he knew that eventually the United States and Baton Rouge would reestablish complete control and the rule of law would be paramount. His organization would either be pushed out or have its influence and power greatly diminished. It would be just like before the collapse, people like him forced to live off the spoils of petty crimes and always worried that the authorities were about to lock them up. He needed a foothold in the legitimate world. He needed his dad's mill operation, his established business, and the timber leases the old man had managed to secure.

There were other strong emotions influencing the crime lord's thinking as well.

His father had been the only person on this earth who had never lost faith in him. No matter how many mistakes he'd made, regardless of his flawed humanity, his dad had always given unconditional love and support. Now it was time to pay him back, to realize the promise his father had always believed was inside of his son.

There was also a darker element to Blackjack's mindset. Revenge.

When he'd been arrested, the entire town had turned their backs on him. No one would make eye contact when he passed folks on the street. Not a single friend, football teammate, or even the pastor asked to hear his side of the story. Yes, he'd struck his mother, but the assault was justified.

Then there was Dallas Plummer, outstanding citizen and keeper of the peace in Forest Mist for decades. He was known as an honorable gentleman, respected by the community to the point where no one bothered to run against him in the elections. Blackjack knew better and loathed the man for his deceit.

Ketchum's mind traveled back in time, to that fateful day in early October of his senior year. He could still remember that afternoon as clear as if it had happened yesterday. Football practice had been canceled due to a nasty stomach bug working its way through the coaching staff. He was home early and worried about the upcoming game.

At 6'4" and 235 pounds, Ketchum's life, future, and religion were football. There had been scouts coming to see him play, serious-looking men crowding the packed bleachers, busy with their clipboards and stopwatches. Some whispered that these strangers were from sacred places like Oklahoma, Alabama, Notre Dame, and the holy grail of them all, Texas A&M.

High school football was everything in rural Texas, the stadiums full of passionate, exuberant crowds every Friday night. College basketball may have touted Marsh Madness, but in the Lone Star State, it was a pigskin and the gridiron that intoxicated the population into a weekly frenzy.

Across the entire region, from the corner gas station to the main street diner, the talk was always about the local team. Small town newspapers dedicated far more ink to the high school's star halfback than to the stock market or international politics. Grain elevators hung painted banners from their massive concrete silos. Storefronts boasted school colors and mascots. Local politicians made sure they were seen at every game, smiling and waving to the adamant fans. Parades were held for winners, fundraisers for losers.

159

Referees had to be given police escorts to and from the games.

Ketchum was what his coaches called a "triple bonus." His grades were excellent, his size considered perfect, and best of all, he could run the 40-yard dash in less than 4.4 seconds. He was considered a shoe-in for a division one, full-boat scholarship.

The police car in the driveway that afternoon only caused young Ketchum a momentary flash of concern. Marshal Plummer was his father's best friend, and it wasn't unusual for him to drop by. "There's an election coming up in November," he chuckled as he entered the front door. "Dallas is probably here trying to get another campaign contribution."

His backpack deposited in his bedroom, the young star's attention immediately switched to his favorite room in the house – the kitchen. "I wonder if there is any of that ham left in the fridge."

He was just reaching for the icebox when it dawned on Ketchum that his mother hadn't appeared to greet him with her always-cheery smile. His mind then returned to the mysterious police car in the driveway. Was something wrong?

He stepped to the sliding-glass door that led to the back porch. No one was there. He then checked the small laundry room adjacent to the back door. Again, no sign of his mother or the marshal.

"I hope she doesn't have that virus that's going around," he ventured, heading toward the far side of the home and the bedrooms that resided there.

The master bedroom's door was closed. As he approached the threshold, he heard an unusual noise from within. Leaning his ear close, Ketchum heard grunting, slapping, and other animalistic sounds coming from inside.

Thinking his mother was being attacked, Ketchum charged in, bowed for combat.

Three steps inside the door, the 17-year old realized what was going on. There was his mother, naked, straddled atop Marshal Plummer and in the throes of passion.

"Ketchum!" his mom spouted, her face blushing bright red as she rolled off the man beneath her. "What... you're home early... oh my God!"

It that microcosm of time, at the very moment, three lives were altered, none for the better.

Reeling from the realization of what he'd just witnessed, Ketchum pivoted and did what he did best. He ran.

He nearly knocked the back door off its hinges as he raced from the house from the betrayal and pain that now echoed within its walls. He couldn't get far enough away from the place that had comforted him since birth. Everything was crashing around him, his teenage mind unable to process the horror welling up in his soul.

His parent's bedroom, a place of sanctuary from childhood nightmares and monsters under the bed, was now soiled... his beautiful, loving mother, now degraded to a cheap, cheating slut. That king-sized bed, always so welcoming when midnight thunderstorms drove a small, frightened boy to its warm, secure covers, was suddenly a place of betrayal, stained with evil sin. He couldn't erase the image of Plummer's hairy frame driving into his mother's body. It was gross. Disgusting. Sickening in a way that he'd never experienced before.

Ketchum ran like the wind, his mind swirling to grasp what his eyes had just taken in. He subconsciously sought out his favorite boyhood haven, another spot that had comforted him since he could remember. The pond by the back pasture. A place of solitude and peace.

As the minutes passed, Ketchum began to change. He's always been an aggressive kid, often using his size and strength to intimidate rivals and smaller boys. While some might have called him a bully, others viewed the oversized teenager as merely strong willed. There were limits as to how

161

far he would go. He had never seriously hurt anyone, his violent acts limited to a few schoolyard scuffles.

Now, after the shock of his mother's unfathomable betrayal, the dark fibers of Ketchum's being began to emerge. The impulses of hatred, ferocity, and wrath grew and multiplied, the goodness residing within him unable to cope with the overwhelming surge of anger. He was being pulled down into the depths of emotion, sucked into a quagmire of pain, a drumbeat of evil pounding on his consciousness, thrashing his capacity for love and other positive feelings to a pulp.

He paced around the millpond, ignoring the frogs that urgently leaped into the water, almost as if they could sense the darkness filling his core. He circled the shoreline, once, twice, and on the third pass, stopped when his mother appeared on the bank.

Tears burned Ketchum's cheeks as she approached, her dark tresses no longer shiny and soft, her green eyes appearing to him as being empty and cold. "Why?" he hissed, unable to control the pain that roared in his chest. "Why?"

"Ketchum," she whispered, stepping toward him, "I'm so sorry. Your father and I... we've been having issues for a long time. I don't know why this happened. Dallas came by. He made me laugh. It was innocent at first, and then it just happened. I'm so very, very sorry."

He started to turn away, her words serving to both infuriate and confuse him.

She reached out for her only child, some inner desire desperately not wanting him to turn away. When her palm closed on his shoulder, he was repulsed, started to retch, and then lashed out.

His first blow struck her on the jawbone, her head snapping back from the force driving his massive fist. As his mother staggered backward, Ketchum felt the first relief since walking through the bedroom door.

Power flowed through his body, his pain lessened by imposing his will upon the source of his anguish. It felt good, a welcome decompression, and he hit her again.

The second jab sent her reeling, landing in the weeds and barely maintaining consciousness. Blood began oozing from her lips as she tried to blink away the waves of agony ripping through her skull. She wanted to stand, but only managed to rise to an elbow as her eyes filled with water.

"You bitch!" Ketchum screamed, now looming over his mother with balled fists. "I'm going to kill you! You are going to die!"

It took her a second to focus on her son, her brain trying to unscramble the impulses of pain. When she finally managed eye contact, her next words were barely a whisper. "Go ahead. I deserve it."

As his weight shifted forward, Ketchum's muscles tightened for the final assault. A nanosecond before his tortured mind gave the command to pummel the woman who gave him life, he paused. The source of his agony was right there, helpless, unable to control her destiny. He was in control. He could do anything he wanted. All that she was, all that she would ever be, was in his hands.

"No!" he snapped, "That would be too good for you! Death would be too quick!"

Without another word, Ketchum stormed off, leaving his weeping, bleeding mother in the pasture, alone with the consequences of her actions.

Again, he ran, this time to a teammate's home.

Over the weekend, Ketchum stayed secluded, telling his friend's parents only that his mom and dad were having issues, and he wanted to stay with them for a few days until the storm clouds cleared.

On Monday morning, as he started to enter the school, Dallas Plummer and a deputy were waiting. Ketchum was handcuffed and lead away to a waiting police car, a ring of his stunned teammates and friends gawking in silence. It was humiliating, but he no longer cared.

It was on the way to jail that Ketchum learned that his mother had run away, leaving the town where she'd been born and raised, and the husband who had given her a home and a son. No one knew where she had gone. A simple note, left on the kitchen table, carried a handwritten apology.

Ketchum was booked for assault, the teen having no clue that he had suddenly become a pawn, a bargaining chip being used by the town's two most powerful men. Dallas Plummer wanted to remain the town's marshal but knew his reputation would never survive if the scandal was exposed.

An hour later, Ketchum's father appeared outside the cold, iron bars, his face having aged a decade in only a few days. "I know why you did it," Whipsaw began. "She told me. Confessed to everything. You're all I have left now. I'll get you out of this, Son."

Most of all, Whipsaw wanted the only remaining member of his family to be free and clear. But he was still painfully aware of the dark cloud that now hovered over the Jones household. He was embarrassed, prone to bouts of self-criticism, spending countless hours wondering if it was his fault his wife had gone astray. In the end, he was more than willing to keep his mouth shut in exchange for his son not going to prison.

The deal brokered by Plummer and the county prosecutor was the only way out. In exchange for Ketchum's release, Whipsaw bargained away his son's dream of college scholarships and a football career. At least the military would offer Ketchum a new start and the potential for a good life.

"And the rest, as they say, is history," Blackjack mumbled.

"What? I didn't hear you, sir," VooDoo responded. He could sense Ketchum's dark mood, and he was certain that his cloudy demeanor meant somebody was going to have a bad day.

"Oh, nothing, Sergeant. I was just thinking out loud," Ketchum replied.

It was another minute before Blackjack stopped pacing and squared to face his trusted sidekick. "Gather the men. All of them. I want everybody issued a full combat load, as much ammunition as they can carry. We're going to put an end to this, Sergeant, today. Our enemy believes they have issued us a setback. We have a very small envelope of opportunity to regain the initiative and hit them before we're expected. Hurry, VooDoo. The sooner we roll, the fewer assets we'll lose."

"Yes, sir."

CHAPTER 9

Something about gunfighting always made Bishop extremely thirsty. The spent cordite was exhausted inches from his mouth and nose, so he could not escape his weapon's gases. While inhaling gun smoke played a role in his condition, he could spend all day training at the range without experiencing such a severe case of cotton mouth. Some other factor was at play.

No doubt the physical exertion contributed, but again, he could run, lift, and sweat for hours without feeling like his throat was lined with sandpaper.

He was sure that combat's unequaled adrenaline dump was the main culprit.

Sitting at Carlie's kitchen table, nursing his third glass of water, the hounded witness recounted his engagement at the park between gulps of the cold liquid. Carlie was shocked, Terri clearly worried.

"So, one of them got away?" Terri asked, somehow always managing to hit her husband's most sensitive button.

"Well, now, let's not forget that I was overwhelmingly outgunned. And yet I still managed to take out seven of their murdering asses before they could make mincemeat of me," Bishop countered, hoping to garner a smidge of sympathy before continuing. "But yes," he continued, lowering his gaze to the floor. "I screwed up. I lost focus, and the ringleader got away. Sorry."

Terri's expression made it clear that second-guessing her husband's performance wasn't the intent. "No, don't worry about that," she replied, lovingly patting his hand. "I'm thankful you're here in one piece. I'm worried about Ketchum's reaction. He's going to know we're here at Carlie's."

"Huh?" Bishop blinked.

166

"His men came here. Carlie sent them to Rocky Falls. You were there waiting in ambush."

"I didn't ambush them," Bishop corrected.

Shaking her head with a soft smile, she countered, "You said one man drove off, that he was their leader, right?"

"Yes."

"And what report do you think he's going to make to Ketchum? Do you think he's going to admit that one guy, hiding in the weeds, managed to kill seven of his henchmen? I'd bet a chocolate cake that this VooDoo fellow runs home and tells daddy that they were ambushed... that an unknown number of men bushwhacked them out of nowhere. That the drygulchers had a good plan and had been waiting."

It took Bishop only a few blinks to realize his wife was probably right. "Shit. I didn't think of that."

Terri didn't waste another moment, turning to Carlie, she insisted, "We all have to get out of here. Quickly. I know this home and farm is all you have left, but it's not worth your life. They will be coming back, and they're not going to be nearly as friendly this time. You should pack up some things, and all of us should get out of here as soon as possible."

"They'll burn down my house!" Carlie responded, her eyes full of horror. "Even if we're not here, they'll destroy everything! Oh my God... what am I going to do?"

"You can rebuild," Terri said, trying to sooth the terrified woman. "As long as you're alive, there's always hope. If we stay here, chances are we'll all be killed."

"I can't leave," came Carlie's determined voice. "Like I said before, I'd rather die."

"Oh, you'll die all right. But before the end comes, they'll torture you," Bishop stated coldly. "These are evil, cruel men without a once of conscience or moral fiber. Their goal is to stop me from testifying against Whipsaw, and they will stop of nothing short of seeing me dead. Now, unfortunately, you're caught in the middle. Ketchum is probably convinced that you know where I am hiding. They'll make you talk.

Everybody talks, and after what they'll do to you, you'll welcome death's release."

Shivering at her husband's words, Terri wrapped her arm around the frightened, confused woman. "You have to go, Carlie. There's a chance that Ketchum and his men won't hurt your house if they find it empty. One way or the other, you can't be here when they come back."

"No!" Carlie protested. "I won't leave my home. Thor and I have no place to go. No money, no hope of starting over. Like I said before, if I run, I'll be in the same shape as all those poor drifters out there. Homeless, desperate, and at best ignored by most of mankind... more commonly loathed by everyone. I'd rather die, no matter how horrible a death."

After throwing her guests a look brimming with tears and determination, Carlie stormed off, Thor on her heels. Bishop started to go after her, but Terri's hand on his chest stopped the attempt. The sound of a slamming bedroom door followed a moment later.

"She'll come to her senses," Terri said to her husband. "She has to."

"I don't think so," Bishop replied, returning to his glass of water. "Think about how long we stayed in Houston. Think about how scared we were, how difficult it was to leave our home."

"But we did bug out," Terri responded.

"Yes, and we had resources... a place to go... hope for the future, and most importantly, each other. If we hadn't had the ranch and all our supplies, we would have been in the same condition as these other poor folks," he pointed out.

"That's true," Terri agreed. "So, what do we do?"

Bishop didn't have an immediate answer. "I don't know; this is a tough one. If we were back in West Texas, I know a dozen good men who would come to our aid at the drop of a hat."

"Can you get in touch with Pete? Ask him if you can borrow some of your employees?"

Shaking his head to the negative, Bishop said, "First of all, I would have no idea how to get in touch with him. Secondly, the guys who work for me are security types, and we're short-handed as it is. I can't ask Pete to get involved in something like this. It's out of his lane."

"What about Nick?"

Bishop rubbed his chin, "I've thought about using Marshal Plummer's shortwave and letting the big guy know what we're up against. But, according to DA Gibson, he and Diana are already up to speed. That's why they sent her. I'm sure that our fearless leaders are up to their armpits in more serious problems. It seems like that's always the way it is these days."

"There's no way Nick knows how bad it is... especially after your little party at Rocky Falls."

"There is a chance that I've eliminated enough of Ketchum's boys that he's now short-handed. I have no idea about his resources, but I did put a hurt on them today."

"Were some of the men who attacked you the same ones who were on Carlie's front porch today?" Terri asked, hope returning to her voice.

"Only one that I noticed, but the others... I can't be sure," Bishop frowned, thinking about the bodies in the exploded SUV. "The guy that got away is a lieutenant. He most likely has a military background and is very competent. I underestimated them before, and that won't happen again."

"Maybe we should just pack up and go home, Bishop," Terri pondered. "Sometimes you get the bear, and sometimes the bear gets you. I liked Nathan, and I want to see Jones face the scales of justice. On the other hand, there are already seven people dead and probably a lot more to die before this is all over. Is seeing one man pay the price for his crimes worth all of that?"

She had a point. Carlie's livelihood and family home were at risk, as well as the woman's life. The same could be said of the waitress from the café. Bishop didn't want to think about Terri trying to raise Hunter without him, or vice versa.

Yet, the concept of running away from the bully didn't sit well with the West Texan. Retreating from any injustice was never right, but in this case, Bishop felt like there was a lot more at stake.

"Look, I hate it that this mess is endangering innocent people's lives. I get it, and I wish it wasn't that way. On the other hand, how many others like Nathan are going to die if we just turn our backs and walk away? If Whipsaw gets away with this, you might as well declare open season on any stranger traveling across Texas. Hell, on our way home, someone could easily mistake you and I for immigrants or drifters and open fire."

Nodding, Terri said, "You were always the one yelling at the cable news before the collapse, wanting the president to build a wall, to keep the undocumented people out, and to deport the criminals back wherever they came from. Why the change in heart?"

Bishop got defensive, "Yes, that certainly has always been my stance, and I still feel that way. I've never been against immigration. Hell, my great grandparents came to Texas from Germany. We've always been a nation of many cultures, and I firmly believe it has made us stronger. I also think the same of Texas. We need strong people who have a dream more than any time in our history, but...."

"But what?"

"But it has to be controlled. There must be rules. One of the main reasons why I'm sticking to my guns on this mess with Whipsaw is that I hope that Alpha and the council will get the message. The borders are, and will continue to be, an issue. Our leadership needs to set up the rules and enforce them, or we're going to have more situations like Forest Mist."

Smiling, Terri couldn't help but poke her husband one last time. "All these high and mighty words from the man who used to get upset every time an illegal alien murdered someone or caused a traffic death."

Bishop knew he was being prodded but couldn't let it go. "Do you remember the argument that was used against people who wanted open borders before everything fell apart?"

Terri had to think for a second, "You mean the one about locking your doors at night?"

Nodding, Bishop responded, "Yes, that's the one. If you lock your doors at night to keep out undesirables, why wouldn't you want to do the same with your country? If you support open borders, why not just let anyone into your house that wants to come in?"

"I remember your using that logic one time," Terri grinned. "I think it was at my bank's Christmas party, if memory serves."

"That's right," Bishop agreed. "And I still believe strongly in that argument. But here's the difference between now and then – I wouldn't shoot people who walked into my yard and asked for food. I might chase them off or threaten to do them harm, but I wouldn't slaughter them. The penalty, even for stealing food or lumber, isn't death. I wouldn't execute another human being just for trying to survive unless they were violent, and then it would still be a tough call. Do you understand?"

Smiling, Terri's eyes twinkled with delight. "Yes, and for once, we agree wholeheartedly on a political point. You're absolutely right; we must stop Jones and those who support his twisted thinking. And I promise I'll make sure Diana understands exactly what is going on along the border when we get back. Now, how do we make sure this comes out the right way here and now, in Forest Mist?"

The couple continued to discuss the possibilities while Bishop reloaded magazines and cleaned his weapon. Finally, he admitted, "We're going around in circles. You stay here and work on Carlie, use those wonderful diplomatic skills of

171

yours to convince her that a bug out is our one and only option. I'm going into town and ask Plummer to help protect her and update DA Gibson while I'm there."

"Okay," Terri teased. "There you go again, running off and leaving me with the tough job."

The first thing Bishop noticed about Forest Mist was the number of men carrying long guns out in the open, their postures stiff, worried expressions on their faces. The streets of the community were eerily vacant, the townspeople only frequenting establishments when absolutely necessary. Those residents who did venture out of the relative security of their homes acknowledged the witness' pickup with harsh, unwelcoming glances. The coffee shops and diners were practically empty, absent were the chatting patrons and their friendly banter. There was clearly an air of insecurity here, much more so than when he and Terri had first arrived just a few days ago.

The courthouse was as expected, deputies patrolling the grounds and searching citizens as they entered the county seat. Even more officers had been imported to keep the peace. As a result, Bishop didn't know the two lawmen who took his weapons.

He found the marshal in his office, the local lawman's face etched with worry. Peering over his spectacles, Plummer grumbled, "What I wouldn't give for that wife of yours to have settled on a house made of native Texas stone from the Hill Country."

"Careful, Marshal, I might think you were less than ecstatic to see my ugly mug this morning," Bishop teased, trying to lighten the mood. He knew that when tensions were high and firearms prevalent, humor was the first weapon of choice.

"This situation is tearing our community apart," Plummer complained. "I've never seen our town so divided and bitter. Some folks are adamant that Whipsaw acted without regard for the law, and the other half of our citizenry thinks the Alliance has set up a kangaroo court to railroad one of our most prominent citizens."

Before Bishop could respond, DA Gibson appeared at the West Texan's side. "Back again?" she inquired. "Everything all right?"

"As a matter of fact, I stopped by to update both of you," Bishop responded. "In private."

After everyone was seated in the marshal's office, Bishop recounted the events at Rocky Falls. Both Plummer and Gibson sat and listened, neither asking a single question nor requesting clarification.

When he had finished, the marshal's head looked like it was about to explode. "So, you are confessing to killing seven men and destroying public property? Sheriff Watts was right about you... you leave stacks of dead bodies everywhere you go."

The prosecutor shook her head and countered, "First of all, Marshal, I heard a clear-cut account of self-defense. More importantly, there seems to have been an organized and well-executed attack on our primary witness."

"This case is escalating quickly, spiraling out of control," Plummer moaned.

Gibson quickly brought the conversation back to the problem at hand, "So, the information we received about Ketchum's activities seems to be accurate. He has traveled here from New Orleans with a small army, and he obviously has a plan to use it."

"Do you know how many recruits he has," Bishop asked, "and where are they operating?"

Plummer's response was only a few decibels over a whisper. "We don't know any exact numbers, but our informant thinks that at least 40 men accompany him. He also believes Ketchum has set up camp just on the other side of the border."

"Let's go get them," Bishop proposed, "let's nip this in the bud."

"I don't have that kind of manpower here!" Plummer barked. "And even if I did, I can't cross the border into the United States."

Bishop hadn't considered the border, and suddenly, he found himself marveling at Blackjack Jones' wisdom and foresight. He had managed to hamstring the Alliance via geography. Nick, even if he sent reinforcements to Forest Mist, would have the same sovereignty issue. The USA wouldn't appreciate an invasion, no matter how well justified.

"You don't have a relationship with your counterpart in Louisiana?" Bishop finally asked.

"What counterpart?" Plummer grunted with a dismissive hand. "The nearest community is practically a ghost town. Three-quarters of Shreveport burned during the collapse, and the Cajuns who survived fled to areas where the recovery was beginning. As a result, the other side of the old state line is generally uninhabited. People around here call it the 'Badlands.' I've heard reports of an occasional army patrol out of Baton Rouge, or at least large groups of men who are wearing military uniforms, but that's about it from the rule of law perspective."

Patricia nodded in confirmation, "We've had other problems along the border before all this came up," the prosecutor began. "It seems that the major cattle and agricultural operations, as well as the larger farms and ranches, have created their own little versions of city-states, almost like Europe in the Middle Ages. The despots who control them are accountable to no one. We've officially requested help from Washington on two previous occasions and have gotten nothing but polite words and excuses."

"Great," Bishop mumbled. "Just great. So now we're like Uncle Sam's Army was during the Vietnam War. We have an enemy who can sneak across and hit us any time they want and then hightail it back across the border where we can't touch them."

"I'll get on the shortwave and let Alpha know what's going on," the prosecutor promised. "Maybe they can figure out some way to help. In the meantime, I think the best course of action is to put Whipsaw Jones in front of a jury as soon as possible. I'm submitting a motion to change the venue today. I expect the judge to rule on it this afternoon."

"I'm all for a speedy trial, but we also need to get a good defense running here," Bishop interjected. "These guys have already threatened Carlie, and these are not exactly choir boys we are talking about either. Can I get some men to help protect her?" Bishop asked Plummer.

The marshal shook his head in disgust. "There's just no way. I'm barely holding on here. We don't have the manpower to guard Whip 24x7, let alone enforce the law in town and guard every citizen. If we dilute our efforts and spread ourselves too thin, we run the risk of losing control of the whole county."

"Can't you recruit more deputies? Swear in some additional men?" Bishop asked.

"Are you kidding me?" Plummer barked. "The majority of the people in this town think I should let Whip go. The remainder are worried about their jobs. The foreman out at the mill announced this morning that they are shutting down and laying everyone off until the trial is over and might not reopen if Jones hangs. I've already called in all my reserves and pinned badges on the few others that I know I can trust. The manpower-well is now dry."

"In that case, I'm going to get my wife and Carlie out of Forest Mist," Bishop announced, standing abruptly. "I'll be back in town tomorrow if you need me for any reason."

"Good luck," Gibson nodded. "Tell Terri I said to be safe."

Bishop took the long way out of Forest Mist, concerned he might be followed. He wasn't going to underestimate Blackjack again, and the little-used country roads would make tailing him difficult.

Before driving into the back section of Carlie's property, the Texan pulled to the side of the road and waited for a couple of minutes. He rolled down the pickup's window, wanting to use his ears as well as his eyes to ensure that he did not lead his opponent to Carlie and Terri.

He was just reaching for the gearshift when the report of a distant gunshot came from the direction of Angel's Porch. Before he could throw the truck into gear, the steady pop, pop, pop of a full-fledged gunfight echoed through the woods.

"Shit!" he barked, hitting the gas. "How did Ketchum get here so quickly?"

Bishop didn't notice the severe jolting and bouncing as the truck raced down the overgrown lane. His mind was on Terri, his eyes scanning left and right, trying to spot any ambush that might be waiting for him to approach. He had underestimated the speed of Blackjack's response. Again, another foul-up.

A steady stream of gunfire was now loud enough to be heard over the engine. "Somebody's still shooting. Has to be Terri. She's still alive," he whispered, the pickup bouncing through the woods.

Just inside the tree line, Bishop slammed on the brakes and ripped open the pickup's door. It took him less than 30 seconds to throw on his armor and vest. Racking a round into the M4's chamber, he rushed toward the sound of the battle.

Bishop's objective was the barn. It provided an excellent view of the house and offered plenty of fighting positions inside.

Running bent at the waist, he managed 25 strides before movement ahead sent him diving prone. He wasn't the only one who had noted the barn's tactical advantages. Ahead, with their backs turned to him, were four men with long guns crouched beside the structure.

Their attention was fixed on Carlie's house, evidently completely unaware that anyone was behind them. After seeing one of the men raise his weapon and fire toward Carlie's home, Bishop flicked off the carbine's safety and centered his optic.

Before he could fire, another group of assaulters rose from the patch of elm trees to the left and dashed for the house, weapons blazing. There were at least six of them, maybe more. The attackers beside the barn opened up as well, trying to provide cover for the assault team.

Bishop instantly reassessed his priorities, moving his aim toward the new hostiles rushing from the trees. Before he could line-up on a target, someone inside the house let loose a barrage, launching a wall of lead into the charging band of gunmen.

One of the invaders went down, landing unnaturally before tumbling into a thrashing ball of arms and legs. Another simply fell flat on his face and skidded. They were 15 steps from the back door when Bishop's first round slammed into the lead man.

As fast as he could pull the trigger, Bishop's bullets tore into the running attackers. Another, then another went down, the Texan having no way of knowing if it was his lead doing the damage or if the devastating fire originated from Angel's Porch. It didn't matter, as the team rushing for the back door faltered, the few survivors then scurrying in retreat.

Switching his aim to the aggressors huddled beside the barn, Bishop knew they had been confused by his joining the fray. Their heads were spinning right and left like they were mounted on swivels, wearing puzzled expressions that said, "What the hell," all over their faces.

Bishop spotted one of the barn-men go down, another collapsing and languishing in agony as the West Texan adjusted his aim. Right at that moment, Ketchum's boys figured out how the game had changed, one of the survivors pointing in Bishop's direction and then shouting some order to his comrades.

Rounds whizzed over Bishop's head as the invaders realized someone was behind them. The West Texan's aim didn't falter. Evidently loyal to each other, an uninjured duo bent to pick up their wounded buddy. Before they had managed five steps dragging their friend, all three were lying in the dirt.

Knowing he had lost the element of surprise, Bishop rose and ran hard for the barn. Despite having broken the attack at the rear of Carlie's home, the constant reports of multiple gunshots at the front of the property told the Texan that the battle was far from over.

Zigging and zagging toward his objective, Bishop managed the spacious structure just as the aggressors recovered. Puffs of dirt from incoming rounds chased him the last few steps, the West Texan diving through the oversized doors and rolling hard across the hard-packed floor.

Clearing the empty interior was easy, Bishop slamming home a fresh magazine while he swept the stacks of hay and tool bench for any shooters that might be lurking inside.

As he moved toward the side facing the bed and breakfast, the intensity of the battle for Angel's Porch grew exponentially.

The sound of a least a dozen weapons came to Bishop's ears, from the roar of multiple shotguns to the saw-like buzzing of automatic rifles. Terri was in there, alongside

Carlie. It would be pure hell inside, bullets ripping and tearing through walls, furniture, and floors.

"How many men does Ketchum have?" Bishop mumbled, moving to exit the barn. "It sounds like we're up against a fucking army out there."

With the attack against the rear of the house now foiled, the barn didn't have as much tactical value. Bishop had to get around to the front of the Victorian house, and from the sound of things, he had to do so quickly.

Rushing for the door, Bishop stayed tight against the outside wall. He would dart for the same patch of elm trees that Blackjack's crew had just used. From there, he could work his way alongside the western edge of the house and flank the attackers.

Reaching the corner of the barn, Bishop popped his head around to make sure the path was clear. His glance was met with a maelstrom of incoming lead, splinters of wood stinging his face and chasing him back.

Poking just his rifle around the edge of his cover, Bishop sent four shots back just to keep his foe off balance and buy himself a second to reevaluate his plan.

Ketchum's forces had already recaptured the elm patch. With that route cut off, Bishop retreated for the opposite side of the barn. He would have to circle wide to the front of the inn.

Scrambling across the back of the barn, he reached the far corner and poked his head around. Just as before, his exposed flesh was chased back by a dozen screaming bullets trying to chew their way through the wooden planks. They had him cut off. He couldn't get to the trapped women.

There were at least six men on each side of the barn. For a fleeting second, Bishop considered going back inside but dismissed the idea in a heartbeat. They would pin him in there, take their time, and eventually close the jaws of the trap. Yet, he knew that Terri and Carlie couldn't hold on much longer. They had to be running low on ammunition.

Angel's Porch, riddled with so many bullet holes, looked like Swiss cheese.

With no other option, Bishop darted for the tree line, back toward his pickup. His only hope was that enough of Blackjack's men would be stupid to try and follow, and that would reduce the headcount trying to take the house. He might be able to buy Terri some time, and at a minimum, pull away some of the assaulters. He would circle around through the trees and hit them from the rear. It would take a while, but it was the only choice short of suicide.

Bishop had never been so frustrated, felt so helpless in all his days. His wife was under siege, and there was nothing he could do about it. A headlong charge into the enemy's ranks would buy her nothing but a dead husband, yet he knew that it was only a matter of time before Ketchum's men gained access to the inside of the house. That would be the end.

He'd just made the forest when the distinctive crack of an explosion sounded from the bed and breakfast. Before Bishop could turn, another blast battered his ears. "Hand grenades? Is that bastard using hand grenades?"

It took all his willpower to stop from charging back toward his wife and the battle raging there. He knew what Terri was going through, could relate to the fear and panic that must be consuming his soul mate. Growling with fury, he began sprinting through the forest, bound and determined to hit Blackjack's army with everything he had.

"Hold on just a few minutes more, baby. Please, Terri, just hold on. I'm coming," he hissed, rushing through the trees, moving with far more abandon than was prudent.

Three-quarters of the way there, Bishop noticed that the shooting had stopped. After another dozen steps, he heard the sound of several engines roaring to life. "Shit!" he barked, doubling his efforts. "Blackjack's people are leaving. They've won."

Bursting into the pasture next to the house, Bishop caught a glimpse of two motorcycles accelerating away from the B&B. Black smoke poured from two of the home's shattered windows.

In a few short bounds, Bishop landed on the porch. The front door, riddled with bullet holes, was standing wide open. Glass and empty shell casings covered the floor.

Weapon at his shoulder and advancing with short, deliberate sweeps, Bishop moved from the living room into the kitchen. He realized that all of the attackers, at least the ones still alive, had already vacated the premises. He shook his head, trying to fight off the visualizations of his imagination, nightmarish images of Terri's dead, broken body creeping into his thoughts.

His first job was to put out the fire. One of the old couches was smoldering, the curtains over the kitchen sink completely engulfed in flames. Both had been the victims of either hot lead shredding their cloth, or the grenades that Blackjack's boys had lobbed into the home. It took only seconds to extinguish both blazes.

He found Carlie bleeding on the kitchen floor, her midsection covered by an expanding crimson stain. Bishop stepped beside her, lifting her head from the broken glass that was everywhere.

She blinked, opening her eyes and struggling to focus on the man above her. "Carlie, hang in there. I'm going to get to help as soon as I can. Hang on, Kid."

She managed a smile and nodded, then in a croaking voice said, "They took Terri. I saw them dragging her out. She was still fighting them."

A conflicting mixture of relief and rage flooded Bishop's already tortured brain. Terri was still alive. Terri was a hostage, in the hands of a despicable madman. She was still breathing, so there was hope. What would Blackjack do to his mate? What horrible tortures would she have to endure?

In a flash, Bishop's fighting knife cleared its sheath. As gently as possible, he cut away Carlie's soaked blouse so as to

181

examine her wound. The injury demanded immediate attention if her life were to be saved.

The innkeeper had taken a round to the abdomen, the entry point two inches below her beltline. The gash was bleeding a lot, but not jetting or pumping. His hands were a blur as he pulled the blow-out bag from his vest and removed the largest bandage he could find.

Several times he wrapped her mid-section, unwinding the cloth wrap as he circled the wound. It wasn't much.

He scooped up Carlie a moment later, the woman in his arms moaning and wincing in pain. Hurrying out the door, he rushed for his truck. There was a physician in Forest Mist. Her wounds were beyond anything he could manage in the field.

It seemed to take an eternity to reach his pickup. As delicately as possible, Bishop worked the wounded woman into the back seat. "I'm taking you to a doctor," he said in as calm a voice as he could manage. "Hang on. Just don't give up, okay?"

She managed a slight grin, but it was clear she was growing weaker by the moment.

Stealth no longer an issue, Bishop didn't bother with the back way out, instead racing past the barn and house and turning directly toward town.

The doctor's office was one block south of the main square. As Bishop passed the courthouse, he honked his horn, waving desperately at one of the patrolling deputies. It was Allison.

She approached the pickup with a frown. In only a few quick sentences, Bishop told Plummer's daughter what had just happened.

Allison glanced at the wounded woman in the backseat and then motioned for Bishop to get going. "I'll tell dad what's happened."

"They have my wife," Bishop shouted as the truck began to pick up speed. "Make sure DA Gibson knows that Terri is a hostage."

CHAPTER 10

Bishop was dizzy, two pints of his own blood now circulating through Carlie's veins. It had taken a considerable amount of convincing for the doctor to use the West Texan's universal O negative plasma to save the wounded woman. "We should match Rh factors and other elements," the country physician had grumbled. "Still, I can't do surgery with her losses."

The doc remained skeptical about the patient's chances, transfusion or not.

"She'll live," the physician stated calmly, washing his hands after closing the incision. "Or not. That's up to God. I got the bullet out, but she has lost a lot of blood. In the morning, we'll need to move her to the hospital in Texarkana if she's still with us. She needs better care than I can provide here at my office."

"You have worked a miracle, Doc! Now... how long before I can walk?" Bishop asked, sipping the tepid tomato juice the nurse had provided.

"Probably a few hours."

About then Marshal Plummer arrived, Bishop tensing as the lawman entered the office, looking like he had aged another decade in the last few hours. "Watts was right," he grumbled, looking bone tired, dark circles under his eyes. "You *are* the harbinger of death and destruction. Not even during the downfall did I have so many bodies to bury."

"Any sign of my wife?" Bishop asked, ignoring the lawman's editorial.

With a grimace, Plummer shook his head. "'Fraid not. We found 11 lifeless bikers scattered around the property, another half dozen blood trails... leading me to believe that Ketchum is now dealing with his own wounded. At least the body count is less than 20."

"The day is still young," Bishop hissed. "No sign or word of my wife?"

"Afraid not."

"Any idea where Ketchum is holed up?" the Texan asked.

"No."

Something about the marshal's body language lead Bishop to believe that Plummer wasn't being completely honest. "Not even a rumor of where his operations are based? No gut feelings or educated guesses? I'm having trouble believing that, sir."

"This is wide open country," Plummer began to explain. "He could be using any number of abandoned schools, churches, farms, or warehouses. Besides that, our informant tells us that his established base of operations is in Louisiana, and I don't know that area as well as I do Forest Mist. Not by a long shot. Other than being reasonably sure he's using the border for protection, I have no idea where he might be."

Bishop still didn't know whether to believe the lawman, an internal voice screaming that Plummer was lying. On the other hand, the West Texan realized his emotions were running high and might be clouding his judgement. "If my wife is harmed, Marshal, I will unleash an avalanche of hell on whoever I find out is...."

Waving a dismissive hand through the air, Plummer interrupted Bishop's accelerating rant. "She'll be fine, at least for the time being. He has to keep her safe because she is his bargaining chip. She's not the witness Ketchum is worried about. You are, and if I were you, I would expect to be contacted soon. They'll offer a trade, your wife's release in exchange for your agreeing not to testify. And if I were you, young man, I'd take the deal."

"I can't believe you're saying that," Bishop spat. "What kind of lawman are you? You haven't embraced this entire affair since the beginning, despite your oath and responsibilities."

"I'm only telling you the truth as I see it. After forty years of wearing a badge and a gun, I'm too old and too tired to mess around with the high-minded concepts surrounding the letter of the law. My hands are tied, Bishop," he spat in a tone that divulged utter exasperation. "Enforcing that kind of high and mighty sense of justice would require massive resources. That hard truth is that I don't have a hostage rescue team, Bishop. There are no state police, or SWAT units, or any other agency readying to charge in and save the day. Even if I knew where Ketchum was keeping your wife, we'd probably get her killed by attempting a half-assed rescue with poorly trained personnel."

Bishop had to admit that the man had a point. Still, there was something he wasn't seeing, some hidden factor that had been playing a role with Plummer since Nathan's death. After pondering several possibilities, the Texan decided it didn't matter. Who could ever know what truly motivated a man's heart?

Finally shrugging, Bishop said, "I'm going to get my wife back, Marshal. One way or the other. That's the only thing that matters to me anymore."

Something flashed behind Plummer's eyes. While there was no physical change in the man's face, Bishop was sure he'd seen something. Was it gloating? No, he didn't think so. Relief was the word that came to mind.

A truck was parked on Terri's head; its weight crushing her skull. She attempted to move but her muscles would not answer her brain's commands. Something had pinned down her arms.

She tried to open her eyes, but everything was cold, dark, and black. The effort ushered in another wave of nauseating pain, and she moaned at its advance.

"She's awake," a female voice announced.

"Let's see what we've got here," answered a male.

Terri felt movement around her neck. Then without warning, a brilliant white light flashed through her tortured skull. She tried to pull away, strained to squint, struggled to keep from retching.

"She's bleeding from that gash," the female voice announced.

"Clean her up," replied the man, who was clearly in charge. "But do not untie her."

There was motion beyond the light, sounds on the other side of Terri's pain. She heard more movement, and then a splashing sound. All the while, the blinding spotlight aimed at her eyes was beginning to fade.

"I bet you've got a concussion, sweetie," the lady advised. "This will make it feel better."

Something cool touched Terri's thumping head, in the same spot where the truck had been resting just a moment before. She felt a stinging sensation, wriggled to pull away, and then relief... as a cold, wet cloth was pressed against her pounding gray matter.

"Water?" Terri croaked in a hoarse voice, her eyes now able to detect vague images of color and shape.

"Sure. Drink it slowly, Hun. Not too much."

A cup was pushed against Terri's lips, followed by the refreshing sensation of liquid flooding her mouth. She swallowed greedily, almost sucking at the source of the drink.

Opening her eyes, Terri realized she could see. Still confused, her eyes darted around what was a small room. She was secured to a chair, her arms and legs bound with thick, unyielding tape. A woman stood at her side, next to a small end table. On its top laid a hood. Upon seeing the offending cloth cover, the nightmare roared back... the gunfight, Carlie's house, a vivid white flash and clap of thunder. Then darkness.

As she took another sip, Terri sorted through the memory quickly, trying to make sense of her current situation. She had been knocked out somehow. She didn't know how long she had been unconscious, but she could feel her life's blood oozing from her bleeding skull. She was Ketchum's prisoner.

More to divert the pain than any need to know, Terri began replaying the images in her mind. She and Carlie had been packing some essentials. They heard the motorcycle engines – a lot of bikes. The mad scramble to set up a defense and get their weapons ready. The call from outside to surrender.

"Get off my land!" Carlie had answered. "Leave or I'll shoot!"

Bullets had zipped through the house, shattering windows and creating a cloud of choking plaster and wood. The lead had been fired intentionally high, an attempt to scare the occupants. "Come out, and no one will be hurt," the second shouted offer from outside claimed.

Terri remembered the first man she had taken down, a big guy, leather jacket covered with patches. His death unleashed a whirlwind of violence, hot lead shredding the walls as they whizzed past her head. These were clearly no longer warning shots.

It seemed like hours had passed before her rifle locked back empty. Then her pistol was in her hand, Bishop words racing through her mind, "Only use your pistol to fight your way back to the rifle you should have never put down in the first place." However, she simply didn't have any choice. She had felt the icy grip of the frosty fingers of fear for the first time. She hadn't seen any way for Carlie and her to survive the skirmish.

Then the blinding light exploded, the overpressure on her ears making the room spin. It was if she had been transported right into the middle of a thundercloud as it had spewed lightning. She couldn't see. Couldn't will her limbs to move. Couldn't defend herself.

She recalled trying to blink back her eyesight, her head desperately attempting to orient to the blurred surroundings.

There was an image, a brawny invader crashing through the front door. She somehow managed to raise her pistol. It fired.

The last thing Terri could remember was another man standing over her. Again, she tried to point her weapon, but her arm wouldn't move fast enough. She spotted the attacker cock his rifle butt, his eyes seething with hatred and fury. She knew the pain was about to follow and closed her eyes.

"I'm going to put a bandage on your head," the woman beside her interrupted. "You've got quite the goose egg. I bet that hurt."

Refocused on the present, Terri scanned her nurse. The woman was probably in her mid-30s, dishwater blonde hair, and sporting solid tattooed murals on both arms. Her voice had a scratchy, raspy quality about it, evidence of a long-time, cigarette smoker... and the face of a woman who had spent most of her life in the fast lane.

Sensing she was being evaluated, the woman offered, "My name's Kitty, or at least that's what everybody calls me. Ketch said you are Terri?"

"Yes," the injured woman replied, "How is Carlie? Did she make it?"

"I don't know," Kitty answered honestly. "You were the only person the men brought back."

As if on cue, the door opened, and a beefy fellow stepped inside. From the resemblance to his father, Terri knew instantly that Ketchum Jones had joined them.

He was as tall as Whipsaw, with shoulders at least as wide. He carried himself with confidence, a man clearly in charge of his surroundings. Heavily muscled, and sporting a black goatee and mustache, Terri noted the two large images of the jack of spades tattooed on each of his forearms.

"How are you?" he asked.

"My head hurts, but not nearly as much as my pride," she croaked. "What do you want? Why have you kidnapped me?"

"Oh, I think you know good and well why you're here," Ketchum chuckled. "Your husband is getting ready to testify

190

against my father, and I simply can't allow that to happen. It all boiled down to two choices, really. Either I could kill Bishop, or I could convince him not to testify."

Ketchum didn't give Terri the chance to respond. Moving close to the bound hostage, he reached out and roughly held her chin in his massive hand. Forcing her head to tilt and look at his face, he continued, "You are a pretty one, that's for sure. If you were my woman, I wouldn't have run for the woods like your husband did. You know that, don't you? You saw him run away when my men were closing in on him by the barn."

Terri didn't try to look away, nor did she flinch. "Nice try," she answered in a monotone. "I know Bishop, and I know he wouldn't run away from any fight. Save your head games for somebody else."

Grunting, Blackjack let loose of her face. "No matter. You'll learn the truth soon enough."

Without any warning, he reached in and grabbed Terri's blouse, easily ripping it away from her shoulders and then holding up his trophy for Kitty to see.

Surprised and infuriated, Terri thought she was about to be raped. "If you hurt me, there's no place on this earth you'll be able to hide. Bishop will hunt you down and kill you slowly, and *that* is the truth," she hissed with wide eyes.

Blinking at his captive's venomous response, it took Ketchum a minute to realize what was going through Terri's mind. "Oh!" he finally said, "You think I want to have a little fun. While I'm flattered to be sure, you're not my type. I like warm, friendly ladies, not cold-hearted bitches who think they're smarter than everybody else. Sorry to disappoint you, Sweetheart."

He started to leave, still clutching Terri's shirt. At the door, he hesitated and laughed. Glancing at the prisoner over his shoulder, he snapped, "That being said, you killed a lot of my men today. Most of the survivors consider the dead as their brothers, and they would surely like to have a little revenge. If you misbehave in any way, cause Kitty even a tiny problem, I will throw you to the wolfpack and let them pass you around until they are satisfied. Do you understand?"

"Yes," Terri whispered.

After recovering from his donation of blood, Bishop's first stop was back at the scene of the crime.

Despite Plummer's assurance that the kidnappers hadn't left any clues, he wanted... no, *needed*... to see for himself. The West Texan was exhausted from the firefight, deeply worried about his wife, and frustrated by the local authority's lack of support.

"Plummer was right," he mumbled as he pulled into the driveway. "They won't hurt Terri right away. Still, she's got to be scared shitless, and who knows what those animals will do to her."

A single police car sat in the driveway, alongside two pickup trucks. Bishop spotted Allison as he exited the cab. "Just what I need, another hostile in my face," he contended under his breath.

"How is Carlie?" the deputy asked as Bishop approached the shot-up Victorian inn. He was surprised at the softness in her tone.

"The doc got the bullet out, but it's touch and go. He wants to move her in the morning if she's strong enough."

Two men appeared from the backyard, both wearing gloves and paper masks, a sagging, dead body between them.

Bishop and Allision watched as they dropped the deceased onto a white bedsheet, and then unceremoniously heaved the corpse into the back of a pickup. "We will take them out to a nearby field and burn the bodies," the deputy announced.

"Your father is probably pissed about the additional expense coming out of the city's budget," Bishop grumbled, watching as the two undertakers left to retrieve another body.

With a grunt, Allison shook her head, "No. Those two do it for free. They get to keep any personal effects, including weapons and ammunition, in exchange for services rendered. They have a second-hand store just off the town square. Given I know where most of their products come from, I don't shop there."

"I see," Bishop nodded, turning his attention back to the house. "I heard explosions, but don't see any damage to the structure."

"They used flashbang grenades," Allision replied, reaching into a bag at her feet and producing the charred remains of a metal canister. "I was trained on how to use these at the academy and found evidence of at least two of them being deployed against the house."

"So that's how they took her alive," Bishop nodded, reaching to examine the device.

"I was hoping you would come back here," Allision continued. "I can piece together most of this for my report, but there are a few things that don't make sense. Would you mind helping me fill in the gaps?"

He considered her request for a moment. "I can try, if you will share what you've learned with me. Your dad said the attackers didn't leave anything behind that would indicate where they were holed up, or where they might be keeping my wife. I'm not sure how he could have known that already, but I would like to be absolutely positive no clues are being overlooked."

"Deal," the deputy replied. "I know you and I got off on the wrong foot, but I want you to know I'm very sorry that your wife has been taken. That, and the fact that Carlie is a friend of mine...."

"Don't worry about it," Bishop interrupted, waving his hand to clear the air. "You were only trying to protect your father. I would hope my son would act the same way one of these days."

The duo entered the front door and began to walk through the shattered home. Bishop was immediately impressed with Allison's detective skills. "Your wife was defending the front and driveway side of the house, Carlie and her shotgun covering the backyard. Evidently, they saw or heard the hellions coming and pulled together these heavy pieces of furniture to use as fighting positions and bullet stops."

Bishop could see Terri doing just that, and for a brief moment, his chest swelled with pride. She hadn't gone down easy, that's for sure.

"From the piles of shell casings, and the position of the bodies outside, I can attest that this was one intense firefight. I believe your wife ran out of ammunition for her rifle toward the end. We found an AR15, empty, next to her barricade, as well as a 9 mm pistol and a pile of empty magazines for both. I saved those weapons for you."

Bishop thanked Allision and then continued surveying the interior of the home for several more minutes. He found Carlie's hastily fortified position, the floor littered by at least two dozen colorful shotgun shells scattered here and there.

"The one thing I can't figure out is that there were several men killed when they tried to rush the house from those elm trees over there," the deputy said, pointing toward the nearby strand of hardwoods. "Yet the angle is all wrong."

"That would have been me," Bishop explained, holding up his end of the bargain he'd just made with the deputy.

For the next 15 minutes, Bishop walked Allison through the gunfight, or at least what had happened from the time of his arrival. He took her to the barn, pointed out his spent brass, and explained every action and move.

Scratching notes on a clipboard, she listened intently, only occasionally uttering an "I see," or "Now that makes sense."

After their postmortem tour of the battlefield, Bishop noted several bodies near the undertakers' pickups. "Any clues on the bodies? Hotel matchbooks? Restaurant napkins? Any of that stuff that TV detectives always find?"

Laughing, Allison responded, "Well, I'm not Sherlock Holmes by any stretch of the imagination, but no, I didn't find anything that would indicate where they are staying. I do know a few things for sure. These guys were all typical biker gang foot soldiers from what I can tell. Tats from two different clubs, both from the New Orleans area. There was an assortment of weapons, some military issue. They had fragmentation grenades but didn't use them as far as I can tell. I found five of them on the deceased. They had plenty of ammunition, and of course, the flashbangs. About the only thing unusual was that two of them had a bad case of poison ivy."

"Poison ivy?"

Nodding, she said, "Yes, on their arms. But that nasty weed is common around here. They could have come into contact with it anywhere, so its presence isn't much help."

"And the grenades?"

"After the collapse, there were a lot of reports and rumors about National Guard armories and police stations being looted. Without computer databases and crime labs, there's no way I can trace them. I talked to one man about a year ago who told me that when the military bases ran out of food, the troops were selling hardware on the black market. He even claimed that one of his buddies traded a tank for a truckload of noodles."

Bishop had heard similar stories. "Wouldn't surprise me. How long after touching the poison ivy before the rash is visible? How long ago would you guess those two guys were exposed?"

Shrugging, she waved for him to follow and began heading toward the row of corpses. After lifting the third sheet, she pointed for Bishop to look. "See the dermatitis? The blisters are from scratching the itch. I had it a few times growing up. Even got a bad case four years ago, helping dad search a fence row for evidence of rustlers."

"So, these guys might have been out in the forest? Maybe sleeping in a spot where they would come in contact with the noxious plant?"

Without hesitation, Allison ripped open the dead biker's shirt and examined his chest and neck. "It's just on his arms. I'd say he was exposed in the last few days. It doesn't start itching for a while but spreads pretty quickly once you start scratching."

Continuing to discuss the gunfight, Bishop and Allison watched at the undertakers loaded the last of the bodies. "There are 13 dead, ma'am," one of the men reported to the deputy. "We'll be on our way now if there's nothing else you need."

"Thank you," Allison nodded. Then turning to Bishop, she pointed to a line of parked motorcycles at the edge of the B&B's lot. "I know Terri put a hurt on those attackers. They didn't have enough manpower left to take all of their bikes. The county will leave them here for a while, and eventually, we'll auction them off. If you want one, you can have it."

Bishop had no use for a motorcycle. He only wanted his wife back. After the two makeshift hearses had left the driveway, Allision announced her departure as well. "I've got to get back to Forest Mist," she said. "I've got a shift of guard duty in two hours, and dad is going to want this report as soon as possible."

Bishop watched the police cruiser leave, his mind still mulling what little he'd learned from the deputy and the scene. He had to find out where Blackjack was hiding and then figure out how to rescue Terri. It was all that simple at the highest level, but the devil was in the details.

Meandering back toward the barn, the Texan began composing a checklist of his next steps. Stopping to scoop up his wife's rifle and pistol, he mumbled, "I'll keep these safe for you, Terri. You'll have them back soon. I promise."

Pleased to find their apartment unharmed by the recent battle, he began cleaning the weapons, first his, and then Terri's. All the while his mind was working overtime, trying to predict the chess game he knew was about to unfold. Ketchum would probably send a messenger, perhaps a note. Bishop would be ready and follow the man.

His body went through the motions of assembling a quick meal while his mind raced, considering possible tactical schemes and approaches and strategies. No matter how he started, his thoughts always circled back to the same conclusions. The trial wasn't supposed to start for a few more days. Ketchum would have to move quickly. Bishop needed to be ready.

Finishing his food, he trudged to the bed and perched on the edge. He was beat, a combination of stress, donation of blood, and an afternoon of gunfighting. He decided to relax for a few minutes and stretched out on top of the mattress. His last conscious thought was that Terri would kill him for not taking off his boots.

CHAPTER 11

Bishop heard a motor, or at least he thought that was what had rousted him.

Embarrassed that he'd fallen asleep, he tumbled off the bed and reached for his carbine. Yes, there was an engine of some kind heading his way.

Less than a minute passed before he was bounding down the wooden steps. "It's probably Allison coming back... or one of the marshal's deputies," he surmised. "Ketchum wouldn't be so bold as to just roll up to the front entrance. Would he?"

Towing some sort of large machine behind it, a dually pickup turned into the driveway just as Bishop reached the door. The Texan didn't recognize the vehicle or the device on the trailer, but he did notice the absence of a law enforcement logo on the side. Rifle ready in his hands, he began approaching the oversized truck with caution.

Bishop was stunned when Blackjack exited the driver's side door. The Texan's first instinct was that his nemesis was springing a trap, baiting him out into the open.

Scanning the bordering woods and buildings, Bishop didn't detect any other shooters. Ketchum quickly grasped the situation and shouted, "No worries, friend. I came alone. Just to talk. Relax. I've won, and you know it."

"You'll go down first, ass clown," Bishop mumbled, his stride now closing the distance to the man he so desperately wanted to annihilate. At 30 meters, the Texan's carbine was at his shoulder. He made a show of flipping off the safety.

"If you execute me, your wife will be passed around among 30 horny bikers. Thirty large men who know that she just personally slaughtered a lot of their brothers. Don't be stupid," Ketchum warned, his hands in the don't shoot position.

"You came to talk, then talk," Bishop growled.

"I want to show you something," Blackjack grinned. "A little demonstration if you will."

Without waiting for Bishop to respond, the brawny man pivoted and stepped to the machine behind his pickup. "This is a Vermeer model 935 commercial wood chipper, complete with a Perkins 50 horsepower diesel engine. This specific one happens to be borrowed equipment from my father's mill. Have you ever seen one of these babies in action?"

Bishop had no idea where their conversation was headed but saw no other option but to play along. "Nope. Never have, but I get the feeling I'm going to."

Smiling widely, Ketchum moved to a control panel and pushed a series of buttons. The diesel cranked, then started with a puff of blue smoke. The rotating machinery roared to life. Blackjack had to shout over the noise, "We use this to clean up unwanted branches and timber as we harvest the forest. It's cheaper to shred all the scraps to tiny bits, and they eventually fertilize the soil. This particular model can handle branches up to 18 inches in diameter. Here, watch, I'll show you."

Moving to the pickup's bed, Ketchum reached in and extracted a large, recently hewn log. Wrapped around the bark was what Bishop immediately recognized as the shirt his wife had been wearing that morning.

Without acknowledging the horror spreading across Bishop's face, Ketchum carried the wood to the chipper's feeder bin and held it there. Again, shouting to be heard, Blackjack said, "If you fuck with me, I will put your wife into this machine head first. If you really piss me off, I will put her in feet first."

With that, Ketchum shoved the log into the machine and watched as the steel cutting knives effortlessly ripped it into tiny chips of wood. "Do we have an understanding?"

Bishop's rage was near the boiling point, his temper flaring from mildly annoyed to the volcanic brink seconds into the exhibition. Seeing Terri's bloody shirt rip and tear to shreds had pushed him to his very edge. It had been an effective demonstration.

"Good," Blackjack nodded, reaching to turn off the tool. Once the machinery had stopped cycling, he turned to Bishop, his voice becoming low and serious, "You will not testify, plain and simple. Furthermore, you will get in touch with the prosecution's other secret witness and convince them not to talk. You will leave Forest Mist by midnight tonight. Once my father is released, I will deliver your wife to Marshal Plummer, and he can arrange for her transportation home. You will never return to Forest Mist, and you will convince your Alliance friends not seek any sort of retaliation. Agreed?"

For a nanosecond, Bishop considered shooting Blackjack in the leg and then pushing the burlier man's head a few inches from the deadly blades. He was sure Ketchum would talk, positive he could learn Terri's location and end this game. On the other hand, the man before him was obviously in peak condition and reported to have been an Army Ranger. One thing was for certain, only a monster with honed skills... a sociopath with no conscience whatsoever... could build an illicit criminal organization like the one that prospered under Ketchum's leadership in New Orleans. He might not be so easy to subdue, even with a bullet in his kneecap. What would happen to Terri if the West Texan failed? What if he had to destroy the animal before he was able to learn his wife's whereabouts?

"How do I know Terri is alive?" Bishop retorted, his mind still reeling from what the man in front of him had just threatened to do to his soul mate.

"You don't," Blackjack shrugged. "Then again, what choice do you have? I still have a small militia of very motivated, well-armed men at my disposal. By tomorrow morning, I'll have doubled their number with reinforcements from my headquarters in New Orleans. Leave tonight, and don't come back. Once the charges against my father are dismissed, I'll have no use for your wife and will deliver her into Dallas' loving care."

"Okay. Agreed," Bishop nodded, "but you should know that if you fuck with me, you'll beg to be dropped into that chipper machine. You'll pray to be hacked to bits after what I'll do to you. You take very, very good care of Terri. Understood?"

Ketchum actually smiled before nodding his agreement. "You know, in a different place and time, you and I could have probably been friends. I like you, Bishop. You have a pair, and in this world, that's often enough. I will deliver your wife undamaged if you keep up your end of the deal."

CHAPTER 12

Bishop took his time packing, his tortured brain urgently trying to figure some way out of the vice squeezing him from both sides. Ketchum held all the cards, and no matter how many different scenarios he mentally executed, Terri ended up dead.

He was basically alone. Plummer, as well as the locals were zero help. In fact, a nagging voice inside the West Texan's head kept revisiting the same conclusion that someone inside the marshal's department might be helping Blackjack. There had been a lot of odd coincidences in the last few days. The only time Bishop had managed to get ahead of the New Orleans gangster, at Rocky Falls, just so happened to be the one time he hadn't informed anyone at the courthouse of his intentions.

"You can't fight city hall," he grumbled, throwing his and Terri's bags into the pickup's bed.

The worst of it, however, was the possibility that he could do exactly as Ketchum wished and Terri would still end up dead. "Once his father is free, why would Blackjack release my wife?" Bishop kept asking himself.

Yet, he couldn't come up with any other reasonable alternative but to cooperate. Whipsaw Jones would go free. There would be no justice for Nathan Hill, and that was a bitter pill for Bishop to swallow. Carlie, even if she recovered, would find her beloved home ruined, probably beyond repair. And then there was the horror of Terri's kidnapping. *I don't even know what atrocities she is being subjected to,* he thought before slamming his fist on the truck's tailgate, the frustration of his situation nearly overwhelming him.

It was dark by the time he had loaded the pickup, filled his gas tank, and made one last tour of Angel's Porch.

The drive into Forest Mist was ominous, Bishop livid at the town, its people, and its elected officials. What had seemed like a quaint, little community complete with romantic nuances now appeared evil, foreboding, and ugly. "This is all your fault," Bishop whispered to the few citizens still walking the streets. "You have tolerated this. You have supported Whipsaw and his warped philosophy. He will probably be treated like a hero once he is set free."

He arrived at the courthouse, parked, and submitted to the search at the door with a blank, vacant expression. Appearing as a broken, empty man wasn't a difficult role to fulfill.

The deputy at the entrance was polite, almost embarrassed as Bishop was passed through the checkpoint. With all the county offices already closed for the day, the place was hauntingly quiet.

The West Texan was directed to a second-floor room after he inquired where he might find the visiting Alliance prosecutor. After a polite knock, Bishop entered what was essentially a tiny conference room, probably used by the local courts.

Pat glanced up, her face tight with frustration and worry. Bishop could see sympathy brimming in his old friend's eyes. "How are you holding up?" she asked upon seeing him.

"I'm probably doing better than my wife about now," he answered in a low, dejected tone.

"They found your Achilles' heel," she replied, and then added, "but we'll get her back."

"I wish I could be so sure. And even if Ketchum does set her free, what am I going to take home? Who knows what those animals are doing to her, what horrors she's suffering right this moment?"

"I assume then that you're not going to testify?"

"Would you?" Bishop asked, looking Pat directly in the eye.

"No, I wouldn't," the DA answered honestly.

Before Bishop could manage another word, a soft knock rapped at the door, following a second later by Marshal Plummer letting himself in. "I heard you were in the building," the lawman said. "I just wanted to stop in and tell you how sorry I am that your wife is being held hostage. We have some more deputies coming into town tomorrow to help out, and I intend to assign two of them to your wife's case."

Oh, really? You are finally going to investigate her disappearance, huh? Resisting the urge to unload on the man, Bishop merely nodded and then relayed the visit he'd received from Blackjack just a few hours ago. Both prosecutor and marshal seemed shocked. "He's not messing around," Plummer stated after the Texan was finished. "That boy never has had any conscience to speak of. He wouldn't hesitate to feed somebody into that machine if he didn't get what he wanted."

"Do you believe he'll let her go once the charges are dropped against his father?" Bishop asked.

"Yes, I do," Plummer stated without hesitation, which made Bishop wonder about the sanity of the man beside him.

"Really?" Bishop challenged. "I am having trouble following your logic, Marshal. What incentive does this Neanderthal have to release my wife in good health? Why would he even bother? Maybe he would rather send a nasty message instead."

The marshal rubbed his chin between his thumb and forefinger, obviously absorbed in thought. "I can see where you might think that, Bishop. But consider this, I have dealt with this fellow since his juvie days. He has threatened ultimate violence against his personal enemies before, seems capable enough to pull it off, yet never actually has done so unless he had no other choice."

"Really," Bishop countered. "How do you explain the attack at the B&B? Target practice?"

The marshal sent the West Texan a look that was intended as a warning shot to curb the attitude. "His father

205

has to live here... do business here. Ketchum knows that. Whip will demand that his son leaves behind the smallest footprint possible. I think he'll honor his word for his father's sake if nothing else."

The West Texan shook his head, processing the information provided by the local law enforcement official, seemingly still not able to arrive at a decision. Maybe the marshal was right. Maybe Terri was simply a pawn and nothing more. But then, Bishop knew there was the possibility that he was simply believing what he wanted to hear.

"I'll start the paperwork to drop the charges," Gibson offered. "Judge Crawford will have to sign everything before the marshal can release Mr. Jones. He was called away to Beaumont this afternoon but will be back in Forest Mist by late tomorrow. Hopefully, we'll have Terri back, safe and sound within two days. When she is delivered here, I'll request Alpha send a private plane, and we'll get her home just as soon as possible."

"Well, I'm out of options then. There's nothing else to do but head west," Bishop sighed, standing and offering Pat his hand. "Thank you, Miss Gibson. I appreciate everything you've tried to do here."

As Gibson accepted Bishop's offering, the prosecutor slipped a small piece of paper into the West Texan's hand. There was a twinkle in her eyes, just enough of a display to give Bishop's weary soul a glimmer of hope.

He ignored Plummer's move to extend his own hand, pivoting without a word away from the marshal and exiting the door. *You can kiss my ass*, Bishop thought.

With Gibson's message tucked into his pocket, Bishop retrieved his weapons and headed for his truck. He could feel the local's eyes on his back as he entered the cab. Without pomp or circumstance, he turned west and accelerated out of town.

After a few miles, he was convinced that no one was following. Pulling to the side of the road, Bishop turned on the dome light and pulled Gibson's note from his pocket. It read, "Go to these coordinates and stay there until contacted. You'll be happy you did. Pat." Two rows of numbers lined the bottom of the paper.

Frowning at the mysterious act of the normally all-business prosecutor, Bishop punched the longitude and latitude into the truck's GPS. The location specified was about 20 miles away, slightly south of his intended route.

Now intrigued, Bishop plotted his course. The small screen in the pickup's dash gave no indication regarding his destination.

The drive took only 40 minutes, Bishop pulling into what had been a small, regional airport before the collapse. The place looked like it had been abandoned for years.

A small office stood in front of what appeared to be three hangar buildings. A light shone in the window, a single, older model Jeep parked in front.

As his headlights illuminated the building, Bishop noticed a single figure appear in the doorway. More curious than cautious, the Texan put the truck in park and exited the cab.

"You Bishop?" an older man asked, a 12-gauge at his side.

"Yes, sir. Pat Gibson said I should come here."

"My name is Verne. Verne Carrol. I used to manage this airport when it was a viable enterprise. Not too many private planes flying anymore, but I still try to keep the place functional just in case things get back to the way they used to be."

Instantly liking the older gent, Bishop offered his hand. "Do you know what I'm doing here?" he asked after the handshake.

"No, Son, I'm afraid I can't tell you much. Patty was a student of mine back in the day. After I retired from teaching, I spent the next several years enjoying my true passion – flying. After my eyes got too bad to pilot, I still enjoyed hanging around and helping out. Patty was one of my favorite pupils, and she still stops by every now and then to talk law and have a cup of tea. One of her security men delivered a note to me earlier today, explaining that I should be expecting a guest and to have a place ready for you to rest and eat. That's all I know."

"Interesting," Bishop nodded, still puzzled, but happy to at least have a roof over his head for the night.

Verne proceeded to show Bishop a modest room inside the office, explaining, "This is a little setup I had for pilots who were doing long runs and needed someplace to log a few hours of shuteye. They tell me that cot is the most comfortable this side of the Mississippi. There's a bathroom through that door. There's no hot water, but the shower works if you can stand a little cold spray."

After thanking the man, Bishop began unloading a few essentials from his truck. Upon noticing the West Texan's weapons, Verne commented, "You won't have any trouble here, young man. I'm the only person still alive for at least 10 miles in any direction. Besides, I don't sleep so well these days, so I'm planning on keeping an eye on things while you get some rest."

Again, Bishop thanked the kind gent. "I appreciate that, sir. I don't think I'll be able to sleep right now, but I will take advantage of your generous hospitality while I wait to see what Pat has up her sleeve."

While Bishop ate a quick meal, Verne sat at the cluttered manager's desk and pulled a book from the top of a considerable stack. "I like doing crossword puzzles," he explained, reaching in the drawer for a pencil. "It helps pass the time, but still keeps the mind nimble."

After an hour had passed, Bishop caught himself yawning. He had been doing nothing but worrying and fighting for nearly 48 hours. He wouldn't be able to help Terri if he was braindead.

"I think I'll test that cot after all," he announced to Verne. "Don't hesitate to wake me if anything changes."

"I promise," the old man nodded, barely peering up from his puzzle. "Sleep well."

The cot was as advertised, worn enough to have just the right amount of sag yet not so sloppy to kink his back. The sheets smelled old, but not dirty.

Less than 10 minutes after stretching out, Verne could hear the gentle rhythm of Bishop's snore drifting from the back room. "Pat said you were a great man," the old-timer whispered, glancing at the door. "I hope your troubles will be over soon."

Just as Bishop was lying down, Terri was waking up. Eventually, Kitty had cut the tape that bound the hostage's arms and motioned toward a sleeping bag rolled up in the corner. "There's no bed in here, and I'm not supposed to let you out of this room. You can unroll that and sleep on the floor if you're tired."

Terri had gladly accepted the offer, knowing that she would probably need every ounce of strength she could muster. Besides, her head throbbed with every heartbeat. Maybe some rest would help.

They had fed her a bowl of instant oatmeal. She had then been escorted to a restroom, a hood placed over her head before being led into the facility. Terri was reasonably sure she was in some sort of park or other public facility, the stark stalls and industrial sinks strong clues regarding the location where Blackjack had established his headquarters.

That had been at least four hours ago, she assessed, wondering what had disturbed her sleep.

A minute passed, the completely dark room giving no hint about the time of night or day. She sensed it was still dark outside. Probably after midnight. Kitty had left at some point while she had been sleeping.

Unzipping the lumpy sleeping bag, she wobbled slightly as she rose from the cold floor. Terri balanced against the wall and felt her way around the room. Eventually, she discovered the threshold and twisted the knob on the metal entry, but it was locked. Deciding that tripping over something in the dark and injuring her ankle wasn't the wisest course of action, she started to backtrack when a distinctive voice drifted through the door.

"He's left Forest Mist," a male throat announced. "The Alliance prosecutor is starting the paperwork to dismiss the charges against your father, but it will be a couple of days before I can let him go. I've got to tell you, Ketchum, I never thought you'd be able to pull this off, but you have."

"No thanks to you, Dallas," Blackjack tersely responded.

"I did my part," Marshal Plummer countered. "I kept my people out of it. Our score is settled, and as soon as this is all over, I expect you to hightail it back to New Orleans and stay the hell out of my town."

Terri was stunned, her mind racing with what she had just overheard. Plummer was in on the caper? The marshal was dirty? No wonder Ketchum had been one step ahead of them the entire time. Blackjack had an inside man! One hell of an insider, it seemed.

Before she could process this new information, the conversation outside flared.

"I'm afraid that's no longer in my future," Ketchum stated. "I've decided to stay around here and help dad with the mill. He's not getting any younger, you know, and he wants to groom me to take over."

Plummer's voice grew angry, "That's not part of our agreement," the marshal pushed back. "You're not welcome in Forest Mist."

"From where I'm standing, you don't have much say in our affairs, Dallas. So, why don't you just scurry on back across the border and do your job. If you keep your mouth shut, I might decide to let you fish and hunt in peace after your retirement. Hell, I might even help Allison get elected. We could all be friends again, just like old times."

"Don't threaten me, Ketchum," the marshal retorted. "I still have your father in my jail, and accidents do happen. Why, he might be shot trying to escape. You just think long and hard about crawling back to that slime pit down on the river."

"If something happens to my pop, I'll burn Forest Mist to the ground, Dallas," Ketchum threatened.

"You won't do that. Your father's mill needs the men from town to work the lumber. You're not that stupid."

"Perhaps," Ketchum offered. "But if I were you, I wouldn't count on it."

"And the woman? Terri?" the lawman asked.

"She's my property now. She personally slaughtered at least half a dozen of my men, her husband at least that many more. After dad is safely back in my care, I'm going to let the boys have their way with her, and it's unlikely she'll survive more than a few days."

"That's dumb, Ketch. Real stupid. She's nothing to you, and besides, her husband would extract his revenge on your father and his mill. You would unleash the full ire of the Alliance and its resources. Give the woman back like you've agreed, and this can all end well."

"I'll think about it," Blackjack mumbled. "That son of a bitch Bishop is the reason why dad got arrested in the first place. This little adventure has cost us all a lot of time, money, and friends. I think he needs to pay the bill."

"That's a mistake, Ketchum," the marshal snapped. "Why kick the hornet's nest? Why take the risk that you'll lose even more men and money? Keep your word. Do the swap."

"Like I said, I'll think about it. Maybe seeing dad's smiling face will allow my benevolence to finally shine through," Ketchum chuckled.

"Whatever," Plummer responded.

The next sound Terri heard was a door slamming, followed by Ketchum's low, evil laugh.

Terri's head was spinning, both from the wound to her skull, and the new information she'd just learned. Bishop didn't have a chance with Plummer working for the enemy. She pined for some way to warn her husband, now concerned he was walking into a trap. Plummer had said her husband had left town, but Terri didn't believe it. He wouldn't abandon her here, that just simply wasn't possible.

She managed to find the sleeping bag, despite the darkness. Pulling the thick cloth up to her chin, Terri began to sink deeper into despair. She had never felt so vulnerable, even when she'd been kidnapped by those contractors while pregnant with Hunter.

Now, in addition to her own future, she was worried about Bishop. Sheriff Watts had said good things about the local marshal, and she knew that her husband placed a lot of value on things like that. Hell, who wouldn't?

Injured, alone in the darkness, and now worried that her son would lose both of his parents, it took all of Terri's willpower to not break out in hysterical tears. "This is the loneliest place I've ever been," she whispered. "Don't leave me, Bishop. Please, I need you now, more than ever."

Three things caused Bishop to leap from the cot.

First, the sunlight streamed through the window and warmed his face. He would've sworn he had just laid down five minutes ago.

The second was the smell of brewing java.

The third was the sound of a motor... the very distinctive engine noise of an airplane.

Rushing to lace up his boots, Bishop burst into the main office just as Verne was setting down his crossword book. "Been a long time since I've heard that racket here. It's a big one. Multiple engines. I think Patty's mystery is about to be solved."

Both men stared out the window when the plane made its first, low pass over the runway. The old pilot was right, whistling as a huge, 4-engine military transport roared less than a hundred feet above the landing strip. "You must have friends in high places," Verne chuckled.

"What's he doing?" Bishop asked, disappointed as he watched the plane gain altitude and circle away.

"Oh, he'll be back, I'd wager. Probably wanted to get a close look at my strip... make sure he had enough room to land. You might as well have a cup of coffee, Son. It will be a minute or two before he touches down."

Sure enough, just as Bishop swallowed his first gulp of joe, the engine noise returned.

This time the aircraft approached from the north, the lumbering behemoth lining up with the runway and angling down. "This guy is good," Verne noted. "We have a short strip, and he's going to need every inch of it to land that baby."

As predicted, the giant bird touched down toward the end of the runway, bounced once back into the air, and then rolled toward the edge of the pavement. Bishop heard the engines reverse as the pilot braked hard.

Verne and Bishop moved outside, watching as the military transport finally rolled to a stop just feet before running out of concrete. The pilot then pivoted his massive machine and began taxiing toward the office.

As the towering plane advanced, Verne stepped out onto the runway, his arms guiding the pilots to a wide parking area just beyond the office.

213

As soon as the aircraft came to a final stop, the pilot cut the engines and exchanged salutes with Verne. The electric hum of the vast rear ramp then sounded, Bishop watching as the "back door" was slowly lowered to the pavement.

"Nick," the West Texan grunted through his wide smile. "What did you send me, my old friend? A rifle platoon? Armor?"

Three pairs of boots appeared at the top of the ramp as Bishop circled toward the back of the plane. Then legs, and finally three grinning faces.

"Grim! Butter! Kevin!" Bishop exclaimed as he began running for the ramp. "Oh my God, guys! You have no idea how happy I am to see you."

"Heard you needed some help, Mr. Vice President Security Man," Grim smiled. "Some guys will stop at nothing to interrupt my fishing trip."

Hugging each man as he stepped off the craft, Bishop shook his head to clear the shock of seeing his former SAINT team standing before him. "How? When? I just can't believe you guys are here," he stammered.

"I was in my last week at the police academy," Butter explained, embracing Bishop in a rib-cracking hug. "The head instructor got me out of the barracks in the middle of the night. A military car rushed me to Fort Bliss. We took off early this morning."

"Kevin was already at Bliss," Grim continued, pointing at Nick's tall, lanky son. "You are looking at one of the instructors at the new sniper course they've opened up."

"And you, you old fart?" Bishop asked, finally standing in front of Grim.

"Sheriff Watts hired me out to consult with the new SWAT teams they're trying to put together. When I heard Miss Terri was in trouble, the 82nd Airborne couldn't have kept me away," the team's oldest member scoffed.

"So, you weren't worried about *me*?" Bishop laughed.

"Not really. I figure an a-hole like you always gets what he deserves," the ex-contractor chuckled. "Oh," he then added, "I almost forgot. Nick said to tell you he's sorry he couldn't send any top tier people or come himself. According to his royal *high-ass*, things are a little dicey with the United States at the moment, and the Alliance can't become officially involved in this matter. Kept mumbling something about crossing the border."

"I guess the bottom of the barrel is better than no help at all," the former SAINT team leader teased.

Bishop had never been so relieved in all his life. Now surrounded by men he knew and trusted, the Texan couldn't stop smiling. As usual, it was Grim who brought things back into perspective. "We were briefed that Miss Terri has been kidnapped and is being held by some very bad hombres."

"Other than that, they didn't have to time to give us very many details," Butter stated, his massive arms flexing in anticipation. "Just point me in the right direction, sir."

"Come on; I'll get you up to speed inside the office. There's even coffee in there, and it's not half bad."

Once everyone had a cup of brew, Bishop began briefing the new arrivals. He started from the beginning, concluding the saga with DA Gibson handing him the note. "And that's how I ended up knee deep in the hurt," he concluded.

Reaching into his jacket, Grim produced a piece of paper. "Well, I can at least help with one problem. While we were in the air, the pilot received this message. It seems Nick had ordered a military drone to fly along the border during the night. Just so happens it was equipped with a thermal imager. According to the big man, and I quote, 'Tell Bishop to check out these coordinates. I think he'll find what he's looking for there. Bring her back safe, or Diana will never speak to me again, and that would make me most unhappy.'"

Grim handed over the single sheet. After scanning the message, Bishop glanced at a nearby table, the surface littered with diagrams, graphs, and charts.

He had to thumb past the top few sheets before pulling out a large map. After glancing back and forth at the longitude and latitude on Nick's message, the former SAINT leader pointed at the exact corresponding spot. "Crescent Furniture Company," Bishop read from the diagram.

Verne, glancing at the paper over Bishop's shoulder, observed, "That makes sense. There would be facilities and shelter there. It would be an excellent location to bivouac a private army."

"You know this place?" Grim inquired.

Nodding vigorously, their host admitted, "The smokestacks there are the highest manmade structures for 30 miles in any direction. When you're flying a private plane around here, you pay attention to things like that. It's also an easily visible landmark for navigation. Even the local high schools pale in comparison to the size of the structures there."

"We need to scout the area," Grim observed. "From what you've told us, we can't just go barging in and shoot up the black hats. Miss Terri wouldn't last too long if this Blackjack guy is worth his salt."

"I brought my best rifles," Kevin chimed in. "Get me within a thousand meters, and I'll drop a dozen of them before they know what hit them."

Verne held up his hands, indicating they should hold on for a moment. Hurrying to the desk, he began digging through one of the drawers. "Yes, I knew this was in here," he announced, extracting a phone book–sized publication and passing it to Bishop.

"Visual Pilot's Guide, Gulf Coast," he read aloud.

Verne made sure to explain its true value. "There should be pictures of the old Crescent Plant in there. That book is what we used to help navigate back in the day... before GPS or the internet."

Sure enough, beginning on page 107, Bishop found several aerial photographs of the Crescent Furniture Company's manufacturing facility.

Grim, peering over Bishop's shoulder at the pictures, let out a long whistle, "Wow! That place is beyond huge. That is not a furniture manufacturer, my friend. That's a compound. Why would this Blackjack character need such a massive base? How much manpower does he have anyway?"

Bishop didn't like what he saw at all, knowing with just a glance that Ketchum's hideout was a tactical nightmare. "No line of approach whatsoever," he acknowledged, pointing at the photo with his index finger. "Elevated overwatch positions. It looks like a maze of buildings. We're up against both quality and quantity here, and these guys are well led. This looks impossible, even with our team."

Turning away to stare out the window, Bishop's mind tried to assimilate everything he had seen and heard. Again, he found it difficult to think straight, images of Terri being beaten, tortured, or worse serving to hamstring his mental processes. "Maybe we shouldn't try to rescue her. Maybe the best plan is to pray that Ketchum keeps his word and releases her in exchange for his father," the worried husband mumbled.

Grim and Butter exchanged a troubled glance. Bishop looked tired and beaten and was now spouting surrender. Both men were surprised and worried. Mouthing a silent, "Keep him from killing me," to Butter, the old warrior took a deep breath and then stepped back to be just out of Bishop's reach.

"So, you just want to do nothing? Just hang out and wait?" Grim complained. "No offense, Boss, but providing you with moral support isn't why we're here. What happened to the man I knew... the leader I've followed through Hell's gates more times than I can count? What happened to the guy who believed there was always a way? Has being Pete's handmaiden caused your spine to turn yellow? Do we need to start calling you 'Bitchup'? Stop feeling sorry for yourself and fretting like a frightened schoolgirl. Think about Terri, because God knows that if it was you being held hostage, we would have to hold her back from charging in and slaughtering everybody."

Grim's harsh rhetoric caused Bishop to spin, his eyes boiling with rage as his fists balled for combat. "I am thinking of Terri, you rude, grumpy, old fuck," he spat. "Besides, I don't hear any great ideas spewing out of your pie hole!"

Smiling, Grim knew his words were having the desired effect. "So, you do still have a little fire in your belly, eh, Boss? I just had to check, just had to make sure you hadn't gone soft on us. Now that I've managed to verify you still have a pulse after all, why don't you focus all that negative energy on this Blackjack dude? You can try to beat my ass later if you want... after Miss Terri is safe and sound."

He's right, the man from West Texas thought, quickly grasping what his old friend was trying to do. *There has to be a way. Terri is alone, frightened, and suffering through who knows what kind of hell. Think, man! Put your brain to work and come up with a plan. Be professional. Kick ass and take names.*

Kevin, ignoring the two older men's exchange, remained fixated on the pilot's book. "Sir, didn't you say that Ketchum is bringing in reinforcements?"

"Yes, I did," Bishop responded, blinking himself back to the problem at hand.

Rubbing his chin, Kevin began articulating a proposal, "What if we were to take Butter and...."

For the next 30 minutes, the team began seriously dissecting the problems they faced. Kevin's idea seemed to open the floodgates to creative solutions. Poring over the maps and the book, they chewed up that elephant – one bite at a time.

The entire team contributed, rounding off the sharp corners, offering multiple solutions to each obstacle. After an hour, they had formulated a plan.

It was risky, fraught with plenty of opportunity to get them all killed, and held Terri's fate in the balance as well.

To Bishop, everything was wrong with their scheme. First, it was complex, and that violated the cardinal rule of operations planning. Simple was always better.

Secondly, the team wasn't in a prime state of readiness. It had been months since their SAINT unit had been disbanded, and everything from their timing to communications represented perishable skills. To operate as an effective, cohesive unit required constant and consistent training... eating, sleeping, and functioning together.

Lastly, their final design called for the team to be split, their forces divided. They were already badly outnumbered and suffering from a lack of hard intelligence. Hell, they couldn't even be 100% positive that Nick's drone hadn't detected the campfires of some drifter's camp. Yet, there wasn't time for a first hand, eyes-on-target scouting mission. They had to act quickly. They had to run with a lot of assumptions. There was no other choice to save Terri.

As his new comrades sorted and prepared their equipment, Bishop stepped over to Verne with a proposal, "I'd like to offer you a temporary trade. I need a vehicle that the people in Forest Mist won't recognize as mine. I'd like to swap my truck for your Jeep for no more than a couple of days."

After a quick contemplation and a cursory glance at Bishop's wheels, Verne agreed. "Sure. Anything else you need?"

"Actually, I need a second vehicle as well. Do you know of anything dependable in the area that is available? I can't help but notice that the airport's car leasing office seems to be..." Bishop paused, coughed into his hand and smiled, before finishing his thought, "...seriously understaffed, underfunded, and under resourced."

Verne chuckled and shook his head at the jokester before offering another set of wheels for the team's venture. "I've got my Caddy in the garage. It doesn't get very good gas mileage, but it runs like a sewing machine. Its trunk is the size of the Grand Canyon... might help with all your gear."

"Sounds perfect," Bishop nodded. "How much would you charge me to rent it?"

It took the old gent about five seconds of thinking before his face brightened into a broad-toothed grin. "I'll let you borrow it on one condition – I get to sit in the cockpit of that fancy transport plane while it's airborne. Can you arrange that?"

Shortly after arriving, Grim had informed them all that Nick had instructed the pilots that their aircraft and crew were temporarily under Bishop's command. Nodding, the West Texan promised, "I can do better than that, Verne. I can arrange for you to take the stick and actually fly her. Deal?"

"Deal," Verne grinned, Bishop's offer seeming to take five years off the man's face.

"One more question," Bishop said, pointing to a faded sign on one of the airport's hangars. "Did that business over there leave behind any of their equipment?"

It took the older man less than two seconds to realize what his new friend was asking. "Yes," he responded with a grin. "Yes, they did. Want to see?"

CHAPTER 13

Terri heard the lock on the door before the harsh light of morning flooded into the room. A bearded, muscular man poked his head inside, scanned the room, grunted, and then moved out of the way. Kitty, with a tray of food, then entered.

"Good morning," she said with contrived cheeriness. "I brought you some breakfast. It's not much, but you've got to be hungry."

"Not really," Terri moaned, rubbing her still-throbbing head. "But I guess I should eat."

A bowl of lukewarm oatmeal and a glass of water comprised the cuisine. "Gruel," Terri whispered, rising to sit in the room's only chair.

After handing over the platter, Kitty stepped away from the prisoner and rested against the wall. "I heard this will all be over in a day or two," she offered. "You'll be home with your husband and son before you know it."

"Ketchum isn't going to let me go," Terri countered after swallowing a spoonful of the lumpy oats. "You and I both know that. What you really mean is that I'll be dead in a day or two."

Surprised by Terri's blunt prediction, Kitty shook her head. "You kind of figured that out, huh?"

"I overheard a conversation," Terri confessed.

"Whatever you do, don't fight them," Kitty offered, leaning close to whisper her advice. "There's a chance... a small chance... but if you cooperate while they are having their fun, they might decide to keep you around as a toy for a while. You're very pretty and clean and soft. That's rare these days. You never know what tomorrow might bring, sweetie. You might get a chance to escape eventually. If you manage to stay alive long enough."

Shaking her head, Terri responded, "I could never do that. I would rather die a hundred times than pretend I was some sort of nympho who liked being raped. Sorry, that's just not in the cards."

A melancholy look crossed Kitty's face, her eyes shifting as her mind travelled to a place far away. "You remind me of another girl I knew, from before the collapse. She was high-minded and strong-willed, just like you. She died a horrible death. I can still hear her screams at night when I close my eyes."

"What happened?" Terri asked, unable to control the urge to preview her potential fate.

"The cops arrested one of the men from the club. Ketchum and VooDoo were convinced that someone had ratted to the police. They figured it was this girl."

"And?"

"The men took her to an abandoned hotel that had been out of business for a long time. They started passing her around, two or three of them having their way with her at a time. She fought for as long as she could, trying to hit them, punch them in the crotch... biting, scratching, screaming... that sort of thing. She just delayed the inevitable; she didn't stand a chance against so many determined men. In fact, she could barely stand once they finished. When their little party was over, they took her to the empty swimming pool and threw her in the deep end. It hadn't had any water in it for years, and her body made this awful crunching sound when it landed on the concrete. I couldn't believe she was still alive after all that. I remember how she was crawling toward the ladder when they poured in a couple of gallons of gasoline in threw in a match. I have never seen anything so horrible. They made all of us girls stand by the edge and watch her burn."

Shivering at the mental image, Terri then glared at the woman beside her. "You saw this, and you still decided to hang with men capable of such a thing?"

"Oh, they're not so bad if you play the role," Kitty shrugged. "They are very protective and extremely loyal. I had run away from home at 15 and hooked up with the wrong people. You know the story, happened all the time before everything went to hell."

Terri nodded, remembering all kinds of similar, sad situations. Kitty continued, "I was forced to walk the streets and sell myself. My pimp beat the shit out of me on a regular basis. I had VD three times before I was 17 and was lucky I didn't get AIDS."

"Ketchum did this?"

"Oh, no, Ketchum rescued me. I met him in the French Quarter, and he was very kind to me. I used to see him at the same corner every night. He was monitoring a couple of meth dealers nearby, and we would talk while I waited for a John to pick me up."

"You said he rescued you?"

Nodding eagerly, Kitty seemed happy to report something positive for a change, "One night, my pimp had given me a black eye. I tried to cover it with makeup, but Ketch saw right through the disguise. He asked me what had happened and finally, I told him. That night, when a man showed up to collect the money I'd earned, Ketchum cut his throat. I've been with his people ever since. They are my family now."

Fighting the urge to debate the woman, Terri barely managed to hold her tongue. Kitty had been the only person that had shown even an ounce of kindness during her captivity and might be her only chance at escape. *Don't judge*, she thought. *Smile. Pretend you understand. Play nice. You need an ally here.*

Before Terri could conjure up a friendly response, the door opened again, Blackjack's wide shoulders filling the entrance. "How is our guest this morning, Kitty?"

An immediate change came over Terri's benefactor, Kitty standing abruptly and rushing to stand beside Blackjack's towering frame. She was like a puppy dog whose master had just returned home. "She knows what you have planned," the woman spouted as she cast a venomous eye at the hostage. "She overheard a conversation."

Stunned at the betrayal, Terri spat, "Why, you bitch... I... I...."

"You what?" Blackjack laughed. "You act surprised. Why would Kitty's loyalty to me be so shocking?"

Without waiting for Terri to respond, Blackjack turned to Kitty and brushed her cheek gently with his hand. "Do you love me?" he asked.

"Yes," she purred, her eyes spreading wide with admiration.

"Will you do anything for me? Kill? Steal? Satisfy any man I wish, in any way I command?"

"Yes," she emphatically replied, Kitty's voice now a lusty whisper.

"Good," Ketchum nodded. Then without warning, his enormous fist slammed into Kitty's stomach with a powerful jab.

Doubling in pain, Kitty collapsed to the floor, her chest desperately searching for a way to draw oxygen while her gut tried to keep from retching.

Blackjack waited nearly a full minute before bending to help Kitty back to her feet. "I'm sorry," he whispered, gently cradling the weak woman against his chest. "It was necessary. Are you okay?"

Terri was amazed when the just-abused woman's face again filled with unconditional love. "Yes," she croaked, "I'll be okay."

"Good," Blackjack stated, still holding her close.

Ketchum then fixed his gaze on Terri, almost as if he wanted to make sure she was taking in the show. Without another word, he then lowered one hand and began gently brushing it along Kitty's thigh, slowly working his way from just above her knee toward her most private region.

Kitty inhaled sharply at his touch, her eyes squinting in pleasure as Blackjack's fingers worked their way up her skirt. Terri spotted the woman's lips actually quiver in anticipation, her nipples growing hard under the thin material covering her breasts.

Ketchum stopped just short of Kitty's thong and then bent to kiss her softly on the lips. "I'll come by and see you in a little while. Be ready."

Clearly thrilled at the potential of his attention, Kitty nodded and then turned and hurried out of the room.

Ketchum now focused his dark eyes on Terri, his face unreadable. "Did you see that? That is what I call allegiance. That is faith and respect. That was a demonstration of true power."

Not wanting to fuel the man's ego, Terri merely shrugged. "If you say so."

"People like you believe power comes from the counting of votes after an election. Your husband thinks authority is issued from the barrel of a rifle. The Army believed loyalty came from an oath and enforced discipline. You're all wrong. After the apocalypse, I learned very quickly why society failed. It was due to a lack of true leadership, an absence of anyone who had *earned* the right to govern."

"And that would, of course, be someone like you?" Terri retorted, unable to keep the sarcasm out of her voice, yet not wanting to test Blackjack's temper.

"We have survived as a species for thousands of years by letting the strongest, most capable individuals lead our tribes. Somehow, we got away from that," he stated. "I intend to see that we go back to that proven method of governing. The destruction of society is proof that the entire concept of elections and politicians was flawed. I want to take us back to the old ways. It has to be better than what we had."

"So, you believe that the man with the most muscles deserves to govern? That his physical prowess endows him with the ability to lead? That the Mixed Martial Arts warrior champ should occupy the Oval Office by default – simply because he can whoop everybody else's ass?"

"I believe the man who fights his way to the top should rule. He has earned the right. Consider the qualities he must possess to rise to that position. Of necessity, he will have the proper balance of physical strength, intelligence, benevolence, and foresight... especially if he is to remain in charge. Eventually, someone who better embodies those qualities will come along and push out the old guy whose skills weakened. The best man would always be king."

Unable to help herself, Terri pushed back on Ketchum's bloated self-image and narrow-minded view of humanity. "Well, you'd better be prepared to step aside," she said. "Bishop is going to be coming for me, and I don't think he'll just *push you out.* He's going to annihilate you, and I'm going to enjoy watching your downfall."

A genuine belly laugh erupted from Ketchum's throat, the man bending backward with laughter. "So be it," he continued. "If he can kill me, then he deserves to lead the tribe. But... I happen to know your husband has already fled Forest Mist. He was last seen driving for West Texas, his cowardly tail tucked between his legs."

Terri didn't blink, "Perhaps you are right. He does have a lot of very violent friends back there. I'm sure he'll be back."

"Maybe," Ketchum shrugged as he stepped toward his hostage. "In the meantime, I'm in a mood to teach you a little more about true power and respect."

He stopped beside her, running a finger down the smooth skin of her cheek. Recoiling at his touch, she pulled away. In a flash, Blackjack slapped at the tray on her lap, sending the oatmeal flying across the room.

Before Terri could recover, his massive hand roughly grasped her jaw, holding her head still as he bent to kiss her. She waited, her harsh stare boring into his eyes with loathing and hatred.

He thought he was teasing her with anticipation, moving in slowly, ready to pick her ripe fruit. When his mouth was close enough, Terri lurched forward like a striking cobra and bit into his lower lip.

At the same moment that she felt his sensitive flesh between her teeth, she made a fist and punched him in the crotch.

Blackjack inhaled sharply as he sprang back from the baulking lover, his retreat costing him a portion of his lower lip.

She bounded from the chair, spat out the flesh between her teeth, and backed away. With no path to escape, she headed for the corner and stood panting, coiled and ready to fight.

It took Ketchum a moment to recover, a hand moving to his throbbing mouth to inspect the damage. After a pause, he stared down at his fingers, grunting at the sight of his own blood. "I knew you would be a spirited, little thing. I had no idea you liked to play rough."

"I don't like to play with you period," she growled. "Stay away. I'm not interested."

"What you want doesn't matter," he hissed, eyes now full of rage. "You're going to do what I want... when I want it."

He stepped in close, her nose assaulted by a blend of old sweat and Old Spice. She could feel his hot breath on her hair as he reached for her breasts. She waited, remembering the lessons Bishop and Butter had taught her.

When Blackjack's weight moved forward enough, Terri kicked with all her might, aiming at a spot just above his knee.

She hit the mark, the impact sending a white-hot bolt of pain shooting up her leg instead. It was like she had just kicked a tree trunk. Still, he didn't go down.

Ketchum didn't react to her attack for a moment. Then without warning, his hand whipped through the air and slapped her, hard.

227

Terri's ears were ringing, her vision blurred by the strike. Then, she felt his hands at the top of her blue jeans, trying to jerk them down.

She again struck out in desperation, her fingers like claws as she went for his eyes. One hand found flesh as she tried to dig as deep as possible with a raking yank. This time Blackjack reacted, a roar of pain bellowing from his chest.

He responded instinctively, his fist smashing into the side of the captive's head with a powerful blow.

Terri's world went black.

Bishop had to admit, Grim looked funny as hell in Verne's Cadillac.

Fire engine red with a rag top and white leather seats, the monster from Detroit was definitely not a low-profile ride. Grim, for his part, had fallen in love with the borrowed land yacht.

The ex-contractor was given several deliverables required for their mission to succeed. First, with Kevin along for the ride, he was to drive into Forest Mist, act like he was a friend of DA Gibson, and deliver a private message. It read, "We're ready. Let Whipsaw go two hours after sunset. Bishop."

After that, the duo had a small laundry list of items that needed to be accomplished. They were going to have a busy afternoon.

In the meantime, Bishop took Butter to his pickup and began digging through Terri's suitcase. After a few minutes, he held up a small bottle of his wife's waterproof eyeliner and a can of hairspray. "Sorry about my lack of artistic skills, my old friend, but I'll do my best."

Dipping into the black liquid normally used to accent his wife's eyes, Bishop began drawing on Butter's arms and face. "You'd be the only biker in all of Louisiana without tats, big guy," he stated, starting with a spider web. "Don't worry, it will be dark, and prison tats always look like shit."

After finishing some rough drawings on both of Butter's massive limbs, Bishop then ordered his buddy to close his eyes. A minute later, the Texan leaned back and admired his work. A black tear now adorned his friend's face.

Next came the hairspray. "I read someplace that this will make the ink looked a bit faded and keep it from running, even if you break out into a sweat."

Just when Butter thought the terror was over, Bishop produced a razor. "Sorry, but that blonde hair of yours just looks way too wholesome. We're going to shave your head."

Finally finished, Bishop pointed toward a nearby window. "Go look at yourself, Mr. Harley Davidson. Except for your head being bleach white, you look like a kick-ass biker dude."

Butter's initial reaction was a deep frown as he studied himself in the reflection. "I came to destroy those kidnappers and to save Miss Terri," he eventually announced. "This is no big deal. But... what are we going to do about my head? There's no time to get a suntan?"

Again, Bishop dug through their luggage, this time producing a bandanna. "Here, wrap this around that oversized brainpan of yours. Remember, it will be dark."

"God, I hope so," Butter, still staring in the mirror announced with a grimace. "I look nasty mean, Boss. Everybody would be scared of me in this getup."

"That's exactly the idea, Butter," Bishop laughed.

Dropping off the note for DA Gibson was easy, Pat responding to Grim's delivery with an update, "We received a message from Ketchum Jones. He says his father knows the location where the transaction is supposed to take place. Marshal Plummer and a bunch of deputies will monitor the exchange. Tell Bishop I wish you all the best of luck."

After leaving the courthouse, Grim asked one of the deputies where he could find a good secondhand store. The local lawman merely pointed and then added, "One block off the square."

Kevin spotted the entrance first, motioning for Grim to take the next parking space. A minute later, the odd couple strolled through the front door.

"I ride a Harley on weekends," Grim announced. "I'm looking for some good leather riding gear to keep these old bones warm. Got anything in stock?"

The gentleman behind the counter smiled and nodded, "Why yes, we happen to have just received a shipment of such items. Right over there on aisle six, toward the back of the store."

Nodding his appreciation, Grim and Kevin wandered through the musty-smelling establishment. They passed boxes of clothing, mostly sorted into categories by sex, age, and size. It didn't take long before they located several containers full of jackets, pants, wallets with chains, and assorted other riding paraphernalia.

Reaching for a sleeveless denim vest sporting several colorful patches, Grim held it up for Kevin's examination. "Too small," the sharpshooter said. "He wouldn't get more than one arm in that thing."

Grunting, Grim then browsed for another, larger item.

Five minutes later, and three dollars poorer, the duo left the store carrying the largest piece of biker clothing they could find. It was a black leather vest, sleeveless, and covered with numerous patches and pins. "It is from a New Orleans club," Kevin announced. "Probably fresh off one of the guys Terri just shot."

"Poor fellow," Grim smiled. "He probably misses his buddies. Let's go help a few dozen more of them join him."

Their last stop was Angel's Porch, Grim piloting the Cadillac into the driveway as Kevin scanned the row of motorcycles still parked exactly where Bishop said they would be. Each of the iron horses had a signed taped to the handlebars: "Property of the Forest Mist Sheriff's Department."

"Not only are we buying outlaw clothes," Grim chuckled, "but now we're committing grand theft auto."

After scrutinizing the assorted machines from top to bottom, Grim chose one and straddled the seat. A few kicks later and the engine rumbled to life.

"I'll follow you back in the Caddy," Kevin announced. "Try to be careful. Those things are dangerous."

"I've been riding a motorcycle since I was a boy," Grim grunted over the rumbling exhaust. "As for you, young man, you be careful with that exquisite classic car."

It was the chilly concrete that roused Terri back to consciousness, her naked body shivering on the floor in the darkness.

She struggled to prop up her torso on one elbow, every inch of her body aching. Her head hung down as if it were a powerful weight, the concussion's jackhammer slamming against her skull unlike anything she had ever felt. For a fleeting moment, she panicked, as she could make out neither light nor shape around her. *Oh my gosh, I can't even see my hand in front of my face!*

Unsettled by the realization, she banged her fist into the cement. She could feel her heart thumping inside her chest, and her brain was clouded by fear. Opening her hand and pressing her palm to the floor, she managed to half-crawl and half-drag herself toward the center of the room.

Steady yourself, Terri; freaking out will make this worse, she told herself. Knowing that panicking would work against her, she tried to calm herself and check her emotions. After a few heartbeats, she noticed a glow emitted from one area of her cell. Blinking back the confusion, she spotted some light leaking in around the door, the glimmer allowing her to make out various elements of her lockup. With difficulty, she managed to sit, pulling her legs close to her chest for warmth and comfort.

She guessed that she had wakened during the night and wondered how long she had been out. *The first thing every kid who takes on a bully learns is to protect his head,* she scolded herself, knowing the double brain injury put her in a precarious position. After all, losing consciousness twice in a 24-hour period was not going to expand her intellect. *If you are not careful, Hunter will have to tutor you on those ABCs,* she warned.

Cautiously, she felt her head where Blackjack's fist had landed, gingerly moving her jaw and testing her teeth. She could taste the dried blood in her mouth, but nothing seemed to be broken. That was about the extent of the good news.

She rubbed her temples, hoping to interrupt the injury's relentless and rhythmic pounding, but there was no relief. She shook her head, eager to clear a few more of the concussion's cobwebs. As her mind began to clear a bit, she gained an even stronger awareness of her surroundings. A familiar odor assaulted her senses, and she struggled to identify it. *Is that Old Spice?* she panicked. *Oh my God! What happened?* The stench of that Neanderthal lingered in her hair... on her skin... the thought of him touching her sending another shiver up her spine. She wretched at the grotesque image her mind created.

She drew her legs in closer to her body, resting her throbbing head on her knees. Gradually, she became aware of stiffness and pain that permeated her body. She hurt in places she didn't even know she had. As she massaged her limbs, she could feel the heat of bruising in her muscles.

Her movement stirred the air and renewed the stink of him. A single tear slid down her cheek, her fingers brushing the wetness from her face. She needed a shower, desperately craving to wash any of his essence from her skin. She was dirty and soiled, both mentally and physically. She began to sob, the helplessness, fear, and loathing sinking her soul to its lowest depths.

A noise alerted her to movement outside her cell. The door blocked most of the sound, her ears straining to understand the snatches brief conversation and laughter. Her heart froze when someone outside jiggled the doorknob.

Waves of nausea swirled in her stomach and the pounding in her skull heightened as she realized her ordeal was not over. Not by a long shot. Was that animal he coming back for more? *Dear God, please... no, not again*, she silently begged. *I can't take much more of this.*

In her mind, she began to formulate a strategy to survive. *I'll keep my eyes open for any opportunity to get away, but this guy has got some skills. A chance like that might never come*, she thought, *so I need a Plan B.* Terri considered her options, realizing the only thing she had been successful at doing was to provoke him into hitting her.

I can use that, she mused. *I would rather be unconscious than lie awake during such a brutal assault.*

Her thoughts turned to Bishop. Her husband. Her soul mate. If only he were here. She wouldn't have to cower to this monster. He would rescue her and hold her so close to him that he hugged out all her hurt.

Bishop...

Where is he anyway? she wondered. *Why hasn't he come for me? Did he really turn tail and run back to West Texas without me?*

The relentless jackhammer slammed harder and harder into her injured brain. She shook her head to clear the murkiness.

No, she knew that Bishop loved her. He would never simply desert her. He would be back for her. She relaxed for a moment, content in the knowledge of their bond.

But will he want me? Will his feelings change after he knows what has happened? Will he wonder if I could have prevented this? Could I have fought harder? She wondered what Bishop would think. Could things ever be the same between them? She was used goods now. Unclean. Soiled. Filthy. Would he question how hard she had struggled? Would he second-guess her actions prior to the assault? Would there always be a shadow of distrust in his heart?

Terri rested her thumping head on her knees and began to sob again. She knew her life was forever changed, and she had no control to affect that.

Voices beyond the door interrupted her period of introspection. The sound of men talking just outside the walls of her cell shook her to her core. Cold, alone in the darkness, and sure she hadn't experienced the worst of it, Terri considered another option, taking her own life. "So, what if I stop breathing? My life was over the second that bastard violated me. He has taken everything away from me. He's ruined it all. I would rather go out on my own terms than let that monster have any more influence over me."

Now with an 'escape,' in mind, Terri felt around the floor for her clothes. First, she came across her jeans, tossing them aside. Too bad she didn't wear a belt.

Next, she found the replacement shirt Kitty had provided. That, too, was worthless for what she had in mind.

Finally, she spotted the shadowy outline of her hiking boots in the dim light. She rushed to them and immediately began removing the laces. They would be strong enough to hold her weight.

Her plan was simple, push up one of the ceiling tiles and tie one end of her laces to a pipe, or beam, or whatever she could find. She would stand on the chair, drape the other end around her neck, and then kick her support away. It would be over quickly. She wouldn't be forced to endure any more pain.

Her fingers trembled as they worked, making it difficult to properly fashion the noose. Terri was unsure if the shaking was caused by the chilly temperature or by her swelling emotions. She wasn't afraid to die; she was afraid she would fail.

Finding a secure anchor for the hangman's noose proved to be more difficult than she expected. In the corner, she balanced on a chair to push up the ceiling tiles, the motion increasing the speed and strength of the pulsing inside her brain. After steadying herself again, she pushed up several of the tiles and found a pipe running the length of the room. That would do.

Even standing on the chair, she wasn't tall enough to tie a good knot. Determined to complete her mission, she stacked her food tray on her folded clothing and boots in the chair's seat. It was a precarious perch, but those few extra inches got the job done.

Examining the noose that now dangled from the corner, Terri decided she wanted to die with her clothes on. It seemed more dignified, and for a woman who had suffered the ultimate indignity, she was determined to recapture as much of her self-respect as she could.

Methodically pulling on her jeans and shirt, she went through the motions of dressing. "All that's left is a robot, a machine," she whispered. "Like the bland, concrete block walls that surround me, I am only a shell of the person I used to be. I'm so, so very sorry, Bishop. I'm weak. I can't go through that again."

She paused for a moment, having trouble deciding whether to slip on her socks. Her feet were cold, but she had always enjoyed being barefoot. It would be her last indulgence.

It then occurred to her that Hunter hated wearing his socks, a smile coming to her lips as she remembered their daily battles while getting dressed. "He got that from me, I guess. Can't blame all of his bad habits on his father."

Hunter. Her son. The latest love of her life.

Images of the boy's cherubic face floated through her mind. She could hear his joyous cackle. She longed to replace Ketchum's stench with the freshness of his young skin.

Hunter.

She began sobbing, a dark sadness welling up inside. She realized she would never see him again. At least not on this earth.

Doubt invaded Terri's thoughts, her eyes traveling between the noose and the door. Blackjack could stroll through the entrance at any moment, ready to pleasure himself again with her flesh... ready to violate her for his own enjoyment. She might not be unconscious the next time, might have to endure every moment of his gross, disgusting assault. He might bring other men with him.

Hunter. The image of the tot riding on his father's shoulders flooded her mind.

Could she ever welcome Bishop's touch again? Would his passion and longing always remind her of how she had been desecrated? She wept some more, glancing back at the noose and the escape it offered.

Hunter.

Bishop was a great father, a textbook example of the loving, involved male parent. He was Hunter's yang to her soft, loving yin. Together, they created a balanced environment for their son. How would her husband manage rearing a child without his mate? How would her end change their son's life?

Hunter.

It occurred to her that Hunter wouldn't care what Blackjack Jones had done to his mother. By the time he was old enough to know, he would be mature enough to understand. Her son wouldn't judge her actions, would never doubt her resolve to resist. If given the choice between no mother at all, or growing up with damaged goods, she was positive her baby would want and need her. He would help her heal. His love, no matter how Bishop reacted, would see her through.

"Ketchum can never take that away from me," she hissed, glaring at the door. "He can rape me, beat me, humiliate me, and torture me until the end of days, but my son will always love me."

She couldn't do it. Not yet. Not now. While Terri had never experienced such low depths of despair, she still couldn't take her own life.

Yet, she wanted to keep the option open. If Ketchum found her boot laces hanging from the pipe, he might take them away. Or use them on her himself. No, these were her property, and they would be used on her terms when she decided all hope was truly lost.

She struggled to untie the knot and eventually pulled her laces down from the pipe. Restringing them through the tiny eyelets was a chore that seemed to take forever to complete.

Exhausted, depressed, and still suffering from Ketchum's blow, she curled up in the corner and cried herself to sleep.

Butter spent the rest of the afternoon getting acquainted with the Harley on the airport's tarmac, Grim's in-your-face instruction reminiscent of a boot camp drill sergeant. Bishop watched the hands-on training with interest, knowing that the kid had to demonstrate enough skill to fit in with the gang. "I'll be happy when there are more burnouts than crashes," Bishop grimaced after a particularly long skid. Still, the big man was improving, rapidly approaching the point where he could pull off his part of the mission.

Kevin was preparing as well, unpacking an impressive array of sniper rifles and optics. "I've got light amplification, thermal imagining, ballistic computers with GPS accurate altitude adjustments and laser range finders."

Bishop was impressed as Kevin began checking the rifles. "This one's the tried and true .308 Winchester. That one over there is my favorite, a .338 Lapua Magnum. With that baby, I can really reach out and touch someone."

Opening another bag, the sharpshooter extracted a pair of metallic cylinders. "Noise cancelation devices," he announced. "I've even got subsonic ammunition, but that really limits my range. Still, I can put one in your eye at 800 meters while making no more noise than squirrel farting."

"You have studied the charts and pictures more than anybody, Kevin," Bishop said. "You know we're going to need anybody on those smokestacks and water tower to be taken out first thing. That's critical. Can you get close enough?"

Nodding with confidence, Kevin stepped to another duffle and pulled on the zipper. "This should do the job," he beamed, pulling out a Ghillie suit. "According to the picture, there's a drainage ditch alongside one of the parking lots. It has the right angle to see both the stacks and the tower. I'm counting on it being overgrown and not having much water. If I can get within range using that trench, I'll have no problems whatsoever. I'm just not sure the conditions pictured in the book are the same ones that I will find out in the field. I'll just have to play it by ear."

Bishop didn't like it. "That's the issue with this entire mission. We have zero eyes-on recon. Hell, for all we know, half of that damn building has collapsed. Verne said it hasn't been occupied for over 50 years. We're all probably going to end up dead, including my wife."

"At least we'll go out knowing we tried, sir. Isn't that what counts?"

Bishop paused before responding, ambling to the window for a view outside before sighing heavily. "I don't know, Kevin. I love your attitude, but there's just no glory in dying."

Kevin didn't seem to notice his team leader's demeanor as he was busily checking his gear one final time. "Well, I think it's best if I get an early start. We all have our radios. If there's something significantly wrong, I can let you know what the changes are. We'll just have to adapt. There's no other option, for us, or for Miss Terri."

Shaking his head, Bishop repeated his teammate's key word. "Adapt. Why does that frighten me so much? Yet, you don't seem scared. You are definitely your father's son."

Shrugging his shoulders, Kevin responded, "I've got the easy part of this op, sir. You, Grim, and Butter are carrying the heavy load on this one."

"Don't be so sure. I know Blackjack has ex-military personnel among his ranks. He might have his own snipers," Bishop warned.

Bending to heft his rifle, Kevin grinned widely. "I'm ready, sir."

Butter appeared just then, his riding lessons apparently over. The big man was anxious to spend a few minutes with his best friend.

Bishop stepped toward the team's youngest member... his best friend's son... and shook Kevin's hand and wished him well. "I'll see you back here by midnight," the team leader confirmed before walking away. And then turning back, Bishop repeated the mantra of a sniper, "One shot, one kill."

Giving Butter and Kevin some time was the smart thing to do. Having survived an apocalypse at such young ages, they shared many common experiences and fears. The two had formed a bond that had been steeled by some of the most intense combat in the history of fighting. They fed off each other, a mutual effort to build confidence, share doubts, and overcome the empty feeling every warrior had in the pit of his stomach before facing the ultimate contest.

While he would have never acknowledged it, Bishop's recognition of these factors was a big part of why he was such an excellent leader. It was a skill that hadn't been taught in any class or learned from any book.

After Butter insisted on helping Kevin load his gear, the team stood and watched the marksman drive off in Verne's Jeep. "He'll come through," Grim whispered. "He's one of the best I've ever seen. If any man can do it, it's that kid."

239

Knowing how close he could approach the old factory was critical to Kevin's timeline. Too far away, and he would be forced to hump over 30 pounds of gear and weapons across unknown terrain. He had to be in place or the entire maneuver's schedule would collapse. Miss Terri would likely be killed, as well as the men he loved and respected more than any others.

Too close, and he risked being detected and blowing the whole operation.

Assuming the enemy would have eyes on the one paved road leading to the furniture plant, Kevin had marked three potential spots on the small gas station roadmap Verne had provided.

Three miles and two intersections away, Kevin spied a thick line of trees running parallel to the main road. Locking in the Jeep's 4-wheel driver, he spun the wheel hard to cut across what had probably been a field of some sort of planted grain.

Less than 100 yards into the knee-high weeds covering the field, Kevin thought he might have made a huge error. His wheels were spinning, slinging mud from all four tires. If he got stuck... out here in the open....

While Kevin didn't have a lot of off-roading experience, his instinct was to give the vehicle more gas. "Momentum," he hissed, fighting the wheel as the back end started to slide.

His next move was to aim for the highest ground. "It will be drier. It will have drained better."

Finally, the Jeep got traction and began to bump and jump as it accelerated across the rough terrain. Sighing with relief, Kevin steered for an open spot between two trees. A minute later, he was swinging a machete, cutting off small branches and draping them over his escape vehicle.

It took him another few minutes to strap on his armor, vest, and water bladder. Next, he climbed into his Ghillie suit before slinging his backpack and the rather substantial magnum rifle that would be his primary tool in the upcoming op.

Despite not having to carry any rations, sleeping gear, or other essential support supplies, Kevin's pack weighed over 30 pounds. With the load of his camouflage and weapon, he knew this was going to be a grueling, exhausting afternoon.

He began hiking toward his objective, the first few hundred yards spent adjusting straps, studying the terrain, and most importantly, taking note of the surrounding vegetation.

The thick suit covering him from head to toe quickly became a blast furnace. Even with the mild temperatures outside, Kevin was drenched in perspiration before he'd managed a quarter mile. He marched onward, partially motivated by duty and responsibility, partly due to all the kindness Bishop and Terri had both shown him through the years.

At one mile from the plant, Kevin's stride, speed over ground, and demeanor changed drastically. His proximity was now close enough that he might be detected by random patrols, a forward listening post, or any other number of security tactics. Time to step up his vigilance game.

Moments later, it was the carcass of a deer that saved Kevin's life.

Alerted by a swarming, black cloud of flies, he approached the lifeless animal with caution and curiosity. The whitetail's hindquarters had been thoroughly shredded, slices of raw meat and entrails scattered haphazardly over the ground. "Looks like he was hit with the world's biggest shotgun," the sniper observed.

Inspecting the cadaver closer, Kevin realized that no shotgun could have caused that much damage. "What did you run into?" he whispered to the dead animal.

He began pacing in small circles, moving away from the slaughtered beast a few degrees at a time. On his third orbit, he spotted the tripwire.

Whoever had set the boobytrap was skilled, the black metal wire barely three inches above the ground. "Just the right height to catch my boot," he noted.

Following the line with his eyes, Kevin discovered the slight indentation in the earth that no doubt cradled what he knew was a Claymore Antipersonnel Mine.

The size of a shoe box's lid, the Claymore's curved surface was covered in steel balls, each about the size of a small bullet. The rest of the lethal device was comprised of pure explosive.

If Kevin had stepped on that wire, hundreds of BB-like hunks of shrapnel would have perforated his body, just like they had the deer.

"Thank you," Kevin whispered to the deceased animal, grateful for the warning of impending danger.

Kevin stared at the booby-trap, realizing that the device had been craftily placed and fatal in its intent. Further, he understood that the Claymore's presence was both good and bad news.

On the positive side, its installation meant he was unlikely to run into a foot patrol. Even the men who planted such devices didn't like stomping around in a minefield. Accidents, especially in low light conditions, were always possible.

The negative was very troubling. If Blackjack had set up a security perimeter at this distance, there was no telling what the inner rings might consist of. Just as Bishop had warned, they were dealing with professionals.

Reaching into a pouch, Kevin extracted his thermal monocular. What followed was the part of being a sniper that he hated the most, the monotonous process of stalking through hostile territory.

The pattern repeated with painful iteration – three carefully placed steps, followed by a scan with the thermal, followed by a detailed visual search of the area. Every third time, he would identify the nearest cover, just in case somebody started shooting.

The exercise was the ultimate test for a sniper. Mind-numbing dull, after only an hour, a man could easily make a deadly mistake or convince himself to take a shortcut just to avoid the boredom. A professional marksman would patiently stay the course.

Slowly, Kevin altered his route. Blessed with an excellent sense of direction, he knew that the drainage ditch was to his right and didn't want to venture too far into the forest.

When he estimated that he was just under a mile from the target, he spotted the trench. Relieved to see no water standing in the bottom, he then studied the vegetation.

Finding similar samples of plants nearby, Kevin wove cuts of the same weeds and brush into his suit. Color and texture were critical elements to proper camouflage, especially when making a daylight approach.

Finally satisfied with his work, Kevin began crawling slowly to the ditch, keeping his profile below the knee-high weeds and moving at only a few feet per minute.

It was rare for any terrain to be completely flat and level. Small undulations were almost always present, even if an area looked as smooth as a tabletop to the naked eye. Fortunately for Kevin, the drain was no exception.

A big part of his training was to identify the low spots, dense undergrowth, and any other natural features that would mask his approach and use them to his advantage. Movement drew the human eye, and that forced the stalker to progress at a snail's pace. From the time his dad had taught him to hunt, Kevin had been coached that discipline was the most important skill he would ever learn. Today was yet another example of how wise his father's words had been.

Creeping only a few feet a minute while encased in a heavy, hot outfit was an extreme challenge, both physically and mentally. Doing so while dragging along 20% of your body weight in equipment was something only a few could accomplish. The fact that the smokestack and water tower probably housed men who would kill him without warning made Kevin's task nearly impossible.

The good news was that he didn't have to get within his weapon's range while it was still daylight. That step would come after the sun had set behind him.

At first, he'd considered mimicking the proven tactic of using the sun's declination to mask his approach, just like the Japanese pilots who attacked Pearl Harbor. The theory was that vectoring toward a target using the glare of the sky's brightest object would blind any defenders. For a moment, Kevin wondered how many commanders had charged headlong into the enemy's ranks, emboldened by the fact that the sun was behind them?

He had access to the basic information necessary to use that technique. He knew the date, which translated into the day of the year. From there, it was easy to plot the exact point on the compass where the sun would slide below the horizon. The ditch aligned almost perfectly today, the Vernal Equinox only 11 days away.

The problems with that method were many.

The weather would have to cooperate. Any clouds or other atmospheric conditions like a red sunset would serve to reduce the glare. If that happened, instead of hiding his approach, he might be silhouetted against the backdrop of a bright sky.

Then there was the fact that Blackjack's sentries were elevated. Kevin didn't know how high his foe might be positioned. They would be looking down, and without knowing their exact height, it was impossible to calculate how much the sun would interfere their vision.

Even if those two factors aligned perfectly, common, everyday sunglasses could all but eliminate any effect from the sun's position or advantage to the stalker. Kevin had to assume the factory's defenders would be wearing shades.

No, he would wait until darkness fell. Bishop had warned that Blackjack's cadre might be equipped with night vision devices, so he would still have to proceed carefully. The timeline was going to be tight.

He arrived at a small intersection of sorts, a spot where water had naturally eroded a channel into the surrounding earth as it rushed to drain into the ditch. Two large bushes had chosen that place to take root and grow. They would provide excellent cover for him.

The terrain was low enough here that he could relax and move at "normal" speeds. Dropping into the bottom of the dip, he took off his pack and removed a large rifle scope. Throwing the quick release levers, he mounted the optic on his blaster and then slowly crawled back out of the draw.

The laser rangefinder told Kevin he was 1801 meters from the water tower, the smokestack another 210 meters beyond that. Just over a mile.

With regular ammunition, he could hit a man-sized target from this spot. Even with the cancelation device on his rifle, the .338 had enough ass to make the shot. If his mission had been to assassinate a lone individual, or take out a single unarmored vehicle, he could set up right here and avoid the risk of approaching any closer.

Today, however, that wouldn't work. The problem was noise.

It would take almost four seconds for his bullet to travel to the water tower. It would be racing to the target at supersonic speeds and thus create a sonic boom, of sorts. Even if he canceled the report of his weapon's discharge with a silencer, the crack of the incoming round would still be detectable to the men at the factory. They would run, duck, or dive for cover. He'd take out the first target, but things would be exponentially more difficult after that.

In addition to the cancelation device mounted on his barrel, truly silent sniping required the use of subsonic ammunition. That meant the bullet would exit his barrel at much, much slower speeds and would be far more vulnerable to the effects of gravity, wind, and humidity on its way to the target. *I want to be undetectable, so I have to get close when it's time for the shot. The laws of physics allow no other option,* Kevin reflected.

Then there was the Coriolis Effect, the need to correct for the rotation of the earth. At 1801 meters, a regular bullet would move just over 7 inches to the right. If he tried to lob in a subsonic round, the planet would have a lot more time to rotate under the shot. His chances of scoring a hit would be greatly reduced.

For the moment, Kevin wasn't worried about taking anybody out. This phase of his assignment didn't require any shooting. He was here to scout and report.

Shouldering the substantive rifle, he began focusing on the old factory, his fingers making minute adjustments to the scope's focus and magnification. He could zoom in 36 times with this optic, and that was just enough at his current distance.

With a closer view, Kevin immediately validated that his father's analysis of the drone's data had been accurate. Like ants working on their hill, he could see several individuals moving around the complex. There were dozens of motorcycles visible near the main building, as well as several campers, two semi-trailers, and a dark grey Mercedes Benz sedan. Bishop had stated that the presence of the German luxury car would eliminate any doubt about where Blackjack's new headquarters was located. Question number one was eliminated. *Base of operations confirmed,* Kevin mused. *No innocent party over there.*

His next priority was to discern any major changes that might have occurred to the structures, grounds, and facilities since the pictures in Verne's book had been published. Scanning slowly with his optic, Kevin noted the signs of nature reclaiming part of the parking lot, the lack of any window glass, and the partial collapse of a smaller outbuilding's roof. Overall, The Crescent Furniture Company had weathered time and the apocalypse well.

Next, Kevin began searching for security. Sentries, dog teams, patrols, strategically placed vehicles, and of course, any sort of overwatch needed to be pinpointed and plotted on his mental map.

The water tower was the obvious location to assign a marksman or two. Surprisingly, Kevin couldn't see anyone on the catwalk or the domed top of the tank. *Now, that is odd*, Kevin thought, pulling his face from the optic and squinting his eyes as if they were somehow missing something. *If I had been asked to provide overwatch for the complex, that tower would have been my first choice.* He recognized that the lofty structure was centrally located, had unobscured lines of sight, and was the ideal height for sniping.

The smokestacks, at least from this angle, were void of human presence as well, but that was no surprise. The ladder-like rungs protruding up the sides of the massive chimneys didn't offer any ledge or flat surface where a man could set up and have a stable shooting platform. That was good news.

Kevin had just begun to doubt his surveillance skills when he finally identified an overwatch team on the roof of the second largest building. They were tucked between two rusting HVAC boxes. Kevin could barely see them from his angle, and that had probably been the point. They were going to be a problem. Pulling a pencil and notepad from his vest, he scribbled their location on the paper.

He began sketching a diagram of the facility, noting what areas seem to be the most popular, and which sections didn't have any foot traffic. Most of his attention, however, was focused on establishing his target priorities. When it came time to fire that first shot, he would have only fractions of a second to adjust his aim and send another round. From the look of things, he was going to have a very long list.

CHAPTER 14

While Kevin scouted the factory, Butter was zipping out of the airport.

Resplendent with fake tattoos, biker club colors, and a chrome-laden Harley, the undercover gang member waved at his friends, popped a wheelie, and accelerated away.

Returning the gesture, Bishop and Grim shook their heads at the sight. "He might actually pull this off," they both said at the same moment.

Taking the detour to avoid Forest Mist, Butter had a 45-minute trip ahead of him. With the wind whipping past his face, the big man was looking forward to the ride.

The machine between his legs was powerful, the freedom of the open road invigorating. Like millions of riding Americans over the decades, Butter appreciated the experience. "I could get used to this," he grinned.

Were it not for the fact that he had an M4 carbine and twenty full magazines of ammunition onboard, it would have been the perfect evening for a relaxing cruise through the countryside. The late afternoon air was cool against his skin, the light soft, the pavement smooth.

As the miles passed, he repeated Bishop and Grim's instructions over and over in his head. Unlike most of their previous SAINT missions, there hadn't been the time to physically rehearse the team's roles and responsibilities. Still, his task was simple and straightforward. He was to penetrate Blackjack's fortress, mingle among the hostiles, and find out where Miss Terri was being held.

Grim had been fairly certain that the hostage would be in the main building, but given the impressive size of the structure, they needed to know exactly where. It was critical to pinpoint her location before the shooting started. Bishop was positive that Blackjack would execute his hostage the moment he realized a rescue attempt was in process.

He crossed into Louisiana without incident, the sun's rays quickly fading behind him. Turning on the bike's headlight, he thought about Kevin, wishing he had been able to go with the little guy. His best friend could shoot, no doubt about that, but when it came to other forms of combat, Butter worried about his slender buddy. "He's tougher than he looks," he whispered, trying to ease his own concerns. "And a hell of a lot smarter than everybody else."

Making the final turn onto the two-lane road leading to the factory, Butter expected he would be stopped soon. There was little doubt that checkpoints and roadblocks would be in place. According to Bishop, the men they were facing were far too professional to leave any approach unguarded.

Cresting a slight rise, Butter spotted them, three pickup trucks illuminated by the circle of his headlight. They were blocking the road, configured in a triangle.

He remembered Grim's advice, "Slow down, but not too quickly. You're late, in a hurry to follow orders. Always keep the mindset that you belong there. You need to report for duty, or you'll be in trouble."

Two men with rifles sprang from behind the trucks, both of them sporting long beards and wearing biker jackets. One of them held up his hand for Butter to stop.

Putting his boot down to steady the bike, Butter rolled to a stop less than 30 yards from the roadblock. A third man then appeared, apparently happy to remain behind the cover of a pickup, his AK braced across the hood and aimed at the stranger.

"You're in the wrong fucking place," the first biker yelled at Butter.

"I don't think so," Butter snapped back as he leaned forward menacingly. "I was told to report to VooDoo. They said Blackjack needed guns, so I got here as soon as I could."

While one of the sentries hung back, the leader slowly circled Butter, shining a flashlight while reading the patches on his jacket. "Why didn't you come in with the rest of the guys?" he asked.

"I was over in Slidell on a job," Butter answered immediately. "It took a little longer than expected. By the time I got back to the clubhouse, everybody had left. I rode all day to catch up."

"What's your name?" the guard challenged.

"Gus. What's your fucking problem?" Butter growled, trying to play the role of the impatient alpha.

The sentry shined the flashlight beam into Butter's eyes, the big man squinting in pain. In a flash, he dismounted the bike, uncoiling his tall frame and squaring his shoulders as if preparing to fight. "You point that thing toward my face again, and I'll rip your fucking head off," he hissed.

The guard wasn't exactly a small gentleman and was definitely not accustomed to being challenged. Butter noticed the flashlight drop as the sentry gripped his rifle with both hands. Fast for such a large man, the biker's arms were a blur as he raised the rifle over his shoulder in preparation to butt stroke the challenger.

Most men would have ducked, pivoted, or tried to twist away from the rapidly accelerating stock. Butter stepped into his attacker, reaching for the descending rifle before it could reach full speed.

The sentry's eyes opened wide when his thrust was stopped cold by Butter's massive arm. A second later, the big kid's fist slammed into the guard's chin with enough force to lift the 300-pound biker off his feet.

As his foe fell to the pavement, Butter managed to maintain his grasp on the guy's rifle.

Before the air had whooshed out of the downed man's chest, Butter flipped the club-rifle around, and aimed it at the second guard.

Despite being men who were accustomed to violence and brawling, the remaining two sentries were stunned. How could a guy so large be so quick on his feet? They had never seen anybody move like that.

"What is your problem?" Butter barked, his body bowed for round two. "Are you fuckers that bored out here? Really, guys, it would be great fun to hang out and arm wrestle with all of you, but I gotta find VooDoo before I get on his shit list. You know how pissy he gets."

Whether to avoid provoking the giant, or still in shock, the three sentries neither spoke nor moved. Seeing that he wasn't about to be attacked again, Butter bent to offer the man on the ground a hand up. "You should keep your left hand a little higher, brother. You were wide open," he offered with a reconciling tone.

Acting like the fight had been nothing more than a ritual challenge worked for all involved. Rubbing his throbbing jaw and trying to blink away the pain, the leader decided to let the stranger pass. "You can find VooDoo by the gray camper, the big one at the south end of the parking lot... and if you ever hit me again, I'll bleed you while you sleep."

Returning to his bike, Butter kicked the starter and engaged the transmission. As he passed, he flipped the guards a bird, laughed loudly, and then accelerated away into the darkness. "I made it," he exhaled after a few seconds. "Thank you, Lord, I made it. Now, off to find Miss Terri. Bishop and Grim will be coming soon."

Pat Gibson knocked softly on Marshal Plummer's door, a small stack of documents in her hand. The prosecutor wasn't happy.

"The judge has signed the release papers for Mr. Jones," she announced while handing the lawman his copy of the forms. "He is free to go."

Nodding without comment, Plummer rose from his desk and summoned Allison from the front. "Get the men ready. We're going to take Whip to his son and bring back Terri."

"What are you going to do if Ketchum changes his mind?" Gibson asked.

The natural expression on Plummer's face changed instantly, the glare of anger mixed with stress boring into the prosecutor. It was clear she had struck a nerve. He started to say something but then caught himself. Finally, after a deep breath, he muttered, "I don't know. I guess I'll solve that problem if it arises."

"I don't think you want to come back without Miss Terri, Marshal. That's not a threat from me, but it is sound advice. I know Bishop. I know his friends in Alpha and West Texas. He'll take it personally, and I don't think you have any concept of what that man is capable of."

"Oh, I've got a pretty good idea," Plummer snapped. "He's not been in town a week, and we're still notifying the next of kin."

Shaking her head, Pat said, "The last few days have been relatively mild, Marshal. Bishop has, in my opinion, shown remarkable restraint. He has only defended himself; he has not gone on the offensive. Seriously, I'd bring back either Whipsaw or Terri. If you even catch of hint of foul play on Ketchum's part, get back here with his father, and I'll figure out a legal reason to hold him. If you lose that bargaining chip, there's no telling how far this will go."

Butter wasn't impressed.

After rolling into Blackjack's compound, he had followed the sentry's directions toward the camper. He had no intention of finding this VooDoo fellow. His job was to locate Miss Terri and wait for Bishop and Grim.

253

A dozen 50-gallon drums had been repurposed as fire pits, each of the smoking barrels surrounded by small clusters of people. Butter heard laughter, spotted several of the men drinking what appeared to be moonshine, and smelled the unmistakable odor of someone smoking weed. It was, by all appearances, more of a beer bash than an armed camp. *Some professionals! I can not believe I shaved my head for this,* Butter mused, shaking his head at the party animals.

There was also an interesting mixture of people, or more specifically, uniforms. Motorcycle club jackets were the clear clothing of choice by the majority, but Butter also noticed two men wearing the moniker "SHERIFF," in bold yellow letters across their backs. There was a surprising number of women, most of them wearing the kind of clothing that said "eye candy" instead of "Special Forces."

Rolling slowly across the parking lot, he also spotted three men wearing military fatigues, and several others in blue jeans and polo shirts.

He estimated that the mix of men versus women was about 60 to 40 percent. Again, for an invading militia, the number of females seemed high.

He pulled his bike to an area that was apparently a popular parking spot, the big man lining his ride up with 20 other machines already residing in a neat row. After dropping the kickstand and switching off the idling motor, Butter dismounted and pulled on a backpack filled with spare magazines over one shoulder, his carbine sling resting on the other.

Music and laughter overwhelmed the background noise, the ambiance definitely festive. As he began scanning the area, a woman sauntered toward him, tossing back her bleach-blonde hair, a definite wiggle in her walk.

"Hi, you're cute," she giggled, the smell of alcohol strong on her breath. "And a such a big boy, too," she cooed, reaching up to rub Butter's bicep. "Wanna party with me and my friend?"

Without waiting for an answer, she turned at yelled to someone in the distance. "Hey! Ginger! Come over here and see what I found!"

"I've got to find a guy named..." he began to protest.

"Ginger! Get your ass over here, girl. Right now!" the woman shouted again, her barely-covered breasts heaving under the thin tube top.

Butter swept the surrounding clusters of people, hoping the woman's obnoxious, shrill yelling wouldn't attract any unwanted attention.

Sure enough, a red-haired girl abandoned the main celebration, rushing to her friend, scoping out Butter as she approached. "Oh my," she chirped as she gave him the once over, "work out much, big boy?"

Embarrassed, worried that any interaction would blow his cover, Butter stumbled to find a way out of the encounter. Before he could react, Ginger's hand was fondling his crotch. "Are *all* of your muscles as large as your arms?" she flirted.

Noting that several people were now staring in his direction, Butter reached down and scooped up both admirers, easily lifting one in each arm. "Let's go find out!" he laughed, pivoting as if to swagger away with his dual prize.

Laughter broke out from the nearest group huddled around a burning barrel, one of the men there raising his plastic cup in salute of the newcomer's apparent conquest.

Carrying both women toward a darker spot, Butter confided, "Listen, ladies... I just rolled into camp, so I need to wet my whistle before we get started. After that, I hope you girls are up for a good time. Now, which one of you knows a place where we can party in private?"

"We could go to my tent," Ginger offered, "but I think Butch is passed out in there. He snores like a pig, and there's not much room."

"How about the offices?" the blonde suggested, her words a bit slurred. "We can stop on the way and get you a drink."

255

"Haven't you heard?" Ginger countered. "We're not supposed to go around the main building. The guys will get mad if we wander over there. It's off limits."

Butter set them down and pointed to Ginger. "You go get me a cup of something strong." Then redirecting his finger at the blonde, he continued, "And you go find us someplace where we can stretch out and get this little party started. I have to warn you though, I need lots of room to operate. But first, I have to find VooDoo and report in; then I'll meet you both back here."

The two women seemed disappointed at the delay. Ginger pouted, "Okay," as she reached up to kiss Butter on the cheek.

Miss Bleach-bottle lifted her top and squeezed her ample breasts together, "Don't get distracted and forget about these."

After the two girls scampered off, Butter headed for the main building, counting his steps as he walked. Ducking around an inky black corner, he made sure he was out of sight and alone. He pulled an earpiece from his pocket and plugged it into the small digital radio hiding inside his vest. After powering up the 2-way unit, he double-checked the frequency displayed. "SAINT-3? You there?" he broadcasted, using their old team designations.

"Affirmative," Kevin's voice sounded loud and clear. "In position. What is your status?"

"On schedule. No issues. No significant changes detected so far. I'm going to start hunting the primary, over."

"Good. I'll let S1 and S2 know, over."

"Tell S1 and S2 that the main building is approximately 92 meters directly west from the main cluster of fire barrels in the middle of the compound."

"Excellent," Kevin replied. "I'll relay the message, if possible. Hey, while you're there, can you get eyes on the water tower clearly?"

Poking his head around the corner for a quick glance, Butter could indeed see the structure in question from the flickering light of the fires. "Yes," he responded into the microphone.

"I haven't observed anybody manning a post there," Kevin continued. "I'm worried I'm missing something. It's too good a position to simply pass up."

Dropping back into the shadows, Butter dug around in his pack and produced his night vision. Anxious that such an advanced piece of kit might be suspicious, he had intended to wait until the real party began before clipping it onto his rifle.

With only the small lenses peeking around the corner, he scanned the tower. "I don't see anybody either," Butter transmitted. "Maybe it's not stable enough. It looks like there are holes rusted through the sides."

"Wait one," Kevin responded. "Switching to thermal."

It took Kevin a bit to attach his thermal optic to his rifle. After booting the device, he focused on the tower and let out a low whistle.

The advanced optic's display was on a setting of "White is hot." Manufactured to sense differences in temperature rather than the normal visible spectrum of light, people with their 98.6-degree body heat glowed brightly with a halo like biblical angels.

Different types of materials absorbed heat at different rates, which made them discernable as well. The roof's black tar was distinctive and definable compared to the cold, concrete block walls of the structures. Windows were black. Hot motorcycle engines were even brighter than people.

Focusing in on the water tower, Kevin noticed an odd pattern of hot and cold in the circular image of the infrared's display. It took him only a few seconds to figure it out. "Holy cow! They're in there all right," he broadcasted. "They've cut rifle slits in the side of the tank. This is a big problem."

"I don't copy, S3?" Butter whispered into his mic. "What's a big problem?"

"The guards are stationed inside the tank and have made holes in it only large enough to shoot through. At this range, the slits are too small for me to maneuver a bullet through, and even if I could, there's no guarantee that I would hit anything inside, let alone take out one of the overwatches. They'll cut S1 and S2 to pieces from there."

Butter could see it now and understood. Ducking back into the darkness, he said, "Let me see what I can do. Maybe I can get up there and take them out myself."

"We've got to do something," Kevin hissed. "That's a showstopper."

"On it right after I find the target, over."

"Over."

After putting away his gear, Butter hurried toward the main entrance to the big plant. His groupies had indicated that this particular building was off limits, so he believed it was probably being used as the hostage holding area. It was the same structure where Bishop and Grim had speculated Miss Terri would be detained. "On my way, Miss Terri," Butter whispered.

CHAPTER 15

Bishop hoisted the parachute onto his back, his stomach swirling with queasiness. It has been over a decade since he had jumped, the West Texan's mind traveling back to Fort Benning and the three-week course he had attended there.

Grim tried to soothe his friend's jitters. "We'll be fine," the older man assured. "It's like riding a bike, you never forget."

Bishop nervously disagreed. "That's bullshit, and you know it. I did five jumps during that course, and they were all static line departures. I had to close my eyes, pray, and not shit myself. Only one of them was at night, and I was so damn scared, I don't even remember it."

"We'll have on our radios. These fancy chutes Verne found at the airport's skydiving school are far more advanced than those old models Uncle Sam loaned us. They're safer, and you can control them a lot better. Just listen to my instructions as we're falling, and we'll peg the landing."

With shaking hands, Bishop managed to strap on his reserve parachute. That backup device did little to improve his outlook. "Think about Terri," he whispered, trying to push down the fear and replace it with anger.

His plan didn't work very well, nor did hearing Grim's next statement. "I jumped into Panama back in '89 with the 504th. It was the first night combat jump the 82nd Airborne had attempted since WWII. We were all scared shitless as well, but it worked. We only had a handful of guys that were blown off-course."

"Only a handful?" Bishop quipped. "Just a few of the trained paratroopers, who had fresh skills, expert leadership, and top-notch intelligence, didn't land in the right place? What if I break a leg? What if the roof of that big building is rotten and I fall through? This the most idiotic idea ever, from a guy who is credited with a long string of stupid plans."

"Unless you can figure out a better way for us to get inside that factory without your wife being executed, we don't have any choice," Grim countered. "Look at it this way, Blackjack and his boys won't be looking for an airborne assault. They'll figure nobody would ever be so dumb as to try such a thing, and that might just be enough."

Before Bishop could respond, the pilot appeared in the doorway. "Ready when you are, sir."

Given the seriousness of the guards posted outside what had been the factory's offices, Butter was confident Terri was being held inside.

Just to be double-sure, Butter approached the closest sentry.

This guy wasn't a biker, striking the big man as ex-military type. The sentry's expression told Butter that he didn't appreciate the lack of discipline being exhibited by the rest of Blackjack's forces.

"Hey," Butter greeted the man, noting his fatigues and load vest. "I heard the boss is going to let us have a crack at this bitch soon. She killed two of my brothers, and I'm itching to make her pay."

"Your fucking brothers were incompetent," the guy barked. "They were way, way too sure of themselves and got their asses handed to them. I don't know what Blackjack is going to do with that woman inside. Now piss off, before I call VooDoo over here and tell him you're causing trouble."

"Chill out, dude," Butter responded, his arms spreading wide in surrender. "I was just asking.... Jezzz."

Now that Butter had accomplished his primary mission, he started thinking about that damn water tower. Even over the radio, he could detect worry in Kevin's voice, and his friend never got nervous.

"S3, primary objective confirmed," Butter broadcasted to Kevin. "Heading for the water tower. Cover me if you can."

"Roger that," crackled the sniper's voice.

They were wheels up, the vast cargo aircraft barely clearing the trees at the end of the runway. "I'm going to circle west so we can gain altitude. It's only going to be a 15-minute flight, sir, so you'd better go on back and get ready."

"We should have catapulted ourselves in," Grim chuckled, "as close as the drop zone is, a slingshot might have even worked."

"The wind is out of the west at 17-mph at deployment altitude," the pilot's voice informed them a few minutes later. "At 2,500 feet, you'll have an easy drift to the east. It should be enough to keep the hostiles on the ground from hearing our engine noise."

"Roger that," Grim replied, pulling his night vision goggles down from the brim of his helmet. Bishop, his heart pounding like a sledgehammer, did the same. "Going to tactical frequency."

Bishop watched as Grim's gloved hands adjusted the dial on his radio. It was almost a full second before he realized he was supposed to do the same thing.

"SAINT 3, SAINT 3, do you read me?" Grim transmitted.

Faint, with static, Kevin's voice sounded over the airwaves.

"Affirmative, S2, I read you. Conditions are green. I repeat, conditions are green. Good luck."

With his eyes still wide, Bishop watched as Grim again switched his radio and let the pilots know that they were indeed going to jump out of a perfectly functional airplane. The West Texan's mind desperately tried to think of an excuse, any reason whatsoever, why he shouldn't go along with this insanity.

It seemed like only a few seconds passed before the huge cargo door started lowering at the back of the plane. The hurricane-like sound of rushing wind filled the fuselage, Bishop suddenly wondering if he would be able to hear Grim's voice over the radio.

There was a yellow flashing light, then Grim's hand on his shoulder, gently nudging his petrified friend toward the opening.

The light changed colors, switching to a bright green strobe. "Go! Go! Go!" Grim shouted, pushing Bishop toward the ramps. "Go!"

On the weakest legs he could ever remember, Bishop pushed off into the black inkwell that was the night. Memories of his training raced through his mind as the roaring gust raced past his ears.

As he accelerated into the freefall, Bishop's stomach experienced a sensation like that of riding a roller coaster as it dropped off a hill. Already queasy, it took all his concentration not to hurl. The jump was cold, loud, and confusing. "Remember your training," he hissed through gritted teeth. "Spread your arms. Control the horizon. Maintain level descent."

It was like falling into a giant, empty, black hole. From that height, Bishop couldn't see any lights, colors, or features of the ground below. It was only when his eyes traveled high did he see the stars twinkling brightly above. The view saved his supper.

Something touched his shoulder, and for a panicked second, Bishop thought something was wrong. Looking over, he could make out Grim's silhouette, his friend waving boldly as they plunged together.

"Can you hear me?" Grim's voice screeched through the Texan's earpiece.

"Yes," Bishop replied. "Five by five."

"Good. Get ready to deploy in three, two, one. Now!"

Bishop released his pilot chute while tucking his chin firmly against his chest. He heard the main canopy flying from its case before feeling the bone-jarring shock as it filled with air and dramatically slowed his descent from its 120-mph terminal velocity to just under 15 feet per second.

Once he'd recovered his wits, Bishop glanced up to see the canopy full and wide. "At least you're not going to end up a greasy spot in some Cajun's yard," he smiled. "You'll land safely, right in the middle of Blackjack's machine gunners."

"Pull your right riser," Grim instructed into Bishop's ear. "More... more... release."

The ex-contractor had told Bishop that they would be floating in the sky for just over four minutes. Finally assured that his death wasn't going to be due to gravity, the amateur jumper inhaled and took in the view.

After 30 seconds, he could understand why people liked to skydive for recreation. It was so quiet and peaceful, the calm welcoming after the drone of aircraft engines and the initial blast of wind. The air was cool but soft. The darkness was no longer hostile, morphing into a sensory retreat that lacked light, noise, or distraction. The stars above glowed with a splendor that surpassed even his native West Texas skies.

"Left riser," Grim ordered, his voice interrupting the tranquility. "More," the older man repeated. Then, "I see their fires. Our glide is lining up perfectly."

Looking down, Bishop could now see small specks of light below. They were a stark reminder of what was about to come.

"S3 and S4, two minutes. I repeat, two minutes," Grim transmitted to Butter and Kevin. "Engage."

"SAINT 3 to SAINT 4," Kevin transmitted. "I can't get close enough to snipe that tower in time. They'll be landing in 120 seconds. What is your status?"

"I'm climbing up the ladder right now," Butter replied, his hand on the first rung.

"Okay, but be careful. You don't know their process or security."

Butter scampered up, hoping to get close enough to the tank before anybody noticed his trespass. He estimated there were about 50 rungs. He needed to hurry.

Halfway up, he spied the overwatch team of marksmen on the main roof. They had seen him too, the spotter pointing at Butter and shouting, "Hey, what the fuck are you doing, you drunk asshole?"

Waving with a friendly gesture, Butter yelled back, "I'm taking my brother a drink, limp dick. Go fuck yourself."

Climbing rapidly now, Butter watched as the spotter and rifleman debated, and then came to an agreement. He inhaled sharply when the barrel of the serious rifle swung his way. There was no way they would miss at this range.

He could see the glass of the sniper's optic reflecting in the light from the barrels, confirming he was, indeed, the target.

Just over 700 meters to the west, Kevin's .338 pushed hard against his shoulder. Working the bolt in a blur of well-practiced movement, he chambered another round and acquired the second target. It was 2.3 seconds before his first shot would impact.

Just as Butter saw the marksman's rifle fly into the air, Kevin squeezed the trigger for the second shot.

Stunned to see his partner's head explode into a red cloud of mist, the spotter just stood there with his mouth open, trying to blink away the gristle and flesh that had sprayed his face. By the time he started to turn, Kevin's second, massive, 285-grain bullet slammed into his chest like a sledgehammer, shredding both of his lungs while simultaneously powdering five vertebrae.

Butter whispered, "Thanks little, buddy," and was moving again, hurrying up the ladder as fast as his over-sized frame could climb.

He approached the catwalk but kept on going. While he'd never been part of a water tower assault before, he assumed the door would be located on top.

Sure enough, he discovered a heavy metal trapdoor on the tank's sloped roof. As someone inside shouted, "What is going on?" Butter dropped through the opening, his hand reaching for his knife.

There were three of Blackjack's men inside the confined space. One of them had just witnessed Kevin's shots obliterate their brother team. Reaching for the radio, he was desperate to call for help.

The second member was lighting a cigarette, his butane lighter temporarily causing him to lose his night vision.

Team member number three, hearing his buddy call out, moved for the nearest rifle slit with a pair of binoculars in his hand. He barely noticed Butter's boots as they dropped through the air.

The last place any man in Texas wanted to be was in a close-quarters fight with Butter. The tank, however, was soon to hold its own special place in Hell's Hall of Fame.

There was little light inside, and no place to run. Butter enjoyed the element of surprise, and the six-inch blade in his hand was honed to a razor's edge. Within seconds, the tranquil interior of the water tower was transformed into a metal cage of horror.

In a flash, the sentry with the binoculars was down, Butter's slash across his throat so brutal it nearly decapitated the man. Squirting fountains of blood arched across the interior as the big guy pivoted, his second thrust lifting the radio holder's boots completely off the floor as the knife plunged hilt-deep into his sternum.

The guard taking a cigarette break was the lucky one, for a few seconds at least. Losing his balance on the slick, uneven floor, Butter fell, landing beside the remaining sentry with a loud thud.

Before Blackjack's marksman could exhale his chest full of smoke, Butter's palms wrapped around his throat.

It was a natural reaction for the guard to reach for the hands now encircling his windpipe. Grasping for the two wrists crushing his throat, he exerted all his adrenaline-power strength against the hold.

Realizing he wasn't going to move the two iron pipes holding his neck, he tried to strike down on Butter's arms, but the grip on his jugular only tightened. His oxygen-starved brain then went berserk, kicking, thrashing, and flexing every muscle in a vain attempt to twist away.

Not knowing how many men were stationed inside, Butter could not take the time to choke his victim out. Torqueing on the flesh in his grip with an animalistic growl of exertion, his massive arms applied all the force they could muster. A faint popping noise signaled the surrender of the hapless gent's spine. His legs spasmed twice, and then the body in the big man's grip went limp.

Rolling hard, Butter braced for another foe to come forward, but none did. After two deep breaths to regain his composure, he found his radio's mic and panted, "S4 to all SAINT. The tower is clear. I repeat, the tower is clear."

Bishop heard Butter's broadcast, but it didn't register. He knew the factory's roof covered several acres, but from his current position, it looked like a postage stamp.

Trailing behind, Grim kept talking the West Texan down from his heavenly perch. "Left riser," the old contractor's voice ordered. "More. Less. That's good."

Knowing he was going to land soon, Bishop recalled what his instructors at Benning had taught. He could still hear the Black Hats' instructions about how to use the five points of impact at touchdown. "Absorb the energy of the landing by letting the kinetic force travel up your side. Bend your knees and roll. Don't absorb the force up the center of your body. Channel it to the side," they had drilled over and over again.

When he dangled about 100 feet above the roof, it occurred to Bishop that there was no way Grim could have the right perspective. "How could he see where we are heading?" the West Texan whispered. "He's behind and above me!"

Convinced he was going to come down short of the target, Bishop slowed the chute's descent. "What are you doing?" Grim snapped a moment later. "Get down! Get down now! Let her drop!"

Too late, Bishop realized he'd just messed up. Watching as the rooftop began racing under his boots, he spied the edge of the structure coming toward him. He was about to overshoot the ridge, almost out of real estate. He opened both risers as far as he could. At five feet from the gutter, his boots hit the surface. One running step, two, and then the momentum hurled him over the edge.

In that moment, Bishop noticed the ground racing toward him, and then a neck-snapping jerk halted his fall. Surprised he hadn't smashed into the earth, he peered up and soon realized that his chute had caught on the corner of the factory's roof.

Suspended 30 feet above the parking lot below, Bishop had never felt so helpless. His weapon was strapped to the pack on his back and out of reach. He was just hanging there.

After recovering his wits, Bishop thought to pull himself up the canopy's suspension lines. Reaching above his head, he grasped the thin cord and tugged... hard

Climbing the chute's lines was difficult; they were thin, slick, and not designed for scaling. On his third attempt, Bishop heard the sickening sound of tearing cloth right before he dropped several feet.

"Shit," he hissed, realizing that the canopy's thin material wasn't going to hold him.

Grim's head appeared over the edge of the roof just then, "Be still, dipshit. This thing is barely holding you."

Relieved that his comrade had made a safe landing and could now help, Bishop did as Grim instructed. The West Texan didn't know what his buddy had in mind, but given his circumstances, it had to be better than staying where he was.

Bishop could feel Grim heaving and pulling on his lines. He was raised a foot, then another, then another. "You could stand to shed a few pounds," a hoarse whisper from above grumbled.

Before Grim could tug again, movement from below drew the Bishop's eye. A man with an AK47 walked around the corner, his hands fumbling for something in his pocket.

Bishop froze, and so did Grim, both men afraid that any motion would draw the sentry's gaze skyward. That would be the end of it, the Texan the perfect swinging target.

The guard removed a cigar from his pocket and flipped open a zippo. Bishop could smell the smoke drifting upward.

A minute passed, Blackjack's gunman happily puffing away 30 feet below Bishop's boots.

"There you are," another voice boomed, a second man joining the first cigar smoker. "Got another one?"

Great, Bishop thought. *Just great. Next thing you know, they'll be discussing the football playoffs.*

Sure enough, a second stogie was produced, lit, and consumed. The new arrival fancied himself a skilled smoker, blowing perfect smoke rings into the Louisiana night. *Don't look up*, Bishop prayed.

After five minutes, Bishop's mind was screaming for Grim to just shoot them. He had a cancelation device on his weapon, didn't he? He had subsonic ammo. Why wasn't his weapon spitting lead? *Take them out, damn it! Put them down before they kill me and alert the entire compound!* he thought.

At nine minutes, the two men below snuffed out their cigars and retreated around the corner.

Again, Bishop's bumpy elevator ride proceeded. Halfway up the wall, Grim seemed to be running out of steam. "Are you that fucking old?" Bishop hissed toward the roof. "My balls are hanging out here, just waiting to be cut off."

"Don't you give me any shit," Grim's voice gasped from the roof in response. "This isn't easy."

Finally, Bishop was securely positioned on the roof, an exhausted, panting Grim rubbing his aching arms. "You need to hit the road with some running shoes, fat boy," the older man protested. "Damn, you've put on weight. Does Pete serve ice cream in his bars?"

Ignoring his friend's complaints, Bishop went about getting out of the harness and unpacking his weapon. It felt good to have the carbine in his hands.

"Why didn't you just shoot those two?" he finally remembered to ask.

"I forgot to screw on my can before we jumped," Grim admitted, his head hanging in embarrassment. "There was just so much going on... I...."

Bishop surprised his old friend by laughing. "We're not SAINT; we're CLOWNS. Clueless, lost, overwhelmed, whining, numb, shitheads. Forget about it. We both fucked up. Let's go get Terri."

Just as Grim nodded his agreement, strobing blue and red lights flashed across the compound. The two rescuers turned to observe several police cars approaching the factory's front gate. "That would be Plummer," Bishop said. "We're too late. He's here to make the swap."

"Shit," Grim barked, glancing at his watch. "He's early!"

"Not by much," Bishop announced, shaking his head. "We, the newly formed CLOWNS, were late."

"We don't have time to get your wife?" Grim asked, already knowing the answer.

"No. They'll be going in to get her. All that we can do now is wait and watch, make sure the exchange goes as planned," Bishop sighed, the disappointment thick in his voice.

The plan had been to secure his wife before Plummer arrived with Whipsaw. With Terri safely out of Blackjack's grasp, Plummer could have declared the swap null and void. Mr. Jones would remain in custody and eventually face a jury of his peers.

"S1 to SAINT," Bishop stated into his mic. "We're too late. Go to Mission Profile B. Let's make sure they release the hostage as agreed, and then get the hell out of here."

"Sometimes you get the bear, and sometimes the bear gets you," Grim mumbled, moving to take up an overwatch position.

"S4 to SAINT," sounded Butter's voice. "I'll stay in the tower. I've got a good view from up here."

"S3 to SAINT," Kevin transmitted. "I'm now 350 meters west-southwest, still in the ditch. I've got a good angle. Egress to my position after the exchange, and I'll give you gents a ride home."

CHAPTER 16

From the roof, Bishop watched as the five police cruisers pulled into a straight line at the far end of the parking lot. Deputies with long guns began pouring from the vehicles.

Blackjack's end of the lot was full of motion as well, his men all rushing to gather around and witness the victorious event.

Plummer appeared from the middle car, the lanky lawman's western hat visible in the light. He stepped to the car's back door and helped Whipsaw Jones exit the cramped seat.

The marshal fumbled in his shirt pocket for a moment, eventually producing a key and removing the cuffs that were securing his prisoner. Rubbing his wrists, Ketchum's father allowed Plummer to guide him to the circle produced by the squad car's headlights.

VooDoo and Blackjack exited the furniture plant's front door just then. Between them faltered a woman, a sack of dark cloth covering her to the waist. "What an ass," Bishop gripped to Grim, watching from the roof. "Keeping the hood on her to the last moment. This guy must be compensating for his substandard manhood."

They guided the captive down the stairs, the frightened woman stumbling badly at one point. VooDoo barely managed to hold her upright, and after stabilizing the hostage, guided her to the parking lot. "She's so scared she can hardly walk," Grim observed.

"Either that or they've beat the shit out of her," Bishop hissed. He wanted to kill Blackjack right there and then. It would be an easy shot. He could get VooDoo and a dozen more while he was at it.

Knowing his wife would never survive if he initiated a firefight, Bishop held his temper and just watched as Terri was pointed toward Plummer and his crew.

On shaky legs, the hooded woman slowly advanced toward the marshal. At the same time, Plummer pushed Whipsaw forward.

The two former prisoners passed each other at the halfway point, both thinking they were heading for freedom.

When the hooded captive reached Plummer, the marshal quickly reached for the cloth covering her head and torso. Pulling it off, Bishop saw the lawman's eyes open wide as the hostage's head appeared.

In a flash, Plummer's gaze shot to the spot where Whipsaw was hugging his son. Bishop, following the marshal's surprised expression, noticed Blackjack extending the antenna on some sort of remote control device. "Oh shit!" Bishop snapped, raising his carbine.

Ketchum pushed a button.

A red and yellow fireball ripped through the place where Plummer and Terri had been standing, the hostage's vest laced with explosives and wrapped in nails.

Bishop, his mouth open, couldn't breathe, his mind reeling from just seeing his wife... the love of his life... the mother of his child vanish in the blast. "Terri!" he screamed, unable to move. "Oh God! No! No!"

Bedlam erupted in the parking lot, the few deputies who survived the detonation recovering quickly from their shock and awe. Somebody fired a shot, then another. Within 10 seconds, lead was flying from all directions.

Only a handful of Plummer's men had survived the enormous blast, and they were completely outgunned. Bishop couldn't move, his mind still trying to cope with his mate's violent death.

"S1! S1! Come in, Bishop," Butter's frantic voice called out. "Bishop, are you there?"

"What?" the stunned Texan managed to bark. "What do you want, Butter?"

"Did Miss Terri have a tramp stamp?" the big man asked over the airwaves.

"Huh? What are you talking about?" Bishop replied, any thought of radio procedure impossible in his current state.

"A tattoo... just above her... on the small of her back?" Butter asked.

"No, Terri didn't have any ink," Bishop answered, his mind now at the point of overload, barely able to function.

"Then that wasn't Miss Terri they just killed," Butter broadcasted. "I saw that woman nearly fall on the steps as they escorted her out. Her shirt was pulled up, and I swear she had a tattoo on her back. Your wife must still be in the building, sir. Whoever that dead woman was, she must have been a decoy!"

Blinking as he tried to process what Butter was saying, Grim appeared close to the West Texan's face. "Did you get that?" the old contractor was shouting above the firefight below. "That wasn't Terri! Snap out of it! Unfuck your brain! We still have to go get your wife!"

It all suddenly made sense to Bishop. The look of shock on Plummer's face. The long hood as a disguise. Summoning all his willpower, the Texan rose and demanded, "Let's go!"

Kevin's discovery of Ketchum's overwatch team had solved another issue for the rescuers. If there were men stationed on the factory's roof, there had to be some way for them to access their position. Shift changes and bathroom breaks would have demanded an easy way up and down.

Running to the location where the two sniped men were still lying, Grim found a low doorway that led to a metal stairwell. In a flash, they were clanking down the steps, weapons high and looking for work.

They reached the main floor in seconds, the dark interior eliminated by the night vision goggles over each man's eyes.

Silently and swiftly, the duo moved toward the main section of the building, passing by rusting hulks of old machinery and abandoned equipment. Grim pointed toward the floor, a trail of boot prints visible in the dust. "The overwatch teams on the roof left us breadcrumbs," he whispered.

They spotted a door ahead, a small square of glass emitting light from inside the section that contained offices. A man stood there, his attention drawn toward the window. *I hate armchair rubberneckers, craning to see what is happening with all the gunfire while they watch from the safety of all the flying lead,* Bishop observed.

In a flash, Grim's blaster spit three rounds, the incoming bullets sending the sentry into a death spiral as he collapsed to the floor.

A quick glance through the window showed an empty, dark hallway beyond. At the far end, they could discern what appeared to be candlelight flickering its uneven shadow against the wall.

In they went, moving with purpose, one against each side of the corridor, their weapons ready should any human shape appear at the distant wall.

Reaching the intersection, Grim started to pie the crossway, moving his body a few degrees at a time to ensure no one was hiding just around the corner. Seeing what his friend was about to do, Bishop waved him back, pointed the M4, and punched four, neat holes into the plaster at waist level. "We don't have time," he whispered.

They approached a series of doorways, the hall littered with yellowed papers, dusty old office chairs, and disheveled desks. After passing by the last threshold, Grim peeked down another corridor and raised a tight fist high into the air. "Hold," was the unspoken message. "I see something."

Slowly, Bishop took his turn, popping in and out of the opening, exposing himself just long enough to get a glance.

274

Two sentries were posted down there, bookending a single door. This had to be Terri's cell.

Exchanging a nod, Bishop and Grim rushed into the passage, both of their weapons spitting nearly silent bullets. The pair of guards went down, neither managing to even raise their weapon.

The two rescuers tried the knob and found it locked. Bishop was sizing up the metal door, preparing for a kick, when Grim motioned his intent to frisk the dead thug at his feet. A few seconds later, the old contractor produced a ring holding a single key.

With the Texan covering the opening, Grim inserted the key and opened the latch. Inside they found a surprised Terri, sitting in a chair, surrounded by darkness.

With the light flooding the room, she squinted toward the opening. Adjusting quickly, she cried, "Bishop?" a moment before being encircled by her husband's arms.

"Oh my God! Bishop! You don't know...."

"I thought you were dead," he gushed, both of their faces quickly damp with streaming tears. He could see the bruise on the side of her face. He could smell the fear in her hair.

Grim, covering the open door, let them go while he checked the surrounding area. There was another locked office just across the hall, and again, he fished a key from a dead sentry. "Did this assworm have more than one hostage?" he mumbled, working the lock.

Ready to spray the interior, he was shocked at what his flashlight beam illuminated. Inside were cases of ammunition, rockets, two belt-fed machine guns, and several crates of hand grenades. "Holy shit!" the old contractor hissed at the arsenal. "Was this guy planning an invasion?"

For a second, Grim thought about tossing in one of his own grenades but then decided against it. They needed to get out of there. The bad guys would eventually figure out their hostage was missing, and the bigger the head start, the better the chance of their survival.

Pivoting to return to Terri's cell, Grim stated, "I don't mean to spoil the class reunion, but we've got to get out of here."

"Come on," Bishop said, pulling his wife to her feet. "Grim's right. We don't have much time. Can you walk?"

He could see her better now, and she was in bad shape. There was a hollowness in her eyes, a hesitation in her movements. *She's taken a beating, survived a firefight, and has been locked in a dark room,* he assessed. *But she'll be okay.*

Nodding that she could walk, Terri rose and stepped toward the door. As she passed the two dead sentries, she bent and scooped up an AR15. "I am *not* going back in that room," she informed her husband.

They reversed course, Grim radioing their teammates an update, informing them that Miss Terri was indeed okay, and that they were heading for the north end of the factory. "Take anybody out that gets in our way," he ordered. "We'll bug out for the rally point from there."

Butter climbed out of the water tower upon hearing the news. Blackjack's men had just finished off the last deputy and were now gathered around the shot-up police cars. It sounded like a celebration was about to begin.

Clinging to the shadows, he darted toward where he thought Bishop and Grim might come out of the factory with Miss Terri.

As Terri and her rescuers hurried through the plant, she said, "Blackjack will be pissed to high heaven when he figures out I'm no longer his prize. I'm worried about what he might do."

They approached a side door, Grim transmitting, "SAINT, we're coming out. Hold your fire."

Pushing out into the night, the trio then started hustling for the ditch where Kevin would be waiting. More than once, Terri tripped and almost fell. She was struggling to keep up.

Butter appeared from behind a pile of discarded lumber just 20 meters away, waving to his teammates to follow. The big man smiled broadly when Miss Terri came into view.

"Are you okay?" he asked, jogging to catch up with the team. Before she could answer, she stumbled again. In a flash, Butter scooped her up in one arm and then began sprinting.

"Thanks," Terri said from his shoulder, breathing hard from the exertion.

It took 15 minutes for them to circle around and rendezvous with Kevin, the team's marksman hugging Terri with glee. "I thought there for a second...."

"Her name was Kitty," Terri sniffed, her emotions welling back up to the surface. "She was about my height and size. I overheard Ketchum convincing her to put on the vest. He said the explosives were fake, that they just to play a joke on Marshal Plummer. I think she knew they were real. I think she understood what was about to happen."

"Let's get out of here," Bishop suggested. "Who knows what Blackjack is going to do now."

"He has his father back," Butter offered as the team prepared to move. "Why would he do anything but crawl back into his hole?"

"I'm with Bishop," Terri said. "That man is evil, and doesn't like to lose, even a portion of the game. We need to get out of here before he figures out I've been snatched from right under his nose."

With Kevin in the lead, they began hiking for the Jeep. Careful to avoid the boobytraps, their marksman led them through the woods using the exact same route he'd taken on the way in.

They arrived at Verne's Jeep and began pulling off the brush and limbs Kevin had left for camo. With five in their party and a lot of gear, Grim and Butter were forced to ride on the running boards. The extra weight soon proved to be a problem.

Despite trying to avoid the low area that nearly snagged him on the way in, Kevin struggled to keep them moving while mud flew from all four tires. Halfway back to the road, the Jeep stopped moving.

"No problem," Butter announced, jumping off with a grin.

After passing Terri his weapon, the big guy stepped to the back and said, "Give it some gas, Kevin."

Grim joined him a second later, both of the warriors putting their backs into the effort. After a few turns of the tires, the Jeep lurched forward. "Keep going!" Butter yelled, "We'll catch up at the road."

"Speak for yourself, Kid!" Grim complained, hustling to keep up as Kevin accelerated toward the pavement. "I've got blisters."

Five minutes later, with Grim and Butter jogging along behind, Kevin pulled onto the safety of the blacktop. "It's going to take you two whole days to wash Verne's Jeep," Bishop teased. "You should really be more respectful of other people's property!"

Laughing, Butter and Grim returned to their positions on the running boards, the duo reminding Bishop of riding on the rails of a Little Bird helicopter back in the day.

"Wagons Hoooo!" Kevin shouted, waving his arm through the air like the trail boss in an old Western movie.

Ketchum was pleased with the results of the evening. Patting his father on the back, the two wandered away from the crowd gathered around the dead cops. A party had already broken out, the survivors in the mood to celebrate their awesome triumph over the despised police.

"Come on, Dad, I've got a surprise for you," Ketchum said to Whipsaw.

Following behind his son, Whip was led to a large motorhome at the far end of the lot. Instructing his father to stay put, Blackjack stepped inside and emerged a minute later carrying a single bottle of scotch whiskey. "It's a Macallan, single malt, over 25 years old," Ketchum bragged. "I've been saving it for a special occasion."

Whipsaw smiled, indicating that his son should open the bottle. Ketchum was happy to oblige, producing two glasses from his pocket like a magician pulling a rabbit from his hat.

After the two men had downed a shot of the fiery liquid, Whip smacked his lips and said, "Damn, that is good. Given I've been rotting away in a jail cell for the last few days, I believe I'll have another."

As his son poured a second swig, the older Jones turned back to glance at the still-burning police cars. "I don't mind you killing Dallas Plummer at all. Believe me, late at night in that closet he called a cell, I planned that old bastard's demise a dozen times. I am sorry about the woman though. She was connected out in Alpha. I'm worried that might come back to haunt us."

"Oh, I didn't kill Bishop's wife," Ketchum grinned. "That was some crack-head biker bitch that tagged along when we left New Orleans. Terri is still inside the office, locked away and under guard."

"Really?" Whipsaw brightened. "You had me fooled there, Son. What are you going to do with her?"

Ketchum shrugged, "She's an insurance policy until we verify that the Alliance isn't going to bring charges against you sometime in the future. After that, well, I'm sure I can find some value in her company."

It was clear Whipsaw was uncomfortable with his son's scheme, but before the older Jones could formulate a protest, VooDoo rushed toward them.

"Ketch, the woman is gone. Three of my men are dead! They must have rescued her during the exchange."

Blackjack was surprised, "How in the hell did they manage to get by...." His gaze shifted to the water tower and then the roof. "Check the overwatch positions."

It took only a few minutes before Blackjack had his reports. "Damn it! Damn it all to hell!" he swore upon hearing that eight more of his men had been killed. "Mount up! I want every last man ready to go in 30 minutes."

"What are we doing?" VooDoo asked, almost as if he was afraid of the answer.

Blackjack was fuming, his rage near the boiling point. "We're going to burn Forest Mist to the fucking ground, that's what we're doing. Plummer set us up, that son of a bitch, and now, we're going to make them pay!"

Whip didn't like it, but he held his tongue. The people of Forest Mist had never given his boy a fair chance in his opinion. His son had been shipped off in shame while Dallas had gotten away with all his sins. Hell, the marshal had even prospered.

The older Jones realized he'd been harboring that resentment for a long, long time. His recent stay in the local lockup had only served to reinforce those feelings of betrayal.

"If Ketchum wants to burn down the town, I don't blame him," he finally decided. "The chickens are coming home to roost."

Kevin had to drive slowly with his two teammates hanging onto the side of the Jeep. Still, everyone was in good spirits and would have agreed that the measured pace was better than walking back to Texas.

When they arrived at the bypass, Kevin naturally steered to take them back to the airport using the same route as he had taken before. "I want to go into Forest Mist," Bishop ordered. "Turn left."

"Why do you want to go into town?" Terri asked, cramped in the back seat by the team's gear.

"I need to give DA Gibson an update, let her decide what charges to refile against Whipsaw, if any. The man has to come back to Texas if he wants to run his business, and I think the long arm of the law should be waiting. That, and I think somebody needs to tell Allison what happened to her father."

Nodding, Terri then told Bishop about Plummer's visit to the factory where she'd been held. "I could hear them talking outside my door," she explained to her husband. "I guess it doesn't matter now with the marshal dead, but Ketchum had inside information all along."

"So much for dying a hero of the Alliance," Bishop spat, wishing he had gone with his gut from the beginning. Then, after another mile had passed, his feelings softened. "I guess Allison doesn't need to know about her father's treachery. I can't figure out how telling her would serve any useful purpose."

They drove into Forest Mist expecting to find a sleepy town that was relieved to have been rid of Whipsaw Jones. Instead, they pulled into the courthouse square to a scene that could only be described as mayhem.

Anxious people rushed in all directions, the church's bell ringing as if a madman were pulling the rope. Every face was covered in fear. Women kept their children close to their skirts. Nervous men huddled in small groups on the lawn.

The SAINT team found Allison giving orders at the top of the courthouse steps. "Get everyone to the church. I'll take the last few officers we have left, and we'll make that our Alamo," she barked. "Let the older women and children in first. Make sure every able-bodied man has a weapon and plenty of ammo."

Relief painted the deputy's face when she spotted Bishop and his team. "Man, am I glad to see you, Bishop. Do you think you guys can help us? We're way short on firepower at the moment."

"Firepower? Allison, what's going on?" the West Texan asked.

"My dad had a deputy in the woods near the plant. He didn't trust Ketchum. Our spy saw everything and radioed about the bomb. Ten minutes ago, he reported that Ketchum was gathering his men, pledging to burn Forest Mist to the ground."

"So, he observed our rescue?"

"He saw strange activity, and I just assumed you were doing something to try and save your wife. When our spotter reported that he noticed three men and a woman sneaking out of the compound, I figured it was you."

"How many men is Ketchum bringing?" Grim asked the clearly-shaken deputy.

"At least 120," she responded. "Maybe more. I don't have an exact count."

"And how many do you have to protect the town?" Grim continued.

"Less than 30. A lot of our men work for Whipsaw and probably won't get involved for fear of losing their jobs. That, and so many of our young people have left to find work in other places. We lost the cream of our crop when Ketchum ambushed my father."

Grim looked to the right, noting two deputies who were marshaling the town's men. He wasn't impressed. Most of the guys gathering there were older. He noted shopkeepers, farmers, and loggers. While they might have been brave enough, the shotguns and deer rifles in their hands weren't going to hold off a determined assault. His mind drifted back to the room he had found across from Terri's cell and the heavier weapons stored inside. Blackjack not only had superior numbers but an impressive advantage in firepower. He said as much to Bishop.

"These guys have belt-fed M249 SAWS, RPGs, and cases of hand grenades, Boss. There's no way they can hold this town," the grouchy man announced, pointing toward the gathering defenders.

Bishop, after a quick assessment of Allison's conscripts, had to agree. Yet, he didn't feel like this was a battle he wanted to join.

Motioning for his team to gather around, the Texan said, "The people of this town did nothing to help after Whipsaw killed Nathan. The vast majority simply wanted to turn their heads and ignore a murder. As far as I'm concerned, this isn't our fight. We rescued Terri, and now it's time to let them simmer in their own stew."

DA Gibson appeared just then, interrupting the team meeting with a joyful greeting. "Terri! Oh, thank the Lord above you're okay. I knew Bishop and the guys would get you out. I just knew it."

Terri, in kind, was happy to see her old friend. "Bishop told me what you did to help. How can I ever repay you?"

Evidently, Pat knew of the latest threat, "We'll talk about who owes whom later. Right now, I'm trying to get help for this town. Unfortunately, there are no Alliance military resources that can get here in time."

"So, you've been on the shortwave with Alpha?" Bishop asked.

"Yes, I just spoke with Nick. He's going to try to get a couple platoons of infantry onto helicopters but said it would take at least two to three hours before they were airborne. I think this will all be over by then."

Bishop had to agree. "Why don't we all head out to the airport and get on that great big, pretty airplane you sent in for us, Pat. Everybody can be safe and headed back to West Texas in less than 30 minutes."

"I can't leave," Gibson announced, surprised that Bishop would even suggest such a thing. "This is Alliance territory; these people are citizens of the Lone Star Nation. While I'm as frustrated as anybody with some of their attitudes, they are under the government's protection. Assholes or not, they're my responsibility."

Butter piped in before Bishop could say another word, "She's right, Boss. We can't just let anybody roll in and burn down our towns."

"It's not our fight, guys," Bishop spat. "None of you should have to risk your lives."

Grim shook his head, "Sorry, Boss, but the rest of us still work for the government, and the prosecutor is right, we have a responsibility. Why don't you and Miss Terri head on back to the airport? We'll do our best to make a stand here."

Scanning the faces of his friends, the men who had just risked their lives to save his wife, Bishop saw that all of them agreed with Grim. "Shit," he barked, realizing he was the lone man out.

Pat moved toward him and leaned in close. In a soft voice, she said, "You fought for the Alliance as hard as anybody. I know you find this town disgusting, but think about the bigger picture. I'm asking you to stay and help. Besides, there are people here like Mr. Yarborough and the waitress at the café. Good people. They deserve our protection."

"It's going to be a massacre, Pat," the West Texan countered. "Our energy would be better served getting everyone to safety. If that's what you want us to do, then I'm all in."

Before anyone could continue the debate, Bishop noticed his wife was missing. "Where's Terri?" he asked his team.

"She was just here a minute ago," Grim answered, scanning the grounds.

"She had to use the facilities," Pat offered, motioning toward the courthouse with her chin. "She'll be back in a couple of minutes."

Bishop thought it was odd, Terri leaving during such an important discussion without letting him know. She'd been acting strangely, but then again, she had just been through hell.

"I'm not making any decision on my participation until I can speak with my wife. I don't think she's doing well, and I might have to get her medical attention," Bishop declared.

It was another five minutes before Terri reappeared. The first thing her husband noted was her hair. It was soaking wet.

"So sorry," she blushed. "I had to take a shower. I just used the one in the jail."

"Are you okay?" Bishop asked softly, his brain telling him that something was seriously wrong.

"That room was filthy," she replied. "I was sleeping in mouse turds and roach piss. I needed to clean up."

"Okay," he nodded. "Now that you are back, we need to talk. Pat and the guys want us to stay and help hold off Blackjack and his troops. I didn't want to make a commitment until we had a chance to talk it over."

"Why wouldn't we?" she shrugged.

Frowning, Bishop couldn't believe his wife was taking that position. "Hunter, for one thing," he answered.

"I would rather Hunter grew up knowing his parents died for a cause they believed in than have us around trying to explain why we ran away from a fight. You started this, my love. You were the one who stood up and declared what was done to Nathan was wrong. We have to finish the job... see this through."

He knew she was right, but that did little to quell a strong urge to get the hell out of dodge. He was worried about his mate, her entire demeanor just a little off-center since she'd been rescued.

Terri, sensing her husband's indecision, voiced her own, personal feelings. "Besides, that rat bastard tortured me. I'm probably going to have nightmares for a year. I want to see him put down like a rabid animal. I want to make sure no one else ever has to go through what I just endured."

Bishop could see the pain in his wife's eyes. "Even if we stay, there's no certainty that Blackjack will be held accountable," he whispered.

"At least I'll know we tried," Terri countered.

Turning to escape the intensity of her gaze, Bishop had to admit that he had a score to settle with one Mr. Ketchum Jones himself. He thought about Carlie and her ruined home and future. He replayed the detonation of Kitty's explosive vest, and the deputies surrounding Plummer – good men who had paid the ultimate price, all under the banner of trying to rescue Terri.

His stance brought the men of Forest Mist into view, the nervous gathering idling around while they waited on Allison's instructions. They reeked of fear, shuffling here and there, nervous eyes traveling in random directions. They were scared, and the West Texan didn't blame them.

While he watched, a woman stepped toward the group, a young boy about Hunter's age in her arms. Both mother and son had tears rolling down their cheeks.

They approached a man standing among the defenders, the family embracing for what they all thought was the last time. Bishop estimated dad was probably 21 or 22 years old, dressed in worn bib overalls, and wearing a dirty, tractor-logo baseball hat on his head. "I'll be okay," the father kept trying to reassure his wife and child. "I'll be fine."

"What will we do if something happens to you?" the hysterical wife wept. "You have to come back... you just have to."

Bishop had experienced his share of emotional departures, he and Terri often struggling to reconcile his leaving her behind while he went off to face imminent danger. It was painful to watch another family go through the same struggle.

What really swayed Bishop, however, was the memory of Nathan Hill's lifeless body hanging from Whipsaw Jones' signpost. When he considered that both father and son were going to get away with their crimes, his temper began to rise.

His fury continued to build, the injustice of the entire affair coming back to eat at his core. It wasn't all about Whipsaw and Ketchum, or Forest Mist's ingrained discrimination and bias. There was plenty of blame to go around, including the officials in Alpha who hadn't thought securing the borders was a high enough priority.

As he scanned the shops and stores facing the square, Bishop noticed several older people milling around, anxious to know what the future held. Among them stood several small children, Forest Mist's next generation. *They would most likely die tonight*, he thought. *Blackjack won't be discriminating. He'll slaughter them all.*

Terri and Pat are right, he finally determined with a grunt. *This has to end, here and now.* "Okay, I'm in," Bishop announced, spinning quickly to address their small gathering. "Pat, can you spare us any of your security men?"

"You can have them all," the prosecutor answered with a smile. "They're all the time complaining about how boring their job is, so they're chomping at the bit to experience a little excitement."

Nodding, Bishop then brightened with an idea. Without sharing the revelation with his friends, he made a beeline for Allison. "How many weapons have you taken from Blackjack's men? Fifteen? Twenty?"

"More than that," she nodded, "Over the years, we've stockpiled dozens and dozens of weapons. Between the B&B and your little shootout at Rocky Falls, we've added quite a few pieces to the arsenal. Why? What's up?"

"Where are they stored?" Bishop asked.

Pointing over her shoulder with her chin, she answered, "In a storage room... in the courthouse's basement. In fact, it's almost overflowing, given all the trouble we had around here. But our problem isn't barrels; it's having enough fingers to pull the triggers."

"I understand," Bishop nodded, waving for his team to join the conversation. "Terri and Pat, I want you two to take on a critical mission. I've got an idea on how to double the number of Forest Mist's defenders."

"Okay," Allision offered suspiciously. "Just how are you going to do that?"

"The Smokers," Bishop smiled. "Outside Highland Hardwoods is a shanty town. There must be 40 or 50 able-bodied men there. If we arm them with the weapons you've collected, they might just be enough to hold Blackjack's army at bay until Nick's troopers arrive."

"They wouldn't fight for us," Allison replied. "They've been shunned and hated by the people of this town since crossing the border. What makes you think they would lift a finger?"

"Because it's the right thing," Bishop stated. "Because we're asking them to."

After Terri and Pat exchanged a quick glance, both women nodded at the same time. "I think we can convince them to pitch in," the prosecutor said. "Terri is one of the most skilled diplomats I've ever seen, and I can speak in an official capacity for the Alliance. It's definitely worth a shot."

"You really think they would stand with us?" Allision asked, still not convinced. "After all the things we've done to them?"

"Yes," Bishop said. "Besides, what choice do we have? Even with my team, we're so badly outnumbered and outgunned it's not even going to be close."

Shrugging, Allison called over two of her men. "Start loading up weapons and ammo. Put them in the backs of pickup trucks and get some volunteers to drive these women out to the Smokers... err... refugees' camp by Highland Hardwoods."

Bishop turned to Kevin and asked, "Where is that map you have? We need to plot a strategy and do it damn quick. The key, gentlemen, as I see it, is to keep Blackjack's boys out of Forest Mist. If we can make this fight happen out in the open terrain, there won't be as much collateral damage to homes, businesses, and innocents. Besides, as we all know, the absolute worst type of fighting is urban. If those guys get in the middle of all these structures, there is no way we can push them out."

A minute later, the team was gathered around the hood of Verne's Jeep, a flashlight illuminating the map. After studying the chart for a moment, Bishop looked at Kevin and Butter. "There's only one road that connects the Crescent Furniture Company with Forest Mist, at least until you get close to town. You guys have driven more of that stretch than anybody. Is there any natural feature... any river or creek... or narrow gap that we can use to our advantage?"

The two younger men stared at each other, both of them mentally traveling down the stretch of two-lane highway leading to the old plant. Almost at the same time, they both answered, "No, not really."

"There are no significant bridges that I remember," Kevin added.

"It's pretty flat, Boss. If we did try to do a roadblock, they'd probably just drive around it," Butter offered.

"They've had too much rain around here to set any of the fields on fire. Hell, you saw how soft the ground was," Kevin continued. "You guys had to push us out of the mud."

"Can you remember any place where the trees are close to the road, where there wouldn't be enough room to go around a barricade?" Bishop asked.

Butter shook his head, "I only drove it once, Bishop, and that was at night. I don't remember seeing anywhere like that."

All eyes turned to Kevin and waited, the youngest member still trying to recall his trip in the Jeep. Finally, he responded, "About a mile further west from where I almost got stuck. There's a similar field and tree line right there, but a little bit narrower. If that field is as wet as where I went in,

Blackjack's boys would have a hell of a time getting through."

"Show me on the map," Bishop ordered.

They all watched as Kevin's finger tapped a spot just inside the Texas border. Grim, looking skyward, declared, "Too bad we can't make it rain on Blackjack's parade."

"Maybe we can," Bishop replied, his gaze now focused on a building at the far corner of the square.

One by one, his teammates followed the West Texan's gaze. Soon, they were all smiling, staring at a sign that said, "Forest Mist Volunteer Fire Department."

"I want to drive the fire truck," Grim announced. "Always did want to do that."

"Can I wear one of those cool hats?" Butter asked.

Dismissing the childhood career fantasies of his teammates, Bishop found Allison again. "Are the firetrucks functional?"

"Yes," she nodded, obviously confused and scanning the horizon for smoke. "Why? Is there a fire?"

"No, not yet. Actually, what I need is a flood. Where are the firemen?" Bishop asked.

"Most of them are over there with my volunteers," she replied.

Bishop produced the map and quickly explained his strategy. "We're going to try and keep them out of Forest Mist. If the firetrucks can make the land impassable on either side of this spot, we can slow Blackjack down. In fact, once they're empty, we can use those trucks as our barricade. They'll be very difficult to move."

"We need those trucks," Allison started to protest. "Fires have been a big problem, what with everyone burning candles and lanterns, and then the spotty electricity coming and going after so many years."

"If we don't stop Ketchum, you're going to need a whole lot more than a couple of tankers, Allison."

Nodding, she signaled her agreement. "You're right. Let me get you some firefighters."

"When Terri and Pat come back with the Smoker brigade, send them to this spot," Bishop added. "You keep your manpower posted around the church to protect the civilians. If Ketchum gets past us, let him have the town. Maybe burning it down will be enough, and he'll leave the people alone."

"Maybe," she sighed. "Good luck."

Bishop followed the fireman out of Forest Mist, the town's fleet of three trucks each occupied by two men who also happened to be reserve deputies.

Kevin and Butter were riding in the lead vehicle, Grim getting his wish and piloting the second. Bishop brought up the rear, Verne's Jeep packed to the gills with ammunition.

They came to the narrow spot Kevin had indicated on the map. Sure enough, with their hoses fully extended, the firefighters could reach the dense forest and hopefully saturate the already-soft ground.

Watching as the volunteers began unrolling their hoses, Bishop issued orders to his own team. "Take some wire and boobytrap those woods on either side of the road. Use as many hand grenades as you can. If I were Blackjack's lead element, and I got stuck in the field, I would try to flank us using the forest for cover. Make them pay for every inch of that ground. Understood?"

Grim was obviously thrilled with the prospect of generating carnage and said as much. Motioning for Butter to heft a case of grenades, he grunted, "Come on, children. Let me show you a couple of old playground tricks I learned from the Mujahideen. Those bastards were the best at rigging a trip wire."

As arches of water saturated the East Texas pasture, Bishop busied himself plotting the positions for his tiny force of defenders. He had ten men, counting himself. Job one was to put Kevin's deadly accurate firepower in a spot where he could do the most good.

Five minutes later, the police radio Allison had given Bishop blared with a message. "Blackjack is on his way," the new marshal reported. "My deputy said he's bringing every man and woman from his camp. Multiple trucks, vans, pickups, motorcycles, and campers are in a long convoy heading directly at you. Good luck."

"We'll be ready," Bishop transmitted. Then in a whisper only he could hear, "I hope."

CHAPTER 17

Terri instructed the three truck drivers to pull off the road a mile from the Smoker camp while she and Pat approached alone.

They rolled toward the area where the roadside men for hire job fair had been, finding nothing but a few oil stains alongside the highway. Through the trees, they could see a multitude of campfires.

On foot, the two women headed for the shantytown, Terri with her M4, Pat carrying no weapon but her smile.

The hour was late, most of the fires having died down to glowing embers. Terri approached the first people she saw, two men sitting beside a group of tents, their empty gazes fixed on the dying flames.

"Hello there," Terri offered walking into the light. "Who is in charge here?"

Looking at each other with blank expressions, the two men said, "No one is in charge. What do you want?"

"My name is Terri," she introduced, ignoring their question for the time being. "Did either of you know Nathan Hill?"

"The guy they hung a few days back? Yeah, I knew him. Poor bastard," the older man answered.

"I'm the lady who hired him to take my lumber back to West Texas," she began. "My husband is the man who was going to testify against Whipsaw Jones."

They instantly relaxed, their expressions making it clear that they had heard most, if not all, of the story. "We also heard you'd been kidnapped... were being held hostage."

"Yes," Terri nodded. "My husband rescued me just a few hours ago. Now we need your help."

"Our help? You need someone to haul your lumber?" the younger guy asked.

293

"No," she smiled. "Actually, it's the Alliance that needs your help."

For the next five minutes, Terri explained to the two men what was going on. After hearing her story, the fire watchers stopped her and said, "We need to get everybody together."

The older man produced a whistle and blew it once, then again. That signal was evidently the local alarm, the surrounding woods suddenly bustling with movement. "Stand over here beside me," the man advised.

The people streamed in from all directions, at least two dozen men and women. Most of them held axes, shovels, or other tools. A few had weapons, but they were mostly hunting rifles that looked like they had seen better days.

"It's alright! Everything's cool!" Terri's new friend announced. "We all need to hear what this woman has to say."

It took a few moments before the commotion settled down, another dozen people eventually arriving in ones and twos, most of them looking like they expected to fight. Finally, the impromptu town meeting began.

Again, Terri explained the situation, her voice strong as she made eye contact with the tired faces and blank expressions staring back at her. Given the flickering, low light, she had no idea how her spiel was being received.

She finished by saying, "I know you've not received a very warm welcome here in Forest Mist. I'm sorry that has occurred, and I promise you that DA Gibson and I will make the leadership in Alpha aware of your plight. Please don't judge the Alliance by the reaction of just one, small town."

Pausing for a moment to let her words sink in, Terri then continued, "I can also tell you that the people in Alpha appreciate those who help themselves. They respect people who work for a greater cause, who are willing to sacrifice for the greater good of the community. While I can't make any commitments or promise you any specific solutions, I can, without a doubt, tell you that Diana Brown and the council will hear about your assistance if you decide to help us today."

A woman stepped forward into the light, Terri instantly recognizing authority in her demeanor. While she looked like the typical grandmother, there was a certain confidence in how she carried herself. Probably around 50 years of age, her wrinkled, brown skin bespoke of both a Cajun heritage, as well as someone who had struggled to survive the last few years. Still, there was an unmistakable fire burning behind her eyes.

Terri also noticed that the others immediately stood just a little straighter when the matriarch moved toward the center of the gathering. Even the largest men seemed to respect her words. "Why should we help Forest Mist?" she replied in a low voice. "Their citizens have done nothing but persecute us. We've been accused of petty crimes, theft, and all manner of sins. You're asking us to put faith in the Alliance... a government that has, so far, ignored us."

"What is your name?" Terri asked, confident she had finally met the community's leader.

"Pearl," she replied. "I hail from Morgantown, lived there all my life. But we can't get diesel for our fishing boats or nets for our shrimpers, so we had to move elsewhere to survive. I didn't want to be here. None of us wanted to leave our homes."

Pat stepped forward, and after introducing herself, she said, "I can't make any promises about what the Alliance will or will not do to help you. What I can say with certainty is that if Forest Mist burns, or is taken over by Whipsaw Jones and his son, you will all be attacked next... and you will probably be killed as well."

"There are good people in Forest Mist. Mr. Yarborough has given you all a place to camp. He is just one example," Terri added. "Others were willing to stand up to Whipsaw and Ketchum, even when their lives were endangered... on behalf of one of your own. Others are simply scared or uninformed.

They've become so caught up in day to day survival, they've forgotten how to think of others."

"I am still not sure I want to help those people. How could Whipsaw and his boy be any worse than what we've endured so far?" Pearl ventured.

"Other than a few isolated incidents, nobody tried to kill us," one of the men countered. "In fact, there hadn't been a single murder before Nathan was hung," he said.

"Yes, yes, you're right," Pearl nodded.

"Two wrongs don't make a right," Terri reminded the throng. "I'm asking you all to prove to the people of Forest Mist that you are good souls. Do the right thing. Take the high road and show everybody that you didn't deserve to be treated this way," Terri finished.

"Give us a few minutes, please," Pearl asked.

"We'll be up by the highway," Terri nodded.

It took nearly ten minutes before Pearl and two of the men walked out to inform Terri and Pat of their decision. "You say you have arms and ammunition for several men?" Pearl questioned.

"Yes, we certainly do," Terri nodded, her eyes full of hope.

"How many?" Pearl asked.

"Dozens," Pat answered.

"We have 37 volunteers," Pearl smiled. "A lot of them served in the military, all of them are young and strong. Where do you want them to go?"

The firetrucks were empty, Bishop praying it had been enough water. After testing the ground with a few steps, he could definitely testify that the earth was sloppy. Would it be enough to stop Blackjack's convoy? They would certainly find out soon enough.

They had just finished maneuvering the big red vehicles into a reverse "V" formation to block the road when Bishop heard the first motorcycle engine. Kevin's voice, broadcasting from his elevated perch in an elm tree just 30 meters away, confirmed what the Texan had just heard. "S3 to SAINT, I have two bikes travelling down the road. Repeat, two bikes, each with a single rider."

"Let them through," Bishop ordered.

Between Blackjack and VooDoo, Bishop knew the approaching forces would well led. It was a safe bet that Ketchum would be leery of an ambush and deploy scouts at the front of his main body. It's what Nick, or Grim, or any competent leader would do.

That tactic, however, was about the extent of what Bishop expected. Blackjack would have no way of knowing that he was up against anything more than Allison and the men of Forest Mist. Yes, his prisoner had been snatched right from under his nose, but that could have been Plummer's doing. Terri was certain that Ketchum believed her husband had left for West Texas.

"Motorcycles are slowing down," Kevin reported. "Now stopped."

For the Nth time, Bishop scanned their defenses. He had three men on the right, including Butter and two of Allison's reserve deputies. On the left was Kevin, along with Grim and two more of Forest Mist's brave defenders. Bishop, with the remaining volunteers, remained in the middle. They would fight from the ditches for as long as they could.

"More headlights approaching," Kevin transmitted. "Looks like one or two SUVs."

"Let them through," Bishop repeated. "We're here to delay, not to defeat. Let them take their time."

Again, he checked their positions. Bishop had ordered extra ammo to be pre-stocked at each fighting hole. Grim and Butter also had a case of grenades. Both the left and right side had prepared two shallow trenches for each man. It wouldn't take Blackjack's boys long to zero in on any single position. Having an alternative, or a haven for regress, would make it twice as difficult for the bikers to successfully return fire.

"I've got dozens of headlights now, lining up along the road. It looks like they are dismounting," Kevin's voice crackled through his earpiece.

"Expect an infantry assault," Bishop ordered. "At 900 meters, make them pay for every inch, S3. Everybody else, hold your fire until my order."

"Roger that," Kevin replied.

Bishop didn't anticipate that Ketchum would needlessly sacrifice his troops... especially this far away from his primary objective – Forest Mist. If Grim had been standing beside him, the West Texan would have probably tried to get the old warhorse to wager how close Ketchum's men would get before turning back.

"I have 14 armed tangos illuminated and verified via thermal imager," Kevin transmitted. "900 meters. Requesting permission to engage."

"Fire at will," Bishop responded into the microphone. "And so, it begins," he added in a hushed voice.

Unconcerned with sound suppression, Kevin used regular ammunition. The pop of his rifle sounded a moment later, followed a few seconds afterward by another shot and then another.

"Tangos scattering. Three confirmed hits," the next status report updated.

While the sniper's battle was too distant for him to see, Bishop could just imagine what was transpiring almost a thousand meters away on the road. VooDoo had ordered a dozen of his shooters to dismount and approach the firetrucks. He needed to know what they were facing, required hard intelligence before deploying the main body of his forces.

Now, those dozen scouts were dying before they could even get close to the roadblock. Darkness was no longer their friend. They did not have the element of surprise on their side. "I wouldn't want to be in your shoes, Blackjack. Kevin doesn't miss," Bishop mumbled.

Again, Kevin's rifle thundered in the quiet night. "Four down," the kid reported. A moment later, the number was five.

"Tangos withdrawing," sounded the next report.

About now, VooDoo was wondering what in the hell he was up against. Without thermal of his own, there was no way Blackjack's men could return fire. Bishop hazarded a guess that Kevin's marksmanship was generating quite a stir in the enemy ranks. "You're wondering who is killing you," the Texan whispered, waiting for Ketchum to make his next move. "Is it the best deer hunter in all of Forest Mist? Is he having the luckiest night of his life? Or is it something else?"

"They are regrouping," Kevin reported a few minutes later. "Spread wider this time. Leapfrogging and buddy rushing."

The sound of Kevin's weapon cracked again, then again, and quickly a third time. "They're learning," the kid transmitted. "Six confirmed kills."

Bishop knew his sniper's effectiveness would diminish now. It took almost three seconds for his bullets to cover the distance to their target. In that time, the "aware," tango was bobbing and weaving, zigging and diving. "Cease fire until they're within 400 meters," he ordered.

At that range, Kevin's bullets would arrive in about one second. Their maneuvering wouldn't help much at that point.

"They're spreading out," Kevin reported. "Staying 40 meters on each side of the road. Count 9 targets, four on the left, five on the right."

"I got 'em," Grim's voice announced across the radio. "Leave a couple for me, Kid."

It seemed like several minutes passed before Kevin's rifle split the night again. Two more shots, and then Bishop heard Grim's team engage.

"Check 320 meters to your right, S2," Kevin advised, informing Grim that one clever fellow was trying to flank his position. Then, a few seconds later, "He's down, S2. Nice shot."

"They're bugging out," Kevin then advised as he fired again.

"Don't let them get back," Bishop snapped into his mic. "We want our positions to be a mystery."

Several rifles were now in the fray, Bishop climbing to the top of the front firetruck, more from boredom than any need to join the battle.

"No movement," Butter broadcasted.

"No movement," Grim added.

"No tangos," Kevin confirmed.

"Your move," Bishop whispered toward the distant convoy.

Bishop was wrong about Blackjack being stumped. Ketchum had found the parachutes, and after seeing an entire team of his men sniped, he knew Terri's husband had indeed returned to Forest Mist.

"So, his reputation isn't exaggerated," Ketchum declared to VooDoo.

"The roadblock appears to be professionally positioned," Blackjack's second cryptically answered.

"Yes, but that also tells us that he's shorthanded. If he had the manpower, they would have set up an ambush. We need to get around that barrier and do so quickly," Ketchum replied.

The crime lord paced for nearly a minute, his lieutenants standing silently, waiting on the orders they were sure would soon come. However, their confidence was beginning to waver.

First, the rescue, executed against what they had all believed to be an impenetrable security configuration. Who parachuted in at night? Who had the skill to take out both overwatch teams without anyone on the ground knowing?

That bit of fieldcraft, now combined with over a dozen of their brethren being killed without firing a shot, had shaken Blackjack's men to the core.

Ketchum knew it as well. This was one of the battle's fulcrums, a tipping point that could result in victory or defeat. He had to conjure up something good, or he would start to lose discipline in the ranks.

His mind returned to his training as a Ranger while he searched for some way to eliminate the roadblock. What would his officers have done if faced with a similar dilemma? An airstrike was the first thing that came to mind, but he didn't have that asset.

An armored vehicle would have been the next option.

"Empty that semi-trailer," he ordered, pointing at the closest big rig. "Take the pallets inside and build a bullet stop. Shovel dirt or cut logs if you need to."

VooDoo got it instantly, smiling at his boss's brilliance. "You heard the man," he snapped at the gathering. "Get your asses moving. We don't have all night!"

"Movement," Kevin's voice announced.

"Finally," Bishop whispered. "It's been almost an hour."

During that time, the Texan had been worried that Blackjack was somehow scheming to bypass the roadblock. The man did have local knowledge, and it would have been the smart thing to do.

Yet, the firemen stationed around Bishop claimed there wasn't a single passable log trail, farm lane, or back road within 15 miles in any direction. "He has to come this way," they kept trying to reassure the team leader. "He's got no choice. If he backtracked, it would take over three hours to get to Forest Mist. The Red Creek bridge has been out since the first flood after the downfall. He would have to go north, almost to Arkansas, before crossing into Texas, and who knows what those roads are like."

Another volunteer piped in, "To the south is even worse. Lake Morse has been over its banks since the collapse. When the power failed, the gates at the dam automatically closed. It floods after every rain."

In a way, Bishop would have welcomed Ketchum taking the three-hour detour. By then, Nick's infantry should be arriving, and he would be happy to let them mop up.

"I've got an 18-wheeler rolling our direction," Kevin announced. "But... well... it looks like it is coming backward."

"S3, expand," Bishop commanded. "What do you mean, backward?"

"It's travelling in reverse. Trailer first. Going real slow."

Before Bishop could digest what he'd just been told, Kevin added, "I see two lines of armed tangos following it. Looks like at least 50 shooters."

"Can you thin them out?" Bishop asked.

"Negative. They're hanging behind the semi. The driver is having trouble backing it in a straight line and swerved a bit. That's the only reason I could see them."

Rubbing his chin, the Texan wondered what Blackjack had dreamed up. Grim's voice then crackled over the airwaves, "Are the back doors of the trailer open?"

"I can't tell," Kevin responded. "It looks like it, but there's no thermal signature inside the cargo area if they are. Switching to light amplification."

The defenders waited what seemed like several minutes before Kevin transmitted again. "Yes, the cargo doors are open. I can see what appears to be stacks of logs or boards inside."

"Shit!" Bishop barked, realizing instantly what Blackjack had configured. "We can expect at least one of those belt-fed machine guns to be nestled in the back of that trailer. Everybody get ready."

The up-armored semi continued to approach, closing the distance to the firetruck barricade minute by minute. When they were 400 meters out, Kevin delivered more bad news. "New contacts. Multiple headlights roaring up the road. Looks like several pickup trucks bringing up the rear."

Bishop could see it all clearly now through his optic. As he prepared to issue the order to engage, the racing pickups cut off the road and into the open pasture on each side. Several of the marching shooters scurried to follow, hoping to use the vehicles as cover as they advanced.

"Hold your fire," Bishop ordered, not wanting to give away their positions until the last minute.

The lead 4x4 then charged headlong into the man-made swamp the firemen had just created, its bouncing headlights slowing dramatically. Bishop could hear their engines, racing to give more power to the wheels now flinging liquid dirt and muddy water.

"Hit the infantry and pickups! Fire at will!" Bishop transmitted. "Give them everything you got!"

Grim and Butter's teams did just that, unleashing a burgeoning volley of lead. Headlights began popping out, flashes and sparks indicating the defenders were hitting their marks. Bishop could see men diving for the ground on both sides of the road as their comrades began to fall.

The semi kept advancing, now within two football fields of the lead firetruck. Kevin managed to transmit, "Movement in the cargo..." before the M249 machine gun began firing a stream of bullets into the roadblock. It was the defenders' turn to duck for cover.

A second gun opened up from the back of the fortified trailer, laser-like, red lines of tracer-laced ammunition stringing left and right. Firing at a rate of over 14 rounds per second, they were an extremely effective force multiplier.

Bishop could hear the deadly weapons, the noise not unlike the saws at the lumber mill. He knew they had to take out those machine guns or this battle would be over quickly.

"Kevin, Focus on those guns! Get those guns!" he shouted into the microphone while bringing his carbine into the fight.

"Roger that," the kid replied. "Not going to be easy. They have quite the nest built inside that trailer."

Centering his optic on the white muzzle flashes spitting from the semi, Bishop began pulling the trigger. He'd managed just half a magazine when someone shouted, "RPG!"

On Butter's side of the road, a bright plume of horizontal flame appeared, followed by the whoosh of the rocket's motor igniting. "Get down!" another man shouted as the warhead streaked through the air.

There was the flash of detonation, then a ball of flame as the six pounds of Russian explosives sent a blast wave over Butter's position.

A second after the fireball had diminished, Bishop spotted the man with the rocket launcher dance and jerk as several bullets ripped through his flesh. Butter's team was still in the fight.

Before he could return to focusing on the semi's gunners, another explosion ripped through the East Texas night, the lead firetruck struck by yet another rocket-propelled grenade.

Huge chunks of shrapnel tore through the air over Bishop's head, a wall of glass, metal, and rubber expanding in all directions. A nanosecond later, the truck's fuel tank erupted, shoving a boiling wall of flame billowing toward his position.

The skin on Bishop's arms felt like it was melting as his buried his face into the ditch. It was over a few seconds later, the Texan having to roll twice to extinguish the flames trying to consume the cloth of his pants.

The volunteer next to the Texan wasn't so lucky. Fully engulfed in flames, the shrieking man rose, his tortured brain demanding that he run away from the fire that was consuming his flesh.

With arms waving wildly in the air, he made it three steps before a dozen bullets tore into his body. It was a mercy killing from Bishop's perspective, far better than being burned alive.

A new sound was introduced onto the battlefield, the distinctive "whoop," of hand grenades flying from Grim's position. Bishop spied the silhouettes of men from both sides chucking the heavy explosives at each other. It was just another indicator of how much trouble they were in. Blackjack's forces had advanced close enough to warrant such short-range weapons. It wouldn't be long before the defenders were overrun.

Behind him, in the tree, Kevin's rifle was firing as fast as the kid could work the bolt. While it was reassuring to know they were inflicting considerable damage, Bishop knew they wouldn't be able to hold. He had managed to delay Blackjack less than two and a half hours, and that wasn't nearly enough.

A series of blasts boomed from the forest on Butter's side of the road. Apparently, some of Blackjack's men had tried to use the trees as cover to flank the big man's position. They had encountered the boobytraps and surely had suffered significant causalities. Bishop smiled, but only for a moment.

"Fall back," he ordered into the radio. "Fall back. Kevin, get down from there. We'll cover you. Come to me."

Bringing his carbine up, Bishop began firing at shadows in the distance, trying to provide his withdrawing teams, or what was left of them, cover. Looking over at the wide-eyed fireman to his left, he snapped, "Get that weapon into the fight!"

There weren't any clear targets for his team to engage, but Bishop had seen plenty of situations where even a few sizzling bullets flying overhead would keep an attacker down. All the while, the two buzz saws in the back of the semi kept the pressure on the defenders.

Just over a quarter mile to the rear of the roadblock, they had staged the Jeep and one of the firemen's pickup trucks. That was their rally point.

"We hurt them," a breathless Kevin managed as he fired another shot into the darkness.

"Not enough," Bishop countered, spraying five rounds to the left.

"S4 to SAINT, coming in," Butter announced.

A moment later, Bishop spotted the big guy running his way, the body of a wounded man over one shoulder, Butter's rifle firing wild bursts from the other hand.

As soon as Butter was in the ditch, Bishop ordered the two remaining volunteers to carry their wounded buddy back to the getaway cars. "Take the pickup. Get him to the doctor."

"S2 to SAINT, right behind the kid," Grim broadcasted, his weapon on full automatic as he dashed to join Bishop on the road. "They're 50 meters behind me," the old warrior reported breathlessly as he dove for the trench. "Probably 15 of them. I did the best I could."

Bishop then noticed Grim's leg was bleeding. "Took one through the thigh," the old mule acknowledged. "Another ropey scar to show the grandkids, I guess."

"Can you still move?" the Texan asked.

"I got here, didn't I?" Grim growled, sending a long stream of automatic fire at the men chasing him.

"Leapfrog!" Bishop ordered as a new wave of incoming rounds began impacting all around them. Blackjack's men had just realized that the only remaining enemy was on the road. Geysers of dirt and stinging blacktop began erupting as the second firetruck exploded in a huge fireball. Both machine guns now focused their fire on the center position.

Motioning his team back, Bishop and Kevin fired blindly into the night, four rounds left, five right, three up the middle. Giving his retreating comrades ten seconds to dart away and find cover, the Texan yelled at Kevin, "Our turn. Move!"

Bishop rose to a crouch, his weapon spitting lead. Bullets whizzed past his head as he turned and began moving, each footfall chased by a growing volume of incoming rounds.

He passed Grim and Butter in the ditch, both men prone, keeping up a steady cadence of death to cover their teammate's retreat. Bishop and Kevin kept on running another 20 steps and then dove for the drainage area.

Over and again, for six iterations, the egressing defenders scurried away from the burning roadblock. On the fourth dash, the final firetruck went up in a whoosh of flame.

With fewer rounds singing past, Bishop ordered the entire team to make the final sprint for the Jeep. "We just got our asses kicked," the Texan growled, helping his friends throw their gear into the back of the vehicle.

"We issued them an ass full of pain," Grim countered, already wrapping a bandage around his thigh. "It was like the Alamo; they paid a heavy price for a worthless strip of real estate."

"The guys defending the Alamo died," Bishop grumbled as he jumped into the front seat.

"Get that fucking semi turned around and push these trucks off the road," Ketchum screamed at two of his men.

While he appeared to be angry to keep up the pressure on his men, deep inside, Blackjack very pleased. He had regained the initiative. Momentum was on his side. He had broken the defenders' best effort and sent them running.

VooDoo appeared just then, standing silently until his superior acknowledged his presence. Instead of the anticipated query, "How many men did we lose?" Ketchum asked, "How many do we have left?"

Frowning, VooDoo answered without any editorial comment. "We have 61 men left."

"What? That's it?"

"There are 27 wounded, and probably only half of them will make it," VooDoo observed. "Taking those firetrucks required quite a lot of our resources."

Before Blackjack could respond, the front bumper of the semi contacted the charred shell of the first firetruck.

Racing its powerful diesel engine, the over the road truck shoved the metal skeleton to the side of the road, screeching metal protesting the move. "Just clear one lane," Ketchum shouted to the driver. "We have to move quickly, before they can regroup."

Whipsaw marched up to his son just then, the older Jones' face wrinkled in disgust. "Ketchum, we need to rethink this for a second. This isn't worth it."

Putting a hand on his father's shoulder to guide him away from any prying ears, Blackjack's response was harsh. "Now is not the time to be weak, Dad. We've got them on the run. We need to press that advantage."

Glancing over at the burned, mangled bodies being laid out in a straight row, Whipsaw exhaled a deep sigh. "There's been enough killing, Ketch. Look at all these dead men. Both sides have paid too high a price. End this, please."

For the first time in his adult life, Ketchum was disappointed in his father. Poking a finger into the older man's chest, Blackjack spat, "You're soft, and you always have been. If you had even a hint of a spine, you would have slaughtered Plummer back when you found out he was fucking your wife. But no, not the upstanding, local businessman and deacon at the church. No, you let them arrest your son for doing what was right."

"I always supported you," Whipsaw countered. "I always sent you money and my love. You know that."

Shaking his head in anger, Ketchum replied, "No, you sent me money out of guilt. You know damn good and well that what I did was justified, yet you threw me under the bus in order to save what little face the Jones name had left."

Sadness filled the father's eyes, "I'm sorry you feel that way, Son, but regardless of my past sins, you have to put a stop to this madness. The people of Forest Mist have suffered enough. Stop the killing."

"I have no intention of doing that, *Father*," Ketchum hissed, an accent of disdain on his last word. "If you want, I'll have one of the men drive your cowardly ass back to New Orleans, or wherever you want to hide out. I'm going to take over Forest Mist and the family mill. I'm going to make that town pay for what it did to me."

"The Alliance won't let you do that, Ketchum. They'll come with tanks and helicopters and thousands of men, if necessary. Even if you're holding the entire town hostage, they'll eventually wear you down and execute you."

"They might, and they might not. I'm not planning to hold some backwater spot in the road hostage. I have much larger aspirations. If they try to push me out, I'll burn down the entire Great Piney Woods. In New Orleans, even as we speak, there are 40 tanker trucks being filled with gasoline from a barge I've been saving for a rainy day. I will disperse those trucks all through the forests for 50 miles. They'll drive along the road, spewing the fuel and then we'll light a match. The Alliance can't afford to lose all this lumber or the dozens of towns along the border. They'll negotiate, or I'll start the biggest forest fire Smokey the Bear has ever seen."

Blackjack gave his dad a few moments to respond. When it became clear that Whip wasn't going to utter another word, the son waved a disgusted hand through the air and stomped off.

CHAPTER 18

Bishop's arms hurt like hell, the burning sensation a serious distraction now that his adrenaline was bleeding off. Grim's leg was still leaking blood, but the old war dog didn't seem to be worried. Kevin was nearly out of ammo for his sniper rifle, and Butter was complaining of spasms in his back.

"Aren't we just a fine, fucking mess," the West Texan grumbled as the Jeep raced back toward Forest Mist.

"We gave them hell, Boss," Butter remarked, trying to get his massive frame comfortable in the tiny seat.

"How long until Nick's cavalry arrives?" Grim asked.

Glancing at his watch, Bishop shook his head. "According to the district attorney, Nick estimated it would take up to three hours until they launched. Another two hours of flight time, give or take, if they don't have to stop and refuel. They're not going to get here in time. We didn't delay Blackjack long enough."

"Okay, Mr. Sunshine and Roses, what's the plan then?" Grim asked.

"I don't know," Bishop snapped back.

Before the team leader could expand on his lack of an idea, a pair of headlights appeared in the distance, soon joined by several approaching vehicles. "Help from Forest Mist?" Kevin ventured.

"Or some of Blackjack's boys that got behind us," Bishop snapped. "Pull over... right there."

The Jeep hadn't come to a complete stop before the team was piling out and taking up defensive positions. The approaching convoy stopped, a lone figure appearing in the headlights.

"You guys okay?" sounded Terri's voice.

"Thank God," Bishop sighed, rushing to meet his wife.

"I've brought help," she cooed. "Lots of help. We ran into the firemen bringing that wounded guy back to town. They told us what had happened. Are you guys all right?"

Bishop showed her his burned flesh, but quickly dismissed his injury. "We can still fight. How many men do you have?"

"Forty," she replied, "counting Pat's security team."

Glancing at the waiting line of pickups, Bishop didn't think it was enough. They were irregulars without any command structure, radios, or experience operating as a coordinated fighting force.

On the other hand, they were all that stood between Blackjack's column and Forest Mist. Bishop could hazard a good guess what Ketchum would do once he was inside the city limits, and the mental image wasn't pretty.

Grim's voice interrupted the West Texan's thinking. "This is as good a place as any to make a stand, Bishop. We can spread them out along both sides of the road and spring an ambush. It's going to take Blackjack a while to clear those firetrucks and regroup."

Bishop's eyes traveled to the surrounding terrain. Just like the location where they had set up the initial roadblock, there was a cleared area for 50 meters on both sides, dense forest beyond. About the only feature that was unique was a huge oak tree thats trunk was so massive, the road crew had altered the 2-lane highway to go around it.

Grim had a point; the trees would provide excellent cover. "I wish we had some way to drop that oak," Bishop pined. "That monster would make an excellent barricade."

"I've got a chainsaw in the truck, Mister," a voice from the shadows offered. "I've worked lumber since I was a kid. I can lay that old girl into a bed and tuck her in if you want."

Rubbing his chin, Bishop responded, "Can you get her to the point where she is about ready to fall? Close enough to where, say a hand grenade will take her the rest of the way over?"

"Sure," replied the old-timer. "You want it to block the road?"

Bishop paused for a moment before nodding his head. "Get your saw, and get those trucks off the road!" he turned suddenly and commanded. "I want every man and woman to gather around. In five minutes, you're going to learn how to execute a proper ambush. Move! Hide those wheels!"

A flurry of activity followed, Bishop's team directing traffic as each truck discharged its bed full of shooters. Turning to Kevin, the team leader said, "Take one of those trucks and go a couple of miles back toward Blackjack's convoy. When you see them coming, get on the radio and give us some warning while you hightail it back here. I'll be behind the oak."

As soon as the final headlights had disappeared, Bishop was addressing an anxious throng of ragtag fighters.

"We're going to form what is called an 'L ambush.' The first rule is that nobody, and I repeat, nobody fires a single shot until you hear my rifle. Is that understood?"

After seeing every head go north and south, Bishop held up his arms to form the letter "L," and then oriented his limbs with the roadway. "The first 30 men are to form the long portion. The remaining 10 will make up the short. Count off, and hurry."

Before he could continue, the sound of a gas motor being pull-started interrupted the makeshift classroom. A chainsaw then sputtered to life, and a moment later, was cutting into the base of the centuries-old oak.

Rather than slow down the most critical part of the operation, Bishop waved everyone off the road so he could be heard. For the next five minutes, he did his best to educate them in the dark.

"The most critical thing we have to do is stop those semi-trucks. We must take them out, no matter what. Shoot the engines, the tires, and the drivers. Turn them into Swiss cheese. Is that understood?"

After receiving conformation and asking for any questions, Grim and Butter began helping everyone to a good fighting position. Bishop, with Terri at his side, went to see the lumberjack and check his progress.

The man sawing on the ancient oak stopped a minute later, shutting down his saw and turning to Bishop with a smile on his face. "A good breeze would take her over," he bragged. "One of those little bombs of yours will surely do the job."

"Great!" Bishop replied. "I hate to take the old girl down. She's older than the road. On the other hand, if we don't stop these people...."

"It was dying anyway," the lumberjack replied. "She only had a few years left at best. Maybe she'll appreciate going out a little early for a good cause."

Kevin's voice interrupted their conversation. "They are a mile behind me," he reported. "I'll be at the rally point in two minutes. Don't shoot me."

"Hold your fire!" Bishop shouted. "Friendly coming in!"

Throughout the forest, the team leader could hear his orders being repeated up and down the lines.

"Where do you want me?" Terri asked, chambering a round in her rifle.

"Back in Alpha, safe and sound," he grinned. "Just stay with me, I think you're pretty," then he pretended to gush.

Kevin's truck raced by without any headlights. Bishop had to laugh, knowing the kid was driving by using his night vision and keep the vehicle dark so Blackjack's boys wouldn't get a glimpse of the Alliance spy. Slamming on the brakes, he barely managed to negotiate a wild turn onto the old logging road where the rest of the trucks were hidden.

Pulling a grenade from his vest, Bishop motioned for Terri to keep down. Then he stepped to the trunk of the old oak and prepared to pull the pin.

He heard the motorcycles before he saw them. As before, Ketchum was using a pair of scouts – just in case. Bishop would let them pass unmolested.

The two bikers drove by, using their bright lights to illuminate the roadway, heads swiveling right and left.

The main body of the convoy was a half mile behind. Again, Bishop heard the herd of engines rolling their way before he spotted the first vehicle. He began counting when the lead unit's headlights appeared.

Estimating they were traveling the same speed as the scouts, Bishop added four seconds for the grenade's fuse, and another two seconds for the tree to fall. He pulled the pin, wedged the device into the chainsaw's cut, motioned for Terri to start moving, released the spoon, and ran like hell.

The couple made it halfway across the field before the dull "whomp" split the night. Turning to run backward, Bishop saw a cloud of dust and smoke at the base of the oak, and for a minute, thought the tree wasn't going to fall.

He heard the cracking and popping of splintering wood, and then noticed the canopy start to lean, hang in the air for a few seconds, and then fall. The timing was perfect, the thick truck gaining speed just as the lead vehicle in Blackjack's convoy reached their position.

The massive oak landed on a 4-wheel drive pickup, its mass crushing the hood and cab like they were a cheap, plastic toy. Shouldering his rifle, Bishop sent a string of slugs into the convoy. A moment later, the entire forest erupted in a maelstrom of hissing lead.

Deadlier than the incoming fire was the chain reaction of the lead element's sudden stop. One by one, Blackjack's drivers rear-ended each other, several of the bikers forced to turn their machines onto their sides as they skidded in a shower of sparks across the pavement. Other, slower-reacting riders went flying as they rammed into one another.

Bishop saw the first semi's windshield explode in a shower of glass as the front tire blew. The driver, his rig completely out of control, plowed into several motorcycles and sent a dozen bodies rocketing into the sky. The carnage was off the scale.

The team leader observed a couple of survivors running up and down the pavement, screaming for their troops to rally. A surprising number responded, moving, crawling, or being dragged to the far side of the road and going prone.

The majority, however, didn't make it.

The entire roadway was as bright as the field of a night baseball game, headlights from trucks, motorcycles, and semis providing the ambushers with clear targets and an excellent field of fire. Bishop contributed, his optic centering on motorcycle club jackets, old military fatigues, and any other human outline the light identified.

Over and over, Bishop watched Ketchum's men die. Some were stupid, rushing into the open to help a downed comrade. Others were simply unlucky, unable to find cover and taking a bullet while looking for someplace... anyplace to escape the hailstorm of lead tearing through the night air.

There was very, very little return fire, which told Bishop they were winning.

Despite having 30 men on the long axis of the ambush, their kill zone was only 150 meters long. Blackjack's convoy was at least three times that length, which meant the back two thirds only had to deal with braking unexpectedly and rear-end collisions. No gunfire had come their way, and by Bishop's line of thinking, that was unacceptable.

"We wouldn't want you to miss out on the party," he whispered.

After three minutes, Bishop was convinced that everyone in the kill zone was either dead, wounded, or in shock. Sure that the short side of the L could handle what was left, he motioned for Terri to join Kevin and help with mopping up the stragglers.

"Where are you going?" she asked, not exactly happy to be left behind.

"I'm going to go running through the woods and hope I don't run into a nest of snakes. Want to go?"

Frowning, she shook her head. "Come back to me, my love," she said, and Bishop responded by blowing her a kiss.

The Texan began working his way up the 30-man line. "Follow me," he ordered again and again, quickly gathering his troops.

Keeping them in the woods while running parallel with the road, Bishop lead them past the rear element of Blackjack's convoy. One of the volunteers asked, "Why are we going past them? Are we going to let them go?"

"We're going to hit them from the last place they expect," Bishop grinned. "We're going to put a boot right up their ass."

"We're going to hit the back end of that convoy," he then announced to the anxious ears waiting on his command. Grim, Butter, Kevin, help them form a skirmish line.

They were slow by Bishop's standard, but in reality, it was less than two minutes before Grim announced they were ready. "Let's get this over with," Bishop barked and began moving out of the trees.

All of Blackjack's headlights were pointing away from Bishop's group, which allowed their approach to be masked by the darkness. Not that anyone would have noticed them anyway.

Halfway to the road, Bishop began to hear a chorus of confused voices, desperate shouts, and the high-pitched screams of the wounded. He could see several men gathered around one motorhome, its front end crumpled underneath the rear bumper of a pickup. They were trying to pry open the door and rescue the passengers inside.

People scurried in every direction, their forms distorted by headlights and shadows. Bedlam now ruled Ketchum's caravan, and the man from West Texas was determined to make things worse.

Bishop positioned his skirmish line on both sides of the highway, keeping Grim and Butter with him in the center. With a wave of his arm, the team leader motioned them forward.

Bishop spied VooDoo's bald head as he tried to rally his troops, frantically waving his arms and shouting orders. A second later, the red dot of Bishop's optic centered on his enemy's chest, and he squeezed the trigger.

Surprise colored the lieutenant's expression as three 5.56 NATO lead pills tore into his torso. The men he had managed to assemble were next, a dozen rifles ripping into their ranks. Bishop kept moving. He wanted Blackjack. He had a score to settle.

After hearing gunfire booming from the rear of the convoy, Ketchum's forces scampered away from the ruckus, their ranks in complete disarray. Before Grim could shoot the next two men darting from behind a pile of motorcycles, one of their own panicked and opened fire, taking both of them down.

Slowly, methodically, Bishop worked his way up the line of vehicles. A trail of blood and dead bodies was left in his wake.

Twice, the team leader encountered women, nearly shooting two of the females as they scrambled out of a camper and into the ditch. One of them was topless, the sight distracting Bishop long enough for a second look, saving her life.

By the time his group made it to the center of the column, somebody had managed to regroup a dozen shooters. Interspersed between a motorhome and Ketchum's Mercedes, they opened fire.

Realizing he had finally found Blackjack, Bishop dove for the drainage area, Grim and Butter racing for the other side of the littered highway to hell.

Dozens of bullets ripped and crashed into the pavement next to Bishop's head as he rolled hard to get away from the barrage.

Before the Texan could get his weapon into the fight, his friends alongside the road answered, their counter-fire slamming into Ketchum's personal guard.

Bishop wanted the man who had kidnapped his wife and ruined the lives of dozens, if not hundreds, of people. Images of Ketchum dropping Terri's shirt into the log chipper flooded his mind, driving a bloodlust unlike anything he had ever experienced. The man he sought was pure evil. He had to be put down.

With a growl of fury, the West Texan rose from the ditch and charged, weapon firing as fast as his finger could work the trigger. One man went down, another howling with agony as holes appeared across his chest.

His charge broke the last of the resistance, the few remaining defenders dropping their weapons and reaching for the sky. Only sporadic gunfire reached Bishop's ears.

Finally, he relaxed.

A strange euphoria began to engulf Bishop's core. He had felt it before. It was a unique emotion, a combination of combat's stress vacating his body while the elation of having survived took over. It was a feeling that came only after victory, from holding the field after enduring life's ultimate test. He wanted to shout to the heavens, "I'm alive! I made it!"

He didn't, however. Before being completely consumed by that sense of ecstasy, the ugliness of the battlefield began to rear its grotesque head. Overwhelming amounts of blood and gore assaulted his eyes, his ears tormented by the cries and pleading of the wounded. The air was thick with the sour, copper scent of oozing human life.

Intermingled with that foul odor was the stench of urine and feces. Large and small intestines had been torn from their hosts, spilling their sickening contents onto the earth.

Bladders had been ripped open by high velocity projectiles or emptied by fear. There was no glory in war, only images the soldier sought to vanquish from his mind forever. Bishop realized that he would never be able to erase what he saw around him, that the horrific images would revisit him in his dreams.

Dozens and dozens of bodies lay strewn across the earth. These men would never feel happiness or joy again. Some of them had left behind loved ones who would never feel the warmth and comfort of their presence again. Bishop could feel their ghosts around him. Confused. Puzzled. Drifting aimlessly across their gray landscape, unsure of where to go or why they were there.

As he plodded toward Terri's last known position, he passed scene after scene of terror. The dead were everywhere, lying at unnatural angles, limbs or sections of their torsos missing. He stepped over an entire arm, separated from its owner at the shoulder. The skin was stark white against the dark pavement, a small pool of crimson leaking from the strings of flesh and muscle at one end. A wedding ring encircled one of the remaining fingers.

He continued his trek, weapon high just in case any of the stragglers decided he wasn't going to be taken alive. Bishop wanted to find Terri, but his real purpose of the gory tour was to verify Blackjack was lying dead on the road.

He approached another Class-A motorhome, a heap of bodies sprawled near its door. Bishop drew closer, hoping to find Ketchum's carcass among the dead. Something moved in the bloody mass.

Vigilant, Bishop advanced cautiously, M4 at his shoulder. Reaching down, he pulled off the corpse of a biker and dragged the dead man away. A familiar figure laid beneath, the Texan staring at Whipsaw Jones.

The old logger had taken two rounds to the chest, red bubbles of frothy blood expanding through his shirt. After verifying the old man didn't have a weapon within reach, Bishop took a knee and simply stared at his former nemesis.

Somehow, Whipsaw sensed Bishop's presence and opened his eyes. "Water?" the dying man croaked. "Would you have some water?"

Bishop had been there before, a severe loss of blood causing the worst thirst imaginable. Already saddened by the carnage around him, benevolence directed the Texan's mindset.

"Sure," Bishop replied, extending the hose of his water bladder to the wounded man's mouth.

After a few swallows, Whipsaw nodded his thanks. It was then that he realized who was kneeling above him. "You... it's you," the old man croaked.

Bishop expected to see hatred in Jones' eyes, but the opposite emotion shone through. "I'm sorry," Whipsaw mumbled. "All of this is my fault," he managed before a rough bout of coughing afflicted the old man's frame.

Not knowing what to say, Bishop just stayed there. Somehow, his loathing of the man beside him was melting away. It was funny how death could do that.

"I want to make amends for what my son has done," Whipsaw whispered, the light fading from his eyes.

Barely able to hear the man's weak voice, Bishop leaned in closer as Jones began what the Texan assumed was going to be an admission of guilt, as well as regrets. He'd listened to deathbed confessions before.

A minute later, Bishop bolted upright, his eyes boring into Whip like two laser beams. The older man merely nodded, confirming what he had just said was true. "He said it was a barge full of gasoline. In New Orleans. He'll burn the entire forest down if somebody doesn't stop him."

Two coughing spells later, Whipsaw's chest heaved off the ground, and then the old lumberman died.

At first, Bishop wasn't worried about Blackjack's sinister plan. There was no way Ketchum had survived the firefight, let alone escaped.

As he continued down the line of shredded, wrecked and shot-up vehicles, Bishop began to seriously worry. "Have you seen Blackjack?" he asked every survivor he passed. None of the Smoker men had, nor had any of the wounded.

He had explored almost the entire kill zone, having almost reached the lead section of the convoy when a deep moaning sounded from inside of an overturned pickup. Again, with weapon high, Bishop approached. He prayed it was Ketchum.

The team leader noticed a bloody arm dangling from underneath the crushed cab. Bending low to get a better look, Bishop spotted the muscles in the limb flexing. Something was in his hand.

Bending lower, Bishop's flashlight illuminated VooDoo's face.

Recoiling backward, Bishop was sure he'd killed the man at the beginning of the battle. "How in the hell had he...?" the Texan grunted, trying to make sense of it all. Did this asshole have on body armor? Had he only been grazed?

"Fuck you," VooDoo smiled as his determined gaze bored into Bishop. His hand opened. A fragmentation grenade rolled out of his fingers.

Hissing, "Oh shit," Bishop dove for the ditch. Everything slowed to individual frames, time moving into the slow lane as his brain accelerated to hyper speed. He landed hard on the roadway's shoulder, then cringed as the hand grenade hit the pavement just a few feet away. He saw the green, oblong metal ball bounce once, roll, and then the world went white.

Bishop felt his body being raised into the air as a dozen sledgehammers hit him at the same instant. A blinding whiteness filled his vision. Then, as he floated above the earth, it began to shrink, darkness closing in from the edges.

He watched as the single, tiny, pinpoint of white disappeared, and then the world was black.

He was inside of a maelstrom. He could hear the wind howling, could feel the debris blowing against his face. Lightning burned his vision, thunder pounded in his ears. The only thing that was missing was the rain.

Opening his eyes, Bishop squinted to clear his sight. He was on his back, several fuzzy globes hovering above his head.

The first face that came into view was a stranger. He wore a helmet, a red cross painted on the Kevlar surface. "He's awake," the head mouthed.

Next, Grim appeared, the grouchy old fart's pie hole gaping wide enough to display every tooth in his head.

Beyond Grim's ugly mug, Bishop spied blinking red lights floating in the sky. The hurricane's wind was stronger now, dust, pine needles and twigs blowing everywhere. *Why weren't the people standing over him seeking shelter*, he wondered? *This storm is getting bad!*

Terri's face was next, the glowing image of his wife making him smile. The gesture hurt like hell, but Bishop didn't mind. He tried to lift his arm, wanted desperately to caress her cheek, but sadly, he couldn't will his limb to move.

The red lights drew his eye again, the outline of a helicopter overhead becoming clear. With his brain still scrambled, Bishop thought to warn the pilot about the storm.

Nick's face came into view then, his smiling friend reaching down to gently touch Bishop's shoulder. "You'll be okay," he mouthed under the roar of the thunder.

Turning back to Terri, he tried again to raise his hand. When that attempt failed, Bishop attempted to inspect his unresponsive limb, praying it was still attached to his body. "You've got an IV in your arm. It's strapped down. Don't move. Okay?" his wife's voice somehow managed to penetrate the din. "You have a concussion and a nasty lump on that thick skull of yours," she added with a smile.

"Blackjack?" Bishop asked, it all coming back to him in a rush.

Terri's expression answered his question before her words. "He got away," she responded, her gaze dropping to the ground.

EPILOGUE

Bishop stood beside his wife, watching as the Blackhawk helicopter flared to land. The couple raised their hands at the same instant, shielding their eyes as the propwash created a miniature hurricane of twigs, grass, and debris.

Glancing down at Terri, the West Texan could feel the quiet intensity of emotion her eyes betrayed. His wife was consumed by a question that demanded to be answered. It was the same query that she had made for the last three days.

An infantry lieutenant, waiting for the last of his squad to exit the helicopter, made eye contact with them. The young officer was aware of Terri's need for closure as well. From sunup to sundown, she had remained at the operations center, watching as the search parties deployed and returned since Blackjack's escape. The LT's glum expression answered her without his speaking a single word, only shaking his head in the negative. "We didn't find him," the motion clearly indicated.

Bishop wrapped his arm around his mate, pulling her close to offset the disappointment. Glancing up, she smiled, but it was a hollow gesture, lacking any real warmth. A moment later, the couple ambled back toward the parking lot, both deep in thought.

"We should go back to West Texas. I don't want to be here anymore," she announced over the background din of the ongoing military actions. "I desperately need to see Hunter and get started on the new house. We've been gone for too long."

Surprised and reassured by her reaction, Bishop enthusiastically nodded his agreement. "Yes, we should be getting back. It will be good for us to focus on the construction while Nick and his men continue the search. The Alliance will eventually find Ketchum if he's still alive, and when they do, justice will be served. Hell, I'd wager that monster is already dead, and we just haven't found his worthless carcass yet."

Terri seemed to brighten, but only for a moment. "Seriously, you think he's dead?"

Before answering, Bishop took his time, choosing his words carefully. Terri was acting peculiar about this entire Ketchum Jones thing, and her attitude troubled him. Sure, his wife had been in a full-fledged firefight, knocked silly by a stun grenade, captured, beaten, threatened, and abused. It made absolute sense that she would want to see the person responsible for all that pain pay a price. Given her resolve to capture the brute, the West Texan was positive Terri would execute the bastard herself given the chance. As for Bishop, he would gladly let her pull the trigger.

She had been through hell, and her mate knew there was no way he would ever fully understand what she felt, or how she had managed to endure. A dozen times, he'd tried to draw her out, made a wholehearted attempt to encourage her to share with him what had happened in that cell.

It had taken Bishop years to realize that talking about the horrors of combat served to dilute the foul, raw images trapped inside his head. Speaking the words... sharing the ghastly, disturbing memories served to water down their corrosive effect on the soul. There was no cowardice in admitting the trauma of such life-altering events. It was normal to feel differently after enduring the pure hell of warfare. He knew from experience that talking it out began a healing process that nothing else did.

He had justified her state by telling himself that she would eventually trust him enough to share what she had suffered, no matter how vile, primitive, or inhumane the memories and thoughts in her head.

Yet, her day-to-day interactions seemed off kilter, and not in a way the dutiful husband would have expected. Bishop had been trapped in similar situations before and knew that he would have emerged "come out fighting" angry. Yet, Terri never displayed even a hint of fury. Bishop would have demanded to be on the front lines of the search effort. She only wanted to sit at the Forest Mist High School's football field, waiting as wave after wave of helicopters deployed and returned, eager to see a bound and captive Blackjack Jones dragged from one of the birds in chains.

"We interrogated over a dozen of Ketchum's injured men," Bishop began, Terri's face reminding him that he owed her an answer. "We know he was wounded and bleeding. We know he picked up a downed motorcycle, turned tail and ran like a cowardly fuck. My guess is that he left a trail of slime as he crawled back across the Louisiana border and eventually bled out alongside the road. I hope the buzzards are feasting on his rotting flesh."

"But we don't know how bad he was hurt. We don't know if he had help. He could still be alive," she stated in a matter-of-fact, rather monotone voice.

Again, Bishop sensed an outpouring of dread from his mate. That specific reaction puzzled him. He could have understood a burning need for revenge, would have fully endorsed rage, could have even related to terror and fear. But dread? That didn't make any sense to him as a method of dealing with post-traumatic stress. *She's a woman*, he justified. *She deals with things differently. Show her unconditional love, and she will eventually get better. After all, isn't that what she has always done for you?*

"No, we don't know much for sure," Bishop continued softly. "What I can say for certain is that Nick has an entire combat brigade searching these woods. Sheriff Watts has brought in lawmen from all over the Lone Star Nation to help. Diana has called the president and asked for his assistance in expanding the hunt to Louisiana. If Ketchum is still alive, he'll probably show up in New Orleans. Wounded animals always go back to their holes to lick their wounds, and if he does show his ugly mug, men with guns will be there put his ass down. That spineless coward wouldn't dare show his face in Texas. If he survived, that's the last place he wants to be."

Terri seemed to marinate her husband's words for several minutes. Finally, she merely shrugged and conceded, "You're right. Now take me home, Cowboy. I want to see my son, sleep in my own bed, and watch my new house being built. Take me back to our desert, my love. I need it... and you... now more than ever."

THE END

32927111R00202

Made in the USA
Lexington, KY
07 March 2019